THE
KILLING
FOG

杀雾

ALSO BY JEFF WHEELER

The Harbinger Series

Storm Glass

Mirror Gate

Iron Garland

Prism Cloud

Broken Veil

The Kingfountain Series

The Poisoner's Enemy (prequel)

The Maid's War (prequel)

The Poisoner's Revenge (prequel)

The Queen's Poisoner

The Thief's Daughter

The King's Traitor

The Hollow Crown

The Silent Shield

The Forsaken Throne

The Legends of Muirwood Trilogy

The Wretched of Muirwood

The Blight of Muirwood

The Scourge of Muirwood

THE KILLING FOG

杀雾

THE GRAVE KINGDOM SERIES

坟王国系列

JEFF WHEELER

47NORTH

Text copyright © 2020 by Jeff Wheeler
All rights reserved.

Published by 47North, Seattle

www.apub.com

Amazon, the Amazon logo, and 47North are trademarks of Amazon.com, Inc., or its affiliates.

ISBN-13: 9781542015011
ISBN-10: 1542015014

Cover design by Shasti O'Leary Soudant

Printed in the United States of America

To Bingmei & Pengyu

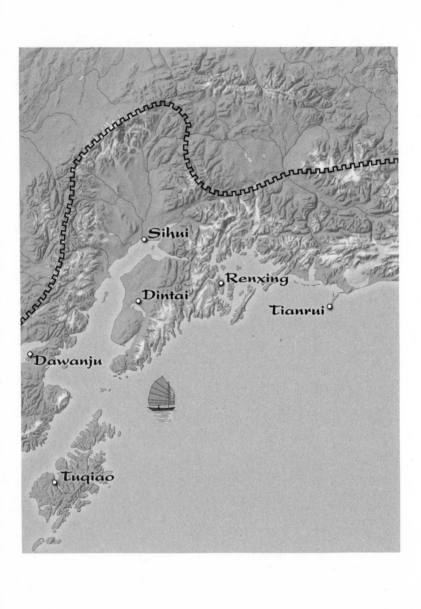

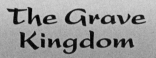

The Grave
Kingdom

THE DEATH WALL

Fusang

Bingmei's
Quonsuun

Kunmia's
Quonsuun

Yiwu

Wangfujing

Shilipu

Yonfeng

Sajinau

Xidan

GLOSSARY

Dianxue—点穴—a long-rumored skill of rendering killing/paralyzing blows by touch

Ensign—舰旗—a band of trained warriors for hire

Jingcha—警察—the police force in Sajinau

Meiwood—檀香—rosewood, a hardwood used for magic and construction

Namibu Desert—纳米比沙漠—a coastal desert far to the south

Ni-ji-jing—逆戟鲸—killer whale

Qiangdao—强盗—roving bandits

Qiezei—窃贼—a thief, cat burglar, picklock; professional criminal

Quonsuun—寺庙—a temple, fighting school

Xixuegui—吸血鬼—the undead

杀雾

Where there is no history, there is no past.

—Dawanjir proverb

PROLOGUE

Revenge

Bingmei awoke in the darkness before dawn to the sound of wind. The sky was marbled with heavy clouds that hung low, obscuring the nearby mountains normally visible through the upper windows. Leaves were chased from the limbs of crooked trees and herded into the courtyard, scraping and rasping against the stone as they went. The air had the smell of ice, the portent of a storm. The season seemed to have shifted overnight, sliding toward winter. Too soon. A spike of worry pierced her chest. Her parents were still not back from their journey. An early winter meant death to anyone caught in the vast wilderness.

Bingmei rose and ate her morning meal of fish and yarrow tea, anxious to be in the training yard. Practicing saber techniques usually tamed her fears, but as she swung the sword in the usual arcs, her eyes kept straying to the spruce limbs swaying wildly above the quonsuun's high walls. Raindrops pattered her head, reminding her of the shift in the weather. She worked until her arms and wrists were sore, her knees aching from holding the stances so long.

Grandfather Jiao came to watch her practice. She knew he was there because of his smell—warm bread with sugary honey drizzled on the crust. A peek revealed that he stood at the edge of the training yard, smiling indulgently as he stroked his long white beard. Her nose never lied, which was why she was unnerved to note a vinegary edge to his scent. Was it worry? Had the sudden change in the season alarmed him as well?

After practicing for several hours, Bingmei climbed the wooden ladder within the training yard to reach the outer wall of the quonsuun. Patrolling it with a pike was Zizhu, who kept his eyes on the horizon. The interior roof was heavily curved, which helped protect the guards against the drifts of snow that would soon pummel the mountains. A fierce wind rippled his cloak, as if determined to yank him off the wall and throw him down to the gorse below.

He turned as she walked toward him. "Get down, young miss!" he said with a scowl. "You're light enough to blow away!"

She hated being reminded of her size and gave him a scowl in return. "I'm not a leaf to be blown away," she said. "What have you seen?"

The low-hanging clouds veiled the ridges. Rumbles of thunder sounded in the distance.

"I can't see a thing," Zizhu complained. "They could be hiking up the trail from the fjord, and I wouldn't know it."

"It doesn't help that you're half-blind, Zizhu."

"Blind? Come closer, and I'll rap you with my pole!"

"You could try, Zizhu, but how would you hit me if you can't see? You might fall and stab yourself with the pike."

"Another insult! You should respect your elders."

She gave him a grin. He smelled like chestnuts. "When you're too old to climb the ladder, then I'll start respecting you, Zizhu."

"Agh, you are cruel, young mistress." He smirked at her, shaking his head. "Your parents named you too well!"

Bingmei smiled. Their banter was all in good humor. Her name meant "ice rose." It wasn't that it suited her because her skin was so pale, although it was, or because she was beautiful, because she wasn't. Her face was too big, and she was too short and skinny.

No, Father had named her Bingmei, a rose that blooms in winter, because he wished for her to embrace her thorns.

Her parents owned the family ensign, the security and bodyguard business her grandfather had started when he'd served the ruler of Yiwu. But boundaries between the kingdoms shifted like the winds and the river deposits.

The banner of their ensign was a mountain leopard, which were more common in the mountains where Grandfather had grown up. Her family had a reputation for their martial skills. They were feared by the lawless groups of Qiangdao, who owed allegiance to none of the kings and who pillaged caravans or snuck into towns to rob the estates of the wealthy. Each season, emissaries climbed up the mountain to the quonsuun, seeking their help.

As she stood on the wall, she turned her head and gazed down at her home. No one knew who'd built it. The thick stone walls and mei-wood timbers were solid, and although speckled with lichen, they had defied the ravages of time and weather. While the roof tiles had been patched over the years, the curving slope did well under the onerous weight of snow. Some ancient civilization had constructed the quonsuun and many of the cities within their world. It was unknown what had become of the ancients, but their buildings had outlasted them, and so had the symbols they'd engraved in their architecture and art. Like the leopard, a creature that had come to symbolize the taming of cruelty. When her father and mother had arrived at their destination, having successfully protected the caravan they'd been hired to accompany, the leopard symbol was received with joy and gladness.

What the sign had meant originally, no one knew. There were some creatures depicted in statuary and ornamental designs that still mystified those looking at them. Did those kinds of animals even exist anymore? Had they ever existed?

So much of the world was a mystery to Bingmei. Where had her ancestors come from? Why were so many languages spoken throughout the kingdoms? Why was so much of the year spent in shadow, the other in light? No one understood, but the change had been attributed to the dragons of myth—the light half of the year was known as the Dragon of Dawn, the dark half as the Dragon of Night.

Worry began to bubble up again as she sniffed the cold, sharp air. If winter came too soon, her parents wouldn't be able to finish their journey. She didn't want to spend the Dragon of Night without her parents, trapped in the quonsuun without news of their adventures.

The rain began to fall in earnest then, striking at Bingmei and Zizhu viciously as the skies began to seethe.

"Have you seen any sign of the fog?" Bingmei asked worriedly, wiping a drop that had landed on her nose.

"No, young miss. Try not to worry. They'll be back. I thought I heard a noise in the distance. I know it must be them."

"Shout when you see them coming," Bingmei ordered.

He frowned at her. "I am Zizhu, a free man! You cannot order me about, little miss! You are only ten years old."

"I'm twelve! Now promise me you'll shout, or I'll throw stones at you from down below!"

"If I thought you could hit me, I'd be worried," he said. "Now get out of the rain before your petals fall off."

She bounded back to the ladder, glancing into the distance one last time, but her view was impeded by layers of storm clouds. A shiver ran down her back.

The storm made practicing in the training yard unpleasant, so Bingmei worked on her fist techniques within the quonsuun itself. It smelled like spoiling fruit, but she burned incense to banish the stench. Only Bingmei could smell it, but a feeling of unease hung in the air, which had everyone agitated.

Grandfather didn't seek her out, but she saw glimpses of him on and off throughout the day. Pacing. Watching the walls and the storm raging outside, his hands clasped behind his back. It was unlike him to brood, which only heightened Bingmei's sense of dread. Servants splashed through the courtyard as they ran for cover between their duties. The quonsuun housed twelve servants, but most of the living quarters were vacant since the bulk of the warriors had gone on the mission with her parents, leaving Zizhu and seven others to guard it in their absence.

After the storm ended, late in the afternoon, Zizhu called down from his post on the wall, his cloak hanging heavily on him, drenched with rain. "They're coming! They're coming! I see the ensign!"

Bingmei ran out to the courtyard, nearly slipping on the wet stone tiles in her eagerness. Water dripped from the edges of the roof, pattering noisily down the drainage chains. None of the lamps had been lit yet, for fear they'd be extinguished in the storm, but they would be. She saw Grandfather emerge from the quonsuun, a relieved smile on his face. A delicious smell accompanied him.

Perhaps all would be well after all. Perhaps she'd worried for nothing.

"You see them, Zizhu?" Bingmei called up. "Are you sure?"

"I'm not blind, no matter what you think!" he shouted back. "They're not far off. Unbar the doors."

Servants of the quonsuun were suddenly rushing around. Some scampered up rickety ladders, beginning to hang the lit lamps from the iron stays. Others rushed forward and raised the heavy crossbar holding the door closed.

Bingmei hurried forward, bouncing on the balls of her feet in excitement.

As the servants set the crossbar down and began pulling the heavy doors open, the smell of fresh rain-soaked grass filled the courtyard. She saw the group marching toward the gate wearily, heads bent low against the weather. No doubt they'd marched through the storm to get there by dusk. They would be tired, surely, but she hoped Mother and Father would have enough energy to tell her and Grandfather stories of their journey. Just a few minutes and they'd be home.

Then the wind shifted, bringing the smell of the group rushing to her. The smell of rancid tubers afflicted her, making her eyes water. The overpowering stench made her step back, gagging.

This was not the smell of her parents. It was a death smell.

Bingmei's heart pounded fast as she stared out into the gloom of the failing light. She recognized the family banner, the depiction of the leopard. But her nose could not be deceived.

The pretenders had her parents' leopard banner. What did that mean?

"Shut the door," she said in a strangled voice, shaking her head.

Grandfather arrived next to her, hands clasped behind his back. "What's wrong, Granddaughter?"

Bingmei covered her mouth and groaned. "It's not them," she said, shaking her head, wanting to banish the horrid stench. "It's a trick. It's not them! Close the doors."

"Do as she says," Grandfather commanded.

The servants, looking worried, began to push against the doors.

There was a clattering noise, startling them, then a crash as Zizhu landed in the courtyard next to her. His pike had fallen first, the noise jarring everyone. One of the servants screamed. Zizhu tried to lift his head, his eyes dazed in pain and surprise, but Bingmei saw the arrow protruding from his chest. He slumped back, his chest falling still.

The servants shoved hard at the doors. Bingmei went to help as the group outside charged toward them. Shouts and yells from outside added to the confusion. The servants managed to wrestle the doors shut and were fumbling with the crossbar when something heavy smashed into the wood from the other side, knocking them back. One of the doors inched open, preventing the crossbar from fitting into the cradle. The smell that came through the gap made Bingmei want to vomit. A flash of metal, a saber, cut through the gap—and through one of the servants holding the beam. He cried out in pain and dropped his end.

They had lost the protection of the walls.

Grandfather looked at Bingmei. "Get my saber and the cricket!" he said, his face contorting with emotion, his cheeks twitching with barely suppressed rage. Bingmei vaulted from her position, rushing back into the quonsuun like the wind. She heard voices, shouts. The few remaining guards came rushing past Bingmei to defend the compound.

Panic urged her on. The smell filling the courtyard was horrible, but she sprinted to her grandfather's room. His saber was suspended on the wall, the meiwood hilt capped in gold. The saber, a relic of the forgotten past, had seen many years of duty.

She pulled it down and then found the little box that contained his wooden cricket. It, too, was made of meiwood, and she knew it was magic. Artifacts like this were as coveted as they were dangerous. But her grandfather had let her play with the cricket before. She knew how to invoke its power. Perhaps this was what the Qiangdao were after. She had no doubt that these were some of the infamous brigands who roamed the world seeking prey and ill-gotten gains. Why would they *dare* attack a quonsuun? She took the box and stuffed it into her pocket, then grabbed the saber and hurtled back toward the training yard.

Voices. Threats. Laughter.

"You've returned at last, Muxidi?" rasped Grandfather Jiao.

"Only to bring you their heads, old man," said the leader of the Qiangdao. Bingmei arrived just as a leather sack, bulging and dripping, was flung at her grandfather's feet. It brought a whiff of a smell. A smell she recognized as her parents, mixed with the stench of death.

No!

She stared at the bag in shock, unable to believe what she was witnessing. The guards who had passed her moments before lay sprawled on the ground, some still twitching as they died, others motionless. A band of ten Qiangdao stood in the area, wearing the thick leathers and hides favored by the thieves. There were no colors in their clothes, no fashion. They smelled like rotting flesh.

"Your ensign is ended!" shouted the leader to her grandfather's face. "You killed my grandfather. So now I take my revenge on you and on your seed. Die, old man!"

Bingmei, still frozen, watched as the leader brought up his saber to strike off her grandfather's head. She still gripped his weapon in her hand, her body too frightened to move.

The killing blow came, but her grandfather ducked at the last moment. With a blur of his fists, he struck at the leader, knocking him down to the wet stone tiles. He was old, but he was not powerless. Two of the bandits yelled and attacked him. Grandfather twisted, evading a thrust, and struck back. He took down one of them and kicked the other in the knee. The crack of breaking bone snapped Bingmei out of her haze.

She raced forward just as the leader's saber sliced down her grandfather's front. Muxidi used both hands to amplify his force, one on the hilt, one atop the blade. She gaped in shock as her grandfather sagged to his knees, his eyes wide with pain and surprise. If he'd had his own weapon . . .

Turning his head, Grandfather saw her charging toward him. The grief on his face ripped at her heart. The wound was mortal. She could see the grin of satisfaction on the bandit's face. Then he pulled his sword free and kicked Grandfather down.

A scream came out of Bingmei as she charged the man. She yanked the saber out of its scabbard. There was no hope of winning against so many. But if she died killing this man, it would be a good death. Why not join her parents beyond the Death Wall? And her grandfather too? They would go together.

Muxidi saw her in time, and he effortlessly blocked her thrusts and slashing motions. How could he not? She practiced daily, but she was only twelve. Tears streaked down her cheeks. He was toying with her, letting her expend her energy. His ruffians formed a circle around her, boxing her in. They laughed as though her efforts were an enjoyable diversion. If only she could steal a little blood from the man before she died.

But Muxidi wouldn't grant her any. He mocked her as he defended himself, holding her off as if she were a dandelion seed dancing in the wind.

"Are you the daughter?" he said. "No wonder they were too ashamed to speak of you before they died. You're pale as a ghost. Look at her!"

Laughter followed. She screamed at him, trying again to stab him. He parried her strike easily, then kicked her in the chest, knocking the wind out of her.

She lay on the wet stones, seeing her grandfather swallow. He stared at her, the final smell of him washing over her. He couldn't speak, but she could see the urgency in his eyes. The plea. He wanted her to run.

"You aren't even *worth* killing!" the leader said. "But I don't want to be haunted by any ghosts!"

He was going to kill her. And all the rest of the servants at the quon-suun. There would be no one left to claim a blood debt against him. Her parents had only one child—her. Only she could avenge them.

Bingmei remembered the little box in her pocket. She fished her hand into her pocket, opened the box, and felt the small wooden cricket.

She gripped it in her hand and rubbed it with her thumb, invoking the magic. She smelled the rich, beautiful aroma of the wood as the power of the artifact enveloped her. Its magic infused her, thrumming outward from her hand. And she leaped, springing out of the circle of killers, rising in an arc to land gracefully on the sloping rooftop of the quonsuun.

"Shoot her!" yelled the leader, his voice drained of humor.

Bingmei rubbed the cricket again, and the magic made her spring even higher, clearing the peaked roof of the ancient dwelling. She heard the twang of a bow, but she landed safely on the other side of the wall. Shouts and commands to find her, to kill her, filled the courtyard behind her.

But it was dark.

And it was impossible to find a cricket in the dark.

杀雾

Be not afraid of growing slowly, be afraid only of standing still.

—Dawanjir proverb

CHAPTER ONE

Kunmia Suun

Bingmei sat on a wooden bench, feeling the sway of the boat as the smell of the salmon in the nets filled her nose. The fisherman and his son adjusted their ropes, positioning the scalloped sail to take advantage of the wind, which seemed to change its mind spontaneously. The stars were partly masked by the tall peaks of the mountain fjord.

Zhuyi and Mieshi, her bond sisters in the ensign, were asleep on the bench across from her, huddled in their cloaks. The fisherman and his son had agreed to sail during the night to hide their group's movement from prying eyes. Kunmia Suun preferred to travel in secrecy.

Bingmei shifted her gaze to the front of the boat, where her master sat beside the fisherman. One of the few women to run an ensign, Kunmia had become her teacher, her adopted mother, her mentor, her friend. It was Kunmia's ensign that had come to Bingmei's grandfather's quonsuun in search of survivors once the Dragon of Night gave way to the Dragon of Dawn. Bingmei had watched them arrive from her hiding place in the abandoned, plundered building. She'd lived there for months, hiding from Muxidi and his men and surviving on what little food she could steal. The Qiangdao had disposed of the dead by abandoning the bodies outside the quonsuun to be devoured by the wild animals prowling there. The only thing she had left of her family was her grandfather's saber and the meiwood cricket. At first she'd feared Kunmia's ensign were Qiangdao, but their smell had assured her that they could be trusted.

For four years Bingmei had trained with Kunmia Suun. This was the first voyage she'd been allowed to make with the ensign. They'd spent the summer crossing the deep fjords into the wilderness, looking for the ruins of another quonsuun. They'd found it, but it had already been plundered. However, they'd managed to secure some artifacts for their employer. They were on their way back to Wangfujing, their journey nearly at an end.

Kunmia smelled like thyme and the subtle fragrance of peonies. She was soft spoken but very serious, her long hair wound up on her head, bound with leather ties. She was never without the meiwood staff she cradled in her arms, an intricately carved weapon that was of ancient origin, its story lost to history. Her eyes were severe, her mouth neutral. She would not be at ease until their duty was fulfilled.

Honor meant everything to Kunmia, and because of that, it meant something to Bingmei as well. Under her tutelage, Bingmei's skills had improved. With her grandfather's saber and meiwood cricket, she felt she could defeat any foe. Even Muxidi. She itched to face off with the brigand, but Kunmia still thought she wasn't ready to kill. And she disapproved of revenge.

"When we reach Wangfujing," Marenqo said, his head bent low, his arms wrapped around his knees, "I want one of these salmon. Roasted on a strip of cedar." He enunciated each word carefully. He was looking at Kunmia but mostly talking to himself as he always did. "A little bit of parsley. A pinch of salt. White pepper, of course. Cooked to perfection. Just a little pink. That is what I want."

"You are always thinking about food," Lieren said, snorting. He was not a tall man, but although he was well into his fifties, he was just as fit as the youngest on the fishing boat. His eyes scanned the dark shoreline, looking for light.

"And you, my friend," Marenqo said, "eat your food much too quickly. You don't even enjoy it."

"I am an efficient eater. There is no sin in this."

"There is a sin. You don't taste the food. How many years have I watched you, shoveling the bowl into your mouth, as if it were a race? As if your belly were that of a starving man?"

"Hush," Kunmia said, trying to forestall another round of teasing.

Bingmei smiled. Lieren was one of the oldest bodyguards at the ensign. He had been everywhere, seen everything. With the stamina of someone a third his age, he walked so fast that the others were hard-pressed to keep up. At any sign of danger, he was always the first to engage. Marenqo, while a passable fighter, was there because of his ability to speak multiple languages. He knew six or seven, and even if he didn't know a local dialect, he could usually communicate with his hands, his eyebrows, his facial features. He arranged their transportation, their lodging. He loved to talk about food, and he loved to tease the others, Lieren most of all.

"Did I say anything that was untrue, Kunmia?" he asked, pretending to be affronted. "Does this man not worry you he will choke on a fish bone?"

Kunmia never argued with him. She merely cast him a glance before turning away.

The boat was small enough that they could hear each other easily. The water's lulling embrace had made Bingmei sleepy, but she was determined to stay awake as long as Kunmia did. The leader of the ensign always worked harder than anyone else.

"And *you're* talking so loud, Marenqo, that the Qiangdao can hear you from the shore," Bingmei said.

"Did I wake you, Bingmei? I'm not sorry if I did. I really want some cooked salmon right now. We haven't had a decent meal in . . . a very long time. I think I have the right to complain about a fish. And when someone eats too fast to appreciate a fine meal."

"And what do you propose?" Bingmei said. "Lighting a fire on the boat?"

"Maybe a little one. I'll even pass on the cedar plank, although you must admit the smoke adds to the flavor of the meat."

"And risk catching the boat on fire?" Bingmei said, laughing softly.

"Isn't a well-cooked fish worth the risk? I think so."

"You're teasing me now."

"You're insufferable," Lieren grumbled.

Marenqo cocked his head. "Am I? Can you be sure I'm teasing, Bingmei? This is your first journey with us. You don't know me as well as you think."

"Four years is long enough to know someone," Bingmei said. Marenqo was a conglomeration of smells. Spicy and intricate, like a feast. Lieren reminded her of the smell of grain. Simple, uncomplicated. Healthy.

Her quip earned a low coughing chuckle from the fisherman's son, who was tightening a knot.

The young man's father, the fisherman, shifted the mast again, and the boat changed course. He spoke their language with a strange inflection but knew it well enough to understand the warriors without Marenqo's help.

"We are near the end of the fjord," he whispered. "The berth we agreed on."

"Thank you," Kunmia said. She glanced over at Bingmei. "Wake the others."

Bingmei nodded and slipped off the bench, staying low, and hurried over to Mieshi and Zhuyi. She gently roused them.

"I wasn't asleep," said Mieshi with a throb of anger, sitting up.

Marenqo barked out a laugh, and she glowered at him.

Zhuyi rose and yawned. Blinking quickly, she stared up at the sky. "We traveled farther than I thought. Are we at the end of the fjord?"

"Yes," Bingmei said. She envied her bond sisters' ability to read the stars. They'd been training with Kunmia Suun for much longer. While Bingmei knew the stars that dotted the sky above her family's former quonsuun and the base of Kunmia's ensign, which was much farther east and south, the constellations she'd seen on their journey north had confused her.

They prepared to disembark as the boat approached the shore in the dark. The fisherman barked orders, and the young man promptly obeyed them, untying and retying knots to achieve the proper angle for the scalloped sail.

"Can I buy a fish before we leave?" Marenqo asked. "They may not have salmon at the nearest village, and I don't want to wait until Wangfujing."

"Not now," Kunmia said, her tone absolute but not angry, as she watched the black shoreline approach. "Quiet."

They all obeyed. The only sound was the boat's creaking timbers as the fisherman and his son edged it up to a quay that had been invisible up to the moment of arrival. Kunmia smiled and nodded. The man knew his business.

One by one, the warriors disembarked. Lieren marched ahead, scanning the gloom for signs of trouble. Zhuyi and Mieshi quickly followed, while Kunmia and Marenqo settled the account. The fisherman's son was staring at Bingmei, holding on to the mooring rope with both hands. Was he staring because of her unnaturally pale skin?

She stuck her tongue out at him and turned away.

"Thank you, sir, for the fish," Marenqo said, bowing and saluting the man. "You've made me the happiest of men. At least until I've finished eating it. I might even share."

Kunmia started walking away from the boat, staff in hand, and Bingmei fell in beside her as Marenqo continued to offer his effusive thanks.

They'd just caught up to the other two women, the long grass hissing against their boots, when Zhuyi stopped abruptly, holding up her hand. There were rocks and scrub trees everywhere, making shadows of varying sizes in the dim moonlight.

Kunmia halted. "What do you hear?"

A sickly odor struck Bingmei's nose. She could feel the stench of malice like a rising haze.

"Qiangdao," Bingmei whispered.

"They were expecting us," Zhuyi said.

"How many?" Kunmia demanded. "Lieren!"

Some of the shadows were moving. Bingmei had time to draw her saber as they charged her group, weapons out and ready. Her heart thumped rapidly in response to the surprise attack.

"Back to the boat, now!" Kunmia said. She whirled her staff, striking one of the attackers in the skull with a resounding crack. Commotion erupted around them. Bingmei tried to make sense of the darkness. Even her sense of smell was muddled, her friends too close to her foes. But she responded to Kunmia's orders as they'd all been trained to do, and when a strange man's leering face suddenly appeared in the starlight, she swung her saber into his middle. He fell with a groan. It surprised her that her training worked so well, that she'd already wounded and maybe even killed her enemy. What startled her more was that it didn't disturb her as much as she'd thought it might. But then, she'd been training to fight and seek her revenge against the

Qiangdao for years. The man had attacked her and would gladly have killed her—she'd taken him down instead.

Backing toward the boat, she saw Marenqo suddenly, a staff in his hand as he parried an attack and countered.

He dealt a killing blow, then gestured for Bingmei to come with him. "Quick!"

Light flashed over her shoulder, and she glanced back. One of the attackers, the leader probably, had drawn a double-edged sword with a wavy green blade. The light glowing from it revealed the mass of attackers. She felt a tug of envy, a strange impulse that the blade should be hers. Although she'd seen magical artifacts before, none of the others had pulled at her in such a way. She forced her gaze away from it. Lieren was surrounded, fighting off four or five at once, separated from the group. Zhuyi and Mieshi were whirling their staves, crushing skulls and dropping Qiangdao all around them. Even outnumbered, they were capable of withstanding the onslaught. No wonder the leader was desperate enough to summon his sword's magic.

Roaring through a mouth twisted with hate and fury, he came at Kunmia. The blade hissed as it sliced through the air; she jumped back just in time.

Kunmia's staff glowed to life as she activated its power. The light emanating from the weapons illuminated the scene, including the first tendrils of creeping fog, curling and reaching. Bingmei's eyes widened with fear, and her heart thumped in worry. If the battle didn't end soon, they would all pay the price.

The sword met the staff, and both weapons sparked with power. Kunmia moved swiftly, dodging, blocking, striking in return. Each time the green-tinged sword struck Kunmia's staff, its glow decreased. Bingmei smiled fiercely. The bandit didn't know the power of Kunmia's weapon. It *drained* the magic of others. Although it was dangerous to use any of the spelled weapons, Kunmia's staff worked quickly. It had saved the ensign many times before, or so Bingmei had heard from the others.

"Bingmei, come!" Marenqo said, his tone urgent. Zhuyi and Mieshi had both broken off their attack and rushed toward them. They all knew time was short.

The leader of the Qiangdao shouted something, but the words were lost in the rush. Bingmei followed the others to the boat and found two of the Qiangdao there. The fisherman was on his knees, a blade in his belly. His son was struggling against one of the enemy, trying to break free.

Mieshi whipped out a dart and sent it flying. It struck the brigand's neck, and he released the boy, his hands flying to the spot where he'd been struck. It was over in a moment, the two brigands dead. And so was the fisherman. The son, probably Bingmei's own age, knelt by his father's body, wailing in pain as he clutched his father's tunic. Bingmei's heart winced at the sound of his raw grief, reminded of the awful day she had lost her family.

Marenqo hurried to the young man, kneeling beside him. "We must flee!" he told him, his tone urgent. "It's coming! If we don't go, we'll all die! Help us."

Bingmei turned back to watch the struggle between Kunmia and the Qiangdao leader. If only it were the man who had murdered her grandfather. She'd hoped to find him this season, to make him pay for what he'd done. But this was the first band of marauders they'd come across.

Kunmia's weapon was soon the only one shining, and the fog's sickly haze was drawn toward it like a flock of moths. Magic lured the fog. It was why the artifacts were used sparingly, if at all.

And then the leader went down, his skull cracked by the staff.

"Lieren!" Kunmia shouted in warning. The valiant man continued to fight, not seeing the creeping mist that licked at his adversaries' ankles as if to taste them. He was still surrounded. And then the fog suddenly surged forward, engulfing him and the others near him.

"Please!" Marenqo gripped the young man's arm, hoisting him to his feet. The fisherman's boy saw the fog then, the scene illuminated by the glow of Kunmia's staff. No further warnings were needed. The boy leaped into the boat and began unfastening the ropes, working quickly. Screams of panic started. The fog had begun its deadly work.

"Kunmia!" shouted Zhuyi. "The boat!"

Kunmia stood transfixed, gripping the weapon that had helped summon the death of her friend, her companion in arms. Bingmei saw the anguish in her face, which was quickly replaced by implacable determination. The leader of the ensign rushed toward the boat, the staff's glow slowly decreasing. Still it lured the fog to follow her. Knee-high tendrils of mist snaked through the grass, chasing after Kunmia.

Despite the danger the staff posed, it was too valuable to be left behind.

With help from Zhuyi and Mieshi, the boat was soon ready to depart. Bingmei hastened aboard, willing her mentor to run faster. She watched as Kunmia sprinted through the grass, the fog rising like a wall behind her, blocking the view of everything beyond it.

The young man was working the mast, trying to catch some wind to propel them away. Kunmia reached the boat and jumped onto the deck, her landing causing it to rock wildly. Marenqo had brought the fisherman's dead body aboard as well.

The young man worked at the mast alone, for no one else knew what to do. It seemed they wouldn't make it, but then the sail bulged as it captured a breeze. The boat lurched away from the quay. Kunmia was breathing fast, gripping the staff, staring at the fog as it drifted over the water. When the last of the artifact's magic dried up, the fog would be blind to them again. They would be safe.

But not without a cost. The fisherman had fallen. And so had Lieren, one of the warriors who had come to rescue Bingmei from her grandfather's quonsuun.

Bingmei felt part of her heart harden as she watched the fog dissipate. The staff finally went dark, the magic winking out, and Kunmia Suun bowed her head. She did not weep, only clenched her hands tightly around the staff and its awful burden.

But Bingmei could smell the pungent grief roiling inside her master.

CHAPTER TWO
The Phoenix Blade

The fishing boat glided listlessly on the water. The sail had been lowered, and dawn crept through the clouds over the eastern mountains. Everyone was sullen, still mourning the death of Lieren in their own private ways. The fisherman's son sat dejectedly on his haunches, his eyes rimmed with red. A blanket covered his father's face.

"We have to go back," Kunmia said after what felt like hours of silence.

Bingmei stared at her, aghast. Mieshi and Zhuyi exchanged a glance before turning to her as one.

"Why?" Mieshi asked in a troubled tone. "I don't mean to be disrespectful, Master, but the killing fog may yet find us."

It was Marenqo who knew the answer already. His hands were clasped together, his brow furrowed in thought. "The sword."

Kunmia nodded. "We cannot leave it behind."

"Hasn't it brought enough death?" Zhuyi asked.

"It is our duty to prevent it from causing even more harm," Kunmia said. "Imagine if it's found by someone who doesn't know it's an artifact? A peasant might accidentally invoke the magic and destroy their entire village." She shook her head. "We'll take it back with us to Wangfujing."

Bingmei didn't like the thought of returning to the place where they'd been ambushed by the Qiangdao, but she trusted Kunmia's judgment, which was never sentimental. Her master always did the right thing because it was the right thing. And because honor and duty were her creeds.

Marenqo's brows needled together. "Would you sell it to Budai, then? You know he'll want it for his collection."

"Would it be safer anywhere else?" Kunmia asked pointedly. "Or perhaps we'll bring it back to the quonsuun."

Their employer, King Budai, ruler of Wangfujing, did indeed possess a collection of magic artifacts. He was crafty, manipulative, but genuinely appreciative of Kunmia's ensign and paid them well for their finds. His patronage was self-interested, however—he often turned around and sold the artifacts they'd brought him to other wealthy buyers or would-be warriors seeking to form their own ensigns. Yes, he would want the sword, even though they hadn't found it at the ruins they'd searched, which meant he had no claim on their discovery.

Bingmei didn't trust him because he smelled too much like the lemony scent of greed.

Kunmia turned to the fisherman's son. "I am sorry for the death of your father."

"No, I am sorry," Marenqo said glumly. "I didn't react quickly enough. It is my fault."

"It is not your fault," Kunmia told him. Not to placate his feelings. Bingmei knew she was scrupulously honest. Kunmia looked back at the young man, her eyes serious, her expression grave. "Have there often been Qiangdao nearby? Did you know they would be waiting for us?"

The young man looked her in the face. He shook his head no.

Kunmia then turned to Bingmei and tilted her head, a silent request for her opinion. Because of Bingmei's gift, she had a way of divining people's intentions. She knew when someone was honest because of how they smelled. She couldn't explain her ability, but it was an instinct that had been with her all her life. The boy smelled like fish. It wasn't an unpleasant smell exactly. Or a surprising one considering his vocation.

Bingmei nodded to Kunmia.

"You are trustworthy," Kunmia said, reaching out and touching the young man's shoulder. "Tell me of your family. What is your name? Where is your mother?"

He sniffed. "I'm Quion. I have no family now."

Kunmia's eyes lowered with compassion. "Your mother?"

"She died when I was little. It's only been my father and me." He blinked quickly, then rubbed his eyes. "There's a debt on the boat. They won't let me keep it until I'm older." His glum expression struck Bingmei's heart. She, too, had no family.

"So you have nowhere to go?" Kunmia asked.

He shook his head. "The man who owns the boat is in Wangfujing. We were going to sell the salmon we caught at Shilipu because it's closer."

"No, come with us to Wangfujing. I will make sure the debt is settled. Who owns the boat?"

"Mao Zhang."

"I know him well," Kunmia said. "There will be no obligation. If you sell the fish in Wangfujing, you will get a better price. Come with us, Quion. Maybe another fisherman will take you on. You're a hard worker. You will not go hungry."

"Thank you," Quion said. His expression had brightened a little, although it drooped again when he caught a glimpse of his father's covered body.

"Please take us back to the quay."

He swallowed nervously. "But the fog."

"If it's still there, we won't stop. But I think it will have settled by now. Do as I say."

There was no way a fisherman's boy would countermand someone with her authority, so it came as no surprise to Bingmei when the young man nodded and set to work.

As they sailed back the way they'd come, Kunmia came and sat by her, putting a hand on her shoulder. "You will fetch the sword, Bingmei," she said.

A quiver of pleasure went through her heart. It was followed by a throb of fear.

杀雾

The air at the quay had an acidic smell to it. When the boat thumped against the damp wood of the dock, she saw the remains of the dead Qiangdao. Dewdrops glistened on the vacant faces, eyes closed as if in sleep. Their chests lay still, but if Bingmei hadn't known better, she would have sworn they were only resting. Their placid expressions chilled her to the bone. She'd never seen the effects of the killing fog before, not firsthand, although the others in the ensign had told her stories. Bodies left by the fog did not rot like they should. No flies would buzz around them, even days later. They said the best way to dispose of the bodies left by the fog was to throw them into the water.

Bingmei looked at the others on the boat, trying to see if they were bothered by the death sleep. They were all different ages, although Mieshi and Zhuyi were closer in age to each other than to the rest. None of them appeared to covet the responsibility for which Bingmei had been chosen. They all looked sickened by the sight of what had befallen their enemies. And Lieren.

She stepped over the edge of the boat and onto the dock, sniffing. A sharp, acidic smell hung in the air, masking all other scents. A bird squawked from a tree in the distance. But nothing living would venture near.

Animals fled the killing fog as well.

She glanced back at the boat, watching the solemn faces stare back at her. Only Kunmia nodded in encouragement.

Mustering her resolve, Bingmei stepped around the fallen and started off into the long grass, hand on the hilt of her grandfather's saber. The gentle breeze made the tips of the grass sway with a shushing noise. She walked deliberately, retracing her steps. Now that it was daylight, the scene looked entirely new and unfamiliar. Her foot struck something heavy, and she realized it was another dead man. She went around him, her heart beating swiftly in her chest.

A new smell struck her nose.

She stopped, freezing in place, her hand lightly touching the tips of the tall grass. The smell of meiwood was a subtle fragrance. Meiwood trees were tall with straight trunks, and the ancients had used them to construct buildings. They were exceedingly rare, and what few groves still existed were guarded day and night. She'd heard it took over a century of waiting to harvest a single tree.

She loved the smell, which reminded her of her little wooden cricket. Kunmia's staff was also made of meiwood, from a limb sheared off a trunk.

The scent came from just ahead. She cautiously started forward again, her boots striking another corpse of the Qiangdao. There were many dead ones nearby, flattening the grass. Then she saw Lieren, and a queer feeling clutched her heart. Even he looked peaceful. The unfairness of it grated on her. He had protected and guided the ensign for decades. Loss quivered in her chest again, though she tried to still the wrenching sensation. Death was something that happened often. It did no good to become too attached to people. Although she pitied the fisherman's son, Quion, she would not let her heart linger on her compassion.

Staying alive was all that mattered to Bingmei. At least for long enough to exact her revenge on the men who'd murdered her family. Then . . . it didn't matter.

The smell grew stronger, indicating she was headed in the right direction, but a strange sensation rippled down her spine. Something felt . . . wrong. Crouching down so that her eyes were level with the tall grass, she gazed around at the small copse of trees where the Qiangdao had concealed themselves. In the daylight it wouldn't have been possible. She could see through the limbs in daylight. So why did she feel that she wasn't alone?

Nearer the ground, she smelled the burnt tang of metal. She parted the grasses until she found the source: an arm and a hand clutched around a dagger. The blade was pitted, discolored. Had it always been that way? She pried it loose of the cold fingers and gazed at it, holding it closer to her nose. The smell was overpowering. She set it down in disgust.

Slowly she searched the grass, using her nose to draw her closer to the meiwood. A huff of wind sounded from above and behind her. She whirled, saber ringing clear of its scabbard. Her arms shook with fear. But she swallowed, steeling herself, and tried to calm her breathing. Nothing was behind her. It was just her imagination. So why were all her instincts screaming at her to flee?

Childishness. That's why Kunmia had chosen her for this mission. So she could overcome her childish fears.

Get the sword. Go. That was her duty. Ignoring the prickling of her flesh, she stepped backward and nearly tripped over someone's remains. The Qiangdao leader. Squatting low, saber held protectively in front of her, she groped with her free hand, searching for the sword. There it lay in the grass. Its blade was not tarnished in the least, a double-edged blade, unlike her saber, which was only sharpened on one edge. There was a rippled pattern in the metal, a technique lost with the ancients. At the nape of the blade, the guard and pommel were made of gold. An intricate carving of a phoenix had been embossed on each, and the meiwood grip looked sturdy and solid.

The phoenix. A creature of legend. A bird that reigned over all other birds. She'd seen them depicted in many of the artifacts retrieved by the ensign, although no two looked the same . . . some resembled roosters, others bore more in common with eagles. Most of the depictions had one commonality—their tail feathers were all different colors, each one representing a virtue, like benevolence, honesty, knowledge, decorum.

These stories and images were all they had left of the past. Upon joining Kunmia Suun's band, it had surprised Bingmei to learn that the legends she'd been raised with differed from theirs. Each village had its own tales, and the degree to which they conflicted made her doubt if anyone knew the truth.

As she stared at the intricate blade, she felt compelled to touch it. It was the most beautiful weapon she'd ever seen. She reached for it, grasping it by the hilt, and lifted it from the grass. Power jolted through her body, frightening and thrilling her. The weapon felt strangely familiar, but she'd never seen its equal in her life.

Holding it, gazing at it, she felt a trance steal over her. Her eyes were fixed on the rippled metal blade, the twin phoenixes on the hilt.

"Bingmei!"

Kunmia's scream jolted her from her reverie as the first wisps of fog crept toward her. The sharp acidic smell had become nearly painful. She bolted.

Although she hadn't intentionally activated the magic of the Phoenix Blade, it had summoned the fog nonetheless. She couldn't send it away, nor could she release the weapon.

She saw Marenqo shaking his head as she raced for the boat. Tendrils of fog licked at her boots, reaching for her. She put on more speed, desperate to escape the eternal sleep that had claimed the corpses in the meadow. The boat was coming away from the dock, the sail catching wind. In that moment, she knew she had to lose one of the weapons she carried in order to use the cricket. Her grandfather's saber meant everything to her, but her duty was to fulfill the trust she'd been given. Besides, she didn't think she *could* release the other blade. So with an ache in her heart, she cast the saber aside and shoved her hand in her pocket, grasping the cricket. The burst of magic propelled her into the air, vaulting her over the fog that was poised to envelop her.

She landed past the boat, falling into the icy river. She began to sink, her thick clothes soaking in the frigid water, but she wouldn't let go of the blade. In fact, she couldn't. It felt fused to her hand. She clawed toward the surface and broke free, choking on the water that suddenly lapped in her face. Confusion roiled her senses. She felt something heavy and rough strike her.

"Grab it, Bingmei! Grab it!"

It was a rope. She gripped it with her free hand, squeezing hard, and they began to reel her in. Her legs were quickly exhausted by the frigid chill of the river. She panted, coughing, and spat out water, but she didn't let go.

A strong hand grabbed her wrist, and another grabbed her elbow. The fisherman's son pulled her into the boat, sopping wet and spluttering, the Phoenix Blade still clutched in her hand. Kunmia and the others gathered around her. The weapon seared her skin, shooting bursts of power up her arm, but she couldn't release it.

Kunmia touched her staff to the blade, and finally Bingmei's hand was able to open. Once it did, the magic of the sword faded. Kunmia took the blade and brought it away from her. Bingmei's hand tingled from it still.

"She almost died," Zhuyi said worriedly.

They were all staring at her, especially the fisherman's son. And she realized her dripping wig was askew, revealing the white hair beneath. The others in the ensign already knew her secret, but now the fisherman's boy knew too. She'd been born this way—pale skin and with hair the color of ice.

You aren't like other children, Father had told her. *You'll be teased and mocked if you go beyond the quonsuun. You must learn to not care what others think of you. You have arms and legs like other children. You have teeth and fingernails. You can fight! Who you believe yourself to be—that is what will define you. People shun those who look different. You cannot change your hair or your skin. But you don't have to. Be an ice rose. Be unique. And always protect yourself with thorns.*

"I'm cold," Bingmei said, her teeth rattling.

But when she saw the blade in Kunmia's hand, she wanted it. She *needed* it. And it was the need that made her afraid of it.

CHAPTER THREE
Wangfujing

Bingmei had changed into warmer clothes and huddled beneath a fur blanket, watching the cavernous walls of the inlet as the fishing boat sailed toward Wangfujing. The coastline was a maze of forested peaks and fjords that stretched north and west to the high glaciers and then west like a giant bow before going south again, hugging a vast sea. The mountains rising from the water were mostly uninhabitable except in a few locations where nature had permitted some settlers in flatlands and meadowed valleys. Villages and towns were also hidden within coves, invisible unless one knew they were there.

Ensign services, like Kunmia Suun's, were paid to know not only the inner secrets of the coastline but also what lay in the hinterlands. The landscape was harsh and unforgiving, and when the winter months came, it was almost impossible to travel. While Bingmei had never been on a mission before, she had visited Wangfujing many times to collect supplies to endure the season changes.

And the end of the season was fast approaching again.

The days were growing shorter, each one ushering in the time when the Dragon of Night ruled the world instead of the Dragon of Dawn. Bingmei hated the winters, the forced confinement, the bitter cold, the long days of darkness, but Kunmia was always quick to remind her of the opportunities the cold season presented. Time to hone and improve her skills, to calm her mind, and to prepare for the spring, when daylight could last all day long. In the warmer months, when the sun and moon were sisters in the sky, the farmers would coax the barren land to life again, hoping for a harvest that would last through the next cycle. The world felt joyful during the season of the Dragon of Dawn, full of delicacies to be tasted, festivals, and color. So much color. Bingmei loved the flowers that survived in the wild—peonies, larkspur, lilies, yarrow, irises, and globeflowers. There were wild berries too, black crowberries and bog bilberries.

"Wangfujing," Kunmia announced at long last, her voice breaking Bingmei's reverie.

They'd been sailing upstream for most of the day, the mountains coming closer and closer. Wangfujing was built on both sides of the river, connected by a series of six arched stone bridges. The first bridge lay ahead, and it was there that the fishing junk would be forced to stop, for the stone bridge was not tall enough to permit the mast through— just the first defense of the highly defensible town. That protection made it attractive, and it continued to grow in population every year. People were willing to pay extra for the promise of safety. It didn't stop the Qiangdao from attempting to plunder it now and then, but King Budai had many guards and officers, and they organized the citizenry to help defend the city.

Although Budai's dominion was not as vast as some of the other kings who ruled coastline towns, Wangfujing was not an easy prey, and Budai knew how to persuade people to serve his purposes. His power had grown. Greed drove him, but at least he was fair to them. Kunmia had worked for his father as well and was trusted in his court. Her integrity and sense of duty fetched a premium in her pay.

"Can we eat before we see Budai?" Marenqo asked innocently.

"You don't think we'll be feasted at the palace?" Mieshi asked, giving him a mocking smile.

"I'm counting on it. I'd hoped to eat twice as much."

His quip earned him grins all around. It felt better to jest than to focus on what they'd endured to get there. The fisherman's son, Quion, began to untie the ropes and brought down the sail slowly yet efficiently. Kunmia approached Bingmei's seat and squatted near her.

"How are you feeling? Warmer?" she asked.

"I'm much better. The old clothes are still wet, but they'll dry quickly enough in front of a fire."

Kunmia nodded. "You will help the boy sell his fish," she said. "See that he chooses an honest fishmonger. Then bring him to King Budai's palace with you."

Bingmei had looked forward to arriving in honor with Kunmia and the others. Her task was distasteful to her, but it was not her place to refuse it.

"Yes, Master," she said, bowing her head.

Kunmia touched her knee in gratitude and then rose and conferred quietly with the young man. When they reached the wharf and tied off, they were thronged immediately by peddlers seeking news of the cargo of the ship. Kunmia passed them, saying nothing. Bingmei saw the Phoenix Blade had been wrapped in a cloak and tied to Kunmia's pack, disguising it. She felt that queer craving in her belly upon seeing it. It was a valuable sword. No doubt the Qiangdao leader had killed someone to obtain it. The others followed the ensign master out of the boat, leaving Bingmei and Quion alone to face the crowd. The young man's father had been buried at sea at the peak of noon with prayers to the Dragon of Dawn to safeguard part of his soul to the afterlife.

There were several fishmongers among the peddlers, and they barged forward to interrogate the young man. He looked overwhelmed by all the voices, some shouting prices at him, others declaring that his fish stank. An inexperienced barterer, then. Bingmei stepped forward and shrugged out of the fur blanket to help him.

"Be quiet, all of you!" she shouted as she stepped out onto the wharf. Although she was young, she used a commanding voice and adopted a posture of power. "Only those who can pay and take possession now, come forward. The rest, go back. Do not waste our time!"

Quion gave her a look of thanks. He went to his nets to fetch a sample.

"Quickly, quickly!" Bingmei said, gesturing to shoo away those who were merely gawkers. She walked down the line of men, inhaling their natural smells as well as the smells of their *intentions*. Some of their intentions were so awful it made her wince. They shouted at her, pressing in around her, trying to outbid each other right there on the dock. Some were lying outright, hoping their high price would scare off others from bidding, even though they were incapable of paying that amount. She knew many of their tricks, having been tutored by Marenqo, who was quite a barterer himself.

Only two of them had the smell of honest men. She went back to the boat and gestured for Quion to produce the samples from his nets. He joined her on the wharf, and the mongers crowded even closer. Some criticized the fish as paltry, too small. Quion opened his mouth to argue, but Bingmei elbowed him in the ribs to silence him and shook her head curtly.

She watched the crowd, listening to the offers, keeping her attention on the two honest men. When one of them backed away and left, she chose the other, which not only stunned him with surprise—his wasn't the highest bid—but incensed the other fishmongers, who railed at her and called her foolish.

This infuriated Quion again.

"Don't speak so rudely!" he blustered, his cheeks turning red.

She butted him again, giving him a scolding look, and concluded the deal with the fishmonger she'd chosen. Soon the others faded away, although some lingered in case the deal failed. She knew it wouldn't. The honest one smelled not only of fish but of mint as well.

The buyer was permitted to board the boat and inspect the catch, which Bingmei saw more than pleased him. There was a reckoning with a local money changer, who accepted the oath of the monger and provided Quion with the agreed-upon cowry shells. Those shells couldn't be spent in Wangfujing, but they could be traded there for bronze coins of higher value.

They had to wait in the boat for the monger's servants to arrive to haul off their catch, which made Bingmei more and more impatient. She wanted to be at King Budai's palace with the others, not stranded at the wharf. Once the deal was concluded, Quion dunked the nets in the river to clean them and then stuffed them in crates, which he secured with a rope lock. She watched in curiosity as his hands deftly tied the knots. He secured the sail the same way, tying off a strange knot with an intricate pattern. She'd not seen that kind of work before.

It was after dark by the time they finally left the boat and paid a guard at the dock a few shells to protect it. Quion had girded himself with a heavy travel pack, complete with small pots dangling from the straps. He would stand out as a foreigner walking through town with all his possessions clinging to his back. But she understood his reluctance to leave his things behind. Trust was a luxury very few could afford. As they approached the inner streets of Wangfujing, the warm light cast by the globe lanterns dangling from rooftops seemed to welcome them.

"Follow me," Bingmei said.

He gazed at the town, staring up in wonder as they climbed the steep steps to cross the first bridge. The murky water below glimmered with the lantern light. They passed vendors with huge steaming skillets full of frogs or seaweed-wrapped delights. As Bingmei walked, she inhaled the savory scents, listening to the bustle and commotion of the street.

"Thank you," Quion said to her, bumping her elbow with his. One of his pots clanked on his back.

She looked at him in confusion.

"For helping me sell my catch," he said.

"I only did what my master commanded me," she answered.

"I know, but I'm grateful. She said you had a way . . . that you knew if someone was dishonest?" He shook his head in confusion.

She wasn't about to confide in him. "It's one of my instincts. I just know. Most people are dishonest. That makes it easier to find those who aren't. That cook, for example." She nodded to a vendor across the way. "Never buy from him. He talks and boasts and seems friendly." She shook her head. "But he robs those who buy his food." There was a rotting odor to the man.

They had to pick their way through the crowded streets, which meant they were moving more slowly than Bingmei would have liked, but the city was beautiful at dusk—the drab gray walls of the buildings glowed with lantern light. As they walked, they passed an intricate wooden stage. People sat on the benches built around it, chatting and eating the food they'd chosen for dinner, but the stage was empty. There was no festival that night, no decrees to be announced. Along the way were shops with carved stone idols, shaped after animals both magical and mundane. Quion stared at everything, which made her grin in spite of herself.

She'd felt the same wonder on her first visit.

Suddenly, the fisherman's son came to an abrupt stop, gazing in horror at a vendor selling scorpions wriggling on sticks.

"They . . . eat . . . those?" he whispered to her, his face showing his disgust.

"They're a specialty here," Bingmei said. "You must try them."

"Never," Quion said vehemently.

"We don't eat them *raw*," she said. She withdrew a small bronze coin from the purse hidden beneath her tunic, then tucked the pouch back out of sight. When she offered the coin to the vendor, he took one of the many sticks of wriggling scorpions and dipped it into a vat of bubbling oil. Bingmei grinned at the queasy look on Quion's face as he watched the vat.

A short while later, the cook withdrew the dripping stick from the vat and doused it with spices from a shaker. The scorpions had all perished, of course, and were brittle and still. Bingmei took the skewer and bit off the first one. It was crunchy and full of flavor.

"You try one," she said, offering him the skewer. Another man shoved past them to buy some for himself. "They come by ship from the desert."

Quion stared at her, then at the skewer, his nose twitching with discomfort.

"Why would you *eat* that?" he asked with a pained look.

"They're good," she said.

A few bystanders had caught on to his discomfort. Their pointing and laughter seemed to embarrass him, and he took the skewer from her, likely just to end the spectacle.

"Don't think about it, just eat it," she said coaxingly.

Quion took a few deep breaths. He was building up his courage. When she'd come to Wangfujing before, she'd seen Marenqo eat four or five of these skewers by himself. He loved the various local fares.

Timidly, Quion brought the skewer to his lips and, wincing, bit off one of the scorpions. He grimaced as he began to crunch into it, and then his eyes widened in surprise as the flavors from the spices delighted his mouth.

"See?" she said, snatching the skewer back from him and taking another.

He nodded vigorously. "That is . . . I'm glad you . . . I wouldn't have thought . . ."

He stumbled over his words and then smiled as she handed him the last scorpion.

A sharp smell hit her, so intense it made her eyes water. The damp rot of dishonesty. A person stumbled and fell against her, knocking her down. He mumbled an apology, trying to help her stand, but he reeked of ill intent.

Bad smells abounded. Someone was pointing at her on the ground, laughing.

And then she saw a wiry man slip the bag of cowry shells out of Quion's pocket while the fisherman's son stared down at her worriedly. He smelled even worse than his friend.

"Get away from her!" Quion said to the first man, trying to wrench him away from Bingmei.

She got to her feet, anger surging inside her as the thief slipped off into the crowd.

"Thief," she called out. She fixed Quion with a look. "Stay here."

She charged into the crowd after the wiry man.

CHAPTER FOUR

The Smell of Greed

Even though Bingmei could not see the wiry man, she could smell him. Angry shouts and disgruntled looks met her as she carved a path through the pressing crowd, weaving around the slower walkers as she made her way down aisles of vendors selling carvings, trinkets, and local dishes. She collided once with a larger man, who scolded her as if she were a street waif. When he tried to grab her to scold her some more, she broke free and continued in her pursuit past ancient stone houses with slanted roofs.

Her quarry had reached another stone bridge that crossed the river, and she caught a glimpse of him before he slipped out of sight. She was tempted to reach into her pocket and invoke the wooden cricket, which would have enabled her to leap up to the top of the bridge and cut him off, but it was forbidden to invoke magic in any town. Although the cricket had never summoned a wisp of fog, using it within Wangfujing would be a greater crime than the theft of cowry shells.

Anger roiled inside her as she ran up the arch of the bridge in fast pursuit, and went down the other side. The thief's scent was still strong.

Following it, she went deeper into Wangfujing, with its assortment of scorpion sticks, frogs, and other delicacies. She was about to pass a stone carver, one who made animals out of marble, when she realized the scent disappeared into his little ramshackle booth. She marched past the owner, who had a sour smell all his own, ignoring his questions, and followed the smell of the thief through the back.

There weren't any lanterns on this side, and the alley lay dark, full of shadow. Her nose told her which way he had gone. The street had broken, uneven slabs of stone, so she slowed her pace, knowing he would need to do the same. The guffaws and noise from the main street masked any noise the man might be making in his escape, and the smell of sewage in the alley made him harder to track. She frowned, judging her way carefully.

Reaching another crooked side street, she smelled him again, along with the scent of several other men. He wasn't alone after all. Or this was where his gang hid in wait for him.

She turned the corner and started onto the smaller street. She heard a few guttural voices, the clink of shells coming from a little area farther ahead.

A voice came out of the dark.

"How did you find me?"

She couldn't see the speaker, who sounded mystified, but she smelled he was near. It was the thief she'd hunted. The scuff of a shoe sounded nearby. A door creaked.

"You stole from someone under the protection of Kunmia Suun's ensign," Bingmei said.

A chuckle sounded. "That foolish *boy*?"

"Yes," Bingmei answered, continuing to move forward. She didn't have her grandfather's saber anymore. She'd lost it to the killing fog. But she didn't need weapons. She might look small, but her body was a weapon.

"You shouldn't have come after it," said the voice. "That was a mistake."

A shoe scuff sounded behind her at the back of the alley. Then another. There were at least four, maybe five of them. Her eyes were still adjusting to the dark.

"You would fight me?" Bingmei said, her insides twisting with anticipation and eagerness as well as a little worry. "You should beg for forgiveness."

"You think we're afraid of a proud little girl?" said the voice.

"You should be," Bingmei said, her tone seething.

She reached into her pocket and rubbed the wooden cricket. It was a risk, yes. But she knew the thieves wouldn't dare report her to King Budai's officers. What could they accuse her of when they themselves were criminals?

The magic swelled in her legs, and she jumped straight up, landing on the rooftop.

There was a grunt of confusion, then one of the roof tiles slid from under her foot and crashed down onto the street. She ran and jumped, and the magic ebbed as she landed, but her maneuver had put her behind the majority of the thieves. Their smell revealed their location, and she attacked swiftly, striking in a series of punches and kicks, feeling the bulk of skin, muscle, and bone quiver under her blows. Someone grabbed her from behind, but she smashed her elbow back into the man's cheek, following it with a tornado kick that sent him to the ground.

A light blinded her. One of them had a shielded lantern, a thief's tool that concentrated the light into sharp beams. She winced in pain but then ran toward the light, jumping into the air in a double kick that caught the man in the chest. He staggered backward, dropping the lantern. The bouncing beam caught on a dagger as it slashed toward her face. She backed away, caught the elbow of her attacker, and flipped the man into the street. The moment he landed, she kicked him hard in the kidney, causing him to wail in pain, then kicked him again before releasing his arm.

She whirled, sensing someone behind her. The spilled light from the lantern was level with her legs, but it opened up her vision to her attackers and theirs to her. She struck the thief once in the chest. He grimaced but grabbed her hair, starting in surprise when her wig came off in his hands. She frowned and kicked him in the groin, and as he doubled over, still gripping her wig in his hand, she sidestepped and did a hammer-fist strike with her fist against the side of his neck.

One more lunged at her. The wiry man. He caught her arm with one hand and smashed his fist into her ribs with the other. It should have hurt. He had hit her as hard as he could. But she was too wild with fury to feel pain. She fought back, hitting him again and again until he staggered back into the wall of a stone building. She struck him where it would hurt and bruise him. His face crumpled with pain, and he tried to pull away, but she continued to hit him until his eyes rolled back in his head and he collapsed, face-first on the stone.

Bingmei, in a low cat stance, swiveled around, hands held in a knife-edge pose, searching for another attacker. Some of the thieves moaned in pain. One was trying to crawl away from her.

She found the pouch of cowry shells on the biggest man, the one who had pulled off her wig. He flinched when she touched him, quivering in fear.

"Who are you?" he whispered in dread.

She snatched the wig out of his hand and gave him a vicious kick. They'd unmasked her secret, her pale hair. That had made her especially angry and resentful.

She gave him no answer. He didn't deserve one. Giving them all a withering look, the kind of sneer that Mieshi was so good at, she tucked the pouch into her pocket. Her knuckles were starting to throb, but it was a pleasant pain. She had trained for years to defend not only herself but those she was assigned to protect.

Even if he was just a fisherman's son.

杀雾

She found Quion wandering the streets, hopelessly lost. She sighed as she approached him, watching him ask strangers for help, something only an innocent fool would do in such a place. She walked up to him and tapped his shoulder. He spun around, looking at her in surprise, and she put the pouch in his hand—maybe a little roughly.

"I told you to wait back there for me," she said, arching her eyebrows.

"I . . . I got worried. What if they outnumbered you?"

"They did," Bingmei said. "Nothing I couldn't handle. You were under our protection. They shouldn't have stolen from you."

He was staring at her again, his eyes looking slightly confused.

"What?" she said, feeling a little stab of self-consciousness in her heart.

"Um," he fumbled, then gestured for her to come out of the road. She noticed others were starting to stare at her as well.

"What?" she demanded, following him.

"Your hair is showing," he said, whispering.

She realized that when the big thief had yanked on her wig, he'd pulled loose one of her braided coils. Quion was right, one of the braids was dangling down her back. She'd been so caught up in the rush of her victory, she hadn't noticed. She frowned and reached back to try to fix it.

"I can help," he said, and reached to assist, but she butted him with her elbow.

"I don't need help," she said. Soon it was tucked beneath the wig. "Let's go."

Quion walked alongside her, quiet, as she led the way to King Budai's palace at the center of town. They crossed another bridge, one of three that led to the main square of the town. This was the hub of Wangfujing, the place where people crowded and gossiped. Bingmei stopped at the peak of the bridge, drinking in the sight of the glowing lanterns on both sides of the river, the noises, and the smells. Several months had passed since she'd last stood there. Soon it would all be blanketed in snow, the days surrendered to the Dragon of Night.

Quion approached and stood next to her, gazing at the river. He rested his elbows on the railing. There were stone carvings of animals on the support stays at regular intervals.

"I'm sorry I didn't listen to you," he said.

She snorted. "You're like other boys. You don't think women can be fighters. But we can. We just have to work harder to prove it."

"You're very brave," he said.

That mollified her a little. "Don't we all have to be? In order to survive this harsh world?"

He nodded in agreement. "You especially."

She wrinkled her brow. "How so?"

"My father told me that some children are born . . . like you," he added, his voice dropping lower. "The winter sickness. It's rare. He . . . he said parents will sometimes abandon a baby if they have it. Being different is dangerous."

His expression was considerate, not mocking. He was perhaps a fool, but he wasn't mean-spirited.

"Kunmia says that once I have a reputation, the color of my hair won't matter. Everyone in the ensign knows. I don't mind you knowing. But if you tease me about it . . ."

He nodded vigorously. "I won't. I promise."

She looked back at the water. "Thank you for telling me. Back there. I hadn't noticed the looks I was getting. Marenqo would have noticed it right away. Well, we should go to the palace to meet the others."

"Does your ensign live here?" he asked her while straightening.

"Wangfujing? No, we have our own quonsuun up in the mountains."

He wrinkled his brow. "What's a quonsuun?"

She shrugged. "That's just what they're called. They were holy places, I think, back when the ancients lived here. Set away from the towns and villages. Most are up in the mountains. It's where we train, where we live. Kunmia's is very prominent. We stay there during the dark season."

"Oh," Quion said. "I'd like to see it."

"You might," Bingmei said. "Kunmia might want you to join us. You have skills that would be useful, I think. Like Marenqo."

Quion pursed his lips and shrugged. He really was a fool. He didn't realize the honor it would be if Kunmia were to issue an invitation.

"Do you want another stick of scorpions before we go?" she asked, grinning.

His eyes lit up. "I'll pay this time."

She let him.

杀雾

King Budai's palace in Wangfujing was girded by a high stone wall nearly three times Bingmei's height. There was nothing that revealed the palace that lay beyond. The commoners who lived in Wangfujing would never be permitted inside. Quion gawked at the wall and the two enormous statues of toads that bracketed the entrance. The doors had probably been replaced recently, for Bingmei noticed the wood was a uniform stain. Each was intricately carved with scenes featuring various animals, and the ring handles were clenched in the jaws of two metal lions. The doorway alone was enough to flaunt the power of the king who resided inside.

Bingmei grasped one of the rings and tapped it against the brass rivets beneath it to knock.

After a brief wait, she heard the groan of the hinges, and one of the heavy doors opened. Inside, torchlight revealed the officers' uniforms. Marenqo stood beside them, his expression impatient, and bid her enter.

As Quion followed her in, he gaped at the lush decorations within the doors, at the marble pathway, inlaid with brass, that led through an arrangement of trees and flowers growing out of tall urns full of earth. A glimpse of the palace could be seen beyond the foliage.

"You're late," Marenqo chided. "I've had to wait for you."

"Has the feast started yet?" Bingmei asked sweetly.

"That will happen later. Come, Kunmia wants to see you quickly."

"Me?" Bingmei asked.

"No, the fisherman's son."

"Truly?" Quion asked, looking flummoxed. He didn't know Marenqo's sense of humor.

"Don't be a fool. She wants to see Bingmei in the throne room. Bao Budai already has another job for us." He wagged his eyebrows at her.

"It's too late in the season to start another one," Bingmei said.

"All the more reason to hurry, then. Come along!" He gave her an enigmatic grin. "Also, there's another ensign here from the kingdom of Sajinau. Budai wants us to work with them on this mission."

That was a strange request, especially since the others were affiliated with a different kingdom. Bingmei felt a throb of concern in her heart. "Why would we need the help of another ensign?"

"I don't know," Marenqo said with delight. "But isn't it curious?"

As they walked along the path, the smell of the fresh flowers made her want to linger, but her desire to learn what was happening drove her on. Although the palace itself was grand, the inner gardens were her favorite part of the estate. The ivy growing on the pillars, the moss thick on the walls. The sound of lapping water from the spring. It was one of her favorite places, surrounded by the fresh flowers cultivated only by the extraordinarily wealthy. Nature masked the obvious.

Inside the palace, the sweaty smell of greed was nearly intolerable.

CHAPTER FIVE

King Budai

Every person had a smell. This was not just the smell of smoke from one who sat too close to a fire. Or the smell of a laborer's sweat. A person's character, their motives and drives, also came off them as a scent. Or at least it did for Bingmei. King Budai smelled like greed, which had a lemony tang mixed with sweat and sometimes cooked yams. Even so, he was not a dishonest man. There was nothing rotten about his motives. He craved power, treasure, artifacts, and boundless wealth. It was a purpose that drove him in all his decisions—and, according to Bingmei's nose, poisoned him.

Bingmei entered the king's throne room alone, Marenqo steering Quion in another direction. The throne room was a collection of the king's trophies, rare and costly items displayed on various decorative pedestals and shelves. There were figurines of animals carved by master craftsmen from every stone imaginable. Many were of giant toads or frogs, which the king loved to collect. Weapons adorned the walls, bound in meiwood scabbards and positioned to highlight their elegance. Delicate fans were encased in glass to protect them from further deterioration. Fragrant jasmine burned on an incense stand, but its sweet perfume could not mask the sharp scent of greed. Guards were positioned at the doors leading in. No one stole from King Budai. His vengeance was swift and terrible.

King Budai was a large man. It was said he'd been a powerful warrior in his youth, but his covetousness extended to a powerful hunger for food. His throne was made of meiwood inlaid with gold, and velvet cushions padded his plump posterior. Two snow leopards were chained at the foot of the dais atop which his immaculate chair was positioned. One of the leopards lifted its head and yawned as Bingmei approached.

Budai's meaty arm lowered, and he began tapping the armrest. Kunmia sat in a smaller chair in front of him, beside a strange man. The man's saber and his martial posture hinted he might be the leader of the other ensign. He had long hair, partly braided in the back, and an arrogant look. The coppery smell of pride made her nose wrinkle.

Her eyes darted to the long wooden box near Kunmia's boot. The Phoenix Blade was in that box—it called to her.

"Ah, there she is," King Budai said as Bingmei approached. "The ice rose. Bingmei. Welcome back to Wangfujing, my dear. Kunmia Suun says you acquitted yourself well. But of course you would. You are the great Jiao's granddaughter." He gave her a broad grin. He loved knowing about people's connections, especially if they had any degree of fame or honor. He'd taken an interest in her from the first time they'd met, and had even promised to help her reclaim her parents' ensign— with a suitable loan, of course. It would take a great deal of money to accomplish it.

"Thank you, my lord," Bingmei said. "I am pleased his memory has not dimmed."

"Everything dims with time, my dear," Budai said. "Look at this palace. Nothing like the splendor of its illustrious past. It must have been a famous port long ago. But now . . . so paltry. I hope to restore it to its former glory. You must be thirsty after your travels. Have some water from our ancestors' well." He snapped his fingers, and a servant was dispatched with a brass pitcher and goblet, which was promptly filled and handed to her.

Bingmei sipped the lukewarm drink gratefully. She was especially thirsty after chasing the thief down. The palace was built over a well, and only the palace's residents and their honored guests could drink of the water.

Two other servants idled in the square-shaped room, Bingmei noticed, and another man walked around examining the collections. He was tall, also long-haired, and had a disinterested look on his face as he stared at the pieces. His dress reminded her of the man seated beside Kunmia. She guessed him to be just a few years older than herself.

"Drink your fill," Budai encouraged after she lowered the goblet. Bingmei nodded and finished the cup before handing it back to the servant.

Budai leaned forward in his chair, the cushion making a squishing sound as he did so. "You are trusted by Kunmia Suun, young Bingmei. Your estimable master will not make this decision without your advice. That speaks highly of you, does it not? That means *I* value you as well. Let us counsel together. Come closer."

Bingmei did as she was asked, coming to a stop next to her master, who sat with a serious expression, her hands folded on her lap. The man seated beside Kunmia eyed Bingmei skeptically.

"This is Bao Damanhur," Budai said, gesturing to the man. "Leader of an ensign from Sajinau. While I prefer baldness, these fellows never cut their hair. Unless"—Budai grinned, his own dome shining in the lamplight, and wagged his finger—"they are defeated in battle! The longer the hair, the more victories! At least, that is what they claim in Sajinau." He chuckled softly.

"A bald man insulting our ways, Budai?" said the other man.

"I am bald because I worry so much about the prosperity of my people," said Budai in sugary tones.

"The prosperity of your people," said Bao Damanhur. "Your words drip with sincerity, great king."

"Alas," Budai said, "Damanhur is not a courtier. But I forgive his insolence because he is a powerful swordsman. The best in Sajinau. Now to the point. He brought me something found by a fisherman last moon. The fisherman wished to sell it to raise money." He snapped his fingers twice, and a servant rushed to a pedestal on which a fragment of broken stone was displayed. The servant hefted it, grunting, for apparently it was heavy, carried it to the king's throne, and set it down on the dais.

As Bingmei examined it, she saw what looked to be a wall crenellation, carved into a pattern of dragons, faint and blemished on the edging. It looked very old. Bingmei crouched to examine it more closely.

"What do you see, young Bingmei?" asked Budai in a silky voice. The lemony smell was getting stronger. The king was keenly interested in this piece of rubble. She'd seen much finer pieces before. Something was special about this one.

She looked up at him. "Where did the fisherman find it?"

King Budai grinned. "That we will not reveal until we have a bargain."

Bingmei glanced at Kunmia, whose eyes were fixed on Budai. She smelled uneasy.

"What bargain?" Bingmei asked.

"It was found by a glacier. The fisherman said it is starting to melt. There's a waterfall coming down. I tell you this only because there are hundreds of glaciers, and the north rim is so vast, you'd never find it without knowing where to look." His eyes glittered. "There was an even larger piece, the fisherman said. He ventured farther north than he'd ever been, trying new waters, and one of his traps got stuck in the river. So he swam down to free it, only to find the stone. The waters up north are as clear as glass. It was too heavy to bring, so he broke off just a piece of it. This piece," he said, gesturing to the stone.

The king steepled his enormous fingers together. "It was found in a place where no artifacts have ever been found. We've plundered from the past so many times, we think there are no troves left. But there are still myths about Fusang, the Summer Palace."

Bingmei had heard many stories about the ancient ones and the palaces they'd left behind. Legends handed down from person to person. Her parents had told her about the Summer Palace, hidden in the mountains far to the north, but she'd never heard it called Fusang. They'd described it as a place full of magic and wonder. Anything could happen there, they'd said, for the killing fog didn't come. One time, her father had gone off in search of it with another ensign, but they'd found nothing to indicate it existed. The sudden memory of her parents made her cheeks tingle.

"As we know, in the highest north, the sun never sets during the summer. Legend says that the splendor of the palace in Sajinau pales in comparison to Fusang. Many people believe it's only a myth, but I have a feeling this fisherman may have discovered a relic from it. I've told as much to Bao Damanhur. I think, my little ice rose, that Fusang is hidden *beneath* that glacier. The force of the ice must have broken off part of the palace and dragged it into the river. But now the ice is receding. The seasons are growing longer. My sages all think something is changing."

Budai sniffed, adjusting his seat. His voice thrummed with anticipation. "I may be wrong. It may just be a fragment of rock that's worth only a few cowry shells. But I have an instinct for making wealth. If it's true, if Fusang is real, then others will try to steal the treasures. I want to get there first. I want my children and my grandchildren and my great-grandchildren to live there someday." He held up two fingers. "That is why I'm convinced *two* ensigns are needed. One to guard it. One to bring its treasures here. It must be kept in secrecy. If the Qiangdao were to learn of it . . ." He shook his head. "They'd find a chieftain and raise a horde that would destroy all of the kingdoms. Think of it. Think of the wealth that may be sitting beneath all that ice."

He leaned back in his chair. "I trust both of your ensigns." His gaze shifted back to Bingmei. "But Kunmia Suun trusts your instincts even more than mine. We must come to an agreement. I insist. We must do this tonight."

"The agreement is simple," Bao Damanhur said, rising from his chair. "I will lead the mission. We cannot have two ensigns obeying two masters. One must lead. That will be me. We found the fisherman who found the rock with the dragon carvings."

Another wave of his coppery scent wafted to Bingmei. He wanted the job. He was determined to have it.

Kunmia rose as well. "Then you can go alone."

"Please," King Budai said, holding up his hands. "Surely we can find a way to accomplish this? Yes, Bao Damanhur, you and your friend found the stone. But without my insight, it meant nothing to you. This is a chance to win a fortune! Don't be proud."

Bingmei noticed Damanhur's companion was watching them keenly. His hair was as long as his master's, and he had an ambitious look in his eye. He smelled of intrigue and deception, but not dishonesty. On further appraisal, he was rather handsome, but what was Marenqo's jest about handsome men?

It's the handsome ones you should be careful of the most.

"Who is that man?" Bingmei asked, nodding to the fellow who had not joined their circle.

"He's my servant, Wuren," Bao Damanhur said. "He's no one. Ignore him as I do." This last statement was said with a chuckle.

It was a lie. A blatant one. Bingmei shook her head. "You speak falsely."

Damanhur's brows lifted. "I'll not have a *child* call me a liar," he said.

Kunmia stepped forward as Bingmei's cheeks flushed with anger. She put her hand on Bingmei's shoulder. "This is why I called her. Something did not feel right when I came in. I understand your eagerness, my lord, but we will not be party to this without understanding the truth. We will go and keep your secret. Find another ensign to make the journey."

She guided Bingmei with her hand and started to leave.

"Wait," Budai said, his voice throbbing.

Kunmia stopped, but she did not turn around. Bingmei felt the tension in the room shift. She was proud of her master's decision to walk away. It was the right thing to do.

"Give me the funds, and *I* will hire another ensign," Damanhur said in a low voice.

A deep sigh followed. "You are a capable master," Budai said. "But I *trust* her. She worked for my father as well. Please, Kunmia, come back. We can work this out."

Kunmia turned. "You knew the truth, yet you did not tell me."

"I was testing *her*," Budai explained, gesturing to Bingmei. "Truly, her instincts are formidable. But let me speak plainly."

"No," Damanhur said, his brows bristling.

"Trust me. You will not succeed without her help. Nor would she without yours. There is a reason I require you both for this mission. There is power in the balance between the sexes. Without that balance, either of you would fail alone. Please, Kunmia. Hear me out."

Kunmia approached the chair again. One of the leopards growled.

"Tush," the king said, jabbing it with his shoe. "Now, let me speak plainly. What Bao Damanhur told you was the truth."

Bingmei squinted at that, and the king held up his hands placatingly.

"It just wasn't *all* of it," he conceded. "As you know, the name Wuren means 'someone without a home.' Without a country. Someone all on their own. That is true. But you were correct in divining he is more than just a common man. That man is Prince Rowen of Sajinau.

Who—I will add—has abandoned his father's kingdom and forsaken fealty to his father. He masquerades as Bao Damanhur's servant, but clearly the disguise did not fool you, Bingmei. A testament to your insight."

As he spoke, Bingmei stared at the stranger more closely. There was something regal about his bearing. There was a quiet discontent in him and, yes, the propensity for deception she'd sensed before. He approached them, eyeing Budai with a small frown.

"I know your father, Prince Rowen," Kunmia said with a tone of disappointment. "He's an honorable man."

"I don't disagree," he replied, keeping his features guarded.

"His father chose his older brother, although they are very close in age, to become the crown prince," said Budai. "A decision that has not settled well with His Highness."

Damanhur snorted and turned away.

"That is all you need know of their sad story," Budai said. "I think it becomes clearer, then, why discovering Fusang is of paramount importance for him. I admire Prince Rowen's ambition. I, too, was a second son, although my father chose *me* over my elder brother. It is my wish that your two ensigns join for this mission. In my heart, I do not believe you can succeed without each other."

"But who will lead it?" Kunmia asked.

"You, of course," said King Budai gravely.

Damanhur turned, scowling, his brows furrowed. "I will not serve beneath someone who has not defeated me."

"Or you will not serve beneath a woman?" Kunmia asked.

"Your sex makes little difference to me," Damanhur said hotly. "Nor would it protect you."

His arrogance was appalling. Bingmei had no doubt that Kunmia would win such a contest.

"That," King Budai said with a chuckle, "was ill-advised. Be sensible, Damanhur. Surely you know her reputation."

"I do," he answered. "But mine is of equal consequence."

"So if she bests you, then you agree to accompany her ensign on this mission? I want it to be clearly understood that you would owe her allegiance for the duration. You would be second."

The man nodded firmly.

"Very well. I find those terms agreeable. Master Kunmia? Do you accept this challenge from your rival? If you are defeated, your ensign will serve under his for the duration?"

Kunmia nodded sternly.

"Excellent!" Budai exclaimed. "When will you face each other? It must be soon, before the Dragon of Night rules the sky!"

"Tomorrow," Kunmia said, bowing her head slightly to Damanhur.

He snorted. "So be it."

Bingmei saw the gleam in Budai's eyes, smelled a hint of satisfaction from him. He was pleased with the outcome. Either way, he would accomplish his desire of unifying their two ensigns.

CHAPTER SIX

Two Masters

Bingmei felt the magic of the Phoenix Blade calling to her, drawing her toward it. She was attracted to it, compelled by it, hungered for it. Never had she felt this way about a weapon or an artifact. The compulsion was so strong it pulled a piece of herself out of her body. She looked down at her body, eyes closed, asleep on the decorative bed in the small state room in King Budai's palace. Then her ghostly form walked away, down the dark corridor, pulled toward the blade. Her ghost feet made no sound.

A few small oil lamps provided enough light for her to see the detailed carvings on the wall panels. The symbols were primarily of frogs and toads. A queer eagerness thrilled inside her, a desperate longing for the sword. It led her to it—down the corridor, to the left at the fork. She could sense its force tugging at her soul. The abandoned corridors were full of small stands demonstrating the king's vast wealth. But they were all trinkets—meaningless. There was only one item of value in the manor.

The Phoenix Blade. And in her heart she felt it belonged to *her*.

She finally reached the last passageway and approached the palace vault. The magic urged her toward the two sentries standing guard, and she cringed internally, fearing they would notice her. She could smell them, even in her ghost state, and they had the sour smell of boredom. She could not see herself, but she could smell herself, too, and wondered if it were a dream or a vision of some sort.

She passed through the door as easily as if she were the killing fog.

There were two men on the inside. One was King Budai's steward, a man named Guanjia. He would get the sword appraised, valued, and find a place to store it amidst Budai's vast wealth. A tall, thin man—as bald as his master—he had served Budai's father for many years. His eyebrows were gray with age. Along with Guanjia was the man Bingmei had noticed earlier, the self-exiled prince. Wuren. Rowen.

The two stood over an open box, rectangular in shape, made of expensive sandalwood with a velvet lining. Within the box was the Phoenix Blade, sheathed in a beautiful meiwood scabbard. She saw tendrils of magic radiating off the hilt, invisible to the natural eye, but quite plain to her in her spirit form.

Rowen was eyeing the blade with keen fascination. The lemony scent of greed hung in the air, stronger here than it had been in the hall.

"And how much do you think Budai would pay for it?" Rowen asked softly, his hands clasped behind his back. He was calm on the exterior, but Bingmei could sense his desire for the weapon burning under the surface.

"It's hard to say, my lord," Guanjia replied with an evasive tone. He was a shrewd bargainer. Especially if he knew he possessed an item someone else coveted. "Can one set a price on so deadly a thing? Kunmia Suun hasn't agreed to sell it yet. She may take it back to her quonsuun when she goes. But I know King Budai will make her a formidable offer."

"Isn't it safer here in Wangfujing?"

Guanjia shrugged. "I should think so. Once word gets out that she has it, there will be many outlaws striving to steal it back. It's a danger to whoever attempts to hold it. Or use it. Another battle could be deadly."

Bingmei did not want King Budai to have it. She felt a strange kinship with the blade, something that had budded inside her the first time she'd seen it, and bloomed when she'd touched it. She'd invoked its magic unwittingly and nearly killed herself. Yet that danger only made it more intriguing to her. With a blade like that, would she be powerful enough to kill her family's murderer, the Qiangdao named Muxidi? The thought tantalized her.

The prince's head turned suddenly, as if he'd heard something. He looked back at the room, searching for something.

"Are you all right?" Guanjia asked.

Bingmei felt a twisting feeling inside her. She didn't understand what it meant, but it was uncomfortable.

"Are we alone?" the prince asked.

Guanjia turned around, gazing at the vault. There were so many decorative chests and boxes around, each one worth a small fortune. The thought of the king owning the Phoenix Blade and stowing it in such a box, another possession to be coveted but not used, made her feel enraged. Or was it the sword's feelings she was experiencing?

"Well . . . yes, we are," Guanjia said. "The guards are outside." He shrugged and held up his hands. "There is no one else here."

The prince pursed his lips, nodding, but she sensed his growing discomfort. "Never mind about the sword. Tell me how much money I have left."

"Your inheritance is dwindling quickly," Guanjia said.

"How can that be?"

Guanjia chuckled. "You chose to stay at the palace, my lord. You knew it would not be for free. King Budai is generous, but he's no fool. You've eaten from his table, sent his servants to do your business, and you've dined well in town, have you not? The clothes you've purchased. All of this adds up."

A sharp smell, the tang of disappointment and frustration, roiled off Rowen, although his exterior remained calm. "It should have lasted much longer than this."

"Allow Budai his games, my lord," said Guanjia soothingly. Yet Bingmei smelled his ulterior motives. His job was to bleed the prince dry, one he had taken to with relish. "Use him as he uses you. With his sponsorship, you're sure to find Fusang. Think of the wealth you will be entitled to! The paltry sum your father gave you as an 'inheritance' will be nothing compared to such a fortune. Go on this journey, and you will soon be a powerful man. More wealthy than your brother and the kings of Sajinau back a hundred years."

The words, and the tone with which they were delivered, were intended to make Rowen covetous. The smell that followed proved they'd had the desired effect.

"I'm counting on it," Rowen said. "Just as I'm counting on *our* agreement. You hear much in this court, information you don't always pass on to Budai. When I rule in Sajinau, you will have a more powerful master who can reward your loyalty even better." He gazed back down at the sword, staring at it hungrily. He reached out to touch it, but Guanjia quickly closed the lid.

"Patience, my lord. I'm certain your diligence will be rewarded."

As the locks were fixed back on the box, Bingmei felt herself wrenched away from the scene. She awoke with a start, breathing fast, feeling as if she'd been holding her breath for a long time. She gasped, trying to gain air. Her skin tingled, and pinpricks of pain stabbed the ends of her fingers and toes, as if they'd fallen asleep. The drapery on the elegant bed fluttered at her sudden movement. The room was dark, but she smelled the sandalwood, the silk sheets. She shivered, heart pounding, a strange but momentous feeling rumbling through her.

Had she dreamed of the Phoenix Blade?

杀雾

King Budai's palace had a training yard that was fully enclosed. Weapons of different styles and shapes were fixed to the walls. Tall spears, hooked blades, glaives, and sai-tam. Bingmei went there to practice and found Kunmia already there, in the middle of a form. Mieshi stood watching her, arms folded, frowning. Bingmei sidled up next to her to watch Kunmia's elegant poses interspersed with blindingly fast techniques.

"I still can't believe that man had the audacity to challenge her," Mieshi told Bingmei. "It's an insult. She is more experienced than that upstart. He's only slightly older than me, but I've come to learn. I wouldn't *dare* challenge Kunmia Suun."

Mieshi was always quick to take offense. She masked her feelings well, but she was highly judgmental of other people. It wasn't an awful smell because she held herself to the same impossible standards she used for others. Her respect and honor for Kunmia was evident. She tried to be a perfect disciple, and whenever she failed, she was her own toughest critic. It drove her to do better, *be* better. Although Bingmei admired Mieshi, she couldn't help but smell the disdain the woman had for her pale skin and hair. Mieshi had never said anything about it, and never would, but she didn't need to speak the words in order for Bingmei to know her true feelings. It didn't help that Mieshi herself was a classic beauty.

"Apparently he has a reputation in his own kingdom," Bingmei said. "But I agree with you. He was foolish to make such a challenge."

"She will win," Mieshi said with conviction. "I know it." But there was worry beneath the certainty. If Kunmia failed, it would lower her in Mieshi's eyes.

A strong smell wafted to Bingmei's nose, one she recognized as pride.

"If she loses, I won't make her cut her hair," Bao Damanhur said, approaching from around a large pillar. "I can't abide ugly women." He'd entered from another side of the room, perhaps hoping to catch them unawares. It might have worked if not for his tangy scent. He leaned against the pillar opposite them, arms folded, looking at Kunmia with carefully cultivated disinterest.

Mieshi's emotions turned instantly hostile and fierce. The intensity of it made Bingmei's eyes water.

"You have no right to challenge her," Mieshi said, keeping her voice low, not wanting to disturb Kunmia's routine.

"I have every right. Don't be stupid."

His words were barbs to her. "You are the fool here. As you soon shall see."

"Possibly. But I was trained by the best swordsman in my land, which is a much more well-known land than these parts. I was his best student. I'm not worried."

"You should be," Mieshi sneered.

"What's your name?" he asked her. Bingmei could smell that he was interested in her. Her defiance and anger appealed to him. He liked spirited women.

"Why should I tell you?"

"It's just a name. Why be coy?"

"Why be so rude?" Mieshi shot back.

"It's not rudeness. I'm honest. I find false humility boring. Your master has a strong reputation. The king of my land admires and respects her. But I don't want to be admired or respected. I want to be—"

"Hated? Despised?" Mieshi said. "Those are great alternatives."

Damanhur chuckled. "Oh, you are a rare pheasant. I'm going to enjoy plucking your feathers."

"I am not a fowl."

"Are you sure? Isn't that a feather on your neck?" He reached playfully for her hair, and she snatched his wrist, squeezing it hard. Her eyes were full of venom, but she was secretly enjoying his attention. Bingmei, on the other hand, was repulsed by him.

"Do not touch me," Mieshi warned in a low voice.

"Are you afraid you will like it?" he whispered back.

Bingmei noticed that Kunmia had finished her form and was approaching them. Some of her hair had come loose from her bun, but she was still elegant and stately.

"Are you ready to face me, Bao Damanhur?" she said.

Mieshi released his wrist, staring at him with new contempt.

A low smile tilted his mouth. "I was ready last night. Shall we call our witnesses, then?"

Kunmia bowed to him.

It did not take long to assemble those who wished to watch their duel. All of Kunmia's ensign came, including Quion, the fisherman's son, who gazed at the training room in wonderment. Bao Damanhur had four men in his ensign, not including Prince Rowen. His disciples all carried similar swords, and their scent bore the same signature.

King Budai and his steward arrived and took the seats at the head of the training yard. The king's chair was not as resplendent as his seat in the throne room, but it still bore a velvet cushion. Some servants arrived carrying trays of sweet meats, wine goblets, and various dishes for the bystanders. Marenqo quickly sidled up to one of them and began sneaking morsels from the dishes.

Kunmia and Damanhur approached the king's chair and bowed before him.

King Budai gestured for them to rise and then motioned for Guanjia to speak.

"We are gathered here to witness a competition of skill. Two masters have agreed to settle their dispute by martial contest. As it is not the goal of the ruler of Wangfujing that either should maim or harm the other, it will not be a trial of weapons but a trial of skill, of cunning, of form. The first to be rendered unconscious is the loser. Both sides have agreed that the winner will lead their combined ensigns on the agreed-upon mission. There will be no use of dianxue and no killing blows."

Damanhur snorted at the reference to dianxue. It was a deadly art that taught the ability to paralyze an opponent and incapacitate them with a single touch. If Kunmia Suun knew the secret of dianxue, she had not revealed it to her disciples.

Bingmei waited in anticipation for the duel to begin. So many feelings and emotions swarmed in the room, each with its own scent, creating an overwhelming stew of conflicting smells. The suspense and dread of not knowing the outcome tormented her. Part of her wanted to wait outside the training room and find out what happened later. But she had to know and did not wish to dishonor Kunmia, and so she endured the discomfort.

Damanhur and Kunmia then walked to the center of the training room and stood facing each other. They exchanged a crisp salute. Kunmia dropped into a cat stance, one arm arching above her head, the other poised in front of her. Her knees were bent, one leg in front, her foot just barely touching the floor. It was a strong defensive position.

Damanhur pursed his lips, eyeing her with a mocking tilt of his head. Then he rushed at her, showing no hesitation at all. Kunmia protected herself, her motions fast and precise. A subtle shift to her neck, and his fist sailed past her head. She counterattacked, and the two whirled and circled each other, locked in singular focus.

There was a flurry of blows, kicks, and the sound of bones striking each other. Kunmia attempted to hook his feet with low, sweeping kicks, but he knew his craft and maneuvered out of reach, blocking her kicks with his forearms. Bingmei stared breathlessly, eyes wide in wonder as she watched strike and counterstrike. She'd seen Kunmia face Qiangdao and knew how ruthless she could be. This was a contest of skill, though, not a fight to the death. Although she thought Kunmia would win, she didn't know.

After a spinning kick by Kunmia, which struck him in the chest, Damanhur staggered back a few paces, grimacing in anger. Her kick was the first blow to have fully landed. But he was not deterred. His style was very different from hers. He kept his elbows in, his fingers like tiger claws as he raked at her face. She rarely stayed in the same place long, keeping her distance from his attacks, forcing him to chase her around the room. She caught one of his strikes and hit him beneath the arm with the sword-hand technique. His face contorted, but he slammed his elbow down on Kunmia's arm, and it connected. This time it was Kunmia who blinked against the pain.

The fight had gone on for several minutes without either contestant falling back, but both were dripping in sweat. Often contests could be decided in just a few blows, the skill of one party far exceeding the other, but these two were more evenly matched. While Damanhur was younger, his master had clearly taught him well.

The match could still go either way.

"I won't object if you yield," he said tauntingly, trying to throw off Kunmia's concentration.

She didn't reply, choosing instead to send a whirling kick toward his head. He ducked, seized her tunic front, and shoved her away. Kunmia flipped in midair and landed on her feet, eliciting a gasp of wonder from the bystanders.

Bingmei bit her lip, feeling the smell of the two fighters wash over her. The anticipation in the room was growing as the two masters grew more exhausted.

Damanhur managed to punch twice in the middle, which made Bingmei wince in pain for her master, but Kunmia replied with an elbow against his nose, which smeared blood down his mouth as he wiped it.

He dropped into a sudden crouch, trying to trip her over his outstretched leg, but she locked her leg with his, levering it against him. Her angle was better, and soon he toppled down onto his back, his head hitting against the stone with a loud smack. Bingmei saw his eyes roll back in his head, but she smelled a spurt of rotten fruit—deception—and knew he was only pretending to be unconscious. Kunmia backed away, breathing hard, staring at him.

Bingmei nearly cried out in warning at the trick. But Kunmia was no fool. She jumped away just as his legs pivoted around, nearly stroking the backs of her knees. When she landed, she kicked the edge of his knee then dropped to a low stance and smashed her knuckles against his brow.

Bingmei felt a jolt of pain go through Kunmia, followed by the scent of worry that she'd broken her hand.

But Bao Damanhur lay motionless on the stone tiles, blood streaming from his nostrils. He was unconscious. Bingmei could smell nothing coming from him. Her master's final blow had concussed him.

Kunmia Suun rose, chest heaving, and then faced King Budai and gave him a salute. Budai chortled, clapping his hands in delight.

The thrill of victory was enough to distract Marenqo's attention from the food. He shouted with glee as Zhuyi and Mieshi gripped each other's arms, flush with their master's victory. Bingmei could nearly taste the sour smell of defeat from their rivals, but her own happiness was spilling over. She clapped and then covered her mouth, nearly sobbing with relief. Quion was shaking his head at her, his grin infectious, and she gave him a quick hug. Looking over his shoulder, she saw Rowen, the exiled prince, staring at Damanhur on the floor. She smelled his disappointment, his dread, and his want of financial means pressing on him. He'd hoped for an easy victory.

He caught her looking at him, and offered a weak congratulatory smile and a nod. But she sensed his growing resentment. It would probably be best to stay out of his way during their mission.

CHAPTER SEVEN

Season of the Dragon of Night

They stayed three days in Wangfujing to recover from their arduous summer journey as well as the contest between Kunmia and Damanhur. The sword master's pride had been humbled, and he had shorn his hair as a sign of subservience to another master's skill. Kunmia had told him it wasn't necessary, but his honor demanded it. Bingmei could smell his resentment and determination to do better, but he was in awe of Kunmia's skill. That emotion was real.

Budai had insisted they leave for Fusang immediately, to try to claim it before winter, but Kunmia had refused. Her long experience had proven that winter came unexpectedly, and she insisted it would be wiser to depart as soon as the snows began to fade. Nature could be a bitter enemy as much as it could be a friend.

Bingmei spent time with Quion during their stay and showed him more of the town. The ensign's payment in coins from King Budai for the mission gave them ample opportunities to enjoy the town's delicacies. Quion's grief at losing his father was still pungent and raw, and she felt he needed a friend. Marenqo was also kind to him, when he wasn't eating his fill at the local hot pots, and the boy's shyness and reserve began to diminish. It was a much needed rest before the journey back to the quonsuun. Bingmei even indulged herself by buying a little scorpion pendant she'd always fancied.

On the morning of their departure, Bingmei sought out Kunmia to inform her that the rest of the ensign was prepared for the voyage and waiting at the gate. She found the master with her gear already strapped to her back, staff in hand, walking through the terraced garden with King Budai. Not even the fragrance of the peonies could mask the sharp smell of his greed today. Although she approached them openly, from the path ahead of them, their focus on each other was such that neither noticed at first.

"Are you certain you don't want to leave the Phoenix Blade here, Kunmia?" the king asked. His craving for her to sell it to him was enormous, but he hid it behind a facade of concern.

"I've decided to take it back to the quonsuun," Kunmia replied. She gripped her rune-carved staff in one hand. Her other hand was still bandaged from the contest.

Relief flooded Bingmei as she approached them. She didn't want Budai to have the sword.

King Budai frowned and nodded. "It's your choice, of course. But wouldn't it be safer here? I would waive the storage fee if you decided to allow me to keep it for you." The ruler glanced up and saw Bingmei. "Ah, good morning, young ice rose." They paused when they reached her.

"Good morning, my lord," she said, bowing in respect.

"It is almost time for you to go," Budai said, looking back at Kunmia. "Unless I can persuade you to linger another day or two? There will be an acrobatic display soon on the stage in the center of town. Surely your younger disciples would hate to miss that?"

Kunmia shook her head. "Each day we delay brings the season of the Dragon of Night closer."

"What caravan will you be accompanying? There are several heading to the mountains."

"I've agreed to protect Jiu Gang's caravan," Kunmia said.

Budai pursed his lips and nodded vigorously. "A wise choice. His grain will feed plenty over the winter. I loathe the dark months. The bitter cold. The unyielding ice. I wish the Dragon of Dawn ruled always." He pretended his palms were weighing scales and lifted one up and lowered the other down. "But there must be a balance. A time to seed. A time to grow. I still wish I could persuade you to start your mission at once. But I know you are too wise to be tempted by money, Kunmia Suun."

And for that, Bingmei was grateful. Although she loved this town, she was ready to be away from his palace and its sweaty smell. And she wished for the Phoenix Blade to be safely away from him.

"What about the fisherman who found the stone? What will he do during the season?" Kunmia asked him.

"Oh, I'll not let him off the hook!" Budai said with a grin. "He will sup and dine, and Guanjia will continue to rack up a mighty debt for him to repay. He believes what he wants to believe, that my steward's loyalty has a price. He's unwise."

"That is not very generous," Kunmia said with a disapproving tone.

"Can I help it if men are weak willed and easily corrupted? I will pay the boon I promised to pay him should his discovery prove to be Fusang. But he will owe me *more* than that. This is how commerce works, Kunmia. Does Jiu Gang resent having to pay you for protection from the Qiangdao? Of course! But if he did not pay you, he would likely be attacked and robbed. By paying you, he prevents that outcome. He may resent it, but it's necessary. No single law governs these coastal towns. It is all ungovernable. And so we must make do with the world we have and not the one we want."

"There could be a unifying law," Kunmia said pointedly.

Budai grunted. Bingmei cocked her head, curious to know more. The king continued his walk, and Bingmei fell in behind them, staying silent in the hopes her presence would be forgotten.

"You speak of King Shulian of Sajinau," he said in a neutral tone. Bingmei caught the odor of jealousy and contempt. It smelled like onions.

"Is he not still seeking to unify the kingdoms?" Kunmia asked.

"Oh yes, he is. King Shulian is an honorable man, for certain." His words belied the strong smell coming from him. "But would it not benefit him and his son, the crown prince, the most? I am a king now. Why would I be content to be merely a governor?"

"I don't seek to persuade you," Kunmia said. "Only to advise."

"I know, Kunmia. And I respect you, truly. Your loyalty to my father, and now to me, is a source of great honor. If I were the last king to bow the knee to King Shulian, I would. Eventually. But I don't antici-pate the other rulers will agree. King Fuchou is a hateful man. He'd never agree to be subservient to anyone. King Qianxu is . . . well . . . modest. I think he'll lose his kingdom before any such unity happens. He's too weak. King Mingzhi may agree to such an arrangement, but will he? I wonder. Yes, it is for the common good, but what king will want to be the first to capitulate? And what about the kingdoms across the sea on the western rim? Does anyone in Dawanju or Sihui feel allegiance to distant Sajinau? I think not. The Qiangdao are a menace to everyone. They war among themselves as often as they attack us. If they were ever to band together, they'd be a formidable threat. But they don't join one another for the same reason we don't."

"Pride?" Kunmia asked, giving him a pointed look and a question-ing smile.

King Budai's face compacted, as if he were giving the matter great thought. "That's not exactly the word I would use. It's more like . . . ambition. Look at this palace, Kunmia," he said, gesturing with his palm. "I didn't make it. Neither did my father. It was built by who knows who? If *they* could not keep their palaces . . . if *they* could not keep from destroying themselves . . . why should we hope to do any better? Perhaps it was banding together as one that caused their down-fall? We'll never know."

They walked in silence after that, and Budai's words struck Bingmei deeply. He was right, in a way. Whatever civilization had built the pal-aces, the Death Wall beyond the kingdoms, the stone wharves with their stone boats, there was no record left behind of what had caused their demise. Different kings had conjured different explanations. Angry gods. Disgruntled dragons. Or the killing fog. There was no way of knowing the truth. What had caused them to perish? No one had sur-vived to tell the dark tale, and so there were only rumors, whispered a thousand times until they sounded like truth.

They were approaching the main gate with the heavy doors. The others waited there. Marenqo had a forlorn look on his face, his pack laden with food and gifts he'd purchased. He always enjoyed their stays in town more than the rest. Mieshi was scowling, but Zhuyi looked at peace. Quion stood there as well with his overstuffed pack, the pans still dangling from it. When he saw Bingmei approaching with the others, he gave her a friendly smile. She returned it. She'd taught him to control his expressions when visiting the town. Smiling too much would make a vendor want to cheat him. It was better to look wary, to appear distrustful. But it was safe to be more free with emotion around others in the ensign.

"You've decided to take the boy with you?" King Budai asked her. "The boat at the dock will be reclaimed by the man who owned it."

"He has no family now. As a fisherman's son, he'll be useful on the journey ahead."

"I imagine so. He could stay here, of course—"

"No thank you," Kunmia said, interrupting him. Bingmei felt a throb of respect for her. Kunmia was giving off a protective smell, the kind that reminded Bingmei of her own mother. A pang of loss struck her heart. Memories of her mother grew more dim with each year. There was no purpose in clinging to them. Only sadness. But Bingmei would always remember her smell, that loving, tender smell that had made her feel safe and loved. The smell of the cinnamon porridge that her mother used to make for her.

But safety was an illusion. There was no safety in their world. Danger was an invisible dragon in the mist. One that couldn't be seen but was always near. Always hungry for another victim.

That dragon had claimed another life that season. They were returning to the quonsuun without Lieren. Yet they would go on, as they must, without him. Kunmia would choose another to lead the way, or she would do it herself. Even with an injured hand, she was formidable.

"Have Guanjia fetch the sword, please," Kunmia said, turning to face King Budai.

The powerful smell of his greed flared up again. He looked calm and peaceful, but there was no disguising his true nature. Bingmei felt a throb of warning.

"Of course," he said. Turning, he snapped his fingers, and Guanjia appeared. The order was given to retrieve it from the treasury.

Quion approached Bingmei. "So we're going to the quonsuun now?" he said in a low voice.

She nodded, unable to take her eyes off Budai.

"The winter months are the hardest, but I know how to fish in the ice."

She wrinkled her brow. "Why would you do that?"

"It's how we stayed alive," he answered. "Are there any lakes by the quonsuun?"

"Several," Bingmei answered. "But don't the fish freeze?"

"They don't. I'll take you."

"Won't we freeze to death in the cold?" she asked, arching her brows.

"Not if you wear the right things. My father said there is no such thing as bad weather. Only bad clothes."

"That's like saying there is no bad food, only bad cooks," Marenqo said sagely, rubbing his mouth. "Anything can be edible if prepared properly. It's all in the sauce."

"Missing Wangfujing already?" Mieshi teased. "We haven't even left yet."

"Look. They're coming," Zhuyi said.

Their smell struck her just after Zhuyi announced them—Damanhur and Rowen, although she called him by his assumed name. Wuren. When there were crowds, it was harder for her to notice individual scents.

Mieshi smelled like satisfied revenge, a syrupy flavor. She gave Damanhur a condescending look. Although his hair was shorn, he still walked with bravado, his sword at his hip. He gave Mieshi a saucy look that said, *You prefer me this way. I know it.*

Rowen, who stood next to him, was looking over their group. Despite his regal bearing, he smelled of smoldering ashes, a smoky smell that whispered of thwarted ambition. The exiled prince would stay in Wangfujing until the season changed, accumulating more debt under the craftiness of King Budai and his trusted steward. He was in bondage and didn't even know it. Bingmei felt a little sorry for him, but someone like him wouldn't listen to her advice. Nor would he thank her for giving it.

"You are leaving, then?" Damanhur said to Kunmia.

"You are welcome to winter with us at the quonsuun," Kunmia replied.

Damanhur chuckled. "I think Wangfujing will provide better amusements during the season of the Dragon of Night. But thank you for your invitation. I will miss"—his eyes darted to Mieshi, and he smiled—"all of you very much. You are protecting a caravan heading out today?"

"Jiu Gang's," Kunmia replied.

Damanhur nodded. "Safe journeys. We will see you again in the spring, when the Dragon of Dawn melts the snow."

As they saluted each other, the other members of Kunmia's ensign followed suit, offering their own salutes to their new allies.

But they could not hold Bingmei's attention for long. She felt the presence of the Phoenix Blade. Its call sang in her blood. Guanjia was carrying the box it had been put in. When he arrived, he held it out to Kunmia. Bingmei felt her hands start to tremble. She hid them behind her back, not wanting the others to sense her covetousness, but she couldn't take her eyes off the sandalwood box.

Kunmia unlocked the case and opened it. The light gleamed on the design of the phoenix carved into the hilt.

"Now that's a sight," Quion whispered in awe.

Bingmei's mouth went dry with want.

Kunmia nodded in respect and snapped the lid closed, which muted the sensation—only a little.

"Thank you," Kunmia said, taking the box from the steward's hands.

King Budai was not the only one who coveted the blade. The acid smell of greed was growing more and more powerful. But not just from Budai. Bingmei looked at Rowen, who wore a completely complacent expression. The smell was strong in him. At that moment, she also smelled a little of it in herself, something that shamed her.

The prince was looking right at her. There were too many people, too many emotions for her to understand what he was feeling. But his look was wary.

As if she were a rival for the sword.

杀雾

Studying is like rowing upstream: no advancement is the same as dropping back.

—Dawanjir proverb

CHAPTER EIGHT

Winter's End

During the long winter months, Bingmei trained by lamplight in the interior training room in the quonsuun, protected from the fierce winds and deep snow. At this point, this quonsuun felt as much like home as the one her grandfather had once possessed. She loved the square-shaped building with the sloping roof edged with designs and embellished with tortoises, eagles, and stags that was a part of her daily routine. The ancients had crafted the ironwork. The ancients had hefted the massive timbers into place. Because the quonsuun was in the mountains, it had been built to withstand a heavy load of snow on the roof. As she went about her business, she could not help but think of those who had come before—and what had become of them.

The skeleton of her grandfather's quonsuun would still be standing, she knew, although she had not gone back there since joining Kunmia. The ancients had built strong buildings. It tortured her to think of her former home in ruins. It would be worse if it were being inhabited by men like the Qiangdao, of course, but she didn't think that was the case. Even after that terrible winter when she'd survived the murders, the Qiangdao had quickly left once spring came for fear of being discovered. Men like that feared justice and laws. They wouldn't make a lair of such a place.

She'd vowed to herself that when she did go back someday, it would be to restore what her family had built. It was the dream that had kept her going at first, especially during that first brutal winter.

This winter was much milder than that one had been, with less snow and milder weather than she'd seen in years. Although the season should last another cycle of the moon, already icicles were dripping and then freezing in puddles overnight, making the outer courtyard a perilous place to cross.

One day, which felt much like the rest, she practiced in the training room with Zhuyi, holding her straight sword in a low stance, mimicking her trainer's movements. When Bingmei had asked for sword training, instead of staff, Zhuyi had been assigned to be her teacher. Although Bingmei could use all the weapons in the training room, she had always been partial to swords over staves. It was in her heritage, she imagined. The souls of her murdered parents and grandfather must have been whispering to her.

Or perhaps the hunger to improve her skills with the sword extended from her connection to the Phoenix Blade, hidden in Kunmia Suun's private chamber. Bingmei knew where it was at all times. She longed to train with it instead. But she did not trust the strange connection she felt to it, and she dared not touch it for fear of unwittingly summoning the killing fog to the quonsuun.

"Lower, Bingmei," Zhuyi said with an exasperated sigh. "Your mind is distracted. Concentrate."

Realizing she hadn't made the transition to the next move, she quickly did so, matching movement to movement again. Parry, parry, duck back—spring forward, sending the sword out like a lance. Twist, low crouch, then thrust both arms out straight, one with the sword, one with two fingers extended. The form was called the dragon straight sword, and she'd been practicing it all winter long. She felt she had nearly mastered it.

They rose as one, bringing their swords up hilt first in a swiveling move, then Bingmei tucked the blade up behind her, lowering her left hand in a salute.

Zhuyi broke her stance first and came around, inspecting Bingmei's final form, her lips pursed critically.

"Your form is good, Bingmei," she said. "What I worry about most is your focus. These movements have to be so practiced they come by instinct. When a Qiangdao is rushing you with a dagger, you must rely on instinct. A moment's distraction can be fatal."

Bingmei knew this. The training yard was much different from the thrill of combat she'd experienced on their last mission. Lieren had been much more skilled than her, and he'd been taken down by the fog. A person's fate was arbitrary. Although she hoped to live long enough to avenge her parents' and grandfather's murders and restore their quonsuun, she realized it may not happen. The real struggle was not only against ambition. It was against death itself.

Some fights could not be won.

"Yes, Zhuyi," Bingmei said.

Although they'd never been close, Zhuyi was a fair and soft-spoken person. Sometimes Bingmei envied her closeness with Mieshi, but she didn't feel she could ever achieve such a connection with either of them. Bingmei's ability to smell emotions sometimes seemed like a curse— she knew how people felt, but most of the time she couldn't act on that knowledge. It made it difficult to become close to others. Even if her winter sickness had not made her looks so disagreeable, her ability ensured she would never find someone to love. No one could be that honest and true.

There were others in the training yard too, new disciples who had been brought in as children, typically orphans. This was one of the rare quonsuuns mostly inhabited by women, although there were men serving as guards and some as instructors. She glimpsed Quion lurking behind one of the support posts, anxious to go fishing again and no doubt hoping she'd join him.

"Do the form again," Zhuyi said, this time watching her closely.

Bingmei sighed. She would rather go with Quion, but learning these skills was paramount. It was by training vigorously during the winter season that they managed to survive their missions in the Dragon of Dawn.

As she ran through the familiar movements, her white braids flapped against her vest and shirt. She loved the freedom of not wearing a wig in the quonsuun. No one here gave her queer looks. Even Mieshi never let her gaze linger on the white braids.

"Faster," Zhuyi said. "Your mind is wandering again."

Bingmei stifled a frown of impatience and delved into herself, clearing her mind of thought as she flowed through the form. She felt herself focusing, her internal energy building. The awkwardness she'd felt the first time she practiced these forms had waned. She was much more confident in the memorized actions, which had been handed down from master to disciple for centuries. These fighting forms were a strange bridge to the obscure past. In performing them, she felt as one with those who had come before her. Her parents. Her grandfather. And other ancestors. They, too, had performed these skills in a quonsuun. As she moved, she experienced a euphoria that accompanied the precision of the movements. Time seemed to fade. It was just her, the blade, the form.

And then it was over, the moment leaking from her like water. Her arm came down in the final salute.

Zhuyi smiled at her. "Well done, Bingmei. That was the best I've seen you perform it. I think you're ready to pass the test for this form. I'll tell Kunmia."

"Thank you," Bingmei said, panting, her cheeks flushing from the exertion and with pride.

"You have incredible gifts," Zhuyi said. "I'm glad you are my bond sister." She reached out and toyed with the end of one of Bingmei's braids. "I still remember when we found you. A child should not have to witness what you did. You spent a season in the dark . . . after losing your entire family." Her lips pressed firmly together. "Only someone very strong could have survived that. And you did."

Bingmei felt her flush deepen. Zhuyi was sparing with her praise, which made it all the more meaningful. "Thank you, Zhuyi," she whispered.

"Quion has been waiting patiently," she said with a little smile.

Indeed he had. He still watched her from behind the pillar, his eyes wide with wonder. It pleased her that he'd seen her run through the form.

Bingmei shrugged. "Our practice is more important than fishing. But he's a good friend."

Zhuyi nodded. "And a capable one. Who would have thought we'd have fresh fish in the winter? I'm glad he'll be coming with us on our mission to find Fusang."

Bingmei nodded her agreement. Quion did not like to call notice to himself, but he was an incredibly hard worker. He'd taken to repairing parts of the quonsuun after arriving, after getting Kunmia's permission.

"Do you think we will go soon?" she asked.

Zhuyi cocked her head to one side. "The winter seems to be ending faster than last year. Yes, I think we are going soon. Back to Wangfujing first."

Bingmei would miss the quonsuun. She gazed at the pillars, at the symbols carved into the metal edging in the stone. This was her home. Her salvation. But she was also anxious to embark on a new adventure.

Especially if they discovered a palace that had been lost for a thousand years.

杀雾

80

The first few times she'd accompanied Quion on his ice-fishing expeditions, she'd questioned the wisdom of seeking fish in the middle of a frozen lake. The ice was slippery, and although Quion had taught her she could keep warm by wearing layers, she'd fallen again and again. But Quion knew what he was doing, and they'd pulled out half a dozen fish from beneath the ice. Marenqo had crooned with delight at the hot fish served at dinner that night. And so the experiment had become a habit.

This day, they'd brought in a trove of fish. Although her hands and feet were cold, the rest of her was plenty warm. The march back to the quonsuun through the knee-deep snow was strenuous, and she felt her lungs burning with the effort. She walked with a spear in hand, using it like a staff. The snow crunched beneath their thick boots.

"We're nearly there," Quion said, huffing, raising a hand, and pointing. Both of them carried fish in their packs, but his was larger by far. If the weight bothered him, he didn't complain about it. Quion never complained.

The wind had picked up and blew snow in their path. The trees were laden with it, and another bank of clouds filled the twilight sky over the jagged teeth of the mountain. The weather could change quickly, bringing a sudden blizzard. They made sure their outings did not bring them far from the quonsuun because of it.

A fresh gust of wind hit Bingmei's face, stinging her cheeks. "It's getting colder."

"It's the start of a storm," Quion said. Just as the words left his mouth, part of the clouds lit up, and a rumble of thunder started.

The timing made them both laugh.

"Zhuyi said we might be leaving soon," Bingmei told him as they put on a little speed. "Are you excited?"

"A little, I think," he replied, huffing.

"Why not more? We might find Fusang. Think of it!"

"We might, or maybe we won't," he said. "It could be for nothing. It's the same as fishing, Bingmei. Sometimes you don't catch anything."

"Where's the fun in that?"

He chuckled. "It means you have to keep trying."

The glow from the quonsuun was just visible ahead when the first flakes of snow started to whip into her face. The clouds were coming down the mountain quickly.

She heard a grunt, a gasp of pain, then a feline growl. Because the wind had been pushing ahead of her, she hadn't smelled the beast stalking them.

Bingmei whirled. Quion was facedown in the snow, struggling to get up, but a lean snow leopard with a swishing tail was lodged on his back, digging its claws into his pack of fish. She saw its tracks following their footsteps in the snow. Its feral eyes were intent on its prey.

"Quion!" Bingmei shouted. She sloughed off her own pack and started back to help him.

The mountain cat hissed at her, raking its claws against the pack again. Quion shouted for help, struggling to rise, but the beast was too heavy for him. He was pinned beneath it and his haul of fish.

Bingmei stomped toward it, waving out her arms to make herself look bigger, but the snow leopard wasn't impressed. It merely hissed at her again as it sank its teeth into the cargo.

One never left the quonsuun without a weapon. She had a knife at her belt, but a knife would require her to get too close to the beast for safety. With half-frozen hands, she swung her spear around and tried to strike the leopard across the head. The animal lunged at her instead.

She tried to bring the spear around to stab it, but it struck her, a jagged claw snagging in her fur vest. It shook her fiercely, growling and snarling, and she dropped the spear. She kicked out with her legs, catching it in the middle, but its claw was still embedded in her furs. A loud ripping sound rent the air, and she felt a gouge of pain in her side. Bingmei yelled and kicked again. The claw dislodged, and the leopard backed away, hissing at her.

She reached for her fallen spear and held the point in front of her, gasping for breath. The pain in her side wasn't bad, but the wound was probably bleeding. She smelled the creature, its wild musk making her tremble with fear. The snow leopard began circling her, snarling again. She came over to Quion, who was finally coming to his knees, snow caking his face. He brushed it away frantically.

The leopard growled again. Bingmei jabbed at it with her spear, and it pawed the tip away as if it were nothing.

"Are you hurt?" she asked.

"It got my leg," he moaned.

The snow leopard lunged again. Her reflexes saved her. Just in time, she raised the spear, and the animal impaled itself on the blade. A shriek of pain sounded, and the leopard fell, then scrabbled away from her. Its spotted fur was drenched in snow, but a bright red stain appeared on its breast, its hot blood steaming. The wound didn't look mortal, but the beast retreated, cringing with pain.

Bingmei gasped, feeling a thrill of victory.

Quion made it to his feet, but his knees were shaking. He gripped her shoulder to steady himself.

"It's hungry," he said, hearing the melancholy snarl as the animal cowered back.

He was right, of course. It had smelled their catch, and hunger had driven it to attack them. Quion tugged off his pack, the back of which had deep gouge marks from the leopard's claws. Some of the fish were already oozing out.

He sighed.

"The storm is getting worse," Bingmei said. "Can you walk?"

"I think so," he said. He winced as he put weight on his leg. "I may need that spear as a crutch." He looked back at the beast, which had slunk away into the trees, defeated. Then he pulled off a glove and wrestled one of the fish out of the slit pack.

"You're feeding it?" Bingmei said in shock.

He tossed the fish toward it, then followed with two more before putting his glove back on.

"It's too hurt to come after us," he said. "It'll take the easy meal. Come on."

She helped him walk, and between her help and the use of the spear as a crutch, Quion was able to keep moving forward as the storm intensified. Before they reached the quonsuun, Marenqo approached them with torches and two servants. They'd been sent to look for them because of the howling wind. It was easy to get lost in a blizzard.

Bingmei explained their adventure as they continued toward the quonsuun, she and Marenqo supporting Quion on either side.

"A snow leopard?" Marenqo said, impressed. "They normally don't come down the mountain so early. It is strange." When they made it back to the quonsuun, they headed directly for the common area. Before a large fire, they stripped out of their wet layers of fur. Quion had some nasty gashes on the backs of his legs, but the servants quickly washed and wrapped them. Bingmei saw a spot of blood on her shirt and a hole where the claw had raked her. It had stopped bleeding before they arrived. Her braids were coming loose, and she was sweating sitting so close to the fire.

She and Quion exchanged a look, taking in each other's dishevelment, then started laughing.

"You laugh? Getting attacked by a snow leopard didn't sober you?" Marenqo said, shaking his head. "You're both lucky to be alive. I once had to escape a pack of wolves. I still shudder when I think of it."

"It was only one," Bingmei said.

Marenqo said, "At least you managed to save the fish."

Kunmia entered the room to check on them. She came to Quion first, asking about his injuries. He was quick to tell her that Bingmei had saved their lives. He was right. He would have died if she hadn't been there. She'd tried to teach him some of the martial skills at the school, but he had no desire to be a warrior. That saddened her. She would have respected him more if he'd tried to develop his skills.

"You did well, Bingmei," Kunmia said, giving her a weighing look. "An ensign must give their all to protect one of their own." The smell of her approval was delicious and stronger than the scent coming from the burning wood in the hearth.

"You would have done the same," Bingmei said.

Kunmia crouched next to her. "I see blood."

"It's nothing," Bingmei said. "His wounds were worse."

"Of course. Tomorrow, I want you to come with me in the morning if this storm ends. We are going to leave the quonsuun."

"Are we going to Wangfujing tomorrow?" Bingmei asked excitedly.

Kunmia shook her head. "No. I'm going to teach you how to use the Phoenix Blade."

CHAPTER NINE

The Curse of Magic

The mountain storm had dropped only a thin layer of snow, and its bluster had worn out well before nightfall. Bingmei had hardly slept that night, waiting eagerly for Kunmia to teach her about the blade she wanted so desperately. She went to the training room early, knowing sleep would not come. That was where Kunmia found her before the morning sun had breached the walls. The Phoenix Blade was already strapped to her back in its meiwood scabbard. Knowing it was there, and that she would soon get to touch it, Bingmei demonstrated a perfect rendition of dragon straight sword. Kunmia declared she had passed it successfully. Another form had been added to her skill set.

The air smelled of grass and pine needles that morning. A scent full of wonder and hope and eagerness—*her* scent.

"You will be wise to dress warmly," Kunmia said, giving her a dismissing nod. She was already dressed in deerskin bracers lined with fur, high leather boots with a fur trim, and a long cloak.

Bingmei, grinning, hurried back to her room. She changed into her favorite red shirt—for luck—before adding her leather girdle, braces, high boots, and fur-lined cloak. The meiwood cricket was stuffed into her pocket. She also strapped on a belt to use for the sword's scabbard in case Kunmia decided to give it to her. Eager to get outside, she hurriedly tied off her pale hair into two braids and left her bedchamber, nearly colliding with Quion in her haste.

"Where are you going?" he asked her. He'd been in conversation with Marenqo the previous evening, and hadn't heard the master's invitation.

"Kunmia is going to train me today," she said.

Quion looked surprised. "What for?"

"I've been working on dragon straight sword all winter," she said. "She wants me to practice with the Phoenix Blade."

Quion's look darkened. "Why *that* blade?"

"Why not?" Bingmei asked back. His normal fishy smell was more pungent suddenly. Worry, concern.

He pressed his lips closed, his look darkening.

She sighed as the weight of his emotions edged away her own excitement and eagerness. He was right to question her. She'd seen the blade summon the fog, yet her feelings couldn't be denied. The weapon called to her, and it fit her hand as if it had been made for her. "Tell me."

"Just . . . be careful," he said, backing away from her.

"Quion," she said, shaking her head. "What's worrying you?"

"I'm not worried."

That was clearly a lie—she could smell it from him, growing stronger by the moment. She'd never told him about her ability to smell emotions. As a child, she'd thought everyone perceived the world that way, but she'd come to realize it wasn't so. Only three people had ever learned of her ability: her parents and her grandfather. At first they'd waved it off as the fancy of an imaginative girl. Bingmei had warned everyone about the scent of a particular student at the quonsuun, but her parents and grandfather had smelled sour and disbelieving whenever she'd brought it up. They'd thought her jealous of the student's abilities. But while he behaved admirably and performed the training with rigor, he smelled spoiled on the inside. Later, it came out that he was dishonest and had stolen from their family, and he was promptly exiled. Her parents and grandfather had respected her gift then. And they'd warned her not to tell anyone else. Such an ability was dangerous—dishonest men and women would sooner kill her than allow her to reveal their lies, and others would be eager to exploit her.

She hadn't trusted that part of herself with anyone since. Not even Kunmia. Her looks already set her apart. No need to make the separation keener.

"Just tell me," she said, trying not to sound exasperated.

"That blade made the killing fog come," he blurted out.

Her brow wrinkled. "I know. We'll be careful. I trust Kunmia. You should too."

"I do trust her. But I'm still worried . . . about you."

"I'll be fine," Bingmei said. His concern touched her. "How is your leg feeling today?" She noticed he was favoring one of them.

He pursed his lips. "A little better. I can't walk very fast. I wish I could go with you."

There was a protective smell coming from him. She didn't want to remind him that it was *she* who had protected *him* from the snow leopard.

"I'll see you when I return," she said. He nodded and watched her go. She could feel his eyes on her back, but more than that, she smelled his worry.

Perhaps she should feel more nervous, but every other sensation was overcome by a rush of eagerness. When she arrived at the heavy door of the quonsuun, she found Kunmia waiting for her there, her breath coming out in a little mist. She cocked her head at Bingmei, who smiled in return, and the two guards at the gate grunted as they pulled it open.

The fresh snow and wind had erased the tracks she and Quion had left the day before.

The sound of crunching snow came as Kunmia led her away. Kunmia smelled calm, but then, she usually did. The sun hadn't risen over the mountain peaks yet. The snow on the trees was already starting to drip. Kunmia didn't take her down toward the lake but up toward the craggy peaks. The hike soon became arduous, and Bingmei felt her leg muscles burn with the effort. They followed a small trail carved into the mountainside, until the trees became sparser and then nonexistent.

It took some time before they reached the peak where a small shrine had been built by the ancients. Bingmei had hiked up to it before, but it was too steep for frequent visits. Although Bingmei's breath was loud in her own ears, Kunmia hardly seemed winded at all. Her master came to a stop at the middle of the small, snow-capped shrine and stared off into the distance. The sun was radiant, exposing a broad track of mountains, gorges, ravines, and distant glaciers. An eagle soared on the wind currents beneath them.

Bingmei stood next to Kunmia, enjoying the view. To the south, she could see the ocean that stretched to the end of the world. The shoreline was riddled with coves and caves, fjords, and ice-fed streams. She imagined some ancient warrior standing on this very spot ages ago, looking at the same view Bingmei looked at. The feeling that thought gave her made her shudder.

"Can you see the Death Wall?" Kunmia asked, turning to look at her.

Bingmei could, although she was so used to seeing it, she'd hardly noticed it. It was a long wall that had been built on a distant set of mountains. Watchtowers dotted its crumbling face, which traversed the length of the horizon. The task of building such a wall defied imagination. She'd seen it from different vantage points during her life, each section built after the same manner. No one ventured beyond the Death Wall, the great wall that followed the rough mountain slopes across all the kingdoms, even past the glaciers. Not even the ensigns would dare attempt it. Although no one knew why it had been erected, they all agreed on one thing.

No mortal could cross it and live.

"I can," Bingmei answered, staring at it with wonder. "How long did it take them to build it?"

Kunmia smiled. "You like to ask questions there aren't answers to. With a few hundred men, it would take a thousand years. But what if more people lived back then? We have no way of knowing."

And yet the questions tormented her. Who had the ancients been? Why had they disappeared? And how had Bingmei's people found this land?

"There are so many ruins," Bingmei said. "I wish they had left us more clues. The legends we believe could be lies, for all we know. They differ from village to village."

"They *did* leave us clues," Kunmia said. She held up her staff, exposing the runes to Bingmei. "They carved animals into everything. We don't know why they left us these symbols. There's no way to know what they truly mean. But I think they were telling us to observe animals in the wild. To learn from them as they did. The ancients taught us that magic is harnessed out of meiwood trees. That, too, teaches us something. We do not live as long as the trees. But when a building is crafted out of them, we live longer than if we lived without shelter."

Bingmei nodded.

"My staff, Bingmei," Kunmia continued, rubbing her thumb over the animal runes, "has the power of the baboon. They are social creatures. They care for one another. And they are very strong. When I invoke the magic of this staff, I feel a deep sense of caring for those in my ensign. An urge to protect and defend them. It's the staff my grandfather gave to me, choosing me out of all of his posterity to continue the traditions of his ensign. When I take an assignment to protect something, I protect it as a mother does her cubs. It is powerful magic. The *most* powerful, I believe. With this staff, I can also temporarily capture magic from other weapons. It's a powerful defense."

Bingmei knew this already, but there was a reason Kunmia repeated the information. Kunmia always had a reason for everything she did. The master frowned, looking away from her, gazing at the distant wall.

"Every time I use it," she said in a low voice, "it becomes more difficult to resist its pull."

Bingmei darted a glance at her, shocked by the revelation. "What does it feel like?"

Kunmia gripped the staff tightly. "I don't know how to describe it. The staff is alive somehow. It senses things. Like there's a partial soul captured inside the wood. Maybe it's the soul of its original warrior. I don't know." She turned, giving Bingmei a hard stare. "I've learned this too, working for King Budai. Only someone with a strong mind can use a weapon like this or the Phoenix Blade. These artifacts wield a strong compulsion, Bingmei. Do not underestimate it. Sometimes a weapon has caused the death of its master."

She swallowed, eagerness twisting inside her. She felt the allure of its power even then. Usually she strived for self-control, wishing to emulate Kunmia, who never acted rashly. Why didn't the compulsion to use the sword frighten her?

She didn't know, except that it felt *right*.

Kunmia sighed, then looked down. "Ever since we lost Lieren, I have felt strongly that you should be the one to wield the blade. It troubles me that my feelings on this matter are so strong." She pursed her lips. "I strive to be balanced, wise, and just. But there is something urging me to let you use the blade. Although you've passed the test for the straight sword, I'm not sure you are ready for such a responsibility."

The doubt in Kunmia's voice caused a pang in Bingmei's heart. Excitement strummed through her once again, but she was determined to keep herself humble and courteous. She bowed her head.

"When you picked it up from the grass," Kunmia said, "all those months ago, it summoned the killing fog almost instantly. Only a weapon with very powerful magic would bring the fog so quickly. The man who wielded it was very powerful. If I hadn't used my own rune staff to combat him, he would have vanquished me. You might all have died that night. I took the risk of summoning the fog in order to protect the rest of you. That's why we went back for the blade. I could not allow it to fall into the hands of someone who might use it for evil."

She looked pointedly at Bingmei. "Before we left, Prince Rowen asked to buy it from me. He craves its power, but I fear it would destroy him. I cannot leave something so valuable, and dangerous, at the quonsuun while we make our journey. No doubt someone would try to steal it. Whoever I give it to, I must be convinced they will not misuse it or succumb to its allure." She leaned her staff against one of the pillars in the shrine, then pulled the strap over her head and brought the mei-wood scabbard around.

Bingmei's fingers tingled with an anticipation she'd felt since she'd last touched the blade. Although part of her feared her reaction, she did believe she could control the blade. That she was *meant* to control it.

Kunmia's lips were still pursed in a frown. She held the sheathed blade in her palms, but not in an offering way. "I have brought the blade up here in order to test it *and* you. It feels *wrong* in my hands. I have tried testing its powers, but the blade will not reveal itself to me. Maybe it will be more open with you. Draw it, Bingmei. But be careful. I don't know what it will do. If you become crazed or enter a trance, I will have no choice but to use my staff to disable you."

That prospect did not sound very enjoyable, but Bingmei's anticipation was heightened all the more by the warning. She nodded. "I will obey you, Master. If it is within my power."

"Draw the sword."

Her mouth dry, she reached her hand tentatively for the meiwood hilt. The engraving of the phoenix on it caught her eye as she slowly closed her hand around it. Then, gripping the scabbard with her other hand, she pulled the blade loose.

The morning sunlight gleamed on the tempered metal. It felt uncommonly light. The edge looked sharp enough to cut stone. A sense of completeness swelled inside her. She released a sigh of contentment.

"How do you feel?" Kunmia asked warily.

"Alive," Bingmei said. It was the first word that came to mind.

"Perform dragon straight sword," Kunmia said, reaching for her staff. She backed away.

Bingmei assumed the starting pose, gripping the sword in her left hand, pommel down, blade up behind her back. She did the salute and then started on the form. It went smoothly, the blade balanced perfectly as she performed the routine. She shortened some of the movements because of the confinement of the shrine, but they came naturally, easily—by instinct. Partway through the form, images began to flash through her mind, startling her. Rows of disciples, all learning together. Fifty or more assembled in a vast courtyard. A memory, but not hers.

She blinked, and the image was broken, shattered like glass.

As she continued the set, another memory came. Someone's mouth on hers in a passionate kiss, utter darkness around them. She had never kissed anyone before. She blinked, the emotion and memory shattering. Her heart began to race as more fleeting images came and left, each one a memory that wasn't hers.

"Stop," Kunmia said.

Bingmei obeyed. She was panting, her body heat trapped within her. She was in a low crouch, the blade extended. She paused, awaiting her master's next command. A trickle of sweat went down her cheek.

"Look," Kunmia said.

Bingmei straightened and went to the edge of the shrine. Down the side of the mountain, she saw tendrils of fog snaking through the tree trunks and over the snow. A vast, hungry fog. It was crawling toward the mountain. Her heart quavered with fear.

"It's coming from the direction of the Death Wall," Kunmia said, frowning. "I watched it start to build. Sheathe the blade."

Bingmei did. They watched, waiting anxiously, preparing to flee if need be. The fog was still a ways off.

"It's dissipating," Kunmia observed. "The fog is blind again. See, it seeks another way. Like it's searching for something it cannot find. The meiwood scabbard masks its scent. Its strength fails."

Bingmei saw that she was right. The killing fog felt *alive*.

"What did you feel when you held the blade?" Kunmia asked.

"I felt a connection with it," Bingmei said, being honest. She couldn't stand the smell of lies. "I always have. Partway through the form, I began having memories . . . that weren't my own."

"Interesting," Kunmia said. "When I saw you at your most focused, that was when the fog started to come. It responded quickly. It's clearly drawn to the blade."

Or to me, Bingmei thought with dread. Was there something within her, some inner darkness, that attracted the magic of the blade and, through it, the fog? Seeing how quickly the fog had crept across the wall had made her curiosity shrivel inside her.

"It's a dangerous weapon," Kunmia said. "But it still feels like letting you use it is the right thing. For now. If I feel you are putting the ensign at risk, I will take it from you, is that clear?"

"Yes, Master," Bingmei said, feeling grateful. If Kunmia felt it was fitting for her to wield the sword, surely she was right.

"We leave for Wangfujing in a few days. I want Quion's wounds to heal more before we leave. I've asked Mieshi to take Lieren's place at the head of the ensign. She will be our guide, the one who alerts us to danger. I would like you to train with her on this journey so that you can take that role someday. Your ability to sense danger will be important where you are going, Bingmei."

Bingmei's stomach squeezed with pleasure. "Do you think that the legend of Fusang is real?"

Kunmia looked troubled. She smelled of wet leaves—concern. "I'm not sure. And I don't know what to hope for."

CHAPTER TEN

Price of Vengeance

There was still snow in the mountains surrounding the quonsuun, but Bingmei could see that the slopes below them were green and thriving. Rivers swollen from the melting ice manifested the inexorable change in the season. The dawn came earlier and earlier each day, and the concealed bulbs of flowers were sprouting green stalks and leaves. Within a few weeks, the mountains would be thick with wildflowers.

Kunmia Suun's ensign gathered in the main courtyard, and the servants and remaining disciples gathered to bid them farewell.

Bingmei wore her wig again, which felt tight against her head, with all the little pins and hooks securing it. Although it took a fortnight or so to walk down the mountain to Wangfujing, they would pass trappers and elk hunters seeking to restore food supplies that had dwindled during the months of endless night. So she wore a wig for the journey, because seeing a maiden with the winter sickness always caused a shock in others. While Bingmei didn't enjoy wearing the wig, she preferred the slight discomfort to the smell of contempt.

Quion looked weighed down by his pack, which was stuffed with supplies and cooking implements. His injuries were no longer troubling him, and he could walk without limping. Bingmei had tried to see if the snow leopard had perished—its pelt would be worth something in Wangfujing—but there had been no trace of it in the snow. Marenqo chatted amiably with Mieshi and Zhuyi while Kunmia gave her final instructions to her captain, Zhongshi, who was also her nephew.

Bingmei had grown a little during the winter and felt more capable than when the seclusion had started. In part, perhaps, it was because the Phoenix Blade was strapped to her back. Although her breath came out in a mist, she wasn't cold. The layers of fur and deerskin made her comfortable. After reaching Wangfujing, they'd be traveling the waterways, especially since the fisherman who'd found the piece of carved stone knew the location of the fjord where he'd found it. No one knew how long they'd be gone. They might return with the winter.

Kunmia finally announced it was time to depart. The smell of excitement was electric in the courtyard. They were all eager to go. Zhongshi led the others in a cheer as they left the courtyard.

With a nod from Kunmia, Mieshi took the lead, and Bingmei went to join her, smiling at Quion as she left him. They continued on in silence, which, while not uncomfortable, was not altogether relaxed either.

杀雾

That night, they set up camp in the shelter of the trees. Quion was expert at starting fires, and he'd gathered a nest of dry sticks and some larger branches. Although they had cured meat in their packs, he'd fished during one of their rests. Bingmei watched him clean his catch while the fire crackled and popped and lazy smoke began to drift up. His head was bent low in serious fashion, and she watched the precision of his movements. Once he was done, he assembled his pans and started to cook. Marenqo hovered nearby, his eyes wide with enthusiasm for a warm meal so soon after leaving the quonsuun.

Everyone gathered around the fire with their eating sticks and shared the hot fish. There was enough for everyone. Quion cleaned the pans afterward, scrubbing them with dirt, which she thought was odd, but they looked good at the end.

As they sat around the small fire, enjoying its warmth, Kunmia offered to tell them a story, a tradition for the first night of a mission. Quion was finished cleaning his pans and sat in the circle with the rest of them, pulling out a rope and tying it into a series of knots. He would then untie them and start anew, tying different ones. Just as she trained with her weapons or her fist forms, so Quion trained in his own skills. It was repetition that brought mastery.

"The story I share tonight is of my grandfather, the founder of the ensign," Kunmia said. "Some of you have heard it before. I don't tell it often, for it is painful. My grandfather was a mighty warrior. He was an expert in the saber. When he was married, his wife—my grandmother—betrayed him with another man. So my grandfather killed the man and banished my grandmother from their house. Because of that treachery, he could not abide those who were not faithful. It was a rule among his disciples that there should be no lechery. To train with him, one had to swear an oath, an oath punishable by death."

Kunmia stared into the fire. "One of my grandfather's disciples decided to forswear his oath. He was a proud man and felt, as his own skills improved, that he should not be held to my grandfather's rigid standards. Even though he had taken the oath, he decided to break it in secret. But secrets do not stay that way for long. Rumors started that he was involved with another man's wife, a woman who cheated on her husband when the man was away on missions. When my grandfather found out, he was furious. The oath had been broken."

Kunmia cracked a stick in half and fed it to the fire. Bingmei listened carefully. She had not heard this story, although she knew the rule against lechery within the ensign and had agreed to it herself.

"Did your grandfather honor the consequences?" Marenqo asked in a low voice.

Kunmia nodded. "He took some of his disciples and went after the man who had betrayed his vow. When the man saw them coming, he fled into the mountains. They hunted him down. It was in the spring that it happened, and it took all summer to find him. A summer when they could have protected a caravan and earned cowry shells. But my grandfather's honor was at stake. They caught him eventually. And killed him. The story does not end there. You see, the disciple had a wife of his own and a son. That boy, when he was very young, came to the quonsuun to kill my grandfather out of revenge."

"A child?" Marenqo asked. Quion's eyes went wide too.

Part of Bingmei shuddered with horror, although she also understood. Had she possessed the ability to defeat Muxidi on the day he'd murdered her grandfather, she would have cut him down without a second thought. But now, years later, it shocked her to think of someone so young doing such a thing.

Kunmia nodded. Her mouth was pressed closed, and she revealed no emotion. But Bingmei sensed a wave of feeling roiling beneath the surface in her master. Of regret, of sadness, of wilted love. Like a flower that had been crushed under a rock for years. Even though she didn't know the story, she knew Kunmia had loved that boy.

"My grandfather nearly accepted the boy's challenge that night. The child would have lost, of course, which would have stopped the revenge. But no, he chose mercy instead. He spared the boy and took him into the quonsuun and trained him. He and I became friends. But there was the cancer within him. The cancer of revenge. When he was twelve, he forsook the quonsuun and left to study under another master. He returned ten years later. And he killed my grandfather. He wanted me to marry him, but how could I marry the man who had slain the one who had raised me? Who had taught me? All because of a forsaken oath."

Kunmia looked so calm as she shared the tale. Like it was just another story. But grief still raged inside her. Although the hurt and sadness had been tamped down by years of self-discipline and training, they were still there. Still potent. Bingmei felt tears sting her own eyes. She could smell the tangled feelings that still lingered in Kunmia's soul like smoke.

"I have told you this tale to remind you of the oaths you all have taken," Kunmia said. "Should my grandfather have exacted vengeance against his former disciple? It was the just thing to do. Yet it led to his own demise. We cannot see the ripples in the future that our actions cause today. Thirst for vengeance is a powerful motivation. Perhaps the *most* powerful. Be careful how you rouse it. When we reach Wangfujing, we will join with the other ensign. Their rules will be different from ours, but they must abide by our customs. There is power in the different energies of male and female. But there is also an inherent danger there." Kunmia looked pointedly at Mieshi, who had received the attentions of Damanhur.

Mieshi looked down. The acrid smell of spoiling squash wafted from her. Bingmei wondered what emotion was being felt.

"Above all, we must trust one another," Kunmia continued, gazing at each of them in turn. "This may be the most dangerous mission we have attempted. Each of you is here for a reason. Be loyal to each other. I've often wondered what may have happened had one man kept his oath. It is always easy to make excuses. But I promise to fulfill my oaths to each of you. To be your teacher, your leader, your guardian. I would give my life for any one of you."

She spoke sincerely; Bingmei could feel it. But as Bingmei gazed around at the others' faces, illuminated by the dimming flames, she realized she was not ready to make the same promise. It made her ashamed to feel the way she did, but as she had seen time and again, the world extinguished life so quickly. Who knew what, if anything, lay beyond? Some believed that life repeated over and over. One might be born again as a newt. Or a blade of grass. Others taught that everyone had multiple souls, one which lingered by the body after death and the other which went to the afterlife beneath the earth. Both ideas felt a little absurd to Bingmei. Because no one knew what really happened after death, life was the most precious thing in the world.

She was determined to preserve her own no matter what.

杀雾

They arrived at the brink of Wangfujing ahead of schedule, having shed their warmer garments after reaching the valley floor. Bingmei had woven a garland of wildflowers along the way and looked forward to something other than fish for dinner. The thought of the scorpion sticks made her mouth water. Her legs were weary from the walking, although it was always easier coming down from the mountains.

At the crest of the hill, they could see down the craggy gorge and into the fjord where the town was nestled. Mieshi and Bingmei saw the flames and smoke first.

They realized they'd arrived to find the town under siege.

CHAPTER ELEVEN
Return of the Dragon

The Qiangdao ransacked the streets of Wangfujing. Several of the shops blazed, and screams filled the air along with smoke as thick as the killing fog. The sobs of frightened children twisted Bingmei's gut. The smells carried on the wind were so overwhelming she could hardly focus on any of them. But the overall stench was rancid fear.

A band of marauders emerged from an alley, carrying sacks of foodstuffs and racks of leathery meat. This was a pillaging party, so desperate for food that they would raid a king they knew was wealthy enough to defend himself. Kunmia charged them, and her ensign followed. Bingmei felt anger burning in her nose as she rushed one of the thieves, her mind summoning memories of the Qiangdao who'd killed her parents and raided her grandfather's quonsuun. She wasn't a little girl anymore. Now she could defend herself. Save others.

One of the thieves dropped his bundle and leaped at her with a dirty knife. She easily blocked it with her staff, then twirled it around and struck him in the side of the head. His eyes rolled back in his head, and he fell to the cobblestones in a heap. Another yelled at her in a language she didn't understand and came at her, but she jabbed the end of her staff into his throat. When he dropped his weapon to grab his neck, she struck the side of his knee to bring him to the ground, then knocked him unconscious.

By the time she'd defeated her third man, the others from the ensign had incapacitated the rest of the group. Bingmei saw some faces in the windows above, the townsfolk gazing down at them with relieved looks.

"To the three bridges!" Kunmia shouted to the ensign.

Bingmei had last been to the common square, connected by the three central bridges, with Quion, and the memory made her turn to look for him. His face was ashen with worry, and he gripped his walking stick defensively, his head swiveling to take in the dangers around them. She whistled to get his attention and motioned for him to follow. The others were already obeying Kunmia's order.

Quion nodded and hustled to follow her into the mayhem. Exiting the alley onto the main street on the east side of the river, they ran into a small group of Qiangdao who were also carrying provisions. As soon as the Qiangdao saw them, they ditched their haul and fled. Mieshi was about to give chase, but a curt command from Kunmia stayed her.

The haze from the smoke made it difficult to see, but they came across some of King Budai's guards, who charged at them through the smoke with spears until they recognized Kunmia.

"Master!" the leader said, bowing quickly.

"Where is Budai?" Kunmia asked.

"He's at the palace surrounded by fifty men. We were just sent to support Bao Damanhur, who went after their leader. This way!"

The ensign ran with the guardsmen, dodging past broken crates and the dead. Bingmei's eyes were red and watery with the stinging smoke. It was difficult to recognize the familiar streets. She'd never heard of Wangfujing being attacked like this before, although she imagined it had happened in years past.

Some of the buildings began to look familiar through the haze, and she realized they were approaching the plaza with the three bridges. The fishy smell from the river confirmed it moments later, and they met another band of King Budai's guards.

"There!" someone shouted, pointing.

In the middle of the plaza stood Damanhur. Wounded and dead bodies lay all around him as he single-handedly protected the crossroads. He held his saber behind his back, turning in a full circle.

"Where is your leader!" he shouted. "Does he fear to face me? Stop sending underlings. Come yourself."

"Who leads this group of Qiangdao?" Kunmia asked the guard who had led them there.

"We don't know," he stammered. "They have at least two hundred. We haven't been attacked by such a force in years."

Kunmia nodded, her expression stern. "They are robbing the townsfolk while the attention is here. Go street to street and protect the families. If they all perish, King Budai will reign over nothing. We will assist Damanhur."

"Thank you!" he said, looking relieved. He imparted orders to his men, who departed to fulfill her command.

"You clearly lack bravery. Do you lack pride as well?" Damanhur shouted. "What? More lackeys?"

As Kunmia's ensign approached the nearest bridge, Bingmei saw a group of at least a dozen Qiangdao cross the bridge closest to Damanhur. They mounted the steps calmly, as if there were no threat awaiting them. Although the smoke impeded her vision, they looked mean-spirited and deceitful. These men did not wear patchworked clothes and furs. They were dressed in finery.

The leaders of the Qiangdao.

"Ah, now things will get interesting," Damanhur taunted.

A huge man with a giant glaive gripped in his hand and a straight sword at his waist pointed at Damanhur and barked a command. Bingmei didn't know how the ranks of authority worked within the Qiangdao, but the strongest and most ruthless men were usually the leaders. She suspected this man might be the one Damanhur wished to face. His arms were bulky and heavily sinewed, and his black vest, secured with gold-tasseled ropes, seemed to strain over his massive chest.

One of the other men strutted toward the square.

"What?" Damanhur said. "You won't face me yourself?"

Another bark of command and two more men followed, making it three against one.

Damanhur brought his sword arm down, holding his saber in front of himself as he faced off against the three.

"Twelve against one is too much for any man," Kunmia muttered. "Mieshi and Zhuyi, go to the south bridge and cross there. Cut off retreat. Marenqo, go with them. Bingmei—you're with me. Quion—stay out of sight."

Bingmei followed orders and started to reach for the Phoenix Blade when Kunmia frowned and shook her head. "Use the staff."

Damanhur rushed to attack. He was not as big as their leader, but he was faster than a whip, and he'd stabbed two of the lesser captains within seconds. The third put up a fight before he, too, fell to the ground.

Damanhur bowed to the Qiangdao leader. "Shall I cut down all your men before you face me?" he asked in a mocking voice.

Another command was given—again in an unfamiliar language. Six men started forward this time, staring at Damanhur with hatred. They smelled of it too, a stench of ash and fire that stung her nose. Damanhur's face became more serious once he found himself facing half a dozen men. His eyes darted from person to person as they quickly surrounded him.

Kunmia and Bingmei reached the nearest bridge and hurried up it.

"They'll cut him down before we get there," Kunmia said. "Use the cricket."

Bingmei nodded, reaching into her pocket. She rubbed the mei-wood cricket, invoking its power, and leaped up and over the bridge, coming down in the middle of the plaza. Damanhur turned toward her, having seen her movement, and the Qiangdao rushed him from all sides.

Whirling her staff, Bingmei struck at the ones nearest her and leaped again as the magic wore off, this time landing behind Damanhur. The Qiangdao shouted at her in anger, slashing with their long sabers, but her staff gave her even better reach. She struck one on the side of the temple, another on the foot, before she reversed the staff and smashed it into his head, dropping him. It was close quarters, and her heart began to pound wildly at the action when Kunmia finally reached the plaza with her staff.

"Neat little trick," Damanhur muttered to Bingmei, his back to her. "Show me how you did that later."

Then the leader of the Qiangdao charged into the fray. He butted past one of his own men and swung the glaive down at Damanhur, its razor-sharp blade coming to split him in half. Damanhur danced to the side as the blade struck the stone, sending up sparks. Then the shaft, which was made out of meiwood, began to glow.

"No!" Kunmia warned as she rushed him.

The Qiangdao leader grinned with malevolence. He swung the end of his weapon around, missing Damanhur, who ducked, and barked out a roar as he charged forward. The magic had added to his power and strength. Damanhur was blocking and defending, but he was forced to give ground. The glaive came suddenly at Bingmei, and she, too, ducked and jumped to the side. A saber sliced her arm, leaving an angry welt.

Kunmia struck at the leader with her staff, but he looked as if he didn't feel her blows. Once, twice, three times to the head. No impact to him. He roared at her and swung the glaive to strike her down, but she blocked it with her staff.

"Stop it!" she hissed at him, her eyes wide with fear. If he summoned the killing fog, he would doom them all.

Bingmei struck the man who had cut her, knocking him down, then delivered a blow to the back of his neck with her fist. She turned, angling the staff, but she felt the Phoenix Blade whispering to her, urging her to draw it so that she might join the battle against the leader. The impulse frightened her, for she knew it would summon the fog. Damanhur struck at him, but the man easily parried his blows.

Kunmia struck at the huge man's stomach, his heart. Hitting vital points over and over, trying to stun him. But his natural strength, bolstered by the magic of his weapon, seemed to prevent him from feeling the pain. He swung at her with the blade of his weapon, and it hit her staff. She had not yet invoked the magic of her staff to draw away its power. Bingmei knew she was worried about drawing the killing fog into Wangfujing.

Bingmei turned and saw the first hint of mist creeping up the river toward them.

"Kunmia!" she shouted in warning, pointing toward the river.

"Drop it, you fool!" Damanhur shouted at the big man.

The leader growled an unintelligible response.

Someone snuck up behind Bingmei, intent on stabbing her in the back. She smelled his awful intention just in time, whirling around and catching him with the dagger poised, his arm raised high. She countered faster, hitting him three times with her staff. The dagger dropped from his hand, and he wilted before her. She kicked him until he cowered, covering his face.

She turned and saw Damanhur and Kunmia striking in tandem against the giant of a man. It took both of them to bring him down, and in relief, she watched the glaive fall from his hands and clatter against the ground. Kunmia struck his skull one more time, and this time he fell, the magic stripped from him.

Kunmia dropped her own weapon, grabbed the fallen glaive, and hurled it off the plaza into the waters of the river. Bingmei's eyes widened as she saw the mist converge where it had gone under. Breathing fast, she watched in fascination and dread as the mist sank beneath the water, becoming cloud-like as it searched for the magic, drawn to it inexorably. Little bursts of green wriggled in the water, and Bingmei realized she was witnessing the death of the fish.

Damanhur stood panting near her, sword still in hand. His gaze lowered to the fallen leader, and Bingmei smelled a whiff of revenge. He stood over the man and raised his sword to strike off his head.

"No," Kunmia said, holding up her palm. "Bring him to the king."

Damanhur wrestled with his feelings. Bingmei could tell he was tempted to defy her. He was an impulsive man, and his blood was up. His eyes questioned Kunmia's authority, but he didn't say the words. Bingmei gripped her staff, wondering if the two of them would start fighting next.

Damanhur sighed and sheathed his weapon. "Yes, Master," he said.

杀雾

The attack on Wangfujing ended in failure. Kunmia's ensign had disrupted the plundering and saved the town. The comatose leader of the Qiangdao was bound and brought to King Budai for judgment. Kunmia's ensign accompanied the prisoner there.

King Budai had a short beard, one he hadn't worn on their previous visits. His bald head glistened with sweat as he sat perched on his throne, gazing down at the massive man who had been forced to kneel before him. The man's arms were bound behind his back, attached to his ankles, shackled with iron cuffs.

Bingmei saw Prince Rowen seated among the advisors of the king. He was looking at her with a fixed stare, not at the prisoner. Cold shot through her. Was he staring at her or the sword strapped to her back?

"What is your name?" Budai asked the leader. His cheek twitched with anger. His emotions were suppressed, but Bingmei could smell them. He'd been very afraid until the victory was assured. Now his fear had turned into fury.

The leader spat on the floor.

Budai grimaced with disgust. He nodded, and one of his guards struck the Qiangdao leader with his staff, earning a wheeze of pain.

"Your name," Budai repeated.

The leader raised his head and started speaking in gibberish.

Budai's brow wrinkled. "What's he saying? What is this?"

"My lord, if I may?" Marenqo said, holding up his hand. When Budai nodded, he approached the leader.

Marenqo tried a few dialects before he found one they both spoke. A few phrases passed back and forth between them. The leader's demeanor was proud, defiant. He already knew he was a dead man.

Marenqo's brow furrowed at whatever he'd been told. He rubbed his mouth as he turned to face the king. "His name is Echion in his language. It means 'reincarnation.'"

Prince Rowen suddenly leaned forward, eyes glittering with interest. He rubbed his mouth with agitation.

"Oh?" said Budai mockingly. "And he remembers his former life, does he? What a privilege. What else did he say?"

Marenqo looked solemn. "He claims he is the reincarnation of the Dragon of Night. If you kill him, he will come back again. But in his next form. The form . . . of a dragon."

All laughter and mocking drained from the room. Bingmei smelled the change in mood from disdain to wariness. It smelled like slightly spoiled grapes.

Most of the legends agreed dragons were real. Although dragon bones had never been found in the ruins of the ancient cities, their images were captured in carvings left in them. It was a symbol of the highest power. Some people had claimed to know someone who had seen one. But Bingmei had never met anyone who claimed to have seen one themselves.

"Bah," uttered Budai, leaning back in his throne. His girth jiggled. "He's the Dragon of Night? Then why not attack during the winter? It is the season of the Dragon of Dawn. Tell him, Marenqo. Tell him!"

Marenqo turned and said a few words to the leader.

The Qiangdao smiled maliciously before he responded.

Whatever he said seemed to have unnerved Marenqo, who clasped his hands behind his back as he spoke. "He knows you don't believe him. But as proof that his words are true, he says he came for the sword. The sword of the phoenix."

Bingmei took an involuntary step backward. She glanced at the gallery. Prince Rowen was staring at her even more intently. A sickly feeling washed through her, and she smelled her own fear.

The leader spoke some more words.

"The phoenix has chosen a new servant," said Marenqo softly. "The Dragon of Night will devour her. And you, Your Highness."

Budai clenched his jaw and leaned forward. "I don't want to hear another word from him, Marenqo. Guanjia—take him below. Execute him."

"Yes, my lord," said Guanjia solemnly. "And those Qiangdao who survived?"

Some uneasy murmuring started up. The worried smell coming from everyone matched Bingmei's own disquiet.

Budai's lip quivered. "If any will be slaves, so be it. Those who refuse . . . the same penalty. Go."

As the big man was taken away, King Budai gestured for Kunmia and Damanhur to approach his throne. Once they stood in front of him, he waved Bingmei over as well. That surprised her, but she did as she was ordered. It disquieted her when Prince Rowen fell in beside her.

"You saved Wangfujing," Budai said, trying to smile, but he looked and smelled rattled. His was a greasy smell, not his normal lemony scent of greed. "I'll admit I am torn about sending you on this mission when things are so . . . unstable." He licked his lips. "But finding what we seek will put my mind at ease. I will hire mercenaries to guard Wangfujing while you are away. I wish you to leave immediately. Tonight, if possible."

"So soon?" Kunmia asked. "That does not seem prudent."

Budai nodded in agreement, but he was determined. Bingmei could smell his ambition flare, his greed. "If you leave during the day, you may be followed. It will be easier to slip out under the cover of smoke and darkness. Find it. You must find it."

Kunmia did not look convinced, but she did not argue with him.

The king then turned to Bingmei. "Was he telling the truth?" he asked in a low voice.

She knew what he meant. But there were so many conflicting smells in the room that she couldn't be sure. All Qiangdao were liars anyway.

"I don't know," she answered truthfully.

CHAPTER TWELVE
Leaving Wangfujing

The night sky was swollen with stars. Smoke from the still-burning town lingered in the air as Bingmei settled down in the fishing boat. Dawn would reveal the damage the Qiangdao had left in the wake of their attack. But the ensign would be long gone by then, leaving her imagination to conjure the images of burned stalls, charred rooftops, and the hosts of dead. King Budai had used most of his guards to protect his palace, allowing the city to be ransacked in part before he sent the men and women out to defend the city. His cowardice bothered Bingmei, but some would likely call it wisdom. The townspeople could be replaced more easily than his treasures.

Servants carried sacks of provisions and loaded them into the fishing boat. The fisherman, whom Bingmei had heard referred to as Keyi, instructed the workers on where to stow the cargo and let everyone know where he wanted them to sit. He fidgeted and had a whine to his voice that grated on her nerves. If he hadn't been the one to find the carving in the first place, Kunmia would never have sought his help.

"No, put it over there, by the ropes. Yes, over there. Now stack that one on top." He muttered to himself and then said, "Now tie the rope down." When the servant started to obey, the fisherman quickly lost patience. He sent the man off and did the knot himself.

"The pickled herring—put the barrel there," he said to another servant, quickly finishing the knot. "Yes, no—not there! There!"

Quion rose from the bench and started to prepare the ropes to secure the barrel.

The fisherman scowled at him. "What are you doing? Sit back down. You're unbalancing the boat."

"Let me help," Quion said. He took two ropes and quickly braided them together, demonstrating the knot for the fisherman when he was finished.

The fisherman's eyes brightened. "Oh good! His lordship didn't mention you were coming. Do you know how to prepare the sail?"

"I do," Quion said, and Bingmei felt a flush of pride for him.

"Good, good! Start on it. Over there. We need to get into the water." With that, he turned and yelled at a servant to bring the next barrel. Marenqo settled in next to Bingmei, and the others filled in as well. Damanhur deliberately sat next to Mieshi, even though there wasn't enough room, and slid in closer. She gave him a hot look of anger, but Bingmei smelled that she secretly liked his attention—it was like the smell of a burning flower. Three other disciples of Damanhur had also joined them, although Bingmei couldn't remember their names, along with the exiled prince. Rowen didn't look at her once as he settled on board. Still, she felt wary of him. The blade seemed to itch against her back.

Once the passengers and supplies were on board, the fisherman and Quion readied the scalloped sail. King Budai was in the safety of his palace, but his steward, Guanjia, had come to see them off. He spoke in low tones with Kunmia, who was the last to board the boat. When she settled into her place, Keyi told Quion to untie the mooring ropes, which he promptly did. The workers on the dock shoved the boat off with hooked poles, and they were quickly embraced by the water.

Keyi the fisherman gave Quion orders about the sail and then took his leisure at the tiller while the younger man did all the work. They snared a favorable wind, and soon everything was quiet and calm, the junk gliding smoothly along.

Bingmei sat thinking, and Marenqo adjusted to a comfortable position and promptly fell asleep. None of them had rested after arriving in Wangfujing, although their wounds had been treated, and they'd been given food. Bingmei should be tired, but the attack on Wangfujing haunted her memories, especially the giant Qiangdao leader. She could still feel the panic rising in her chest as she remembered the killing fog creeping up the river. If Kunmia hadn't acted so quickly, they would have all died. Well, except for Bingmei. With her grandfather's cricket, she could have outrun the fog. Would she have? She blinked, glancing at the darkened faces surrounding her. The ensign was her adopted family. Would she truly have forsaken them to save herself?

In the quietude of the deep night, she realized that yes, she probably would have. Quion caught her eye, and the sight of his friendly smile, which he'd put on just for her, made her emotions flinch. She didn't want to lose him. She didn't want to lose any of them. But death was an implacable, uncaring enemy to be guarded against at all cost. It had taken Lieren. Her parents. Her grandfather. Too many babies died before their first birthday.

Yes, she would have saved herself if there had been no other way. She wished she were braver, more like Kunmia, but in the end survival was an individual effort.

The sword seemed to pulse against her back, whispering to her that it would save her should she need it. That it wished to be used. The Qiangdao leader had been searching for the sword. He'd attacked Wangfujing seeking it. Had he known the other Qiangdao leader who had once held it? He had called himself Echion, the Dragon of Night. What did that even mean? He had also said the phoenix had chosen a new servant. A little tingling went down her back, as if sent by the sword. She shifted, uncomfortable. There was so much she didn't understand. Much she couldn't understand.

She felt her head lolling as fatigue finally swept her away. In her mind's eye, the Qiangdao leader turned his head to face her. He gave her a wicked smile. And then his teeth turned into fangs. He snapped at her.

Bingmei started, blinking awake.

杀雾

Dawn had already come when she finally roused from her sleep. She rubbed her eyes and yawned. Rock hugged the shoreline, the mountains rising from the fjord. Everything was set at steep angles, from the placid river to the craggy mountains on each side of it. The water reflected the green of the fir trees. The trees didn't have deep roots, and some of them had toppled over and crashed into the water. Waterfalls made of melting snow carved paths along the jagged slopes, each one crowded with smaller rocks and smoothed boulders. The veins of water came into the river on both sides, and it was beautiful to look at.

"You're awake," Marenqo said, opening his palm and offering her some pickled herring from the jar in his hand. The air was crisp and cold. The mood smelled inquisitive, like small flowers about to bloom.

"Thank you," Bingmei said, taking one of the little fish and eating it quickly. They would be confined on the boat for a while, so she decided to ask him about the previous day. "What do you make of that Qiangdao leader?"

"Nothing. He's dead."

"What he said . . . did it make sense to you?"

"I understood the words, but he could have meant anything. I wouldn't worry about it, Bingmei. He knew he was about to die. All he cared about was aggravating the king."

"Have you ever heard that name before?"

"What name?"

She sighed. "Echion."

"No," he answered. "There isn't a direct translation of it in our language. That's just what it sounded like. But that is normal in languages. The dialect that man spoke was from far away."

"So they traveled a great distance to attack King Budai."

"Definitely," Marenqo agreed. "That's not a surprise, though. They were probably short on food and took a risk in attacking Wangfujing. I heard from Guanjia that they came up the river in fishing boats. By the time the alarm sounded, the pillaging had already begun. They wanted food, Bingmei. They were probably starving. The Qiangdao only know how to plunder. They don't even have the patience to fish, let alone raise crops. They take what they want and kill anyone who stands in the way."

"I don't understand why the kings won't band together and destroy them," Damanhur said, joining the conversation.

"Because it would require them to cooperate," Mieshi answered with a mocking tone, "and they don't trust each other."

"But they should," Damanhur said.

"To what purpose?" Mieshi asked. "Do you know how long it would take to hunt all the Qiangdao? Years. They hide in caves and secret lairs. Who would protect the crops while the soldiers were away? They'd be slaughtered."

"Doing nothing isn't helping either, my dear," Damanhur said, shaking his head. "Each year the Qiangdao get stronger. People from the towns leave and join them. They do this to feel safer. If we instead made our lands safer, there would be no need to flee."

"You're a fool if you think the kings will work together," she scoffed, her eyes sparking. "They won't."

"But they should. At least can we agree on that? Look at us. Our ensigns are working together. That's a start."

"But our agreement does nothing," Marenqo said. "Would Budai give up his power? Only if he were at risk of losing it. He is only interested in making a profit."

"Without the Qiangdao, he would save money," Damanhur challenged. "It works to everyone's interests to present a united front."

Bingmei was getting bored of the conversation and looked at the trees as they glided past. What Damanhur was suggesting was completely impractical. She'd heard Budai speak of unity in the past, had she not? Marenqo was right—he would never give up his position unless forced.

She looked back the way they'd come and saw Quion resting, arms crossed over his knees. He was gazing absently at the water. He would never join a conversation like this. He didn't like arguing. She appreciated that about him.

He was gazing behind them, his expression solemn. Following the line of his gaze, she saw it too: a huge black fin had appeared in the water. As she watched, it submerged again.

杀雾

They found an island at the mouth of another fjord later in the day, and Keyi advised that they camp there since the strait would offer them little chance to stop until long after dark. Kunmia agreed, and they hauled the boat up onto the rocky shore. Everyone prepared their packs and rolls to hunker out the evening. Although Kunmia had ordered them not to light a fire, they didn't need one for warmth or to cook food. Soon the two ensigns were laughing and swapping tales, eating the cold provisions they'd brought.

Bingmei enjoyed the lighthearted mood, especially when Marenqo launched into a game—he would tell a tale, and the others would guess if it was true or false.

After dark, Kunmia ordered a rotating guard schedule so that most could sleep. Bingmei was part of the first watch. She wandered along the shore to stretch her legs, watching the water lap against the rocks. After some time, she heard voices and smelled Damanhur and Rowen as they walked along the waterline. She ignored them, but they soon ventured close enough for her to hear part of their muffled conversation.

"How much treasure do you think that ruler buried with him?" Damanhur asked. "It will take many trips to transfer anything of size."

"Some of it may be too big for boats," answered Rowen. "That's why we need Budai."

"I hope the fisherman is right about this. If we've found Fusang, it could be more than enough to achieve your dreams."

"I know. It's difficult not getting my hopes up too much. My brother thinks—"

"Your brother is too much like your father. Stop comparing yourself to him. You could do what they've only dreamed of."

"Do you think so?"

Bingmei could smell the ambition. It stung her nose. She kept her back to both of them, not moving. There was something they knew that they hadn't shared with Kunmia. But given their circumstances, it wasn't surprising they would go to any lengths to secure a hidden treasure.

"I know it. Come on, let's get some rest. I put our gear by Mieshi's."

Rowen chuckled, and then their voices faded away.

CHAPTER THIRTEEN

Ruins

As the sun rose the next morning, a pod of enormous whales passed the island, and the ensign gathered around to watch the majestic creatures breach the water.

While they ate their morning meal, the dawn brought a mask of natural fog that concealed the distant mountains and the nearer shores in short order. Keyi did not want to travel in the fog, and so they waited most of the morning for it to clear until he was satisfied that the danger was over. Bingmei and Quion explored the small island, examining the broken rocks and stunted trees. They found a massive eagle's nest high in the branches of a dying tree, and the white-headed raptors eyed them suspiciously as they ventured near. Quion was mesmerized by the birds and stared at them a long while, shaking his head in admiration and wonder.

After they left the island, the wind rose, and the river became choppy. The rocking and jolting of the boat banished Bingmei's appetite. The weather was a constant danger. She was grateful the clouds didn't choose to soak them, but their luck did not hold. Before long, rain began to fall.

The fisherman scowled while he and Quion tried to steer the boat and manage the sail. "We need to find shelter again!" he shouted to Kunmia over the whistling wind. His short cloak was soaked, and his face grimaced in worry.

"What harbors are near?" she asked, coming closer to him so she didn't have to yell.

"The nearest one is Wangfujing, but I don't think you want to go back!"

The boat lifted on a high wave, making Bingmei's stomach lurch. It came slamming down hard.

"What other choices do we have?" Kunmia asked.

"The wind is too strong, and there are no beaches on either side of the fjord," he said. "We'd be dashed against the rocks if we tried to moor there. I think we take the next inlet and try to get out of the weather."

Kunmia nodded in agreement. Bingmei saw the look of determination on Quion's face as he wiped his wet hair out of the way and worked on the sail. He took some additional rope from his pack and made some lashings to help against the strain of the wind. His hands looked cold as he worked at the knots, and every now and again the wind would shift suddenly, swinging the bar around to strike him. Keyi barked orders to him, which he obeyed, and she wished she could do something to help.

After they battled the river and winds for a time, they found an inlet and steered into it. The wind immediately calmed as the passage was quite narrow, the looming mountain walls rising steeply on both sides. Feathery clouds hugged the tips, obscuring the sky and the progress of the sun. The problem with inlets was they could end abruptly and not give a vessel time to maneuver out of them. They could serve as cruel traps if an enemy waited at the end. Hidden boulders could also damage the hull of the ship.

Keyi and Quion paid close attention and communicated frequently. Everyone on board kept alert for trouble, Bingmei sitting on the edge of her seat as they followed the inlet through some twists and narrows.

Waterfalls trickled down the face of the jagged stone. They turned around a sharp bend, and the fisherman called out a warning.

"Ruins!"

There was a dilapidated wharf and the bones of several buildings with caved-in roofs. There were six or so smaller buildings, but none had windows, and the latticework had been weathered to the point of uselessness.

Keyi sniffed. "I've seen many villages like this. Abandoned. Rotten."

"Sail up to the quay," Kunmia said, gazing at the ruins. "It looks abandoned, not ransacked. The roofs fell in because of the weight of snow. Or maybe boulders crashed down."

Within a few moments, they'd steered the fishing boat up to the quay. Quion tied off a rope to secure it.

"Mieshi . . . Bingmei," Kunmia said. "Go scout the ruins."

"There may be Qiangdao hiding here," Damanhur said. "I would like to go as well."

Mieshi flashed him a look of annoyance. The smell of wariness and fear—of rotten things—was superseded momentarily by the scent of sweet peppers. "We don't need your help," she said with disdain.

"I didn't ask if you needed help," Damanhur said. "I offered to come because I'm curious too." He turned back to Kunmia with arched eyebrows.

Kunmia nodded, and the three departed the boat while the others remained behind. Bingmei and Mieshi, each with her staff, led the way, followed by Damanhur, who wielded his sword. They had to be careful traversing the quay because of the rotten wood and broken planks. Bingmei could smell Damanhur's interest in Mieshi as well as feel her bond sister's tension at having him behind them.

After crossing the dock, they entered the small broken village. There was evidence of fire pits in the middle of the rocky street. Wood had been scavenged from the buildings to be burned. Bingmei breathed in, trying to catch a warning smell, as they trod down the street. Bingmei cocked her head, staring up at one of the support beams that was still holding, while another had crashed.

"How old are you?" Damanhur suddenly asked. She turned around, seeing that he was addressing her.

Mieshi looked back and then pressed on.

"What does it matter how old I am?" Bingmei asked in return, following Mieshi.

"Wait," he said, and she stopped, turning in confusion. She felt apprehension.

Damanhur approached, looking at her shoulder. His eyebrows wrinkled in confusion. "Your hair is . . . white."

Bingmei saw that the fierce winds from the boat had blown some of her real hair loose, which had mixed with the dark strands of her wig.

She frowned at him and walked away.

"You have the winter sickness?" he asked incredulously.

Mieshi turned on him, eyes flashing with fury. "Leave her alone." For all Mieshi looked down on Bingmei for her ailment, she wouldn't allow anyone else to call it out. They were bond sisters first.

"Sheathe your fangs, cat," Damanhur said to Mieshi. "I'm surprised is all." He turned to Bingmei. "You've hidden it."

"People think they might get it if they touch her," Mieshi said. Bingmei's stomach was shriveling with embarrassment. She hated that smell on herself. "But it's a myth."

"Of course it is," Damanhur said. "One of King Shulian's stewards has it. He's highly respected. His name is Jidi Majia."

Bingmei had never met anyone else with her condition, and it surprised her to hear the man had achieved such a prominent position.

He looked at Bingmei again. "It's a rare thing. Bingmei . . . I can see that now. 'Ice rose.' Look how your cheeks are flushed. I attributed your pale skin to being from the north."

"I *am* from the north," Bingmei said, her cheeks steaming further.

"And what about your trick?" he asked. "The one that makes you jump?"

"Are we going to just stand here in the street?" Mieshi snapped. Her comment, while impatient, was also tinged with jealousy. Was this because his attention had been diverted from her? Bingmei could only wonder. "We have a duty to perform."

"It's just a question. How did you do it?" he pressed.

Although he had not treated her with disgust, Bingmei didn't trust him. "Let's go, Mieshi." She resented that Damanhur had discovered her secret so soon. She had a dark feeling he might use the knowledge against her someday. If nothing else, she felt sure that he would tell Rowen about her.

杀雾

One of the buildings had a suitable shelter that was protected from the elements. Kunmia had assigned Bingmei and Quion to guard the boat during the first watch. The boat needed to be guarded. The security of their supplies was paramount. The rain still fell with a steady patter, and Bingmei was cold and envious of those who were huddling around the fire that Quion had built within the structure. They would get their turn to be warm after midnight.

Quion sat fishing off the broken docks—he had already caught a stack of eight—while Bingmei paced along the broken wharf.

"Damanhur is a pile of dung," she said, still seething that he knew her secret.

"He is arrogant," Quion said, shrugging. "But if we face more Qiangdao on this mission, we'll be glad he's here."

"I'm not glad he's here."

"Why?" Quion asked, poking his lure back into the water.

She sighed. "He saw my hair. It's the storm's fault."

Quion looked at her. "Why should you care if he noticed?"

"How many people will he tell?" Bingmei countered.

Quion shrugged. "I don't see why you wear the wig at all."

"Because people would stare at me," she said.

"So what?" Quion said. "It's different, but it's not ugly. You're *not* ugly, Bingmei."

He was used to her. He'd never treated her as if she were diseased. Gratitude rippled through her. How she hated to be looked at with contempt, ridicule, and disgust. It made it so much worse that her sense of smell so often confirmed her fears and self-consciousness.

"You don't understand, Quion," she said, shaking her head.

He turned to face her, setting his rod down, and his brow wrinkled in concern. "I don't understand what?"

She swallowed. She'd never told anyone other than her family. But she wanted to. Quion was different. He'd never done anything to make her believe she couldn't trust him. He still smelled like fish, but it was a strangely comforting smell. There was no deception in him at all, unlike Rowen, the exiled prince, who often smelled different from how he acted.

Quion leaned closer. "What's wrong?" She sat down next to him, the words bubbling inside her. Did she dare tell him? The moon was barely strong enough to pierce the clouds. The ruins were invisible in the darkness. Somehow it made it easier to contemplate opening her soul to him.

Still, it would hurt if he rejected her. If his acceptance of her was changed by what he learned. Once spoken, the words could not be taken back. Should she? Bingmei bit her lip.

He gazed at her, and she felt his concern growing. His sympathy smelled like warm grain with raisins and nuts. It made her mouth water.

"The only people who knew my secret were my parents and my grandfather," she said in a low voice.

"You don't have to tell me," he answered. "But I hope you will."

She licked her lips. "It shames me to speak of it." His eyes were filled with such kindness and warmth, she couldn't hold his gaze. The urge to tell him throbbed inside her. She decided to trust him.

"I'm different than other people," she said softly. "Remember when we went to Wangfujing the first time? How I knew which people were honest? I chose some people, even though others offered more cowry shells?"

"Yes," he said, nodding encouragingly.

"It's just . . . I *know* what people are feeling."

He went very quiet. Before he could say anything, his pole started to jiggle, and he quickly snatched it before it could fall into the water. Moments later, he pulled out a huge silvery fish. He grinned at it in wonder. It was the largest one he'd caught so far.

It struggled to break free, but he thumped it with a small hammer, and it lay still. Bingmei could imagine the meat on such a massive fish. As he began removing the hook from its mouth, she heard the sound of others approaching. It was not yet close to midnight.

"Watch the next part, or you'll be taking a swim." She recognized Damanhur's voice, but there were two sets of footsteps coming down the planks.

"I'll be careful." The response came in Rowen's voice.

Quion finished removing the line when they arrived. Damanhur gazed down at the pile of fish and then squatted near it. "You have a gift, Quion. Fortunately, you have many gifts. The fire is almost out, and we're all getting cold. Can you come revive it?"

Quion looked at Bingmei in concern.

"Rowen will take your place as guard with Bingmao. Kunmia said so. Come on." He grinned at Bingmei. He was teasing her, something she could tell from his scent and his tone, but it had a friendly intent.

"Her name is Bingmei," Quion said evenly.

"Isn't that what I said?" Damanhur asked with feigned innocence. "You must have misheard me. Come on. Nothing will dry before dawn without that fire."

Quion pursed his lips. She smelled his reluctance to go. He wanted to stay and keep talking with her, and she wanted it too. The last person she wanted to share guard duty with was the exiled prince. Particularly if he knew one of her secrets.

But Quion was only a fisherman's son, after all, and someone like Damanhur outranked him. Her friend muttered something about bringing the fish along, pulled out a sack from his pack, and quickly stuffed the fish in one by one.

Damanhur stood and waited, and then both of them left, Quion looking back over his shoulder as he walked away.

Rowen towered over her, and she felt very small. His striking looks made her feel insignificant, but his smell told her that he was intrigued by her. Fascinated even. And she could smell his hunger for the blade still strapped to her back.

She turned away from him, folding her arms around her knees as she sat in the quiet, hearing the water lap against the quay and watching the clouds tease the stars.

He said nothing for a very long time, which did not surprise her. She hadn't heard him speak very often. He did more communicating with his eyes. So when he finally did address her, it startled her and made her turn her head sharply to gaze at him. It was not what she had expected him to say.

"If I come into my kingdom, will you lead my ensign?"

杀雾

Words are powerful. We need always be wary
how we speak to others and
even more so how we speak of ourselves.

—Dawanjir proverb

CHAPTER FOURTEEN

Ruined

"What?" Bingmei asked, wrinkling her brow.

The prince sat facing her, his back against one of the dilapidated posts, his arm resting on one knee. He gave her an enigmatic look, one of deep interest. He smelled of raw ambition, along with the subtler scent of curiosity, but his words and feelings were sincere. There was no sour smell of deception coming from him. A little smile curled his lip. "I didn't know when we'd get the chance to speak like this. Privately. So I thought I'd take a chance. I intend to rule Sajinau." He shrugged his shoulders. "Soon perhaps. I wanted you to be ready."

"Why are you asking me this?" Bingmei said.

"King Budai thinks highly of you. He told me the story of what happened to your family's ensign. You train under Kunmia Suun, which is a sign of your dependability as well as your skill. I've seen you fight."

Her brow wrinkled more. "When?" she demanded.

"I'm an observant person," he replied evasively. "I ask you again. When I come into my kingdom, will you lead my ensign?"

"You said *if* at first. Isn't that a more likely outcome? King Shulian is the strongest ruler in all the coast, his kingdom the most powerful. Your brother, the crown prince, has been named his heir."

"Are you going to answer my question?" he asked, smiling again.

"I don't see why I should," she answered, adjusting herself.

"I'll give you three reasons," he answered. He'd anticipated her reaction. His self-confidence smelled like the rind of a melon. It made her even more distrustful, anxious to depart. But she could not abandon her post.

She waited, staring at him. She could see his expression easily in the moonlight. But he did not answer straightaway. He paused, deliberately, heightening her curiosity. Was he toying with her?

"The first," he said after prolonging the silence to the point of discomfort. He paused again, cocking his head slightly. "I can help you reclaim your grandfather's quonsuun. Budai told me where it was. It will cost a great deal of money to restore it. If you let Budai help you, then you will be his servant. You don't want that. I am a much more patient master."

He stopped speaking, watching her face for a reaction. Was he waiting to see if she'd respond? She didn't. He'd said he had three reasons. She wanted to hear them all.

When it became apparent she wasn't going to answer, he continued. "The second." He gave her a friendly smile. "Those with the winter sickness are not persecuted in Sajinau. There's a myth that the founder of Sajinau was a pale-skinned king. My father's own advisor has the winter sickness, and he is highly regarded for his wisdom and loyalty. Those are traits I admire. As the head of my ensign, you would be respected and honored. Think on it."

His words annoyed Bingmei at first—Damanhur hadn't kept her secret for very long, and while Sajinau might treat people with the winter sickness differently, all her experiences with being revealed publicly had been negative. Still, it felt good to have earned the prince's respect. She was flattered, despite herself, but she summoned her will and blotted out the feelings of warmth. *Do not trust him. He hasn't proven himself yet. He wishes to betray his father and brother. He could betray you too.*

She gave him an expectant look, waiting for him to finish.

Her reticence seemed to please him. He smiled again. "The third reason is . . ." His voice trailed off, and then he chuckled and looked down. "To be honest, I hadn't thought I'd make it this far before you rejected my proposal."

"So there isn't a third reason?" she said. His confession had been unexpected.

"Oh, there is. I'm just saying you surprised me. That doesn't happen very often. There are more than just three reasons. Another is that I wouldn't trust Budai if I were you. And that I'll honor you more than he ever would. But here is the third reason. The Phoenix Blade."

She felt the smell of his desire for it flare in her nose.

"I don't imagine you will part with it," Rowen said. "But I must be near it. I have a strong notion that I will not succeed without it. Call it an omen, if you will, but I believe my destiny is bound to that sword. I can't explain it. It draws me in." He licked his lips. "There. You have my three reasons."

He'd put her in an uncomfortable position. His words had conjured her own ambition. Yes, she wanted all the things he had offered, and yet . . . he was only revealing part of himself to her. He was not trying to deceive her. She would have smelled that. But there was something simmering beneath the surface she didn't understand. Nor did she understand the strange tension that had suddenly formed between them.

"How do you aim to defeat your father?" Bingmei asked. She could have suggested ideas, but she wished to know his thoughts first.

"I think he's wrong. Misguided," Rowen said. "And so is my brother. He waits to be *asked* to be the high king. To be *invited* to save the people from the Qiangdao hordes. He doesn't understand the stubbornness of men." His words were raw, full of antipathy. He paused, controlling himself again. She felt the bubbling passion beneath his exterior, the belief that he could do better than what his father had done. Prince

Rowen did not let his emotions get the better of him often. He smiled again, but it was self-deprecating. He realized he'd lost a little control.

"Was your brother chosen because he is more of your father's temperament?" Bingmei asked softly.

The prince shrugged and nodded.

"There has been conflict in your family for some time," Bingmei said. "What makes you think that you will be able to rule your people eventually?"

"It's a fair question, Bingmei." The way he said her name made her feel strange inside. An unfamiliar smell, like the pomegranate seeds she'd tasted only once, filled the air. It was enjoyable, yet embarrassing at the same time.

"Will you answer it, *Wuren*?"

He rubbed his jaw, looking up at the stars. Then he leaned back against the post more firmly and, still gazing off in the distance, answered, "There are families in Sajinau who are discontented with his reign and have managed to stay beneath the notice of the Jingcha, my father's spies. These people want to see *change* happen. They know what they'll get under my brother." He chuckled darkly. "Little. If I return to the kingdom with enough force, then it will compel a discussion with the king's council. Civil war? I don't think it will come to that. I wouldn't murder my father, if that concerns you. I don't want his blood on my hands. He would live comfortably the rest of his days."

Again she smelled his honesty. He wasn't lying to her. That was blatantly clear. Budai knew of Bingmei's ability to discern a person's intentions, although not how she came by it. He also knew she had Kunmia's trust. Clearly Prince Rowen had anticipated he could not deceive her. He was laying out his plans. The knowledge of which, if sent to his father, could ruin him.

"What about your brother?" Bingmei asked.

She felt a sharp scent, one that stung her nose. Jealousy, like fresh-cut onions. His expression, his casual bearing, belied it. But the odor was overpowering.

"I don't think he'll relinquish his position," Rowen said softly. "I wouldn't in his place. He thinks he's doing what is best for the realm." He sighed. "But if we do nothing, here's what will happen, Bingmei. If the Qiangdao unite, even temporarily, they can destroy any single kingdom. It almost happened to Wangfujing! I know I am right. Why wait as the enemy gets stronger? We must unite our strength and attack *them* in the mountains. It will take . . . years." He looked directly into her eyes. "This is a task for the young. My father lacks the will to start something he doesn't have the strength to finish." What he left unsaid implied to Bingmei that he believed *he* did. "Call me Rowen, Bingmei. I want you to call me by my proper name. Will you *be* my ensign?"

His words intrigued her. His promises tempted her. But she would not swear her loyalty so easily. She wouldn't commit herself to a cause she wasn't sure she believed in.

"Maybe," she answered.

His eyebrows knit. "Maybe," he said, then chuckled softly. "That's better than a no."

And it was also quite far away from a yes.

杀雾

When dawn came to the abandoned town, Bingmei awoke near the steaming coals of Quion's fire to the sound of seals barking. She stirred slowly, enjoying the warmth of the fur blankets wrapped around her. Other members of the ensign were already beginning to stow their gear. When she sat up, she saw Prince Rowen talking in low tones to Damanhur. The prince noticed her rousing and nodded to her, offering a pleasant smile.

Damanhur, seeing his reaction, turned and looked at her. "Good morning, Bingmao!" He greeted her with a smirk.

She restrained herself from glaring at him. Not reacting was the best course when someone was deliberately trying to provoke a reaction.

Quion was gone, and his pack too, so she assumed he'd gone to look after the boat. The fisherman, Keyi, was also missing. She rolled up her blankets, tying them with leather straps, and packed them away. She'd slept with the sword in her grip, worried that the prince might try stealing it in the night. Even though she'd spent part of the night on guard duty, sleep had been long in coming. She'd lain awake, thinking about his offer. There was no denying it had tantalized her emotions. Then again, that had no doubt been his intention. She would not be rash in making such a decision. And she would certainly counsel with Kunmia about it.

After they finished packing, they followed the noise of the seals back to the boat and found Marenqo and Quion laughing and throwing fish to a group of seals that had come up on the dock. The creatures were so odd looking, with their spotted hides and long whiskers, they made Bingmei smile. When one of the seals yawned really wide, she laughed along with the others.

Kunmia stood at the dock, gripping her rune staff, and spoke to Keyi in hushed tones. The sky was void of clouds, the weather favorable again. When the rest of the ensign arrived, they began boarding the fishing boat. Bingmei stood by Kunmia, letting the others go first.

"If we take the inland passage, it will take us ten days to reach the point where Keyi found the artifact," Kunmia told her. "The farther we go along the rim, the fewer settlements we'll pass."

Bingmei turned and looked back at the ruins. "I wonder how much time has passed since people lived here?"

Kunmia shrugged. "The buildings are ancient, but they have fallen apart. No one knows how to build like that anymore. We should go."

"Wait," Bingmei said. "I would like to talk to you. About the prince."

Kunmia's brow wrinkled in concern. "Did he offer to buy the sword?"

"No," Bingmei said. "He wants me to join him. He intends to rule Sajinau."

Kunmia gave her a knowing look. "Wanting to rule and being fit for it are two different things." She smiled. "It's always easy counting cowry shells before they're in your hand. This mission may prove fruitless, Bingmei. Fusang may be nothing but a dream."

Bingmei smiled in return and nodded in agreement. "We will talk later, then. I value your advice, Kunmia."

Kunmia hefted her staff. "I value you as well, Bingmei. And I trust you."

The warm comforting smell that came from her master was one of her favorites. Bingmei climbed aboard and found her place. Marenqo finished feeding the seals.

"Why you'd waste a fish on them is a mystery," Damanhur told him after he arrived.

"We had plenty to spare," Marenqo said as he jostled through the group to find his place. "The boy filled the net this morning."

The evidence of it was there in the boat, a net bulging with the catch. The smell of the sleek fish overpowered Bingmei's senses, but all were delighted they had so many. Quion was the last to board. As he untied the ropes from his position on the dock, the seals barked and wriggled, as if pleading for more of the catch.

Quion laughed, showing them his empty hands. Then he finished with the rope and held it while Keyi barked orders with his usual impatience.

The seals' complaints grew louder and more intense. Bingmei looked at them more closely. There were a lot of them on the dock, probably twelve in all.

Something heavy slammed into the side of the boat, making everyone lurch and gasp. Bingmei gripped the edge, watching in alarm as the water sloshed up the side of the boat, and she saw something huge and black in the water. A white stripe marked its eyeline.

The sailboat smashed into the dock, crushing the timbers and spilling the seals—and Quion—into the murky cold water.

A ni-ji-jing.

A fish that hunted men.

CHAPTER FIFTEEN

The Glacier

Icy water splashed into Bingmei's face, blinding her. The boat rocked as it was struck again, and she heard Marenqo cry out in warning that he had seen another ni-ji-jing. Quion was in the water, amidst the debris and the seals, and she felt a pang of desperate resolve surge through her. She couldn't let *him* die. He was her friend, and their friendship meant something to her.

"Grab my hand!" It was Damanhur's voice, calling to Quion.

"You'll swamp the boat!" the fisherman yelled. The boat reeked of terror. Bingmei's stomach wrenched as the floor shifted beneath her. The fishing boat had been struck and was spinning, the current yanking it away. A black dorsal fin sliced through the water near her, the creature's sleek body, black on top with a white underside, gliding past. Then she saw the other one, and her heart shivered with fear. The ni-ji-jing were huge creatures, about as big as the fishing boat if not larger. They preyed on seals, which, she realized, was why they'd sought safety on the broken docks.

She couldn't see Quion, so she rose on shaky legs. Damanhur was leaning out over the side of the boat. He tried to grab something she couldn't see and missed.

"He's under the boat!" Damanhur shouted in warning.

"If one of the ni-ji-jing breaches, it could kill us all!" Keyi whined.

"Look for him!" Kunmia ordered. She was crouching in the boat, her staff held defensively, ready to use it against the man-eating whales. "Where is he?"

Bingmei's heart leaped in her chest when she saw his head bob up from the water. He looked frantic, his hands groping for the hull.

"There!" Bingmei shouted, pointing. She shoved past Mieshi and lunged to reach his hand, but Marenqo grabbed her from behind and pulled her back.

She saw a third dorsal fin appear on the surface of the inlet river, coming straight toward the boat. Straight toward Quion. Bingmei screamed in anger and terror. Marenqo clambered over one of Damanhur's disciples and leaned over the side of the boat. He was taller than her, had a longer reach. He grabbed Quion's hand and arm and started pulling him. Waterlogged and flailing, Quion kicked, his feet churning water. He was so close to safety, but the ni-ji-jing was coming too fast.

Bingmei watched in horror as the one in front surfaced, opening a mouth full of long, sharp teeth.

"Get him in the boat!" someone screamed.

Suddenly, Kunmia pushed her way to the front. She swung her staff up and over the edge of the boat, striking the ni-ji-jing on the snout. The great whale jerked and went another way, missing the boat and Quion. Prince Rowen stepped forward to help, and he and Marenqo grabbed Quion's coat together and hauled him on board.

Quion was pale with fear and cold, his teeth chattering, his hair dripping in his face. Bingmei helped pull him away from the edge of the boat. One of the ni-ji-jing struck the side of the boat again, making it spin even faster as the current caught it. She could see the mess of the dock and hear some of the seals barking.

Keyi was frantically trying to regain control of the boat as they spun toward the other side of the river, where sharp boulders were waiting.

"Are you hurt?" Kunmia asked, leaning over Quion with a worried look.

He shook his head no, but he was shivering so much he couldn't speak.

"Untie the sail! Untie the sail or we're all doomed!" Keyi shouted. He was struggling with the tiller, but the momentum was too great. The chasm of the fjord loomed before them.

Quion's hands were trembling much too badly for him to be of help, but Bingmei had seen him tie the knots for the sail, so she hurried into position.

"Untie them, quickly!" Keyi pleaded.

Bingmei's fingers felt clumsy, but she managed it. Keyi dashed forward, trampling on someone's foot before reaching her. He quickly worked the sail, and thankfully there was enough wind to catch it. The sail billowed out, and the boat jerked in response.

"They're coming after us!" Zhuyi warned.

Bingmei turned and saw a dorsal fin surface again. Keyi grimaced with determination and shoved against the bar, angling it so that the wind was pushing them away from the ni-ji-jing. The boat ceased its reckless spinning and lunged against the river.

"Duck!" Keyi told her, and suddenly swung the sail in the other direction. She was able to crouch just in time.

Then they were gaining speed, faster and faster. The ni-ji-jing gave up the chase and ducked under the water.

"Bingmei," Kunmia said in a tone of command.

She turned and approached her master. Quion was still shivering, although Kunmia had draped a fur blanket over his shoulders. Marenqo sat next to him.

"We need to get him warm again," Kunmia said. "Both of you should be under the blanket with him. That should reverse the cold. Come."

Bingmei and Marenqo sat on either side of him, and Kunmia wrapped the blanket around them.

"That was terrifying," Marenqo said. "I thought about going for a swim myself this morning. I'm glad I did not."

Bingmei gave him an incredulous look, and he smiled. Marenqo did like to joke. Quion's trembling lips tipped into a smile too. Bingmei grabbed his hands and squeezed them. He looked and smelled like relief. The scent of fear was dispersing.

As she nestled against Quion, she realized that perhaps she was not as selfish as she'd thought. He was someone she would have given her life to try to rescue.

There were some people worth saving.

杀雾

The days passed slowly as they worked through the inner maze of the fjords and waterways, staying away from the open sea as much as they could. There were plenty of provisions to keep them from going hungry, and Keyi and Quion's knowledge of sailing allowed them to travel at night.

The voyage continued for days. The inner passage felt like a maze. Bingmei was absolutely lost in the chasm of the fjords, which all began to look alike, but the view of the rugged, harsh land was impressive. Enormous glaciers had broken apart the mountains, leaving the debris of enormous boulders along the rough coastline. Bears roamed the rocky shore to feed on the abundant salmon that were spawning in the spring, and eagles flew gracefully above the snow-capped treetops. As the days passed, it grew warmer, and she could see the edge of snow receding up the mountains, creating giant waterfalls that rumbled and roared. Smaller boats could be seen now and then, some working huge crab cages while others used nets to catch the fish converging at the inlets to swim upstream.

They no longer needed so many layers. Quion asked Bingmei about her scorpion pendant, which she wore above her shirt. She explained that she liked it because scorpions might be small, but their sting was excruciating. She felt that described her well enough. He said looking at it made him hungry to go back to Wangfujing.

Through the journey, she enjoyed the moments of respite when they would beach the boat on a sandbar and walk around and stretch their legs. She worked on her dragon straight-sword form, and it felt glorious to exercise again. When she used the Phoenix Blade, she no longer felt compelled to call upon its magic. Every day it felt more and more a part of her, which lessened her fear of how the blade affected her. Clouds scudded across the sky, the weather often temperamental within the span of the same day.

It took them about ten days to reach the bay where Keyi had found the fragments of sculpted stone. They had to take a winding river through a narrow gorge into the mountains, which emerged into a vast lake. They could catch no wind in the passage, and so they had to take turns rowing to bring the boat against the current. The glacier was an enormous mound of ice that touched the edge of the lake with its teeth. Snow had receded up the sides of the surrounding cliffs, but the mass of ice was thousands of years old and had carved a valley into the mountains.

Adjacent to the glacier was a wide sloping waterfall that flooded down the side of the lower portion of the abutting mountain. The melting glacier clearly fed it, and the sound of the churning water could be heard from a distance. There was a sandbar at the base of the waterfall, touching part of the glacier. The graying chunks of ice from glaciers could shear off suddenly, so it wasn't wise to venture too close to the edge.

"Now that we're here, where did you find the stones?" Kunmia asked Keyi as the boat glided closer to the waterfall.

"By the edge of the glacier," Keyi said, pointing. "I camped on that sandbar right there. Drank from the waterfall. There are lots of fish in this lake."

"Any ice bears?" Damanhur asked.

Keyi nodded. "But plenty of fish for all. They left me alone."

"Let's stop at the sandbar and look around," Kunmia said. They sailed to the edge. It was getting late, and there wouldn't be much time for exploring that day, but at least they could wander a bit. Bingmei was excited by the grandeur of the place. It felt almost familiar, although she wasn't sure why. She'd seen dozens of glaciers before, but this one looked different.

When they beached the boat on the sandbar, Quion asked if he should start a fire. Kunmia shook her head, not wanting to attract attention with the smoke, but asked him to gather firewood with Marenqo. Bingmei walked along the edge of the sandbar, admiring the view of the glacier. The beauty was almost painful to behold.

Chunks of ice floated along the edge of the lake. She hugged herself, feeling the waves of cold coming off the glacier. It would be cold when the sun set. Bitterly cold.

She made her way over to the waterfall. The water rushed down the angle of the mountain, crashing into the lake. She smelled fish and wondered if Quion was nearby, but she didn't see him. The wind shifted, and she smelled Prince Rowen coming up behind her. She turned as he came to a stop beside her. He watched the waterfall for a moment, arms folded across his chest.

"What a savage land," he said.

She wondered why he'd chosen that moment to approach her. "One must be a little savage to survive," Bingmei replied, gazing at the waterfall. The wind shifted again a few moments later, coming down from the mountain. The stench stung her nose, and she realized that there were people hiding behind the waterfall, watching them. She knew the smell, the stench of the Qiangdao. Memories from her childhood struck her. This was a familiar smell, one she'd sought for years. The smell of her parents' killers.

"They're here," she breathed, feeling fear spasm inside her heart.

"Who?" Rowen asked.

And from behind the hidden veil of the falls charged a band of Qiangdao, weapons raised, screaming in challenge as they closed in on her and Rowen.

The others were too far away to help.

The Phoenix Blade shot straight up from her scabbard. She felt the magic of the blade surging through her, invoked by its own command. Aghast, she stared up at it in terrified wonder. When the pommel swiveled down, she felt the instinct to reach up for it. It settled into her hand as if summoned by her.

CHAPTER SIXTEEN

Chosen

Bingmei felt the magic of the blade ripple down her arm as she dropped into a pose from dragon straight sword. Her blood felt like fire in her veins, but she felt no fear. She felt only calm determination. She smelled Prince Rowen's sudden flush of fear, but he drew two long daggers from his belt and set his stance to defend. Some cries of warning sounded from the others gathered around the boat.

"We fight together," Rowen told her huskily, his voice trembling slightly.

Bingmei didn't respond, keeping her eyes focused on the charging men and their weapons. They wore seal skins, hide boots, and leathery armor that was beaten and fire-hardened. Scraggly beards and unwashed faces contorted with hatred. They had all the marks of savagery, of those who dwelled in such inhospitable shores, who raided and plundered and stole. How she despised them. Where was Muxidi? Where was the man who had slain her grandfather?

Before she could spy him, the first of the raiders reached her. Bingmei sprang at them with the sword. The magic augmented her instincts. Her movements felt as light and quick as a feather, yet each stab struck a man in the vitals, the sharp blade piercing the thick hides they wore. Soon the Qiangdao's shrieks of attack were paired with cries of pain and groans of anguish. Bingmei shifted from pose to pose, parrying cudgels as she danced backward, then lashing out with a whip-quick slash to a wrist or chest.

From the corner of her eye, she saw Rowen at work. He, too, was quick and lethal, using both blades at once. He swiveled, turned, and thrust, dropping man after man. They were both engulfed by the tide of men, but their blades held the enemies at bay.

Bingmei's blade seemed to quiver with delight in her hand, and the magic threatened to overwhelm her. Was she summoning the killing fog by using it? Part of her didn't care. The power began to consume her, promising her the revenge she'd hungered for all these years. How many of this band had slaughtered her family? They deserved to die. To be cut down without mercy.

A dart embedded in her arm, thrown by one of the Qiangdao. She plucked it out and threw it back, hardly feeling the pain. She cut down two more before she saw a man whirling a leather sling overhead. He launched the stone at Rowen before she could issue a warning, and the rock struck him in the temple, dropping him instantly. The other Qiangdao roared in triumph and surged forward to bludgeon him to death, but Bingmei shouted in fury and rushed to protect his body. She brought down three before the slinger managed to load another stone. He whirled it again and launched it at her. Some instinct within her, probably the magic, brought the sword up just in time to deflect it. The slinger scowled in anger, already reaching into his pouch for another stone.

Then Kunmia and her ensign arrived, smashing into the Qiangdao. They were still heavily outnumbered, but the odds had improved. The cacophony of battle filled the air. Damanhur was at the forefront of the group from the boat, his sword slashing the chests of enemy warriors in long sweeps, his expert skill outmatching those he fought. Mieshi and Zhuyi were twin sisters of vengeance, using their staves to crack skulls and smash throats. Even Quion was part of the effort, using his fists to strike down those who'd attacked them.

One of Damanhur's men went down from the slinger's stones. Bingmei scowled at the slinger, reached into her pocket and invoked the cricket, harnessing its power to leap over the tide of battle. When she landed near the slinger, who was already reaching into his pocket for more stone, he ducked away from her slash. He scooped a handful of sand and tossed it at her face, but she closed her eyes in time, as the grit stung her skin. She smelled his fear, his dread of her abilities, his hatred—a noxious blend of rotting meat and putrid fish. Bingmei followed the scent, clearing her eyes, and saw him put another stone in his sling. He started to swing it around his head, intending to strike at her at close range, which would kill her for certain, but she leaped forward and sliced through the leather strap. She'd ruined his weapon of choice. Bingmei heard the crunch of sand, the sound of someone rushing up to attack her from behind. Still facing the unarmed slinger, she tucked her blade beneath her armpit and stabbed behind her, impaling a man in the gut. He slumped to the ground.

The slinger gawked at her and turned and ran for his life. Bingmei let him go, turning her focus on another of the Qiangdao. Bingmei's blood was up, she was thrilled by the combat, by the power of the blade in her hand, and the invincibility it gave her. Then a new stench caught her nose, one she recognized with a wrench in her stomach. The horrible man who'd killed her grandfather was fighting Kunmia. He wielded a saber that was the same shape and style as those used in her grandfather's quonsuun. He was dressed in furs like the others, but she could see a flash of color from his underclothes. Kunmia blocked a strike from his saber and then dealt a blow to his head with her rune staff. The man fell to his knee, blinking through the haze of pain and surprise.

Fury filled Bingmei. *No. No!* She needed to be the one to defeat the man.

She rushed forward, slicing down two more enemies who stood in her way. Perhaps a hundred Qiangdao had attacked them. Bodies writhed in anguish on the sand. Bingmei saw at least thirty fallen. The rest were fleeing, running off toward the woods along the base of the rocky slope.

She saw Marenqo using hand and foot techniques, crippling a man's arm before chopping him in the throat. He'd always preferred hand-to-hand combat.

When she reached Kunmia and the crouching leader, she raised her sword to strike him down and exact her revenge.

Kunmia turned, her eyes fierce. She shifted the staff to defend the man against her. "Put it down. Now!"

Bingmei felt her heart explode with rage. It was as if she'd become the core of a raging fire. "He murdered my family," she said, so angry she choked on the words.

"Obey me, Bingmei," Kunmia said. "You promised. Put it down."

Muxidi tried to rise, but Kunmia whacked him on the back with the staff.

Never had Bingmei felt so tempted to defy Kunmia Suun. The man deserved death, not life. Some miracle had brought their paths together to give her a chance at vengeance. It took every ounce of will within Bingmei's mind and heart to lower her weapon. She felt her gaze might melt the man under its heat. Sadly, it did not. He reeked of that memory, the one that had tormented her for years.

Kunmia let out a breath of relief. Her knuckles were white against the rune staff.

Bingmei felt the magic slough off her, as if it had been a second skin. She shuddered, feeling her body as her own again. Her arms trembled. The sword felt suddenly heavy. The rest of the ensign gathered around them, except for Damanhur, who was tending to Rowen's injuries. Quion came to stand by Bingmei, giving her a worried look. His knuckles were bloodied.

She cast her eyes around the sandbar, then saw the fisherman, Keyi, straining to push the boat into the water.

"Kunmia!" she said, pointing.

Her master frowned. "Stop him, Bingmei. We'll go after those who fled later."

Bingmei nodded and quickly sheathed her blade. Invoking the cricket again, she sprang away from the ensign and bounded twice before springing again. Keyi had part of the boat in the water and was shoving it hard. If he got away, he'd strand them on the beach. Perhaps that had been his plan all along.

She landed hard on the sand, but she didn't allow herself time to recover. Keyi howled with fear when he saw her rushing up to him. The smell of his terror was overwhelming. He pushed harder, trying to flee, trying to escape.

"Stop it, Keyi!" she shouted.

The boat started to slide into the water. Keyi's boots tramped and splashed after it. There was a huge groove cut in the sand where he'd pushed it.

"There are too many! Too many! We have to flee!" he shouted at her, shoving harder.

Bingmei grabbed the edge of the boat to halt its slide. Keyi, with a frantic wail, tried to knock her back. She took a blow to the cheek, which startled her, and then kicked him on the edge of his knee. He landed with a splash in the icy water, and she continued to tug and pull at the boat, but its weight dragged her with it. She felt squishy sand sucking at her boots, but no matter how hard she pulled, she couldn't wrest the boat back from the water's embrace.

She heard the sound of running, and then Quion was kicking up a spray as he joined her. His bloodied hands gripped the edge of the boat, and he grunted as he pulled it with all his might. Together, they were able to drag it back to the sand. Bingmei sighed in relief. Keyi wept, sitting in the water, trembling and gnawing at his fingers in worry.

After they'd brought it far enough ashore, Quion secured it to a piece of driftwood with one of his locking knots.

The misery Keyi felt smelled like spoiled cabbage. He continued to weep, although not with the same intensity. He looked like a child at that moment, a confused and frightened child. She felt a little disgusted by him, but she understood why he'd done it. He was desperate to save his own skin at all costs. That was understandable. He'd never faced Qiangdao before. But everyone knew the stories of how they tortured and killed their captives for sport.

"Stand up, Keyi," Bingmei said.

He wiped his eyes, looking at her morosely, but he did as she asked and rose, his clothes dripping. Quion folded his arms, looking at the older fisherman with disgust.

"We're all going to die," Keyi moaned.

Bingmei felt a shudder of apprehension at his words.

杀雾

Muxidi's hands were tied behind his back, and he'd been forced to kneel in the sand. His fur jacket had been ripped open, and Bingmei saw the soiled tunic he wore beneath. It looked like her grandfather's jacket, though stained and blotted. Seeing it made fresh anger surge in her breast.

Although the man hung his head, he had a smirk on his mouth, a look of defiance in his eyes. He still smelled of rotting tubers. If anything, the stench had grown stronger.

As Bingmei and Quion approached with the trembling Keyi, the Qiangdao leader gave her no notice.

Marenqo's arms were furled over his chest. He raised an eyebrow at Kunmia.

"He said they were expecting us," Marenqo said.

Kunmia looked around the beach. Some of Damanhur's men were gathering the dead and laying them alongside one another.

"Bingmei," Kunmia said. "Come closer." When she did, Kunmia turned back to Marenqo. "Ask him again."

Marenqo nodded and repeated the question. The Qiangdao leader, Muxidi, lifted his head a little, casting a glance at Bingmei. His eyes showed no sign of recognition, but why would they? She was a woman grown, wearing a braided wig, and they were very far from the quonsuun where they'd first encountered each other.

Muxidi said some words in his guttural language. She recognized his voice. After all, he'd spent the winter pillaging her quonsuun, ruining all that her family had built. He'd eaten like a king those months. Her resentment burned in her nose since she'd been forced to conceal herself and scavenge for food when they weren't watchful.

Marenqo sighed. "He asked if I was deaf and didn't hear him the first time." Squatting, he gazed at the Qiangdao leader's face and said a few words in a low, menacing voice. Muxidi blanched. He answered curtly this time.

"What did you threaten him with?" Kunmia asked, giving him a little smile.

Marenqo shrugged. "Best not to say in the presence of ladies. He did answer. He said they were expecting people to come."

Kunmia turned to Bingmei. "Is he lying?"

The odors coming from Muxidi were still strong, but his smell hadn't changed. "No."

Kunmia faced Keyi, her expression giving nothing away. "Who else did you tell about this place?"

"N-no one!" Keyi stammered, his words tainted by the smell of his lie.

Bingmei shook her head. "He's not telling the truth."

Keyi looked at her angrily. "I am!" The smell got worse.

"Then why were you trying to flee?" Kunmia said.

"I thought you were all going to die," Keyi grumbled. "But I didn't know we would be ambushed. I swear it on the ghost of my grandfather!"

"That much is true," Bingmei said. "But you still told someone else about this place. That part was a lie."

Keyi began to tremble.

Damanhur sighed, hands on his hips. "Shall we beat it out of him? That would be faster."

Bingmei noticed that Rowen was standing. He had a scrape and some blood on the side of his temple. He smelled of suffering and antipathy against the fisherman.

"Keyi," Kunmia said patiently. "Bingmei knows when someone is honest. She has an instinct for it. If you do not tell me the truth, we will leave *you* behind on the island and return to King Budai. We can come back next spring and try this again. If you want our protection, you must be honest with us. Who did you tell?"

Keyi looked from face to face, his cheeks turning red. "I . . . I . . ."

Kunmia waited, watching him intently.

"I may have shown the pieces to someone *before* coming to Bao Damanhur. There's a little fishing village called Somset." His cheeks continued to flame. Bingmei felt his self-loathing and shame.

"You lied to Budai, then," Kunmia said. "And you're afraid you won't be paid the wealth he promised you."

The fisherman nodded miserably.

Kunmia then walked over to the Qiangdao leader. "What is his name?"

Marenqo asked the question.

The man, whom Bingmei knew to be Muxidi, lifted his head slightly. "Echion."

Another shudder of dread went down Bingmei's spine. He'd lied, but what a strange lie to tell. Kunmia's eyes wrinkled in concern. "That's the name the other Qiangdao leader gave."

The man muttered more words.

Marenqo listened and then said, "He's not afraid to die. If you kill him, he will be reborn. And he will avenge his death in his true form. A dragon."

"The last one said the same thing," Kunmia said warily. "Yet he did not come back as a dragon. Why are these Qiangdao leaders calling themselves the same name? Are they banding together?"

Rowen frowned at that, and Bingmei caught his eye for a moment. He knew something he wasn't saying. It didn't come as a smell, just as a wave of intuition. The reek of the Qiangdao leader overpowered everything around him.

The Qiangdao leader spoke again. Marenqo listened and translated. "He said there's an ice cave here. His palace is buried beneath it. His empire is about to be reborn. We can see it for ourselves."

Everything about Muxidi was insincere. It was impossible to divine whether anything he said was true, although she sensed it wasn't a bald-faced lie.

But she did know one thing for sure. He had killed her family. She still wanted her revenge.

Kunmia pivoted again, gripping her staff, and faced Bingmei. Her expression was full of concern, but there were other emotions playing out inside her. Confusion and even a little distrust. "How do you know this man is the one who murdered your family?"

"I know it, Kunmia," Bingmei said. "And he understands every word we're saying."

"How did you know it was him? I see by his clothes that he stole from your grandfather's quonsuun. But you can't possibly have recognized him. He was wearing a bearskin hood when they attacked. You told me that yourself."

All of their eyes were looking at her, and she felt part of herself shrivel inside.

In order to convince them, she'd have to reveal herself in front of everyone, something she could not do.

CHAPTER SEVENTEEN

Ice Caves

"I can sense people," Bingmei answered softly, hoping a partial truth would be enough. "I recognized him as soon as he emerged." She wanted him dead. The temptation to draw the Phoenix Blade made her fingers itch. Her arms.

"I will not allow you to kill him yet," Kunmia said. "He may be of some use to us. I forbid you to harm him."

The restriction made Bingmei's heart surge with resentment, but she wrestled it down. Kunmia was a good leader, just. She would not forsake her. "As you say, Master. And as I said, he speaks our language," Bingmei declared, eyeing the Qiangdao leader with contempt. "He's only pretending not to understand."

Kunmia turned to face the man, her eyebrow lifting.

Muxidi's shoulders sagged a bit, but a malicious smile twisted the corner of his mouth. "I remember you now," he said in their language, his voice deep and rough, his eyes meeting hers. "You're the ghost. The little girl with the winter sickness."

Kunmia rapped him on the side of the head with her staff, a quick blow. "Now you're speaking to us, villain?"

"We cannot trust *anything* that comes out of his mouth," Damanhur said. "Why not just kill him now?"

"We cannot trust his words," Kunmia said. "But we can trust Bingmei's senses."

"Ice rose?" the Qiangdao leader muttered, still wincing from the blow. "I should have crushed your flower when I had the chance."

His vile smell was overpowered by the protective smells coming from the others. The ensign were her friends, and she could inhale their support, their anger on her behalf. She glared at the murderer in defiance. He was only one man. He would bleed like one. Die like one.

"How many robbers do you lead? How many are here?" Kunmia asked.

"Too many for you, I think," he said with a smirk. "We saw you coming up the fjord. What you faced here on the beach was just a taste. The others are coming. If you kill me, every one of you will be slain. After they've tortured you."

Keyi started to whimper with fear again.

"How many?" Kunmia pressed.

"Do you even know what's hidden here, beneath the ice, or did you just come to pilfer the ruins of another palace? We are at the threshold of the Summer Palace! Fusang!"

"You are educated for a bandit," Kunmia said. "I see you weren't raised in the wilderness. You were trained at a quonsuun, were you not?"

Muxidi snorted. "I was"—he shot a look at Bingmei—"but I razed it to the ground. This is my quonsuun now. My fortress. My treasure. It all belongs to me. I am the Dragon of Night."

"You're an imposter," Kunmia said. "You're not the only one claiming that title. So you've found the lost city. It is no more yours than anyone else's. You may have frightened your followers into believing such lies, but you do not fool us. Where is this ice cave you mentioned? How far is it?"

"We have to hike up to the edge of the glacier," he answered. "It's a steep hike, but not too difficult."

"Why do you camp by the waterfall?"

He sneered at her. "Because it is warmer down here, why else? Everything is ice up there." He wrenched against his bonds, but they didn't yield. He sagged again.

"Bao Damanhur," Kunmia said. "Consult with me."

The two wandered a short distance away and spoke in low voices. The noise of the falls drowned out their words. Marenqo had a sour expression on his face as he glanced at the Qiangdao leader, and Quion openly scowled at him. Rowen approached Bingmei.

"How did you know who he was?" he asked softly, his back to their enemy.

She was not about to tell him. "I just knew," she said.

Now that her blood no longer boiled with the thrill of battle, and the Qiangdao leader sat kneeling in the sand, wrists bound behind his back, the thought of executing him made her queasy. She knew he had trained under her grandfather. He'd come seeking revenge himself, just like the young man in Kunmia's story, the one who'd wished to marry her.

In her youth, the devastation of losing her grandfather and parents had blinded her to everything else. What had driven this man to join the Qiangdao? Enmity. He, too, had wanted to appease his thirst for vengeance. With the blood of her family. The cycle of revenge never ended. She knew if she killed him, there might be someone else who would come after her in retaliation. A brother perhaps? Maybe he had sired children? There was no way to know. And yet she still wanted him dead. Anger and hatred bristled inside her.

"There's more to it . . . but you won't say," Rowen offered with a sigh. It wasn't a question. He walked away from her, heading toward Damanhur and Kunmia.

Because I don't trust you, she thought in return, staring at his back.

She saw Rowen speak to Kunmia, who shook her head no. The prince gestured angrily in response, speaking in low but furious tones. He did not agree with the decision that had been made.

Damanhur shook his head and then put his hand on Rowen's shoulder. "We cannot risk your life," he said, his voice audible. "You'll get your chance to see the ruins. Let the others go in first."

"But I know more than the rest of you," Rowen said. "I've studied with Jidi Majia . . ."

"Not yet. Besides, we promised to obey Kunmia's orders."

Rowen glowered, and Bingmei smelled his discontent. There was something she didn't understand, something that had made him angry.

Damanhur turned to Kunmia and nodded. "We are agreed. Let's tell the others."

Kunmia gripped her rune staff and tilted her head as she turned to face the group. "The only way out of this fjord is by boat. We cannot trust any other source of escape. Which means we cannot possibly trust Keyi with the boat. Quion—I do trust you. I want you to take the boat into the middle of the fjord. Catch some fish for us to eat tonight. Enough to feed many people, including our prisoners. Damanhur's ensign will remain at the beach to keep watch on the prisoners. The rest of us will go to the ice cave." Bingmei saw Rowen scowl at this, but he remained silent. "We'll return before nightfall and decide where to camp. If this is Fusang, the sooner we know it, the better."

"Dividing up your warriors is a good strategy," the Qiangdao leader said mockingly. "At least some of them will survive. But I will take you to the lost city. It's nothing like you are thinking."

Kunmia would not be provoked. "Lead the way, thief."

杀雾

The hike up to the side of the glacier was more difficult than Bingmei had expected. The glacier had crushed the surrounding rock into small fragments, which made the path treacherous, both slippery and jagged. The trail to the ice cave had been trampled, however, so it was not difficult finding the way. They had to cross icy streams to get there, and she was thankful for the hide boots that protected her from the frigid water. When they reached the crest of the first part of the trail, she looked back and saw the fishing boat in the middle of the water. Even from that distance, she could spy Quion with the nets. The dark shapes of Damanhur's ensign could be seen roaming along the beach. They had the few captured foes working on digging graves for the dead.

After they crossed the first peak, the area opened up with thick vegetation, which would make it ideal for an ambush. Kunmia frowned.

"Through the gorse," Muxidi said.

A path of trampled gorse led the way. But people could easily hide along the way if they crouched. Large boulders also provided places of concealment. It amazed Bingmei to see the evidence of the ice's power over the land. The glacier had shattered a mountain, leaving debris in its wake. But it was clear that the glacier was indeed receding. The detritus it had left on the edges was ample evidence.

"And right into where your bandits are waiting for us?" Kunmia said.

"Death is coming to you either way," Muxidi said with a sneer. "You don't know the ways of the Qiangdao."

"And you've forgotten the ways of the quonsuun," Kunmia countered. She turned. "Bingmei. Get up on those boulders, the highest ones. That will give you a vantage point to direct us."

She nodded and was about to proceed, but Mieshi interrupted. "I should go with her. You asked *me* to lead the scouting."

What was that smell? Jealousy? It wasn't the same as protectiveness.

"Stay with us," Kunmia said. "Her skills are better suited for this situation."

Mieshi conceded, but she flashed Bingmei a look of displeasure that came with the sour smell of spoiled onion.

"You'll want to stay near me," said the Qiangdao leader to Mieshi. "You're a pretty one. I'll protect you when my followers come." He chuckled darkly.

"Go," Kunmia said to Bingmei.

She began to creep through the gorse, keeping her staff gripped in her hand. Kunmia had warned her not to draw the sword again for fear it would overwhelm her. But holding a staff didn't give her the same feeling of protection the blade did. It struck her that she could *feel* the blade on her back. A sense of calm emanated from it, as if it were not worried in the slightest about the dangers that lay ahead. Strange that a sword should make her feel emotions.

Bingmei quickly wove through the brush, using her nose to smell for the presence of intruders. There were none. When she reached the bottom of the massive boulder that Kunmia had directed her to, she reached in her pocket and rubbed the cricket. The magic flung her to the top of the jagged stone.

There was already a Qiangdao lying atop it.

He scrambled to his feet, stunned by her sudden appearance, and she butted him hard with the end of her staff. He flailed backward, falling off the edge of the rock down into the gorse with a loud crackling sound of snapping and breaking branches. He groaned in pain down below. Shouts sounded, and she saw men fleeing through the gorse. She counted maybe a dozen in all.

Bingmei whistled and pointed in the direction they were fleeing. They scattered like bugs beneath an overturned stone. Some still crouched in the gorse, but they looked to be hiding to protect themselves rather than lying in wait to attack. The ambush had failed. From her vantage point on the rock, she motioned for Kunmia to come closer. When her ensign reached the boulder, Bingmei jumped down, earning a glare of hatred from her enemy.

"I remember that you could jump," he said in a low, angry voice. "You had his cricket."

She gave him a smug smile, and they continued along the trail.

It took about an hour for them to reach the edge of the glacier. The packed snow and ice had built up in layers over the centuries, or longer, creating a massive ceiling of rippling ice. The edges of it were pressed on crumbled stone, which had been pulverized by the glacier's weight and movement. The great hunk of ice crawled like a beast—a very slow beast—and destroyed everything in its path. The upper layers were crystalline and white, while the lower reaches were mingled with stone and sludge. Part of it was brown, as if it were made out of sand.

The sound of running water came from all around. The melting ice fed streams that both trickled and raged. With every step, the air got colder. It was a hauntingly beautiful sight, but Bingmei's senses were sharp for danger.

"Do you see the opening?" the Qiangdao leader said.

Yes, there it was. Murky shadows gathered beneath a low shelf of ice directly ahead of them. The rocks were all jumbled together, making the footing unstable. It would be difficult going down the slope without falling, but they started, one by one, Mieshi and Bingmei leading the way.

When they were halfway down, a man emerged from the cave. Bingmei recognized him as the man whose slinger she'd sliced, but he held a new one in his hand. He stooped by the edge of the cave, grabbing a stone, and twirled it overhead.

"Watch out!" Mieshi called.

The two of them separated as the first stone whooshed by, missing Mieshi. They scrambled down the slope while he brought out another stone and began twirling it. The rock came straight at Mieshi again, and she leaned sideways so it raced by her face. If it had struck, it would have killed her.

Bingmei felt the ground giving way as she hurried down the slope to the edge of the ice. The slinger scowled at having missed and loaded a third stone. He spun again and loosed it. Mieshi twisted and let out a gasp as the stone struck her arm.

Three of the stones had gone to one person. Bingmei reached the bottom and started to rush forward. The others had started to descend the slope. The slinger was hurrying, his face betraying his worry as he loaded another stone. He sent this one right at Bingmei, who jumped forward in a roll as soon as the missile left its sling. Coming up, Bingmei charged him, but he fled back into the cave before she reached him. Mieshi joined her a moment later, rubbing her arm and grimacing in pain.

"How bad is it?" Bingmei asked.

"I'll be fine," she answered curtly.

They could hear the sound of the man running away. A small rivulet ran out of the mouth of the cave, revealing that the doorway had been carved by moving water. The interior of the cave was rounded and smooth with ice. Muddy puddles around the entrance revealed multiple boot prints. The gap in the ice leading in was taller than a person and as wide as three.

"Do we wait for the others?" Bingmei asked.

Mieshi turned to look back, watching the rest scrabble down the hillside. Muxidi was still tied up and came down slowly. Kunmia guarded him personally. "We wait," she answered.

The frost was already making Bingmei shiver. She pulled on her leather and fur hat to keep her head warm and unslung her pack to get her gloves. Soon she and Mieshi were both garbed for the cold of the cave. They waited at the entrance, and although Bingmei tried to determine what lay ahead, she could only smell the ice and the discomfort coming from Mieshi.

The crunch of gravel and rocks announced the arrival of the others.

"It's *cold*," Marenqo said, chafing his hands.

Their breaths came out in puffs of white mist. Zhuyi pulled off her pack and began adding layers for warmth. Marenqo quickly followed suit. They then watched the prisoner while Kunmia dressed. When she finished, she took hold of Muxidi's arm. "How many caves are here?" she asked. "Is this the only one?"

"One way in. One way out," he said, and his lie made Bingmei's eyes water.

She shook her head no.

Kunmia smiled in appreciation. "How much of Fusang is still intact?" she asked. "Judging by the amount of debris, it too must have been shattered by the glacier."

Muxidi turned and looked at her. "All of it."

"It's all broken?" Marenqo asked dejectedly.

"No." The Qiangdao leader grinned a savage smile. "It's all intact. A city beneath the ice. Waiting to be found again." Then he looked directly at Bingmei. "Welcome home."

CHAPTER EIGHTEEN

Realm of Fusang

His words should have frightened her, but they didn't. It surprised Bingmei that instead of feeling trepidation and fear about coming to this place, she felt instead a vague sense of familiarity. She'd never been to this place before, but it *felt* as if she had. Perhaps each person did live multiple lives, as the stories said, and she was experiencing the echoes of a previous existence. The entrance to the ice cave drew her in, making her long to enter it.

"This is no home," Kunmia said. "Nothing can survive in there for long."

Muxidi smirked. "And what do you know of survival? You hide within your warm buildings, bundled in furs. The Qiangdao follow the laws of the pack, not of men. Even an ice cave can be warm."

"Master," Marenqo said in a warning tone, "should we really bring him in there with us? He is too devious."

"We cannot leave him outside either," Kunmia replied.

Muxidi's nostrils flared. "I know the path inside. You could wander in there for days. The melting ice has carved many tunnels."

"But you are an untrustworthy guide," Kunmia said. "Bingmei—if he attempts to flee or they try to rescue him, you have my permission to exact revenge." She gave Muxidi a stern look. "Your life is in your hands."

"I'm very afraid of the little rose," he said, giving Bingmei a wicked smile.

Bingmei felt her hatred of the man pulsing in her chest. He was the kind of man who could smother a child and feel no remorse. The reek of his presence had not abated.

"Mieshi, Bingmei," Kunmia said, nodding for them to enter first. They gripped their staves and stepped into the small stream of icy water coming from the cave floor.

They entered a new world.

Light from the sun outside made the translucent ice glow a thousand stunning shades of blue and gray. The ice's rippling layers were slick and wet. All around, the sounds of water plopping into the stream echoed through the space. The ground was made of broken rock fragments and rivulets of water. It was cold, but the Qiangdao leader was right. It was warmer inside the cave than out.

The scene was enchanting in its beauty and wonder. It was like a river had frozen solid, trapping the little eddies and current. Bingmei ran her fingers on the ceiling, watching her gloves moisten with the damp. The power of the glacier was beyond her imagination. How thick was the ice overhead? It would take months to chip through it. Yet the melting point had been reached, and the stream was carving paths from beneath. She and Mieshi walked on the dryer portions of the path of broken rocks, frigid air following them like their shadows.

"Which way?" Bingmei asked Mieshi. To go downhill, they would have to start crouching, as the ceiling of ice dropped lower that way. Higher up, it seemed to open into a broader cavern.

"That way," Mieshi said, pointing her staff upstream.

They hiked carefully, choosing their footing and listening for sounds beyond the rush of the water and the constant dripping noises.

Bingmei smelled a man ahead, hiding behind a pillar of ice. She touched Mieshi's sleeve and nodded toward it. Mieshi nodded in return and gestured for Bingmei to go to the right while she went to the left.

Bingmei recognized the smell as the slinger. She slowed her approach, trying to disguise the noise of her steps, but the rocks kept shifting beneath her feet, scraping against each other. Seeing no way to avoid it, she kept advancing. She saw a pale shadow against the ice. Mieshi crept soundlessly toward it.

Bingmei reached the edge of the pillar, keeping wide of it, and suddenly the slinger jumped out, whipping his sling around. A stone whistled past Bingmei's ear as she lunged away. She spun her staff in broad sweeps in front of her, hoping to confuse him as he prepared another stone. He'd just raised the sling, ready to send another missile at her, when Mieshi struck him from behind. He grimaced in pain as her staff impacted against his back. When he dropped the sling, turning toward Mieshi, she hit him in the face. He crumpled to the rocks, unconscious.

Bingmei set her staff down. They both investigated the body and took away the man's weapon and his bag of rounded stones. Mieshi turned him over, and Bingmei produced some leather straps and bound his wrists behind him. They left him on the broken rocks by the ice column, so he'd be easily spotted by the others.

"Let's go farther," Mieshi suggested. Eager to continue exploring, Bingmei did not object.

The farther they went, the higher the ceiling rose above them. The veins in the walls looked almost like tapestries made by nature, and Bingmei continued to be impressed by the beauty of the place. A rock tumbled from one of the massive piles, making them both raise their staves and turn at the same time, expecting another attack. But nothing happened.

A strange sensation rippled down Bingmei's back. She turned again, feeling as if someone were sneaking up behind her. There was no one there.

"What's wrong?" Mieshi asked.

Bingmei squinted, trying to see. She couldn't smell anything, but her whole body felt odd, and she started to tremble. "We're not alone."

Mieshi turned around as well, looking back the way they'd come. "I don't hear anything. Or see anything."

"Neither do I. But something is near—I *feel* it."

Anticipation mingled with fear, and she felt her breath quickening. Danger was coming. Something they couldn't see was hunting them.

"What is it?" Mieshi demanded, turning around again, holding her staff defensively.

It reminded Bingmei of the feelings she'd experienced when she'd retrieved the Phoenix Blade from amidst the bodies left by the killing fog. The sensation of being watched, of knowing something was coming for her.

Bingmei set down her staff and drew the blade from its scabbard.

Mieshi gazed at it in worry and awe. The blade shimmered with greenish light, reflecting off the blue walls of ice. It had, once again, invoked its own magic.

"What are you doing?" Mieshi demanded worriedly. "What if it summons the killing fog in here? We'll all die!"

"I think it's trying to protect us," Bingmei said. She looked around for any traces of the fog.

The sense of danger receded. Bingmei started to feel more at ease. She saw no evidence of the killing fog, not even a creeping mist. Whatever had frightened her, it had withdrawn from the sword. The noise of sliding rocks revealed that Kunmia and the others were approaching. The Qiangdao leader's eyes glowed with lust as he beheld the blade. His awful stench reflected his desire to wrench the weapon from her hand and take it for himself.

Kunmia approached them with a stern look. "Why did you draw the blade?"

Mieshi spoke up first. "She sensed something dangerous."

"The guardian," said the Qiangdao leader.

They all turned to him.

He chuckled. "You thought this place would be left unprotected? Magic keeps those who would intrude here at bay."

"What is it?" Kunmia asked.

Muxidi shrugged. "No one has seen it. It afflicts the mind. It can drive someone mad."

"Does it kill?"

The man chuffed. "Not with claws. It drives people to kill themselves. No one wanders in these caves all alone."

Bingmei smelled the truth in his words.

"We're almost there. Keep going," he said.

The presence Bingmei had felt was gone, so she sheathed the sword again. A look of disappointment crossed the Qiangdao's face. He noticed her looking at him and glared. The smell of banked violence made her walk away. She couldn't bear it.

杀雾

As they walked, it felt as if it was getting warmer and warmer. Before long, Bingmei's fur jacket became unbearable. The rocks at their feet were smoother, less jagged. And then, to Bingmei's surprise, she saw tufts of plants growing out of the gravel. A little farther, flowers dotted the ground. Where the sun could not reach them? It made no sense.

Except she could not deny the light had also grown brighter. Was there perhaps a hole in the ice? She knew from caves she'd visited before that plants did not grow inside mountains. Well, only the strangest of plants did, the lichens that speckled the walls and could trap light from a torch for a little while. But this was entirely different. Farther still, she saw little trees sprouting.

The rocks gave way to dirt and turf and then, impossibly, a street made of carved marble. Overhead, the rippling ice looked like the underside of clouds. There was no hole in the ice. The light was coming from ahead, not above. Bingmei and Mieshi exchanged baffled looks. They were entering an enormous cavern where the walls were made of rock, which soared up to touch the ice overhead. Waterfalls gushed from where the rock met the ice and formed two rivers, one on each side of the clearing. Boulders sat haphazardly around the valley, pocked with larges holes where the water had carved through them.

A little farther along, they reached a wall made of painted meiwood pillars with sloping rooftops, painted a thousand dazzling colors. The shingles on the roof looked to be made out of solid gold. Before the gate embedded in the wall stood two enormous bronze lions, carved in perfect symmetry with each other. Each one was taller than three men standing atop one another. The lions were each perched on a square pedestal intricately carved with designs. Their heads were slightly turned in, opposite each other, as if they were standing guard.

The vibrant reds and blues and greens painted on the wooden wall reminded her of an arrangement of flowers. What kind of craftsman had done such work? The paint on the walls of Wangfujing was all peeled and faded, with hardly anything left. This was fresh and lovely. No Qiangdao could or would have done it.

"Now you see?" said Muxidi. "The wealth of Fusang. It belongs to us."

This was beyond anything they'd imagined.

The light she'd noticed came from behind the decorative wall.

"The gate is open," urged Muxidi. "Go on."

The wall was taller even than the lions, so they couldn't see over it. As they came nearer, the design work became more apparent. How many painters had been required to embellish such an elaborate scene? How long had a craftsman spent fashioning the lions to make them so smooth, so muscular, so lifelike? As Bingmei approached, she saw that each lion had a paw raised. On one of them, the paw rested atop a carved orb.

As they drew nearer to the gate and the carvings, Bingmei felt that strange pressure in her head again, the worry that had risen before.

"Wait," she said, stopping.

Everyone froze. They looked around, trying to determine the danger.

"Go on. Are you afraid?" asked Muxidi.

He smelled rank, but it had a new foul flavor to it. Deception. He wanted them to go forward.

"What will happen if we pass the lions?" Bingmei asked him.

"They're made of bronze. Decorations."

His lie stung her nose. He knew something he wasn't saying.

"You're lying," she said.

"You little . . ."

Kunmia struck him behind his knee with her staff, making him grunt in pain as he fell to his knees.

"You brought us this far only to trick us?" Kunmia said.

"No!" Muxidi fumed. "Just walk in!"

Bingmei shook her head no.

"Maybe we could go around the lions and climb the wall?" Marenqo suggested.

The meiwood posts glistened red with lacquer and looked very slippery. There were no handholds.

"I could jump up there," Bingmei said.

Kunmia frowned. Then she nodded, giving Bingmei permission to try.

Bingmei licked her lips, which were very dry, and walked around the base of the lion on the right. Upon closer examination, the orb on which its paw rested seemed to be shaped like flower petals. The other lion rested a paw on something different, which she couldn't make out from a distance. She feared what lay beyond that wall, but it would be better to see what was beyond the barrier than to rush in blind. She reached in her pocket and stroked the cricket.

To her amazement, nothing happened.

Never had the charm she'd gotten from her grandfather ceased to work.

The Qiangdao leader started to laugh. "What? You're surprised? Your grandfather's toy won't work. This place has magic beyond anything you've seen. Those posts are *made* out of meiwood. Think of it! And the stumps are used to hold up the roofs. I will show you. There is nothing to fear. I will go first." He slowly rose to his feet again, although his legs trembled.

"I don't trust him," Mieshi said with a scowl.

"None of us do," Zhuyi agreed. "Master . . . maybe we should leave this place."

The thought of leaving sent a spasm through Bingmei's heart. *No!*

"Just follow me," the Qiangdao pleaded.

Kunmia's look was intense. She gazed up at the wall. There was a doorway beneath the overhang, but it was dark, lost in shadow. Bingmei could smell her confusion, her unease and ignorance. She wasn't ready to decide yet.

The Qiangdao leader lunged forward and raced between the lions, surprising everyone with his sudden escape.

Zhuyi, the fleetest and quickest to respond, rushed after him. One of the lions suddenly leaped off the pedestal, landing in front of her with an impact that sent tremors through the ground. The Qiangdao man was already past it and sprinting toward the doorway. Zhuyi tried to duck and escape, but one massive paw from the bronze lion struck her, and she collapsed. A low bell-like growl came from the beast.

Everyone else backed away from it, weapons raised.

The lion climbed back on the plinth and resumed its position, resting a large paw atop something that had remained behind. It was a statue once more.

Zhuyi lay still, sprawled on the stone.

Dead.

And the Qiangdao leader was gone.

CHAPTER NINETEEN

Ancient City

The shock Bingmei felt at seeing Zhuyi's crumpled body left her frozen with dread. Again the fragility of life gave her a helpless feeling, made keener by the dread that she would someday meet the same fate. The other members of the ensign stood hushed at the entrance. Mieshi stifled a sob, the smell of her aching grief nearly overwhelming Bingmei's senses.

Kunmia stood transfixed, a look of mourning on her normally calm face. Each member of the ensign was important to her. She gazed up at the massive statues, cold and lifeless once again. Whatever magic had given them power had become dormant.

Marenqo broke the silence. "We do not understand the rules of this place," he said with a worried tone.

"Do we go back?" Mieshi asked, tears strangling her voice.

"We cannot go back," Kunmia said. "We have a duty to fulfill."

"That Qiangdao scum made it past," Marenqo said. "Why didn't the lions crush him?"

"Because he did something to prevent it," Kunmia said. She turned and faced her companions. "He was bobbing his head as he passed."

Bingmei had seen it too, but the shock of Zhuyi's fate had made her forget. "Yes. I saw that too."

"But how do we know for certain?" Marenqo challenged. "Maybe there were also words he muttered that we couldn't hear!"

"We can't know for certain," Kunmia said. "But we must try. That man must be held accountable for the ruin he's wrought." Her brow furrowed. Bingmei had rarely seen her master express so much anger. "He tricked us into bringing him this far. We must proceed with the utmost caution and care. If you sense anything out of order, you must speak immediately. Our lives are at stake. Passing these guardians is only the first task. But we must succeed."

Her speech roused the group's courage. Bingmei struggled to subdue her own emotions, but she did. She clenched her fists and nodded in agreement.

"How will we get past the guardians?" Marenqo said. "I'm not questioning you, Master. I'm afraid. This place is beyond anything I've ever seen."

"Uncertainty always causes fear," Kunmia said. "I will go through the lions myself."

Their master would never ask someone to do something that she herself wouldn't do. It was why they all respected her so much.

"Be careful," Mieshi said.

Kunmia bowed her head and began to meditate. They all emulated her example, trying to find a place of peace within them despite the danger of their situation and their grief at losing a friend. The only sounds in the quiet were the chatter of streams and the creaks and groans of the ice. No other animals lived down there. No birds. No insects. Nothing but them and their enemies.

Kunmia raised her head, her eyes burning with purpose. She gripped her rune staff and invoked its magic. Blue light rippled down it, the sigils sparking to life. She took a step forward and then another. As she walked, she bowed her head to each of the lions. Bingmei held her breath, trying to quell her worry. The others looked on in fascination and hope.

The lions remained still.

When their master reached the crumpled body of Zhuyi, she paused. Neither of the lions had moved. Kunmia stood there for a moment, gripping her staff. Then she stepped beyond the body, farther than Zhuyi had made it.

Nothing happened. The lions remained statues.

"Come," she beckoned to them. "Bow in obeisance as you do." She would wait in the middle to see that the others made it across safely.

Mieshi obeyed first. Her meditation had calmed her agitation, but the closer she walked to her dead friend, the more Bingmei smelled her grief thicken. The stew of emotion worried Bingmei. Would the lions sense it and attack? Mieshi continued forward, walking confidently. She nodded her head to each lion, paying her respects. Neither statue budged. She reached Kunmia, who motioned for her to pass.

"Marenqo," Kunmia called.

His courage was faltering, but he stiffened his resolve. Blinking quickly to calm himself, he strode forward next, bowing to each lion in a more pronounced manner than the others had. He adopted a groveling demeanor, keeping his head low and his eyes on their powerful paws. He wiped the sweat from his brow when he reached the safety of the other side.

That left Bingmei alone.

Kunmia met her gaze and nodded for her to come. Holding herself proudly, she began to walk toward the lions, bowing her head as she approached. Now that she was closer, she saw that the lion on the left had its paw resting on what appeared to be a lion cub, turned upside down on its back. That was the only difference between the two lions. One rested a paw on an orb, the other on a cub.

Both of the lion heads turned suddenly, their snouts facing her. Bingmei's heart quivered in her chest like a wild bird trying to escape a cage. Would they attack? But the statues did not attempt to leave their perches. Rather, both of them bowed their heads to *her*.

She stared at them in awe and wonderment. Why had they done this for her and not the others? Again she experienced the strange notion that this place was familiar. She regretted that she hadn't darted after the Qiangdao leader before Zhuyi could.

A sense of peace and wellness suffused Bingmei's heart. She believed the lions posed her no threat at all. She continued walking and passed them. After she had, their heads swiveled back to their previous pose, and they remained still.

"What did *that* mean?" Marenqo asked in confusion, staring at Bingmei.

"Perhaps it's the sword," Kunmia said. "The phoenix is the king of all birds."

Perhaps that was true. But there was a part of Bingmei that didn't believe it. The sword had not given her any special feeling at that moment. It struck her that the sword seemed to respond to her differently as well. Kunmia had felt compelled to give it to her. Why? She had no firm idea, but the Qiangdao leader who'd attacked Wangfujing had said the phoenix had *chosen* a servant. Did that have something to do with her? She didn't know, but she hoped the answer lay beyond the colorful door directly before them.

Kunmia's eyes were thoughtful. "Bingmei. Lead the way. You may be the only way we can all get in safely."

杀雾

The doorway was perched on a high ledge separating the threshold from the interior, very similar to the ones at the quonsuun. But after passing through the partially open doors, Bingmei saw that what lay beyond was much more vast. It opened to an empty courtyard that had built-in waterways to channel the half-frozen water through it. Stone railings lined the waterways on both sides, and ramps and staircases led up to an enormous manor, at least six times the size of King Budai's palace. With sloping rooftops at multiple levels, the building was as colorfully decorated as the outer wall.

Marenqo breathed out a sigh of wonder as he stepped over the threshold next. Lower buildings, similar in fashion to the palace, surrounded the courtyard on all sides, like walls. Giant meiwood trunks held up the edges of the roofs, each bedecked with decorative illustrations with an assortment of color.

There were so many buildings. Would Muxidi have fled to the central one, the palace-like structure straight ahead? Or one of the many other buildings forming the walls of the courtyard?

Her instincts told her to go to the palace. She led the way, walking across the courtyard, wondering at the labor required to erect such a substantial building. The blue-gray ice overhead felt like the sky, and it glowed with ambient light. There was no evidence of the sun, no shadows cast on the ground as they walked. The strange cold light suffused into them.

As they approached the huge staircase leading up to the giant palace, they saw large urns stationed at the tops of the steps. Bingmei turned around as she walked, looking back at the tall wall they had just passed.

As she turned back to the palace, she caught a faint odorous scent in the air. She wrinkled her nose and readied her sword. From her vantage point in the courtyard, she couldn't see ahead, but she imagined their enemies could see them.

"Be ready," Bingmei said, warning the others.

She started up the steps. The handrail was intricately carved into animal shapes, but the carvings were old and worn and faded by the passing of time. The grandeur of the place filled her with a sense of awe. King Budai would not believe it when they told him. This place had been immaculately preserved under the ice for centuries. Had the glacier not melted, it would have remained hidden for ages to come.

Upon reaching the top of the steps, she searched for signs of their quarry, reassured by the sound of the others climbing up behind her. Two enormous doors lay ahead, each decorated with nine rows of nine golden knobs the size of pomegranates. The plating at the base and top of the doors was solid gold. Huge golden door handles were fixed to the painted doors, each carved into a lion's head.

Kunmia and the others joined her at the top of the steps and gazed up at the huge doors. Was the palace built for a giant?

"I've never seen such wealth," Kunmia said. "Not in all of my travels. This is more grand than the court at Sajinau. Even grander than Tuqiao."

"How did they build this?" Marenqo said. "These stones must be impossibly heavy. How were they moved?"

"I don't know," Kunmia answered. "Why hasn't it been found before? How could this place have remained hidden for so long?"

Mieshi's grief was still roiling inside her. She didn't look impressed. She smelled of disdain as she beheld the opulence of the palace. "Whoever built it abandoned it," she said curtly. "What good did it do them to create this place? It was folly."

"But think of how many lived here," Kunmia said. "We can't comprehend it. Yet it is still preserved. By magic."

Moving ahead, Bingmei approached the doors studded with knobs. The handles were too high to reach, but as she approached, the doors swung open of their own accord, pushing inward, revealing another huge courtyard followed by another palace, even larger. What they had seen wasn't a palace at all, but an elaborate gate leading *to* another palace.

Marenqo exclaimed in amazement as they stepped over the golden threshold and viewed the immense scene that lay beyond. There could be thousands of Qiangdao hiding there, but there was no evidence of smoke or noise. No evidence that anyone else was there at all.

Bridges led across a waterway dotted with chunks of floating ice. They walked to one of the bridges and crossed it, but as they approached the huge palace ahead, Bingmei felt a strong sense of uneasiness creep over her.

Dividing the two sets of stairs leading up to the palace was a marble slab with something engraved on it. As they drew near, she saw it bore a continuous design that stretched all the way up the ramp. The size and weight of the marble was staggering to the imagination, yet it had been held in place by some inhuman force. She had never seen anything like it before.

Her ill feeling grew stronger as they neared the base of the stairs. The cold stone was carved into an elaborate scene of mountains with jagged peaks and a depiction of the Death Wall on its crown. Clouds graced the sky, or perhaps the elegant lines engraved in the stone were meant to mimic the ceiling of ice that towered above them at that moment. Either way, she saw two distinct carvings within those lines—dragons, facing each other, one looming from above and the other crouching and looking up at the other dragon from below. An orb was nestled between their two heads. None of it made sense to her, but the beauty of the sculpture was breathtaking, as if it had been carved by the hand of some immortal.

"We are not bringing that slab back to Wangfujing," Marenqo said with a grin as he folded his arms and shook his head.

"I don't think anything human could lift it," Kunmia said in awe. The image of the two entwining dragons was clearly the focus of the work. A shudder went down Bingmei's back. She looked up and gazed around.

"I don't think we should go up there," she said.

Kunmia looked at her and then nodded. "I have a heavy, brooding feeling. Maybe we can go around the palace?" It was built on tall blocks of stone, making it higher than the gate they had just passed through, but the depth of the courtyard disguised its height.

Stone gargoyles sat along the rooftops to drain water away, but it was difficult to imagine the place being exposed to the real sky. The marbled surface of ice overhead felt surreal.

After rounding the corner, they saw yet another courtyard and another palace beyond, although the next one was set lower. The one they stood beneath seemed to be the apex.

The sword on Bingmei's back began to vibrate. She felt the blade pushing her toward the next palace, as if it were trying to guide her.

"This way," Bingmei said. As she walked, she felt the pressure against her back decrease. Why was the blade bringing them there? She couldn't understand it, but she felt the beckoning sensation. More buildings lined each wall of the courtyard. It could take weeks to explore the entire grounds. Yet the whole place felt shockingly empty, void of life, void of any smells but their own. Still, she knew the Qiangdao leader was hidden somewhere within the enormous compound. She kept turning around, expecting to find him and some of his warriors trailing them. But each time she turned, there was only the vast empty space behind them.

The palaces all shared the same basic structure, the meiwood poles supporting the massive sloped roofs. The shingles of the roofs were all overlaid with metal and seemed to reflect the color of the icy sky. She realized with a start that she was no longer cold. The air felt comfortable and pleasant.

The next palace they approached did not give off a foreboding. Bingmei led the way up the steps. Several urns with lion's-head handles waited for them at the top. Bingmei peered into one and saw that it contained water, not ice. Strangely drawn to it, she was about to scoop some up in her hand, but Kunmia caught her arm and shook her head no.

Bingmei didn't know why she had nearly done it. It could have been poisoned, and besides, she wasn't thirsty. The compulsion reminded her a little of how the Phoenix Blade affected her at times. She stuck her hands into her pockets.

These doors were decorated like the set they'd passed through at the elaborate gate, embedded with nine rows of nine knobs. As Bingmei approached them, they swung open. They stepped over the threshold, and she was struck with wonder at the decorations inside. Everywhere she looked, there were urns and vases, small statues of dragons and phoenixes and lions, of turtles and leopards and cranes. Each one had been made by a master craftsman. Bound and locked chests sat atop each other in haphazard stacks that formed haphazard rows.

But the thing that caught her attention next was the white marble tomb in the middle of the chamber. A man was carved onto the lid. Next to it lay another crypt with a woman carved onto the frieze. Bingmei stared at them in shock, taking in the cold beauty with which the artist had depicted their faces.

How long had these sepulchers been here? And what lay entombed within?

CHAPTER TWENTY

The Phoenix Rune

It was impossible to describe what was in Bingmei's heart. The grandeur of the palace, the wonders they'd seen crossing the courtyards had all led to this moment, staring at the funeral sculptures of these ancient rulers. Husband and wife, side by side. A series of chills shot down her back.

The others shared her sense of awe and wonder. Their reverence smelled of soft peony petals. Every space within this inner sanctum had been hand carved and fitted to perfection. Each dab of blue, green, red, and yellow paint had been applied with precision. No masters lived today who could work stone and meiwood in such a way. It was the final resting place of the ancients' civilization—and it had been preserved intact. What secrets would they learn there? What treasures could be found?

Marenqo wiped his mouth, then asked what they were all no doubt thinking. "Do we dare even touch anything?"

Bingmei felt drawn to the male figure on the sarcophagus. She couldn't explain the feeling, but it felt as if time itself had led her to this place.

Kunmia looked around the chamber. "The wealth in this place is beyond anything I've seen. Why were these left behind?" She reached out to touch the sarcophagus of the male ruler, but hesitated and then withdrew her hand. "I see no evidence of servants or animals other than the carvings we've seen. These tombs were left here . . . abandoned."

A weight pressed down on Bingmei. That was true. There was no evidence of servants in the hall. No bones or scraps left behind. Perhaps even the tombs that lay before them were empty.

"What should we do?" Marenqo asked.

"I have a dreadful feeling," Mieshi said, looking around worriedly. "Perhaps a curse is on this place?"

That made Bingmei wonder, but if this place were cursed, she smelled nothing to warn her of it. Perhaps the cold itself had driven the people from the city, leaving behind two rulers who refused to abandon their dominion? Who, then, would have laid them in their tombs?

She wanted to touch the male ruler's tomb. It drew her to it. She stepped cautiously forward and reached out her hand.

"Bingmei!" Kunmia warned sharply.

But it was too late. She had already touched the white marble. Like so much else in this strange place, it felt achingly familiar. Nothing happened.

Marenqo let out a sigh of relief.

"We should open it," Bingmei said as a strange compulsion came over her. There were secrets buried there. Would she learn why she'd been born so pale? Why the magic seemed to work differently for her than it did for others? Why she could smell people's feelings? The intrigue made her imagination chase off in different directions.

Bingmei caressed the stone.

"Each of you take a corner," Kunmia said. She joined Bingmei at the base while Marenqo and Mieshi went to the head of the sarcophagus. There were grooves and edges along the seam, making it easy to grip.

Bingmei's eagerness to see what lay beneath the marble slab made her impatient. She dug her fingers into the grooves. Marenqo's forehead was slick with sweat. The warmth inside the chamber was stifling. Mieshi squared herself and then, after a nod from Kunmia, they all hefted the marble slab.

It took four of them to lift it, and still the strain was intense. As they lowered the lid to the side, Bingmei caught sight of the corpse buried within. A strange, sweet fragrance exuded from the interior. Not the rotting stench of death. She blinked in surprise.

With a grunt, they leaned the lid against the wall of the sarcophagus.

Marenqo wrinkled his nose. "What a curious smell," he said, sniffing it. That surprised her, because she had believed she was the only one who was experiencing it. "It's . . . myrrh, cassia too—I think. And . . . hmmm . . . camphor?"

"I smell cinnamon too," Mieshi said. The four of them stood gathered around the tomb.

Bingmei had expected to find a skeleton within the crypt, but the body was incredibly well-preserved. Although the man's skin was pale and shrunken, leathery, she could still make out dark eyebrows and pale hair longer than Damanhur's had been when they'd first met him in Wangfujing. There was no mistaking the nose, and the shriveled lips were parted on one side, revealing a glimpse of teeth.

The paleness of the corpse struck her. Could these rulers have had the winter sickness too?

The clothing of the corpse was also preserved. The tunic was made of some sort of fine silk with spiderlike strands that crisscrossed the fabric. The arms were crossed over the chest and she saw four rings, one on the forefinger and one on the fourth finger of each hand. The rings were asymmetrical twists of metal, like the roots of a gnarled tree or skeins of grapes, each quite wide. Around the body's neck hung an amulet with a rune carved into it. The polished stone glimmered in the light. The nails had grown in death and were gnarled and dark.

If the body hadn't looked so grotesque, it might have appeared the man was merely sleeping. She blinked in surprise. Had the killing fog done this? The cheekbones were high, the chin prominent. The crown of garlands that wreathed the head still smelled beautiful.

They gazed at the body in shock for several moments. Bingmei felt a nudge against her back and quickly turned her head, because she was standing alone. No one was behind her, but the feeling came again—the sense that they weren't alone. Gooseflesh rippled down her arms. Then she realized what had demanded her attention—the Phoenix Blade wriggled in its scabbard.

The blade had come home. The idea sprouted in her mind like a candle in the dark, impossible to snuff out. She noticed the way the corpse's hands were placed, as if they'd been resting on the hilt and pommel. Her eyes widened with surprise.

"Kunmia," she said, turning eagerly. "The Phoenix Blade came from this crypt. It belongs here. It's . . . it's been trying to come back."

"But why?" Kunmia said. "Was it stolen?"

"I think so," Bingmei said. "We weren't the first to come here. It was with the Qiangdao, remember?"

Kunmia frowned. "Should we return it and see what happens?"

That *felt* like a good idea. Bingmei was about to reach for the blade when it came out of the scabbard on its own, shooting straight up. She lifted her hand, and the hilt lowered into her palm. A rush of magic filled her as the blade started to give off streamers of flickering light. Marenqo backed away nervously.

Bingmei smelled the emotions of the others as they stared at her. She sensed some curiosity, but the predominant emotion was fear. They were afraid of her.

The heat in the room grew more intense as she approached the edge of the sarcophagus, the blade's pommel cradled in her hands. Light glowed from the core of the sword. Something quickened inside her as she held it over the desiccated corpse. A symbol she'd never seen before rose in her mind's eyes—a glyph, a rune. She laid the blade down on the body of the dead ruler, feeling an overwhelming sensation of relief as she did so.

The image pulsed in her mind, filling her with an overwhelming urge to trace the rune on the side of the sarcophagus with water. Unable to stop herself, she knelt by the edge of the sarcophagus and pulled around her waterskin. After uncorking it, she poured some water into her cupped hand.

The others came around and stood near her, watching with transfixed interest as she dipped her finger into the water and started tracing the glyph onto the side of the sarcophagus. As she knelt there, she felt a strong presence behind her again, as if it were hovering at her back, watching her in eagerness. The skin on the back of her neck prickled. She felt possessed, as if part of her mind and soul had been unlocked. She let the current of fate carry her along.

As she finished the last stroke of the glyph with her finger, the image began to glow, and she saw that she'd copied the sigil over the faint carving of a phoenix. She hadn't even noticed it because her mind had been so focused on the glyph.

The sword also bore the phoenix symbol.

Her hand began to tingle—at first as if it had been drained of blood, and then more keenly, as if tiny needles were jabbing into her flesh. She rose, trying to shake away the pain, but the feeling shot up her wrist and then her arm.

"Bingmei?" Kunmia asked worriedly, seeing the look on her face.

Bingmei backed away from the tomb, shaking her arm again, trying to revive feeling. It felt as if part of her life force were being ripped away. Agony tore at her, causing her to wilt from the pain. She dropped to her knees, groaning, the sensation shooting through her shoulder . . . toward her heart.

She began to gasp, to writhe, and the sound of howling wind filled the palace walls and rattled the urns and vases. The marble floor began to tremble.

"Look!" Marenqo said, pointing.

Despite the pain, which had shot all the way up to her head, Bingmei looked and saw the body hovering inches above the tomb, the Phoenix Blade higher still. Magic flooded the palace. And then they all watched in awe as the figure's hands reached out and grasped the hilt of the blade.

A shock wave rippled through the floor, driving everyone to their knees. The others huddled around Bingmei, who was still tormented by the stabbing pain. It was shooting up her legs, converging around her middle.

The corpse had shifted in the air, and it hovered upright at the head of the tomb. The man's leathery skin began to glow, his pale hair fluttering in the magical wind. One hand gripped the Phoenix Blade, the other lifted and began to trace glyphs in the air with a curled fingertip.

The wind spread the smell of camphor and myrrh throughout the closed space. Blinking with surprise, Bingmei watched the aging of the skin reverse as if time were whirling backward. The power of the magic surpassed anything in her imagination. The ancient ruler was being restored to life again before her eyes, and her intuition told her that it was her hand that had invoked the spell. How she'd done it, she had no idea. She'd been drawn there by a power greater than she could understand.

The leathery skin turned young and pale, the winter hair thick and healthy, not the withered strands she'd seen in the crypt moments before. The dark eyebrows—why were they so dark?—seemed to wrinkle as if this being shared her pain. But the suffering she endured, the awful shooting pain that made her sob, was worth it as she watched the magnificent transformation.

The man's eyes fluttered open, and Mieshi gasped. The spell was broken.

The heat from the chamber vanished, and Bingmei felt a wave of cold settle over her as the man's sandaled feet touched down on the marble floor. The last pinpricks of pain vanished, but she was left trembling. If the assault had lasted any longer, she knew without a doubt she would have died.

Just moments before, she'd been *willing* to die to restore the ancient to life. What had happened to her?

The majestic man took a deep breath and then exhaled.

And that was when Bingmei smelled him for the first time. The reeking stench filled her lungs, making her nauseous to the point of gagging. She choked on the bile that suddenly came up her throat. This stench was so much worse than that of Muxidi. A hundredfold worse. No, a thousandfold. The ancient ruler's outward appearance was regal and wise. A kindly smile stretched his beautiful mouth, but his heart was full of horrors.

What had she done?

The being spoke in a language they did not understand. He greeted them, and when no one responded, those dark brows wrinkled slightly.

Marenqo, his voice quavering, responded in a different dialect, speaking in tones of subjection and respect.

A patient smile followed, and the being drew a glyph in the air with his hand. As his finger moved, sparks of light sizzled in the air, outlining the shape, which quickly faded after his finger stopped moving.

"Do you understand my words?" he asked in a rich, melodious voice.

"Yes!" Marenqo answered for them all. He looked not only startled but delighted.

"You have revived me from the Grave Kingdom," he said. "For this, I will spare your lives. I am a benevolent ruler. You will be among my first servants. I wish to reward you. What do you want?"

Bingmei's instincts screamed at her that this man, this *creature*, could only bring death and despair. His honeyed words belied his true nature, which became more apparent to her each second. Bingmei gripped Kunmia's arm, digging her fingers into her master's flesh to get her attention. But Kunmia was gazing at the ancient man in wonder and awe. Bingmei could sense that all three of her companions were ready to worship the person who seemed to possess such godlike power.

Kunmia looked at Bingmei's face, her brow furrowing when she saw her desperate expression, her livid worry, her consuming fear.

"He is pure evil," Bingmei whispered. "He'll kill us all."

For many years, they had trusted each other. Bingmei had played a part in bringing this man back to life, even though she'd been compelled by forces she couldn't understand, like a puppet dragged on strings. But Kunmia didn't mention that, nor did she question Bingmei's judgment.

The ruler gave them a patient look. "Do not doubt my benevolence. Speak freely. What do you want?"

"Run!" Kunmia shouted, barking the command to the others. She raised her staff, invoking its runes, and attacked the ancient being with it.

The beautiful eyes narrowed coldly.

Bingmei bolted. The fear churning in her stomach made her legs pump with vigor. She was the first to hurtle past the threshold and race outside. The cold from the frozen sky struck her instantly as she started down the steps, vaulting several of them at a time. She heard the sound of chasing steps and looked back to see Mieshi overtaking her. Marenqo had reached the top of the stairs. The three of them raced across the courtyard as quickly as they could, Bingmei's ragged breath escaping her mouth in a plume.

As they reached the far side of the courtyard, Bingmei glanced back. There was no sign of Kunmia.

CHAPTER TWENTY-ONE

Rise of the Dragon

The overriding emotion they all felt was utter terror. Bingmei could smell it in the air as she gazed back at the ancient tomb. *She* had unwittingly opened the cage of a monster. Suddenly, she felt a surge of power. Although she no longer wielded the weapon, she knew the magic of the Phoenix Blade had been invoked. Part of her mind blacked out, and she saw the pale-skinned ruler whipping it around with blinding speed. Kunmia parried it with her staff, but she was giving ground, driven back by the force of his relentless attack. The runes on the staff were glowing, but they seemed unnaturally dim, as if they had no power over this man. The look of calm was gone. He looked angry, malevolent, and he did not attempt to hide it.

The ancient ruler seemed to sense the intrusion of Bingmei's thoughts. His eyes, which were the color of jade, seemed to see her through the walls of stone and the meiwood pillars. His mouth turned into a snarl, and he brought up his hand and drew another glyph, each stroke burning in the air like a shard of fire.

Kunmia fled during the moment of distraction.

A wrenching sensation twisted Bingmei's gut.

"Bingmei!" It was Marenqo, shaking her, ripping her back into her body. She felt the cold tingling she'd experienced in her dream at Budai's palace and then again at the tomb.

Lightning exploded from the meiwood pillars around them, arcs of energy striking the stone effigies throughout the courtyard. The air thrummed with power. Instead of destroying the stone, it seemed to awaken it. The stone creatures became animated and began to shrug and stretch.

The next moment, Kunmia came running out of the palace of tombs at a sprint.

"Hurry!" Mieshi urged. "We should never have come here!"

Blazing sigils appeared on the meiwood posts at the front of the palace, sizzling with energy and power. These glyphs were larger than the ones the revived ruler had drawn in the air, and there were so many of them.

A giant stone lizard scuttled up to Kunmia, but she struck it with her rune staff, knocking it away.

Magic crackled in the air, and blazing runes appeared along the support structures of the buildings at the edges of the courtyard. What were these glyphs, and what did they mean? There was no way to know, but the air had an acrid aroma from all the burning.

"We have to get out of here," Bingmei warned.

They continued to run, hoping Kunmia would catch up with them. Again they skirted the largest palace, the one they'd circled around previously. But it, too, was reviving; the meiwood posts began to hiss and burn with the power of the glyphs hidden under the painted wood.

The aura coming from the huge palace filled Bingmei with dread. The ice overhead reflected the dancing lights that hung and shimmered in the air, giving the impression of thunderheads bulging with trapped lightning. Huge chunks of ice began to fall from the glacier, smashing all around them as they ran. They wove and dodged, trying to avoid getting crushed, until they reached the interim gate. It provided them with shelter briefly, but they raced through it, intent on their escape.

Bingmei had never been so afraid or felt so helpless. Even as she ran, she felt the presence of the Phoenix Blade behind her. She felt the power of the man who wielded it. The ruler had not yet followed them, although truly he didn't *need* to follow them. He was still summoning his magic, but his power had already grown beyond her comprehension. If he wished to find them, he would.

That thought only made her run faster until she had passed Mieshi. The gate lay ahead of them at the top of a stairway, but their path was no longer clear. Men in ragged clothes descended into the courtyard in front of them, wielding tarnished weapons. The Qiangdao. There were at least thirty of them, waiting for the ensign to try to leave.

Muxidi grinned fiercely as he marched down the steps as if he were the master there. Oh, he had led them into a trap all right.

The other Qiangdao fanned out, leering at their quarry. The chunks of ice stopped raining down.

Muxidi raised his voice as they approached him at a full run. "The Dragon of Night, the mighty Echion, bids his new visitors to stay longer in his palace! You cannot leave after you've so recently come!"

The Qiangdao brandished their weapons, grunting and chanting as they did so. The sparks from the glyphs began to light the meiwood posts at the gate.

Bingmei didn't slow down. She decided to try her cricket charm again, but before she could reach for it, she felt herself vaulting through the air, her legs still pumping as she soared over the first ranks of their enemies. Her heart shuddered in surprise. This surge of power hadn't come from her charm. There was no time to think of it, however, for she came hurtling down into the gathering of Qiangdao on the stairs. They converged on her like rats on a piece of meat, some coming up the steps, others down. Bingmei struck out with her hands, feet, elbows. Ducking, dodging, weaving. Just as the men were about to overpower her, that same power hoisted her into the air, causing the Qiangdao to crash into one another. Some tripped and stumbled down the steps. She landed again, arms splayed, and attacked the nearest people. It was an unearthly feeling, a sense of weightlessness, as if she were nothing more than a ball of feathers. The angle of the steps made the whole courtyard seem off-kilter and wrong.

She flipped backward, landing a few steps lower, avoiding a cudgel coming straight for her head, and then jumped forward and smashed her palms into her attacker's middle. A pulse of energy came from her, and the man flew backward, knocking down two other Qiangdao, who then tumbled down the stairs. Mieshi and Marenqo were fighting their way up toward her, but Bingmei was in the thickest part of the battle. Kunmia was still at a distance. In the shadows of the gate, she saw the door leading out begin to swing shut, the golden nobs glowing with power.

Muxidi stepped in front of her, trying to smash her like an insect. Trying to destroy her as he had failed to do all those years ago. A grimace of hatred twisted his face. She dodged his blows, then kicked him in the middle so hard that he, too, went sailing backward and landed on the sharp edge of the steps. His grimace of rage transformed to one of pain.

Kunmia arrived then, her rune staff blazing and hissing with steam. Sweat streaked down her face, but she batted down the Qiangdao around Marenqo, who had blood streaming from his eye.

Of the thirty who had attacked them, only a dozen were left, and they fled the scene.

A deep boom issued from within the lost palace. It rattled the very stones upon which they stood. More splintering sounds of cracking ice overhead made her heart plunge with fear. Would the entire glacier come down on them? She saw dozens of stone animals coming toward them, animated by the ruler's power, intent on stopping them.

The doors were nearly closed. She rushed up the final steps and charged at the doors, which were swinging slowly toward her. The golden knobs flashed against the glossy red paint. She struck the doors to hold them open, but they were too big, too heavy for her to stop them. Mieshi reached the top of the stairs and ran to the other door. Their heels scraped against the stone as they attempted to push the doors, only to be shoved backward.

Kunmia came up the steps, gripping the bleeding Marenqo around the shoulder. They were close, but they wouldn't make it in time. Outside the doors, Bingmei saw the two bronze lions on their perches. It felt as if she were shoving against one of those statues. Impossible.

Mieshi groaned in frustration as the doors continued to close against them. When Bingmei grabbed one of the knobs to better position herself, the metal burned her flesh, and she yelped in pain.

"It's too heavy," Mieshi grunted in anguish, then backed away. The doors were nearly closed. They'd have to leave right then in order to escape. But that would trap Kunmia and Marenqo inside.

"Mieshi!" Kunmia shouted.

Mieshi turned just in time to catch the rune staff, which Kunmia had thrown like a spear. Its glyphs still smoked with power, but the edges of the wood were blackened. Mieshi grabbed it in the middle and shoved it sideways between the doors. The knobs began to flicker as the staff drained their power. The giant doors slowed.

Bingmei rushed to Marenqo's other side, and she and Kunmia helped him cross the stone tiles leading to the threshold where Mieshi grunted with the staff, trying to keep the doors apart. The staff was flexing dangerously, about to break.

They made it through the gap single file, and Mieshi followed them out, twisting the staff and pulling it with her. She stepped over the gold-plated threshold just in time.

The doors slammed shut behind them.

But they were not out of danger yet. Ahead waited the two lion guardians. Zhuyi's body was gone.

"Where is she?" Mieshi said worriedly, and started down the steps.

"Wait!" Kunmia said, gasping for breath. "The guardians!"

Marenqo was trying to wipe the blood from his face. The cut seemed to be at the corner of his eye. A bruise was also beginning to form on his cheekbone. He looked dazed still, and slumped down onto his rump.

Now that the immediate danger had passed, Bingmei found herself thinking again of the ruler, of his inhuman stench. What had they unleashed on the world? Regret flooded her heart, making her want to start crying. But she steeled herself. How could they have known what awaited them? Any knowledge of the danger of Fusang had long been forgotten.

The sweat on Bingmei's brow dribbled in her eyes, and she wiped it away. Kunmia was no longer staring at the lions. She was staring at Bingmei's face with alarm. She smelled confused, concerned, like a slightly sour cucumber.

"What is it?" Bingmei asked in worry.

"Your hair has changed," Kunmia said. She approached and began examining Bingmei's face.

"Master," Mieshi said with urgency. "We must flee! We're not safe here."

"I can stand, I think," Marenqo mumbled. He got up, swayed a bit, but remained on his feet.

Kunmia frowned at Bingmei, not in anger but in apparent bewilderment. "We will solve this puzzle later. Mieshi, the staff. Help Marenqo. I will go first."

Bingmei watched as Kunmia took the staff and quickly marched down the steps. The runes in the staff were fading, the blackened edges of the glyphs revealed as the light ebbed. Kunmia nodded to each bronze lion, but she had a wary pose, a posture of defense, ready to spring into action if either monster charged. They remained rigid and still.

"Bring him down. The three of you, come at once. Nod as you go."

Kunmia stood between the lions warily, staff held at the ready. Trepidation made Bingmei swallow. So much had happened, her mind felt numb. Only through her force of will could she proceed. What had given her—?

"Concentrate!" Kunmia said. "Clear your minds."

Bingmei was grateful for the reminder. She took some deep breaths, banishing her thoughts as if they were a swarm of butterflies, and focused on passing the sentries safely. Marenqo walked on his own, but he still cupped his wounded eye.

As Bingmei passed the lions, one of them, the one to her left, the one with a paw resting on the sculpted orb, swiveled its head to face her.

"The phoenix-chosen must return," said the lion, his voice scraping like metal on metal. *"The others may go."*

Bingmei halted, feeling her heart pound with fear. She wanted to fly away as she'd done on the other side of the wall, but as quickly as the power had come, it had forsaken her. What had felt completely natural to her within the palace gates was suddenly beyond her reach.

Kunmia looked at her and then at the lion. Was it warning they'd attack if Bingmei attempted to leave? "Mieshi, keep going," Kunmia said. "Quickly."

Mieshi nodded, pulling on Marenqo's arm. Soon they were past both of the lions. Fear quivered in Bingmei's stomach.

"Bingmei, go next," Kunmia said.

"What if they attack?" she whispered, her voice trembling. She had no idea what power had overcome her earlier, but it was clearly gone.

"I am not leaving you here," Kunmia said. Her tone brooked no argument. She did not give off any scent of fear, only the determination and tenderness a mother felt for her child. That sweet, delicious smell—of cinnamon porridge—had always made Bingmei long to be near her. Bingmei's heart warmed with gratitude. After losing her family, her ensign, she'd feared no one would ever accept her for who she was. Finding a new home in Kunmia's ensign, and the sense of belonging she'd craved, had felt like a double gift.

Bingmei opened her palm and gestured for her master to give her the staff. She looked into Kunmia's eyes, silently asking for her trust. Kunmia pursed her lips, then cast a wary glance at the bronze lions. Finally, she gave the staff over. Bingmei gripped it, comforted by its reassuring weight in her hand, as she watched Kunmia walk away from the lions.

Bingmei felt weariness ripple through her, sapping her strength. If only this would be easy. She gestured for the others to step away, then tightened her grip on the staff and started to back away from the lions, away from the dreadful city. The other lion leaped off its pedestal and circled around behind her, blocking the way. The one with the orb joined it.

"Follow me," grated the orb lion.

"Bingmei," Kunmia warned.

"Go, Master," Bingmei said. "Please."

The two lions began circling her. She heard one of them issue a rattling growl.

"The phoenix-chosen will return," said the mother lion. The door started to open again, making a grinding noise.

"Am *I* that?" Bingmei asked, glancing worriedly at the door. She turned around sharply, looking at the way out. The ice overhead tapered down as the path neared the caves. If she could make it over there, it would be too narrow for the lions to pass. She watched Mieshi help Marenqo through the rubble they'd crossed to get there. Kunmia hesitated, looking like she wanted to help.

Bingmei shot her a warning look and nodded for her to depart.

The orb lion behind her came forward and tried to butt her back toward the pedestals with its snout. Bingmei dodged it, shoving at it with the staff. The monster snarled at her but did not strike.

It occurred to her that she had one advantage. The lions clearly weren't permitted to kill her. Suddenly, the mother lion came closer, trying to usher her along. They were herding her toward the steps leading to the glowing door.

She dodged one lion, only to find the other had switched directions to confront her again. The magic that animated the metal lions was powerful. They walked and crouched just like real animals. Their metal muscles rippled.

She swatted at the orb lion with the staff, and it struck with a hollow sound, like a giant bell.

And then she heard the flapping of wings coming from the ancient palace. A familiar awareness prickled down her back. The same sensation she'd experienced before with the invisible guardian.

"Run!" Bingmei screamed.

CHAPTER
TWENTY-TWO

Truth of All Things

Bingmei dodged the beasts, rushing away from them. The mother lion was about to snatch her in its jaws when she reached into her pocket and invoked the cricket. She was far enough from the walls that the magic worked, just as she'd hoped. Bounding high and far, she sprang like the creature whose likeness she held in her pocket until she'd outdistanced the lions. Then she ran as fast and hard as she could. Bingmei's heart pounded until it hurt, her lungs burning with the exertion. The broken rocks spilled away, making the footing unstable. But still she felt the presence of the unseen guardian. She risked a glance over her shoulder and nearly tripped. Her vision doubled, and she saw something huge and black soaring over the walls. Something made out of nightmares.

She saw spiny wings and huge yellow eyes that burned like coals. Compared to this creature, the lion sentries were smaller than puppies. It squatted on the rooftop like a man, cords of muscle rippling beneath its scales as it gripped the balustrade with two longer armlike append- ages. It was wreathed in shadow that seemed to exude from it in tendrils like smoke. And then, just as suddenly as it had appeared, it blinked out of view. There and then gone and then there again, sniffing the icy air, staring at them balefully.

She knew it was a dragon, and yet it was nothing like the images she'd seen carved into stone. No craftsman could capture the malice. No artist's skill could evoke such danger. She'd seen its huge shadowy wings hulking on its back. It blinked out of sight again, but she could still sense its presence.

They had awoken a dragon from the past. The certainty of it chilled her heart. The Dragon of Night was not just a season of darkness. It was darkness personified. And although she didn't understand how, she knew in her heart it was an extension of Echion. That the two were inextricably linked.

She felt but didn't see the great beast swoop off the roof toward her.

The panic that flooded her heart made her run all the faster. Kunmia and the others were scrambling toward the ice caves, spurred on by her urgency.

It was coming for her. She pumped her arms, racing against the inevitable. How could she outrun something that could fly?

And yet she reached the low-hanging shelf of ice. She plunged into the tunnel, her strength renewed, and felt the monster veer away. A wave of its stench followed her into the tunnel, and she recognized the smell as that of the man who had awakened from the sleep of death.

Bingmei stopped after turning the corner, huddling against a pillar of melting ice, and began to weep. She gasped for breath, trying to control the raw feelings that raged inside her like a storm, but it was impossible. Again she wondered what she had done. Was it her power that had awakened the monster? She'd drawn the glyph, hadn't she? How had she even known it? Confusion, misery, helplessness, and despair all crashed within her like waves against a rugged shore.

She became aware, a few minutes later, of the others joining her at the tunnel's entrance. Looks of relief crossed their faces. They all were desperate for breath by the time they found her against the ice pillar. Bingmei held out the staff to Kunmia, who silently took it.

A moment passed before any of them spoke. Rarely had Bingmei's emotions been so raw. She knew she'd start crying again if someone looked at her with accusation. None of them did. They all smelled relieved, grateful to be alive. That they had even made it this far was nothing short of miraculous. But the danger was far from over.

"Do you . . . do you think," Marenqo asked, his hand clutching his eyes as he squatted nearby, "that Budai *knew* this would happen?" He smiled a crooked grin. It was just like him to try to lighten the mood at such a time.

Kunmia was staring up at the ripples in the ice overhead. Her rune staff was dormant, the traces of magic spent. Black scorch marks riddled its length. Bingmei realized, shuddering, that they all probably would have died if Kunmia hadn't possessed the staff.

Bingmei reached for her water, wanting to slake her thirst before she answered him, but it was gone, left behind in the burial chamber. Just thinking about the waterskin made her remember when she'd last seen it—she'd used water from it to trace the glyph on the tomb. Another wave of guilt crashed into her.

"No," Bingmei said. "Budai was greedy, nothing more. He wasn't trying to trick us."

"We need to warn him," Kunmia said. "We need to warn all the rulers. This ancient one has power we do not understand. His magic must block the killing fog. Look how much I used the staff. Nothing. Not even a little wisp of it."

Noises reverberated from the direction they'd come, stone claws moving over gravel.

"Let's keep going," Mieshi said darkly, pushing away from the ice pillar. "I wish we'd never come." She looked at Bingmei then, and her scent soured. There were notes of mistrust, jealousy, and even a little fear. It wasn't a pleasant smell, but then again, Mieshi's feelings for her had never been altogether pleasant.

Bingmei understood. Of all of them, she'd been closest to Zhuyi, whom they had lost in the tunnels.

They rose and continued through the ice tunnel at a fast pace. It looked different to Bingmei. The sense of wonder she'd felt was gone, replaced by concern for the future. And as they walked away, she felt the Phoenix Blade flare with magic. Its pulsing magic felt like a snare, pulling her mind free of her body. The vision opened up, and she stood at the gate of the forgotten palace once again. The ancient ruler stood before a group of Qiangdao, including the leader who had murdered her parents and grandfather and led her new family into danger.

The fearsome ancient held the Phoenix Blade in his hands.

"Find her," he said. "Bring her again. She must not die. Do this, and you will no longer skulk in the caves and in the woods. I will make you rulers over many. You will have slaves to bring you food and wine. Do not fail me."

The ancient one handed the Phoenix Blade to Muxidi. When the foul man touched the hilt, his eyes widened with pleasure, and an uncontrollable smile twisted his mouth. She felt his emotions in a way that made her cringe and writhe in disgust, in part because she had reacted to the sword in the same way. She did not wish to understand him, of all people, or to feel anything that he felt.

"Yes, Lord Echion," he said in reverence.

杀雾

As they hurried to leave the ice cave beneath the massive glacier, Bingmei's mind roiled with what she had seen in the vision. *Bring her again.* That phrase kept repeating in her mind.

Again. Again.

When they'd first encountered the Phoenix Blade, it had been in the hands of a group of Qiangdao. A group that had ambushed them when they'd tried to disembark from Quion's father's boat.

The conclusion was inescapable. They had been waiting for *her*. For Bingmei. The blade had led them to her. Although she didn't understand why, she was connected to the blade and it to her. With it, they would find her, no matter where she went.

Feelings of hopelessness surged inside her again. Muxidi was coming for her. She could feel the blade coming closer. Even if they made it to the boat, even if they sailed away, Echion's followers would still come. She thought she knew why.

The other tomb still lay unopened.

"We must go faster," she warned. "They're hunting us."

Kunmia looked at her in surprise but nodded in acceptance.

Marenqo snorted. "I was just going to suggest we stop and eat. Maybe we'll wait until we reach the boat."

He was always trying to lighten the mood, something Bingmei appreciated. The stress of the ordeal weighed on them all. But Mieshi was less patient. "Can you only think about food?" she snapped with anger, her scent raw and unpleasant.

When they emerged from the ice tunnel, the sun was so bright it hurt their eyes. The little streams delivering the melted ice from the cave sloshed against their boots, and the cold quickly became unbearable. They donned their heavier clothes and hastened up the slope they'd come down.

How strange to return to the real world and find it unchanged. The snow-capped mountains, the distant thunder of the waterfall coming down the rocky edge of the slope.

Marenqo's eye was swollen shut and encrusted with blood, but he managed to keep his feet. Bingmei's legs were exhausted from the rough journey, but she, too, was motivated to keep a brisk pace. If they could reach the boat, they'd find shelter on the water, however impermanent.

Was Echion trapped beneath the ice? She hoped his powers did not extend beyond the caves, although she suspected if that were the case, it would not be so for long. If that were so, there was time to warn the kingdoms about him. That thought gave her a modicum of hope. But it still felt impossible to defeat one capable of such magic.

"They're coming," Mieshi warned, causing them all to turn back. Qiangdao were already exiting the glacier and charging up the rockslide hill.

"Run," Kunmia said urgently. "We must get to the boat first!"

The terrain seemed determined to stall them. Every boulder, every slick patch of ice threatened to bring them to their doom. The scenery became a blur in Bingmei's mind as she tore down the mountain toward the sandy shore. The waterfall roared on her left, drowning out the noise of their pursuers. But she didn't need to see them to know how close they were. The Phoenix Blade was calling to her, and its song burned in her blood. It urged her to take it from the unworthy Qiangdao leader. To bring the fight to Echion and destroy him with it. But the magic was tainting her mind, surely, just as it had before. It had made her believe she was special, that it was hers and hers alone, and in so doing, it had led her straight to Echion. She regretted ever laying eyes on it.

Marenqo stumbled as they came down, and she watched him fall down the mountainside in front of her, yelping as he struck a rock. She hurried forward and helped him stand, but he barked in pain and clutched his arm. He'd likely broken it.

But he kept his feet, grimacing in agony, and continued to clamber down the mountainside.

When they reached the beach, Damanhur, Rowen, and the others stood around the Qiangdao they'd captured, who were kneeling in the sand. The boat and Quion were gone. Bingmei's heart sank. She'd forgotten Kunmia Suun's orders. They were trapped on the beach.

Damanhur saw them coming and raced to join them, his look full of concern.

"What happened?" he asked quickly.

"A hundred men are chasing us," Bingmei shouted, looking back. The hillside swarmed with Qiangdao. Their shouts could just be heard over the roar of the falls.

The Qiangdao kneeling on the shore suddenly leaped to their feet. Some fought with hands and legs, others ran away. The mayhem was instant.

"Without the boat, all is lost!" Kunmia said frantically.

"It's hidden nearby," Damanhur said. "Come."

He drew his sword, and they all rushed back to help the others fight the former prisoners. Bingmei, although tired, was one of the first to enter the battle. It quickly became clear that these Qiangdao understood Echion's intentions—rather than attack her, they tried to carry her away. One of the men grabbed her from behind, around the waist, and hauled her off her feet. She smashed her elbow back into his face, but he didn't drop her. Before she could redouble her attack, another one grabbed her legs.

They started hauling her away as she bucked against them, but Rowen stabbed the one holding her legs, in the back. The man screamed in pain, and as he sagged to his knees, Rowen spun around and jabbed one of his blades into the arm of the man who held her. The man let go and fled, gripping his arm, even as blood welled up through his fingers. Rowen stood over Bingmei, nodding for her to get up. Another one of the Qiangdao attacked next, and Bingmei jumped forward, swiveling her legs and kicking him in the face. He slumped onto the sand, unconscious.

"This way," Rowen said, leading her back toward the others. The Qiangdao who had pursued them from the cave were starting to reach the shore. They were a large, well-armed force. These men had not been involved in the earlier battle, which suggested the Qiangdao leader had purposefully lost to them earlier. The whole exercise had been a manipulation to ensure they might deliver Bingmei to the ancient ruler.

Kunmia and the others had not been expected to make it out of Fusang alive.

As they raced across the beach, Bingmei saw Quion dragging the boat out from behind a large boulder that had concealed it. His legs were wet as he stood in the frigid water, but he dragged at the guide rope until it came around. Some of the others had reached the edge of the water and were already splashing into it to get inside. Quion helped each of them up.

The screams of the Qiangdao grew louder as they charged closer, brandishing their weapons. Fear blazed a path through Bingmei. She was the one Echion wanted, but if they weren't quick enough, all her friends would be murdered on the beach.

Rowen sheathed his blades and gripped her arm, ushering her toward the boat. She watched as Mieshi made it inside. Then Marenqo. Some of the members of Damanhur's ensign climbed in. Kunmia waited at the water's edge, gesturing for her and Rowen to hurry.

Bingmei didn't dare look back.

The fisherman Keyi's face was wide with alarm as he hastened to raise the sail, his hands shaking as he untied Quion's knots.

"Get inside!" Kunmia shouted to Damanhur, who arrived next. He shook his head and turned, his sword out.

Rowen and Bingmei arrived and plunged into the water. The shock of the cold couldn't overwhelm her panic. She reached the boat, and Quion gripped her around the waist and heaved her into the boat as if she were a net full of fish. Mieshi helped pull her inside. Rowen made it on board on his own. Then Damanhur and Kunmia plunged into the water, and together with Quion, they pushed the boat deeper.

"I can't undo the knots!" Keyi wailed in terror.

Quion pulled himself on board and quickly, methodically released the tension on the ropes. Damanhur helped lift Kunmia up into the boat next, leaving himself as the only one in the water. A spear flew at him and missed, striking the side of the boat with a quivering thud.

Quion helped Keyi pull and raise the sail. When the arm was yanked to the side to catch the wind, it nearly knocked Marenqo down, but it didn't, and the sail bulged with air and started to move the boat.

Damanhur grabbed the edge of the boat and let the vessel pull him away. Mieshi and another man reached out and grabbed his arm just as he lost his grip.

Against all odds, they'd made it.

Bingmei, shivering, turned in her seat and looked back at the shore where she saw Muxidi standing at the edge of the lapping water, holding the Phoenix Blade. The blade didn't want to be left behind. It screamed at her mind in panic, invoking a torrent of feelings.

She stared at Muxidi's face, and he at hers, and she wished she had killed him when they'd first captured him on the beach.

CHAPTER
TWENTY-THREE
Things Not Seen

The sail billowed with a strong wind that sent the fishing boat clapping on the water, unlike the calm they had rowed against when they'd first arrived. Bingmei sat in a stunned stupor, her mind unpacking the events that had preceded their perilous escape. Relief soothed her agitation as distance separated her from the mammoth glacier. Her feelings calmed, settling into a shallow sense of gratitude that she was still alive.

Damanhur, who sat next to Mieshi, asked Kunmia for their story, but the master shook her head, saying it was not the time. She ordered Keyi to make for Wangfujing in the most direct manner possible. The open sea.

Damanhur stared at her in alarm. The risk was great, especially since they knew they had pursuers. Prince Rowen's feelings ignited with anger and confusion, giving an ugly smell that reminded Bingmei of burnt turnips. After stewing in his feelings awhile, he carefully approached Kunmia and whispered something to her. The master listened, then shook her head no.

"I will tell you when we've reached calmer waters," she said pointedly.

He wasn't satisfied by the answer, but he made his way back to his seat. The faraway look in his eye told her that he was thinking of the Summer Palace. He had bet his fortunes on discovering treasure in the lost city. There was plenty of treasure there, although it was not available for the taking. Bingmei could smell the festering disappointment he concealed, sour and bitter, like the rind of the spiky durian fruit. "No one answered me earlier," Damanhur said softly to no one in particular. "Where's Zhuyi?"

Mieshi shook her head, tears in her eyes. Her mood was dark and sad. Her grief was deep.

When the sun finally set, Bingmei felt embraced by the dark. Rations were handed out, including hunks of smoked fish, which Quion had already prepared for a later meal. It was salty and fragrant with spices. Their supplies had been intended to last for some time, so Kunmia was liberal with the portions. Memories from the palace streaked through her mind like lightning between storm clouds.

The boat had entered another fjord leading to the sea when Kunmia finally spoke. Although they were on open water, they were far from danger. Far, at least, from the danger Bingmei had unwittingly released in Fusang. She had lost nearly all sense of the Phoenix Blade by this point. Its power over her was definitely strengthened with proximity.

"I wish to tell you what we faced. What we *lost*," Kunmia said, her voice calm. But Bingmei could smell the concern, the worry that lay beneath it.

Foreboding hung in the air. There was enough light for Bingmei to see the faces of her companions. Keyi, the fearful fisherman, looked despairingly at her. Bingmei hung her head low, dreading the tale.

"More importantly," Damanhur said, "why we are running from Fusang? The Qiangdao had greater numbers than we thought, but their ability is nothing compared with ours."

"That was the only option to survive," Kunmia said. "If we hadn't run, you'd be dead."

Damanhur shrugged. "Maybe if we'd all been together, perhaps it would have turned out differently."

Bingmei thought his tone was too disrespectful. Although Damanhur was not as arrogant as she'd thought at first, he had never relished being second in command. She glared at him.

"You don't know what you're saying," Mieshi snapped.

Kunmia was unruffled. "There is a series of palaces hidden under the ice that not only rivals but dwarfs that of Sajinau. We only witnessed a portion of it, but it's all intact. Even the paint seems new. Magic preserves and defends it in a way I struggle to understand. The Qiangdao discovered it first. I think many of them are living hidden within the walls."

Damanhur nodded. "How many do you think?"

"Several hundred, I should say, but they aren't the true threat. We're not going to Wangfujing to raise an army. We're going to warn King Budai. And then King Shulian. And then all the others."

Rowen stiffened at the mention of his father's name. His brow furrowed with agitation. This was not the victorious return to Sajinau he had planned.

"What did you find there?" Damanhur asked worriedly, catching on. The lemony smell of greed laced the air around him and the prince. The hidden city was there, just as they'd thought, and they wanted their treasure.

"This is not a matter of what we found, but of what we awoke. We found a slab of solid stone, marble I should think, bearing effigies of two entwined dragons. There were two stone tombs in one of the palaces, made out of pale marble and carved into the likenesses of two rulers, male and female."

Rowen and Damanhur exchanged a long speculative look. A smell of excitement passed between them. Bingmei wondered what they already knew, what myths had driven them to seek out Fusang. They clearly knew more than she had, more—even—than Budai.

What had they set into motion? Had they done so knowingly?

"Which one did you open?" Rowen asked.

"We opened the tomb of the male," Kunmia said. "The corpse within had been painstakingly preserved. It had not decayed to the point of bones. There was still leathery flesh and hair. Pale hair."

Rowen's eyes turned to Bingmei in surprise, and perhaps some alarm, and she felt her cheeks start to burn.

"Did the corpse rise?" Damanhur said with curiosity and some fear. "Was it a xixuegui?"

"I don't know," Kunmia said. "But I don't think so. It came back to life."

"Then it *was* a xixuegui," Damanhur insisted.

"In those legends, they speak of the dead who have only one soul walking and feasting on the living. This one returned to life, yes, but he became *young* again. Alive. Whole. The corpse's flesh was restored."

Both Rowen and Damanhur looked shocked by that news. Their smells confirmed it. Whatever they'd expected, it wasn't this. At least they hadn't set out to raise Echion.

"Where is the Phoenix Blade now?" Rowen asked, his voice full of dread.

Kunmia turned to face him. "The sword belonged to this ruler. Bingmei felt a powerful urge to place it on the corpse. Then she drew a glyph on the side of the tomb."

"What?" Damanhur said. He looked at her as if she were raving mad. "Why would you do such a thing?"

Before she could speak, Rowen gripped Damanhur's arm and shook his head.

Her voice sounded small. "It compelled me."

"The glyph invoked a powerful spell," Kunmia continued. "The ruler was restored to life. He said he was awakened from the Grave

Kingdom. He intends to reclaim his empire. He performed glyphs himself, tracing strange symbols in the air with his finger. The air would spark and burn for a moment before fading. His power was beyond anything, and the myths of Fusang must be true, for none of it brought the killing fog. He summoned a dragon to chase us after we fled."

Keyi choked on his portion of fish, and Quion had to thump his back. Those who hadn't experienced it stared at her in disbelief.

"He didn't summon a dragon," Bingmei said, squirming in her seat. "The dragon is part of him. Echion is *the* Dragon of Night."

Kunmia turned to look at her.

"Did he threaten you when you woke him?" Damanhur asked Kunmia.

"Not at first, no."

Damanhur's brow wrinkled, and he smelled of confusion and frustration. "So why did you allow him to make an alliance with the Qiangdao and not us? If he's as powerful as you say, surely there was an opportunity there. I imagine he was grateful to have been awakened. And you say you saw a real dragon?" Doubt tinged his words.

Kunmia's brows knitted together. "I did see it."

"We should go back," Damanhur said. He wrestled with his patience. "Perhaps a deal could still be made. It would be foolish for us not to try to form an alliance with such a man."

"No!" Bingmei said, shaking her head.

"We've lost the Phoenix Blade," Damanhur said, "and you brought nothing else with you. You lost one of your disciples too."

"Maybe *you* should go back," Mieshi said with rage in her eyes. "You'd be killed by the guardians before you even made it through the gate!"

The air was getting difficult to breathe, ripe with smells of anger and distrust.

"When we get back to Wangfujing, you may do as you like," Kunmia said. "But for now, you have sworn to obey me. Do you still have your honor?"

Damanhur scowled at the rebuke. "It's not that I distrust you, Master," he said. "It just seems that you may have fled before understanding all the facts. Perhaps you even unintentionally caused offense. Why not go back and see if we can reason with him?"

"Because he is untrustworthy," Kunmia answered.

"And how could you judge that so quickly?" Understanding flamed in his eyes, and he shifted to look at Bingmei. "Because of you?"

She met his gaze. "Yes."

Damanhur shook his head. "And what gives *you* such insight? Why should we all trust your word on something so important?"

"She's never been wrong," Kunmia said.

"But does it stand to reason that because she's never been wrong before she can't be wrong now?" Damanhur challenged. His lips twisted into a scowl. "We are leaving that place to be plundered by the Qiangdao. They will use whatever they find there against us. Weapons. Artifacts. If so many of them have gathered together under such a leader, they will be a threat to the kingdoms." He cut the edge of his hand against his other palm. "Wisdom dictates that we return and challenge them now, before they have a chance to gather others to their cause. If they have two hundred, then we face them in smaller groups. Ambush. Attack. Retreat. This is what King Budai would want. We're doing the wrong thing out of childish fear."

His words caused a hot stab of pain in Bingmei's chest. She was about to come out of her seat, but Kunmia shook her head, her expression firm.

"Stop defending her," Damanhur said. "Let her answer for herself." He looked at Bingmei. "How do you know whether someone is honest or not? You are no more worldly-wise than I am. It will take a few days to reach Wangfujing. Perhaps the right course is to go back now. Explain yourself."

Anger, toward herself as much as Damanhur, flared inside her. Her own scent became an overpowering one of burnt metal. He was backing her into a corner, asking her to reveal herself before everyone.

"Damanhur," Rowen said warningly.

"Why does it matter how she does it?" Kunmia said. "It is a gift. An instinct. It's proven itself in a hundred situations."

"There is too much at stake," Damanhur said, shaking his head. "I want an explanation. We deserve one." His eyes never left Bingmei's. "How do you do it? Why should we trust what you feel?"

She licked her lips and tried to swallow. The anger had faded, leaving her vulnerable. He wasn't wrong. They'd taken her gift on faith before. But circumstances had changed. She wouldn't be able to convince them of what she knew without telling them how. If she refused to speak, the trust her companions had in her would be damaged.

Bingmei swallowed again. Her throat was thick with anger and thirst. "I . . . I can smell emotions."

None of them, including Kunmia, had expected the answer. Confusion emanated from them in waves of ginger and old fish.

"I *know* when someone is angry or disappointed or even embarrassed," Bingmei said, the words gushing out. "I can sense their character. Someone who is dishonest has a certain scent to them. They appear one way but smell another. It conflicts. The worst smell I've ever known, up until now, was the Qiangdao. They murder without remorse or guilt. They *hate* in a way that you cannot understand."

She paused, looking around at them, waiting a moment to see if they questioned what she said. Their surprise was still evident on their faces. She sensed no disbelief, not yet, but they grappled with what she'd told them.

Sighing, she continued. "Believe me when I say the Qiangdao smell *nothing* at all like the stench inside that tomb. The corpse itself smelled sweet, of burial spices, but after Echion came alive, he could not conceal his true nature from me. I nearly vomited." Her voice trembled slightly. "I've never smelled something so horrid, so deceiving, so murderous before. And my parents and grandfather were murdered by Muxidi, the man we captured. Echion has killed . . . countless others. Thousands or thousands of thousands. More. I cannot even describe how much blood taints him." She swallowed again, watching their widening eyes. Her gaze caught Quion's for a moment. A little smile played on his mouth, and he nodded at her, silently reassuring her. She was grateful for his unwavering belief in her.

Damanhur looked more subdued. By his look and his confused smell, he hadn't expected such an answer. "Why did you revive him, then?" he asked with worry.

"I couldn't control it," Bingmei said. "The palace looked beautiful. The level of craftsmanship . . . it's impossible to describe. So many colors and hues, all in the same style of the buildings and art left behind by the ancients, but restored to perfection. It felt like it was my . . . my *fate* to awaken him. The sword whispered as much to me. I don't know how I knew the glyph of resurrection. But it came into my mind while we were there, and I felt compelled to draw it. Once Echion's depravity was revealed to me, I warned Kunmia to flee. Staying would have meant death for us all." She sighed. "He will hunt for me," she added. "I'm connected to the Phoenix Blade still. He gave it to the Qiangdao leader and sent him to bring me back. He wants me to revive his queen. His consort." Bingmei turned to Kunmia. "It felt as if I'd been there before. In a past life."

"Maybe you were," Kunmia said with worry. She reached out and stroked Bingmei's cheek. There was no blame or anger in her. No disbelief or mockery.

The boat continued to rock and creak as it lumbered down the fjord. Little splashing noises from the hull filled the air as everyone fell silent.

Kunmia, after some silence, turned to the rest. "I faced the ruler to give the others time to run. If I hadn't had the staff, he would have killed me in moments. His expertise with the Phoenix Blade is beyond anything I've witnessed. His reflexes were faster than mine. I couldn't even touch him." She fell silent for a moment. "I was afraid of him."

Damanhur nodded. "Perhaps both of us could have killed him."

Kunmia shrugged but didn't insult him by speaking the truth—if they'd both stood against him, they both would have died.

Damanhur looked pointedly at Bingmei. "What am I feeling now?" he asked her.

There were so many smells on the boat at that moment that it wasn't easy picking out a specific one. But Damanhur's emotions were not very subtle.

"You're afraid," she said. It probably wasn't what he wanted to hear, but it was true.

They were all afraid.

杀雾

It was nearly dawn when Bingmei awoke for her shift at guard duty. Kunmia nestled under her fur blanket to get some sleep before the others awoke. Quion stood at the tiller, gently steering the boat while Keyi slept. Bingmei carefully picked her way past the others and joined her friend at the rear of the boat. The others breathed softly, hunched and leaning against one another. Mieshi's head rested on Damanhur's shoulder.

Bingmei sat down next to Quion, pulling her blanket more tightly around her, then wiped the sleep from her eyes.

"Any ni-ji-jing following us?" she whispered to him.

He shook his head. "No, but I spotted a whale."

They were quiet for a while. The moon was down, and the stars were their only light, but the sky was growing paler. Quion glanced at the horizon occasionally, but the fjord was guiding their path.

"The other night," he said softly. "You were about to tell me that, weren't you? About what you can do?"

She nodded, wishing she'd taken the chance to tell him sooner.

He wasn't disgusted by her, she knew. In fact, he was impressed. Even a little in awe. "What . . . ?" Then he shook his head and looked away.

She butted him with her elbow, raising her eyebrows.

"It's foolish," he said sheepishly.

"Tell me," she insisted.

"I wondered . . . I wondered what *I* smelled like. To you. Am I . . . trustworthy?"

She'd expected someone to ask her. Maybe all of them. Would they start treating her differently now that they knew about her special instinct? Some of her companions would probably be wary around her. But not Quion. He was still the same.

"You smell like fish," she said, butting him with her shoulder again. "But that shouldn't surprise you."

"Stinking fish?"

She shook her head, smiling at his question. He had always had a simple smell. He was naive and hardworking. Faithful, above all. She was glad he was part of the ensign. Glad they were still friends.

A memory stirred inside her, one that had been lost during the chaos. She reached up and undid the pins of her wig and then pulled it off.

"It's changed!" Quion whispered, his eyes widening with surprise.

The first rays of sunlight shimmered on her hair. The braids were no longer pale but bright as polished copper.

杀雾

She who knows her heart mistrusts her eyes.

—Dawanjir proverb

CHAPTER TWENTY-FOUR

The King of Wangfujing

It had taken them just six days to sail back to Wangfujing. They had stopped only rarely, enough to stretch their legs and practice their forms, always remaining watchful. The waterways were crowded with fishermen seeking to make their fortunes.

Memories from the glacier continued to haunt Bingmei, but they dimmed as they reached familiar country.

When they arrived, the market in Wangfujing was overcrowded with buyers and noisy with commerce. Some of the buildings had burned down, but the mess had been cleaned up, and only a few scars remained from the attack. If anything, the traffic and commotion showed an improvement in Budai's fortunes, for each visitor was taxed on the cowry shells exchanged to trade there. The vendors' huge vats of roasted frogs and steamed buns were nearly empty, and it was only midday. The jostling crowd made Bingmei long for the quiet of the boat. Marenqo crammed a still-steaming bun into his mouth and moaned with pleasure. The wound on his eye was still scabbed but healing.

Another thing they had noticed upon entering Wangfujing was the mercenary force King Budai had hired to protect the town from the Qiangdao. Their black tunics bore a leopard badge instead of Budai's frog, and they patrolled the streets in groups of four. Their silk hats made them easy to notice.

Quion jostled Bingmei's elbow and offered her a scorpion stick he'd just purchased. She accepted it with a smile.

Another man suddenly accosted Kunmia, demanding to speak to Prince Rowen.

"That man owes me a great debt!" he declared hotly.

Rowen's eyes flashed with malice. The smell of an indebted man was an unusual one. It was the bitter smell of worry, like onions, only it never faded. Its odor had increased the closer the boat had come to Wangfujing, and Rowen had become increasingly sullen and withdrawn. He was intrigued by the transformation of Bingmei's hair, just as they all had been, but that secret was hidden beneath the dark wig again. The change was inexplicable.

Kunmia told the man to appeal to King Budai.

"But I want my share of the money first! Not after Budai has claimed his due! He's owed even more than I am, and I'm just a poor moneylender."

His words stunk of a lie, but Kunmia didn't need Bingmei's assistance in discerning it.

"Appeal. To. The. King," Kunmia said, enunciating each word, and they continued.

As they passed the frustrated moneylender, he scowled and shook his fist at Rowen.

Rowen refused to meet the man's eyes. He seemed impassive, but she sensed the shame and anger and despair that lay beneath it.

"I think that man is offended," Marenqo said after chewing and swallowing. "What do you think, Wuren? He looked positively upset."

Marenqo's attempt at a joke didn't land. Rowen glowered at him.

"Did I say something amiss?" Marenqo asked innocently, but he was ignored.

They reached the palace doors and found four of the black-silk guards stationed there with heavy glaives.

The chief gave Kunmia a wary look. "State your business."

"I'm Kunmia Suun," she answered, saying nothing more.

The man's expression changed. "Ah. Pardon me, Master Suun. I'm new to this duty." The words were clipped and rough, his accent one Bingmei didn't know offhand. "I report to Captain Heise. We are mercenaries from—"

"Tianrui," Marenqo interrupted. "I recognize your accent." He addressed the guard in his own language, and the man's face brightened. They conversed quickly, eagerly, and Marenqo then gestured to the door, which the man readily opened.

The knobs on the door reminded Bingmei of the forgotten city beneath the ice. The doors had all been huge, tall enough to fit a dragon. The thought made her shudder.

After a few more pleasantries were exchanged, they stepped into the interior of the garden. The vines were flowering, and the buds wafted a sweet smell at odds with the greed that still lingered in the air.

In short order, they were met by Budai's steward, Guanjia, who approached them with a look of grave concern.

"You're back suddenly," he said with a tone of suspicion. "The season has only just begun. Why do you return so soon, Master Kunmia? Have you quit so easily?"

"Take us to the king," Kunmia answered. "We have come for good reason."

"He will not be pleased to see you, I should think," Guanjia said. "This is highly unusual."

"So are the circumstances of our return," Kunmia answered. "Take us to Budai at once."

Guanjia gave Damanhur a probing look, but the warrior merely folded his arms and nodded for the steward to depart. The man nodded, although he looked less than eager, and quickly went ahead. The throne room was full of servants bearing trays of food. Budai had eaten well during their brief absence and seemed even thicker. Guanjia whispered in his ear as the group made their approach.

There was a new man present, wearing the black silk jacket but no hat. His hair was braided in a queue down his back, and a straight sword was belted to his waist with a red sash. His arms were folded over his chest in an imperious manner. This was Captain Heise, no doubt.

The captain turned to look at the arrivals, which was when his smell struck Bingmei like a fist. She *knew* that rancid smell, having just come from his palace beneath the ice. She gagged at the stench, her eyes watering, fear sapping her strength. The captain's gaze took them in one by one, his lips twisting into a cruel smile.

That smile seemed to tell her that a dragon could fly faster than a boat. Although his resurrected body was far, far away, the part of him that lived in the dragon had preceded them there. It had possessed this man's body or transformed itself into an exact replica of it.

It was abundantly clear to her that Echion had control of this man.

Worry and panic seethed inside her.

Before she could warn Kunmia, her master was striding forward to approach the king. Then she noticed the other guards stationed along the wall, pacing around the columns and watching the new arrivals like prey.

"What is the meaning of this?" King Budai said, giving Kunmia a distrustful look. "Why have you returned so early in the season? If you've found what you sought, you should have left half of the ensign behind to guard it as we agreed. This is unlike you, Kunmia Suun. Surely you have much to account for."

"I do, my lord," Kunmia said, walking past the pretend captain.

"What's wrong?" Quion whispered to Bingmei.

He'd seen her shudder in horror. Bingmei tried to control herself. The Dragon Emperor was staring at her, a knowing stare. Did he know that she had detected him?

She kept her gaze fixed on Kunmia, not wanting to give herself away if she hadn't already.

Kunmia reached the base of the dais. The two chained leopards lifted their heads. One growled at her, earning a pointed kick from the king's foot.

"May we speak in private, King Budai?" Kunmia asked.

Budai looked at Guanjia, who frowned and shook his head.

"I would hear your explanation now," the king said. "These are all my trusted servants. What do you fear, Master Kunmia?"

"I fear causing a panic," she replied. "We did as you asked."

"But did you succeed?" he said. It was impossible to smell him over the awful presence of Echion in the room, but Bingmei could see that doubts had been planted in his mind. Bingmei squeezed her eyes shut, realizing the danger they were in.

"We did," Kunmia said.

Guanjia smirked.

"And what evidence have you brought with you?" Budai said in a feverish tone.

Bingmei couldn't take the suspense any longer. She walked directly toward the throne, keeping the imposter in her peripheral vision, her gaze fixed on the king and Kunmia. After reaching the dais, she knelt before the king. Kunmia had a reproving look on her face, but the interruption could not be helped.

King Budai looked down at Bingmei with equal wariness.

"Wangfujing is in danger," Bingmei said softly. "Your palace is overrun."

"W-What?" Budai said with an astonished chuckle.

"You are already overrun," Bingmei said. The message wasn't truly for the king. It was for Kunmia. Bingmei prayed in her heart that her meaning would be understood.

"You speak nonsense, child," Budai said, his mouth twisting with offense. "Wangfujing has never been more powerful. My guards are loyal. I had hoped both of you were loyal as well."

Kunmia narrowed her gaze. "Can we not speak in private, my lord?"

The king sighed. "Very well. We will retreat to my private chamber. Just the two of you, though. And Captain Heise."

A jolt of fear shot through Bingmei. "Not him," she whispered.

"I've paid him very well for his loyalty," Budai countered. "This is all so highly suspicious. You claim you've been to the Summer Palace, but did you bring anything from it to prove your words?"

Kunmia straightened. "When there is trust, no proof is necessary. When there is none, no proof is possible."

Budai pursed his lips and glanced at Guanjia. The steward still looked skeptical.

Bingmei saw a shadow on the floor touch them. Looking up, she saw Echion standing at the base of the dais in his new body. "Is everything all right, my lord?" he asked with concern. Although his man at the gate had a thick accent, he did not have one at all.

The hairs on Bingmei's arms stood on end. A shudder went through her, and she leaned away from the man.

Budai shifted uncomfortably on his throne. "Can you excuse us . . . Captain?" he said, tilting his head. He looked as if indigestion were wreaking havoc on him.

"Of course, my lord," said the captain. He backed away.

"On second thought," Budai said. "Take your men and patrol the perimeter of the palace. Secure the walls."

"As you command," said the captain, bowing in reverence. He shot Bingmei a weighing look.

When they departed, Bingmei started breathing again.

"Is it the captain?" Kunmia asked as soon as the hired guards were gone.

"Yes," Bingmei said emphatically.

"What nonsense are you talking about?" Budai asked in confusion.

"Echion," said Kunmia. "The Dragon of Night is real, my lord, and we have awakened him."

"Now you are talking of superstitions," Guanjia said disdainfully.

"They are," Kunmia said, turning on him. "And the Dragon of Night is here in your palace, just as the leader of the attack on Wangfujing prophesied. How long has Captain Heise been here?"

"He arrived shortly after you left," Budai said. "With all his warriors."

"How many?" Kunmia demanded.

"Two hundred. Why?"

"It's more than that," Guanjia said.

The king turned on him. "Explain yourself."

Guanjia's face lost color, his manner changing. His smell of self-satisfaction faded. "The washerwomen, the ones who clean the uniforms, told me there are at least three hundred. More keep coming in."

Budai's look turned fearful. "More keep coming? Why didn't you tell me?"

"I wasn't sure at first. But haven't you noticed a change in Heise since he came, my lord? Of late, his suggestions have been more . . . useful. Wiser. As if he were a different man. I hadn't thought much of it until now. I've also heard that he frequently absents himself from the palace and doesn't return promptly. He's the one who warned me that Kunmia Suun might try to steal the treasure of Fusang for herself."

Sweat had appeared on Budai's face. "He has grown more useful. You're right. When he first came, he was taciturn and quiet. I thought he was stupid at first."

"When did he change?" Bingmei asked.

The king and advisor exchanged a look. "Within a few days of his arrival," Budai said.

Kunmia nodded. "That was when we freed him. Echion has been reborn, my lord. He comes to reclaim his lost empire."

"But what do we *do*?" Budai implored. He mopped his sweating forehead with a silk kerchief.

Damanhur and Rowen approached the dais.

"What's going on?" Damanhur said worriedly.

Bingmei turned to him. "He's here. Echion. He's taken possession of Captain Heise."

Damanhur's brow furrowed. "You're certain?"

There was no mistaking that stench, which had left the chamber as soon as he'd gone. Bingmei nodded quickly.

To her astonishment, they believed her. She smelled it, saw it in their faces.

"We can't stay here," Rowen said, glancing at the door.

"But where can we go?" Budai said.

Kunmia folded her arms. "Sajinau. We must warn King Shulian. Wangfujing is already lost."

CHAPTER
TWENTY-FIVE

When Ravens Flee

The king's face became ashen, and he struggled to control his emotions. Bingmei smelled them simmering beneath his perpetual greed. He was afraid, but he was also unwilling to part with the wealth and artifacts he had accumulated. With a sidelong glance at his steward, he shook his head no and leaned back. Then he rose and gestured for them to follow him out of the throne room.

When they reached the corridor, he kept his voice low. "I cannot walk away from my . . . people," he said hesitantly. "And I'm not as vulnerable as you likely think. Am I to abandon Wangfujing without a fight?"

Kunmia kept in stride with him. "You do not understand. None of us truly know what we are up against. This being, this ancient king, possesses magic we cannot hope to defeat."

"But I have magic artifacts too," Budai said, his tone growing angry. The mixture of fear, anger, and greed stung Bingmei's nose. "One that protects me. Others I haven't dared use. Perhaps one of my artifacts can defeat him? Damanhur . . . you are brave. Do you agree with Kunmia's plan to run away?"

Bingmei bristled at his choice of words and shot Damanhur a look.

The warrior frowned and cocked his eyebrow. "Think of it this way, Budai. If Echion unites the Qiangdao, he will destroy everyone. All they have lacked is a strong leader. I agree that we must warn King Shulian at once."

"Of course we must," Budai said. "But send a messenger. Why not defend Wangfujing first? You are both capable masters with strong reputations. I cannot abandon my people." He shook his head. "I will not."

"Be sensible," Kunmia said. "Although the city is highly defensible from outside attack, Echion has three hundred men inside your city walls. If you come with us, we have a better likelihood of convincing Shulian of the truth. You do not care about your people as much as you pretend to."

Budai's eyes flashed with anger. "Are you chastising me, Kunmia Suun?"

"I am speaking the truth when you most need to hear it. Abandon your treasures. They are not worth losing your life."

Bingmei felt a prickle of awareness go down her spine. She sensed the approach of the unseen presence she'd felt before. The dragon. It was approaching the corridor.

"Be still," Bingmei warned. She looked around the space, taking in its expensive decorations and artifacts. "He's coming."

"I thought you commanded him to secure the walls?" Guanjia said.

The invisible presence entered the room. Nervous warning thrummed inside her. She couldn't see the dragon, nor did she understand how it could fit in such a tight space, but she could nonetheless sense its blackness, the inky shadows of its wings. She felt unmistakably that it was watching them.

Kunmia watched Bingmei's face. "No one speak," she said.

The flesh on Bingmei's neck prickled as if something were about to touch her. Fear churned in her heart at the unseen enemy who was among them. She felt the raw terror of a helpless animal in the presence of a predator.

Then, in an instant, she felt a spark of savagery flare in her chest. Magic burst out of her fingers and toes, chasing the black feeling out of the room.

She had no idea what was happening to her, but it felt like she had somehow driven away their unseen enemy.

"It's gone," Bingmei whispered.

"This is utter madness," Budai exclaimed. "Kunmia Suun, you are being deceived. This girl has convinced you of some whimsy."

"Hardly so, my lord," Kunmia answered. "Just because we cannot feel the danger she does, it doesn't mean the danger is not real. Come with us to Sajinau."

"No!" Budai said. "I will defend what is mine. You work for me, Kunmia, not Shulian. I order you to stay and defend Wangfujing. I will command Captain Heise to step down and take his soldiers away. What you've told me is preposterous. I won't abandon what I've won on the word of one small girl."

Kunmia's mouth turned down. "I will not obey this order, my lord."

Budai's eyes flashed with arrogance and anger. "Then you will not be paid. None of you will." He shot Rowen a vengeful look, then faced Damanhur. "Will you obey my commands?"

Damanhur clenched his jaw. "You owe us payment for our efforts."

"What for? You brought me nothing of value," Budai said curtly. "In fact, you owe me for your stay. Obey me, and I will clear the debt."

"I will not be part of this any longer," Kunmia announced. "You've lost your honor, Budai. Your greed has finally consumed you."

"Well, Damanhur?" Budai said, glaring up at him. "What will it be?"

"You're a fool," Damanhur said. He looked to Kunmia and nodded. "Shall we go, Master?"

Budai's face went black with rage. "You will regret those words. And your choice."

"Perhaps," Damanhur said. "But I doubt it."

"Guanjia, secure the treasury. Then order Captain Heise to see me alone. I want twenty of my own trusted guards at the ready. Alone, Guanjia. See to it."

"Y-yes, my lord," Guanjia answered nervously.

"We go to Sajinau," Kunmia said.

As Bingmei turned, she saw that the fisherman, Keyi, was already gone.

杀雾

Kunmia led the way toward one of the opulent palace's back exits. Torches lit the halls as there were no windows. Bingmei did not smell or feel the presence of Echion. The desire to escape made her walk quickly.

"That went about as poorly as I could have guessed," Marenqo grumbled.

"I suspect Keyi has gone back to his boat," Quion said.

"You think?" Marenqo chuckled. "He wants what he was promised more than anything. He'll not take us to Sajinau."

"I know other merchants who will," Kunmia said.

As they reached the door that would lead to the rear gardens of the palace, a voice called out to them.

"Master, wait!"

It was Guanjia.

Kunmia turned and gave the steward a dismissive look. "More threats? Does the king intend to waylay us?"

"No," the steward said, hurrying to catch up with them. "I believe you."

Bingmei smelled that he wasn't lying. He was loyal to his master, but despite the cool welcome he'd given them, he'd realized the error of his ways. The error of Budai's ways. The conflict roiled within him, giving off fumes.

"Will you come with us?" Kunmia asked pointedly.

Guanjia rubbed his brow and shook his head no. "I cannot abandon my master. But don't go yet. I will try to persuade him to go with you."

"We cannot delay," Kunmia said firmly. "The situation is urgent."

"Please! I implore you. I know of a merchant ship preparing to sail tonight for Sajinau. Its cargo finished loading yesterday, and the crew lingered to enjoy one last day among the pleasures of Wangfujing before setting sail. Captain Guoduan."

"I know him from Sajinau," Damanhur said. "He's a good man."

Guanjia nodded excitedly. "He is! And trusted. King Budai gives him certain artifacts to sell to interested customers."

"I can secure passage without your help, Guanjia," Kunmia said. "Budai broke my trust."

"Please," the man begged. "Your words unsettled him too much. Give him time to come around. Wait until nightfall, at the least. You can hardly call that a delay. I will ensure, Master Kunmia, that payment for your services is sent to your quonsuun immediately. I am empowered to discharge Budai's debts."

Kunmia gripped the rune staff, her knuckles turning white. "I do not want his money. I will not accept it unless he begs my pardon. You and I both know he will not."

Guanjia bowed his head. "I beg it on his behalf, Master Kunmia. Give me time to help him reconsider. Sunset is all I ask."

Bingmei couldn't feel any deception in Guanjia's words. But she doubted the steward could convince Budai to change his mind so quickly. Kunmia glanced at Bingmei, her brow wrinkling slightly.

It was an implied question. Was Guanjia being truthful? Could he be trusted in this?

Sighing, Bingmei nodded.

"Sunset," Kunmia said. Then she turned and walked away.

"Captain Guoduan's ship is a junk with two masts. The sails are black. The ship is called the *Raven*."

They exited the palace, finding two of Budai's guards standing outside. The men nodded, however, and let them leave without question. The rear garden featured a huge boulder that had been dredged from a faraway river. Running water had worn holes through it in various places. It was surrounded by trees and a little fence to prevent people from touching the smooth stone. The dappled daylight was pleasant, but Bingmei's nerves were taut. Quion looked worried too, and kept glancing back to see if they were being followed.

So far, they were not.

After passing the pleasant garden, they reached the eastern gate of the palace compound and found the black-silk guards blocking the way. Twenty of them stood at attention, holding pikes and swords.

As they approached, one of the mercenaries stepped in front of the others. "No one is to leave," he said curtly.

Kunmia did not slow. "We are not staying."

"Captain Heise has ordered everyone to remain within the palace." He gestured with his chin to the other mercenaries, who sidled up near him, forming a wall of flesh before the wall of stone.

Kunmia stopped when she reached the man. "Open the door," she said, nodding to it.

"Captain Heise—"

She swung her staff into his gut, making him bend double, and then cracked it over his skull, dropping him to the ground. The combined ensigns charged the mercenaries. One of the black-shirts tried to escape, and Bingmei used her cricket charm to fling herself after him. She landed on his back, knocking him down, and delivered a punch to his kidneys. He groaned and then lay still as she straightened and looked back. The gate was no longer defended.

As she walked back to the others, Kunmia was gesturing for them to leave. A shout rose in the distance. Two patrolling black-shirts had just witnessed the ambush. They sounded the alarm and ran away, bellowing for other mercenaries to come.

But they weren't about to wait around for an attack. The gate was unguarded, and they quickly left, entering the abandoned alley behind the palace. Soon Bingmei and the others were blending in with the sizeable crowd.

"Separate," Kunmia instructed. "They'll be looking for us as a group. Everyone meet at the *Raven*."

杀雾

Quion and Bingmei went together, as they'd done before, crossing the bridges and changing their course multiple times. Within an hour, the black-shirts' pursuit had begun in earnest. Groups of six or more stormed past, carrying weapons in their hands, mostly sabers. They shoved aside anyone who didn't clear away fast enough, and the mood in the market darkened with their hostility. Some passersby were randomly accosted and questioned, but the crowd was too vast for them to find the ensigns.

So far, Quion and Bingmei had managed to escape notice, but Quion smelled nervous and agitated. Every time a group of mercenaries passed, he would deliberately look away, trying not to be noticed.

"Stop that," Bingmei said with exasperation after it happened for the third time.

"Stop what?"

"Looking away from them. It makes you look guilty. It draws attention." Another group of mercenaries turned the corner, and Bingmei grabbed Quion's arm and pointed to one of the merchant stalls. "Oooh, look at that jade carving! It's beautiful! Buy it for me?"

He looked at her in confusion. "You want me to buy—?"

Bingmei tugged on his arm and approached the stall. "How much?" she demanded of the merchant.

"Fifty cowry shells," the man grunted. "It comes from Dintai!"

"It's not worth more than twenty," Bingmei said. "Who cares where it came from?"

The mercenaries passed, and Bingmei quit the negotiating, tugging Quion with her as she left the stand.

"Oh!" he said, looking back at the merchant, who barked out another bid. "You didn't *really* want it."

Bingmei shook her head in wonderment at his innocence, but it was endearing. Crossing another bridge, they continued toward the edge of the town where the ships were docked. No ship with a tall mast would be able to make it under the arches. Merchants passed them, pushing carts stacked with goods, including ones full of fish. It was the most prosperous time of year, and the season was still new.

As they passed people, Bingmei felt a little envious of their ignorance of what was coming. Would Echion band the Qiangdao together at last? In her mind's eye, she recalled the devastation of the Qiangdao's attack on Wangfujing mere weeks before. There were still char marks on some of the walls from where the flames had ravaged the buildings. It was hard to imagine Wangfujing being razed.

But it could happen. The being she'd raised in Fusang would change everything.

"I see the *Raven*," Quion said. He pointed at it, and she pushed his hand down, giving him a scolding look. "I'm sorry," he muttered.

The junk did have two masts, and the furled sails were indeed black. The boat looked heavy in the water, laden with cargo. As she and Quion ventured closer, walking down the dock, Bingmei saw Kunmia standing on deck, speaking with a large man with folded arms.

They approached the ship, but a commotion rose behind them on the docks. Turning, Bingmei saw Guanjia with a long box clutched in his arms, running and wheezing down the dock, his robes flapping behind him.

And then she saw a group of mercenaries chasing him, shouting for others to stand aside.

"Stop that man!"

Two men loitering on the docks suddenly stepped into Guanjia's way. Bingmei saw his eyes light with terror as they grabbed him.

CHAPTER
TWENTY-SIX
Passage to Sajinau

Bingmei was racked with uncertainty as she watched Guanjia's capture. She was the closest member of the ensign, the one with the best chance of helping him, yet doing so would put her in conflict with the black-shirt guards. That, in turn, could prevent their escape from Wangfujing.

Kunmia was too far away to give her orders, and Quion was useless in a fight. What should she do?

Guanjia saw her and shouted her name. "Bingmei! Help me!" She frowned in frustration, her decision being forced on her.

She gripped Quion by the arm. "When I free him, get him to the junk."

"Ten guards are following him!" Quion said.

"Do as I say," she replied firmly and started walking toward the men who had taken hold of Guanjia. The guards were still battling their way through the crowd, so she made it there first.

"Unhand me!" Guanjia said in a fearful voice. "I'm King Budai's steward! Let me go!"

One of the men wrenched the long box from his arms. "How do we know that? Maybe you're a thief!"

"Give me that!" Guanjia snarled. He tried reaching for it, but the man held it up and away.

Bingmei slammed her fist into the man's ribs, surprising him. He wilted in pain, dropping the box as he bent double to hold his wounded side. Bingmei caught the box and pitched it to Quion, who was still approaching. He caught it.

The other man restraining Guanjia shot Bingmei a fearful look.

"Let him go," she said in a low voice.

Whatever he heard in her voice must have chastened him, for he released Guanjia and backed away.

"Thank you," the steward gasped, his face streaked with sweat. Fear came off him in waves. "He stabbed my master!" Guanjia said in a choking voice. "Heise tried to murder him!"

She felt as if she'd been punched in the ribs. "Get to the boat."

"Stop! By order of King Budai, stop!" shouted the nearest blackshirt. He shoved aside an onlooker who had stopped in confusion. Bingmei gave Guanjia a little push toward Quion and turned to face the approaching guards.

The area quickly cleared, leaving her to face them alone.

"You let him go!" the first guard shouted.

"He's the king's steward," Bingmei said, watching as the others fanned out in front of her.

"He betrayed the king!" the man rejoined. "Captain Heise has ordered him to be brought back."

"She's the one," said another of the other guards in a furtive voice. She needn't ask what that meant.

The leader's eyes narrowed, and they all rushed her as one.

Bingmei had expected it. She slipped her hand into her pocket and stroked the cricket charm. As their hands reached to grab her, she felt the magic jolt her legs against the ground. She jumped above and over them, watching as the mass of black-shirts collided with one another where she'd been standing. A gasp went up from the crowd.

The first to recover launched himself at her. She deflected a punch sent at her face, trapped his arm between her forearms, and broke his elbow with a quick scissoring move. The man shrieked in pain. She kicked him down, but two more men were already punching and kicking at her. Although she sent one tottering backward with a low, sweeping kick, the other one avoided her tactic and did a hammer-fist strike against her head.

His speed startled her, as did the sudden concussion of pain. Her vision spotted with black, and she struggled to rise, but it felt as if a cart had landed on top of her.

"Get her! Hold her!"

Her muscles felt sluggish, and she couldn't summon the energy to fight. To escape them. Someone yanked at her hair, and she felt the pins holding the wig scrape painfully against her scalp.

"She *is* the one! It's her!"

Someone kicked her ribs, knocking the wind from her. Unable to breathe, she clawed her fingers into the face of the closest guard, then heard him cry out in pain. A single gulp of air made it into her lungs, but it left them just as quickly. Someone grabbed her middle and squeezed, lifting her. She managed to get in a kick before her legs were also encircled. Three or four men were holding her, and she wished she'd run as soon as she'd seen Guanjia captured.

"Bring her to the palace!" came a guttural voice, groaning with pain. "You four, arrest the steward!"

Bingmei struggled against her captors, her vision finally beginning to clear. Pain throbbed in her skull, but she was desperate to escape. Teeth. She tried to bite the one holding her, but no matter how she stretched her neck, she could not reach him. The crowd shrank from the violence. No one stepped forward to help—she saw only fearful looks.

Until Marenqo pushed through the crowd, having come up from behind the guards on the way to the junk. His eye was still bruised and scabbed from his wound at the Summer Palace, but he was quick and decisive as he strode forward and struck the neck of one of the men holding her legs. He grabbed the second man from behind, sending him flailing backward. With her legs free, Bingmei flipped them up and crossed them around the neck of the man who held her arms. She punched him where it hurt a man the most, and he sagged down on his knees, unable to bear her weight any longer.

Marenqo grabbed Bingmei's arm and helped her stand, and she threw her arms around him, giving him a fierce hug before turning and kicking another man in the chest.

It was then the smells hit her. The crowd that had gathered around them could see her hair and its freakish color. Her wig was nowhere to be seen. The smell of revulsion, disdain, abhorrence was like the smell of garbage left to rot. It came at her from all sides. She put her hand to her mouth, trying to block the stench, but it seeped through her fingers, filling her lungs.

The looks they gave her brought out all her dread, all her fear. She was an object of disgust.

"Come," Marenqo said, putting an arm around her, and led her toward the junk. Someone spat at them, which seemed to break an unseen dam. Others began to spit on them. To fling insults. The words were thick with scorn and contempt. It roused in her a deep-seated anger. These were the people they struggled to help? She never wanted to return to Wangfujing. Ever.

"It's all right," Marenqo soothed. One of the gobs of spit struck his face. His nose wrinkled in disgust, but he did not pause to wipe it away.

Suddenly, Quion was walking on her other side, shielding her from the barrage as they passed. Her stomach felt empty, sick.

"Get back!" Quion shouted. Someone hurled a piece of spoiled fruit at them, and it struck Quion in the shoulder as he hunched closer to protect her.

Her anger increased to a blistering outrage. Not only were they humiliating her, but her friends as well.

"Back off!" Marenqo shouted at them.

She felt some things pelt them from behind and realized the crowd was following them, throwing taunts and insults along with the debris. Bingmei shriveled inside, wanting the nightmare to be over. She glanced ahead, her skull still throbbing, as more rotten food pelted them. The smell of the food made her nostrils twitch, but it was nothing compared to the stench from the crowd. If she'd been alone, she sensed some of them would have been frightened and disgusted enough to try to drown her in the river.

The smell changed abruptly to fear, and the crowd backed up. Lifting her head, she saw Damanhur and Prince Rowen, blades drawn, stalk down the dock with menacing looks. As the crowd parted, she saw the five black-shirts who had gone after Guanjia kneel on the dock in submission.

Damanhur snarled, whipping his sword around in an elaborate twirl. He charged at the crowd to terrify them, and the effect was immediate. They scattered like rats.

"We made it," Marenqo said. They had reached the junk. Kunmia removed her cloak as she came down the ramp. She swung the thick cloth around Bingmei's shoulders and lifted the cowl to cover her copper hair. Mieshi was already there, holding her staff, ready to fight, but she couldn't hide her feelings. Part of her loathed Bingmei as the crowd did.

"Thank you, Marenqo," Kunmia said with relief.

"No one snatches our little ice rose," he said, squeezing Bingmei's shoulder with affection. They climbed onto the deck, where they found the stern captain, Guoduan, speaking with Guanjia furtively. He was a massive man with long hair braided in a queue.

"We must set sail at once, Captain!" Guanjia insisted. "There is no time to delay. Budai is dead. I saw the dagger go in his belly. Please, we must go!"

"How did you escape?" the captain asked. He glanced at Bingmei and Quion with a frown, but the steward held his attention.

Bingmei lost the thread of their conversation as Quion led her to a bench. He wiped his face and then started picking scraps of spoiled fruit from her shirt. His eyes were dark, and she smelled the burnt odor of his anger as he struggled with it. He, too, was angry at the mob who treated her with such scorn. She saw tenderness in his eyes, smelled an almost sugary scent coming from him. He knelt by her and moved aside the cloak so he could brush off the bits of filth. As she sat, her teeth chattering, she saw that something spoiled, like an eggplant, had smashed against her upper leg. She hadn't even felt it.

Quion scooped up the mess from her leg, his lips twisting with the unpleasant feeling, but he made no complaint about the vile task. The rage and hatred had burned out, leaving her with an empty feeling in her chest. Like she would never *feel* again. But she did, and it was a small pulse of gratitude for Quion. She should be cleaning herself, not letting him do it for her. She looked into his face, into his eyes, and he didn't smell quite so much like fish in that moment.

"Thank you," she whispered.

He wouldn't meet her gaze, just shook his head like nothing he was doing was out of the ordinary. And maybe it wasn't, for him, but although he was a simple man, he was an extraordinary one. She appreciated him.

Marenqo came over to join them. He picked a spoiled hunk from his shirt and flung it into the water with a sigh. "That was rather disgusting."

"Thank you, Marenqo," she said.

His mouth quirked into a smile. "I think I've soured on Wangfujing for a while." He gazed over her shoulder at the bustling town. "Maybe they deserve what's coming. Ah, Kunmia and the others are back. It looks like we'll be off before more of those mercenaries arrive."

Bingmei's resentment usually ran deep, but her heart still felt dull. Brittle. She watched as the loaded junk cast away from the dock and began trudging up the river. The black sails rippled as they groped for wind.

"I'm glad you made it," Mieshi said to her. The words were well intended, but there was a sour smell coming from her. A tangled conflict roiled inside her. She'd lost her bond sister, Zhuyi. Bingmei wasn't a suitable replacement.

Wangfujing began to lurch away from them. Bingmei wondered, deep inside, if she'd ever return. She reached in her shirt for the scorpion pendant. Gripping it hard, she yanked it fast. The chain broke. She let it drop to the floor and nudged it away with her boot.

杀雾

Night had fallen, but the junk plodded through the choppy waters of the fjord. Night was welcome. Night concealed. Captain Guoduan had ordered the lanterns to be covered to disguise their passage. Some of his crew watched the waters ahead.

Bingmei's mood had darkened with the fading light. Her anger was reviving again, but it was manageable. At least she was gone from Wangfujing. But her ears still rang with the insults flung by the crowd. And she remembered the smells. Every splash from the river that landed on her reminded her of the spit.

Marenqo had left to eat, and when he returned, he said that Kunmia wished to speak with her. Bingmei still wasn't hungry, but she followed him to the back of the ship, where the captain stood gripping the massive rudder. The ship had about five other crew members to work the sails. Kunmia, Rowen, Damanhur, and Mieshi were also gathered at the back. Marenqo left her after bringing her up to them. Some of the crew huddled under the wooden roof beneath the main sail and slept. This junk was much bigger than Keyi's fishing boat.

Bingmei gazed up at the constellations and felt an overwhelming sensation of insignificance. The others smelled normal to her, but the captain was concerned. He did not smell of disgust or trepidation, only the pungent aroma of worry. When he looked at her, he nodded in greeting.

"Did you get any rest?" Kunmia asked her in a kindly way.

Bingmei shook her head. "I'm not tired."

"How is your head? Does it still hurt?"

Bingmei nodded, and the sensation made her a little dizzy. She winced.

Kunmia put her arm around her and pulled her closer. "We have time to get some rest. Captain Guoduan knows the safest route to Sajinau."

The bitter smell of resentment came from Prince Rowen. His expression was neutral, but she felt emotion roiling off him in waves. His fortunes had been ruined. He was returning home with dishonor, and worse, he needed help. The smell of onions stung her eyes.

"How long will it take to reach it?" Bingmei asked. "It's quite a distance."

"Yes, that's true," Kunmia said. "But a junk can travel much faster in open water. We'll reach the high seas tomorrow, and then we'll sail in the ocean to reach Sajinau. We should be there by the end of the week. If we're lucky." She paused. "There's something else we learned from Captain Guoduan."

Damanhur sighed, his hands on his hips. The smell of onions grew worse.

"What?" Bingmei asked in concern. It clearly wasn't good news.

"King Shulian isn't at Sajinau. He left last season to visit a quon-suun deep in the mountains on the western rim past Sihui. He hasn't returned. His son, Crown Prince Juexin, is ruling the kingdom in his absence."

Bingmei looked at Rowen, who was staring overboard, his feelings becoming even more pungent.

Kunmia put her hand on Bingmei's shoulder. "We don't know how the crown prince will react when he learns his brother has returned."

CHAPTER TWENTY-SEVEN

Brothers of the Blood

The news caught Bingmei by surprise and more than explained the shift in Rowen's scent. She didn't know much about the circumstances surrounding Rowen's departure, but she did know he'd planned to rule in his brother's stead. She didn't relish the idea of facing a family rift.

"I see," Bingmei said. "In other words, we may not be entirely welcome when we get there."

"Quite the contrary," said Captain Guoduan. He had a steady look about him, and his manner of dress had a certain flair—there were sea turtles stitched onto his cuffs, and he wore a gold medallion shaped as a raven. An actual bird perched on a rung near the tiller, and its beady eyes watched them. A nearby cage sat empty, but apparently the raven was trusted to be loose. The captain had clearly grown rich in his trade. "Prince Rowen will be welcomed home. He's popular in many quarters."

Rowen glared at the captain but said nothing in reply.

"Why would King Shulian travel so far from his kingdom?" Bingmei asked.

"We don't know that," Kunmia answered. "Captain Guoduan said he has become more introspective of late. More concerned about death and what will happen to Sajinau after he's gone."

The captain was more than willing to speak for himself. "Personally, I think he's left to give his eldest son the chance to rule. Since naming Juexin crown prince two years ago, he has handed over more and more responsibility to him. Much like a captain grooming his second to take his place. King Shulian is very wise."

"That is true," Kunmia said. "But these are dangerous times, and his leadership is needed now more than ever. Word must be sent to him immediately. As I explained to you, we face no mere mortal threat. Echion has already proven that he can travel great distances and wear the guise of another person."

"What happened after we left Budai's palace?" Bingmei asked worriedly. "Where is Guanjia now?"

"He's sleeping. His mind is very disturbed. Following our departure from the palace, he went to the treasury room. It's a vault, and only he carries the key. He chose several magical artifacts to aid us and a great deal of money. Those were in the box that he carried. After securing the vault, he went to the throne room where Budai was waiting. They spoke, and Guanjia persuaded Budai to come to the *Raven*."

"Guanjia persuaded him?" Damanhur said incredulously. He rubbed his mouth. "I'm surprised. Budai was stubborn."

"Indeed. But he was cunning too. It won't be easy for Echion to steal his treasures. But that's beside the point. Budai trusted his steward, and Guanjia is persuasive. The decision had barely been made when Captain Heise—or Echion—came as summoned. We had already caused a stir by defeating the guards left at the east gate, and Heise demanded the authority to arrest our ensign. He had no other guards with him, as instructed, and Guanjia had summoned at least twenty guards he believed loyal. Budai ordered them to arrest the captain."

Bingmei's heart raced in anticipation as the story was told. She'd visited the throne room many times and could picture the events in her mind. Budai had not often let anger get the better of him, but his rage, when it came, was terrible to behold.

"The guards rushed to apprehend him. Guanjia said he attacked with just his fists. He was clearly a practitioner of dianxue, and could incapacitate a man with a single blow. He struck quickly, leaping high into the air at times, as if carried on invisible wings. It shocked and horrified them. Budai loosed his two leopards and tried to flee, but Echion soared across the room and blocked the door. He then drew his blade and stabbed Budai's belly. When Guanjia saw his master fall, he tried to save his own life, grabbing the box and leaving the palace through a secret passage. He managed to evade the black-shirts until just before reaching the docks, when he was spotted. He thinks it's possible Budai survived. He has a meiwood charm. But if he did, he's helpless."

The news sickened Bingmei. She was grateful they had made it out of Wangfujing at all.

Damanhur breathed out sharply. "With Echion's ability to transform into other people . . ."

Kunmia nodded. "We have to assume he can take on Budai's identity and rule Wangfujing in his stead."

"Could an army hope to defeat him?" Damanhur wondered.

"Eventually? Maybe?" Kunmia said, shrugging. "We don't know. Which is why it is imperative that King Shulian be summoned back to Sajinau. Our only advantage is that his disguises cannot deceive Bingmei. That makes safeguarding her one of our primary duties." Kunmia gave her a sharp look. "And why we must avoid danger. You were almost captured."

"I'm not reckless," Bingmei objected hotly. "Guanjia shouted my name!"

"No, you aren't reckless," Kunmia said. "But there is something different about you. And not just the color of your skin or your unusual hair. When Echion was reborn, I first thought he was an old man because of his white hair. But it's not white. It's just . . . pale. It's different. You are connected to Echion in some way. One of his people, I think."

Kunmia's words chased around in her mind and her heart. Had she not wondered the same thing upon seeing him?

"The more I've pondered this, the more I realized that you were *summoned* to Fusang," Kunmia said. Her words only confirmed what Bingmei had felt all along.

"How can that be, Master?" Damanhur said, his brow furrowed, his tone fierce. "Who summoned her?"

Kunmia sighed. "The Qiangdao found Fusang before we did. Likely they also found the Phoenix Blade in the tomb. I don't know the truth; I'm just hazarding a guess. Echion was unable to revive himself. That much is clear, or he would not have needed Bingmei to do it. After our mission last summer, the Qiangdao were waiting for us. They ambushed us. Was that an accident? Or did Echion send some Qiangdao with the blade to find her?"

Damanhur tilted his head. "It could be coincidence."

"No," Rowen said, shaking his head. "There was something about that blade. I felt it drawing me as well."

Damanhur looked at him in surprise. "I thought you just wanted to buy it."

"It was more than that," Rowen said. He looked at Bingmei. "Wasn't it?"

She remembered the strange ghostlike vision she'd had. She'd never told anyone about it. At that moment, she wasn't sure whether she should speak of it or not. Kunmia's words made sense to her. Had she not wondered at the sequence of events? But she still felt wary around Rowen and his conflicting emotions.

She couldn't trust him.

杀雾

The *Raven* rushed up and over the huge ocean swells with the ease of its namesake bird. Bingmei admired the power of the wind the captain and his crew harnessed with the massive black sails. She'd hardly seen Quion at all during the voyage. He was enamored with the vessel, and Kunmia had arranged with Captain Guoduan for him to lend a hand. He was already skilled with knot tying and knew the essentials of sailing, but traveling in the vast ocean was an entirely different type of sailing.

When the sky poured down rain, everyone crowded beneath the teakwood roof in the center of the boat. There was little room in any of the compartments below deck because of the cargo. Bingmei enjoyed exploring the boat to drive off the monotony of the voyage. They were so far from land that only the vague shape of mountains could be seen in the distance. The sea looked like a field that went on for eternity.

Captain Guoduan had a map that had landmarks on it to help guide the journey, but he mostly used the stars at night. He'd let Bingmei gaze at the map, and it looked like the land was just a huge bow of islands and inlets scattered from west to east over a vast ocean. At the center of the bow was nothing but glaciers, and it was at one of those that they'd discovered Fusang. In fact, she saw that a recent sketch had added a palace in the midst of the ice fields. She wondered if Quion had pointed it out to the captain.

Bingmei brooded constantly about being the one who had freed Echion from his tomb. She couldn't even understand *how* it had happened. How had she known the glyph that had revived him? She thought on it over and over until her head hurt. At night, she had difficulty falling asleep. Her skull still throbbed from the blow she'd been dealt in Wangfujing.

The sky was often devoid of clouds, and an overwhelming sense of nothingness would wash over her as she stared up at the stars. Her ignorance ran so deep she felt like crying. What were the stars? How had the world come into existence? Why did she need to breathe? What was the purpose of it all?

In those moments, the utter chaos of the world pressed against her, and she shivered beneath her fur blanket, feeling as small as a mote of dust flitting with a breeze. She'd heard the various myths of creation, of course, but there were so many. All different. Which one should she believe in? The tales of death were equally confusing. Why did some people believe that the afterlife was a giant labyrinth, like the fjords that riddled the coastline, while others believed in rebirth? A cruel king could be born again as a quivering worm in order to teach him humility. What would Budai be reborn as, then? A frog? Or perhaps he'd been a frog in his previous life, and he'd collected sculptures of them because he was compelled by a forgotten memory? There were so many myths, yet nothing satisfied the craving for purpose in her soul. Why had she been born with the winter sickness? Or was it even a sickness at all? Why could she smell in a way others could not? There were never any answers to her questions.

On the fourth night of the voyage, she was struggling, again, with sleeplessness. The moon hadn't risen yet, and the darkness seemed especially deep, as it did during the season of the Dragon of Night. She sat still, staring at those who slept. Of her group, Rowen was the only one still awake. She spied him at the prow, leaning against the front, watching the junk slice through the water.

Her feelings of loneliness were so terrible that she rose from the bench and carefully picked her way over to him. Whenever she'd tried to share her sullen feelings with Quion, he'd looked at her in confusion, unable to relate to her grim feelings of purposelessness. His mind never wandered that far or plunged into the deep. But she had an instinct that Prince Rowen would understand. He brooded more than her, it seemed.

Rowen glanced back when he heard her coming. The wind struck from the west, and so she didn't smell him until she was practically next to him. She leaned against the rail, staring down at the breakers striking against the hull of the junk. He said nothing to her, although it wasn't a mean-spirited thing. He smelled thoughtful, worried, and morose. It was a pungent blend.

It was up to her to break the silence.

"Do you hate your brother?" she asked, gazing at the water that seemed to never end. It was difficult believing that Sajinau lay ahead in the gloom. There was no trace of it, no light on the horizon to reveal it.

"I do," he answered simply, then sighed. "But it's more complicated than that."

"Tell me about him," she said. The spray from the water made her face damp, but it felt strangely soothing.

"Why?" he asked with a chuckle.

"Because I'm about to meet him, and I'd like to know more about who he is."

His lips pursed just a little. "I don't want to influence you. You may end up liking him."

A little whiff of jealousy accompanied the words.

"Why do you say that?" she asked.

He sighed again, but his voice, when he spoke, was full of loathing. "Because everyone likes him. He's perfect. Handsome. Strong-willed. Dutiful. Commanding. Insufferable."

"Was he cruel to you?"

"Never," Rowen said. "He's arrogant, to be sure. Demeaning to others who do not meet his level of perfection. He always tried to make me more . . . like . . . him." He snorted. "It was like having *two* fathers. And my sister usually took his side."

"You have a sister?"

"Yes. Eomen. We used to be close, then she became insufferable too. I don't see things the way they do. My brother tries so hard to be just like Father. I think he's never had an original thought in his life," he muttered at the end.

"How does he feel about you?" Bingmei asked. His feelings matched his words, but he was still jealous. Jealous of his brother's popularity. Of his father's preference for him.

"That's what we're about to find out," he said, turning to face her. His eyes gleamed in the starlight. "That is what I most want to know. And what I most dread." His eyes narrowed. "Your power frightens me, Bingmei. We are all laid bare."

CHAPTER
TWENTY-EIGHT
Unspeakable Grief

Marenqo had attempted to describe Sajinau's splendor to Bingmei before they arrived, but even he was at a loss for words.

"Just wait until you see it for yourself," he said. "It's not as grand as what we saw under the ice. But it's impressive. You'll see."

They arrived at the port of Sajinau the following day, after an especially turbulent night at sea. Captain Guoduan had arrived in record time, for which Bingmei was grateful. She watched eagerly as the snow-peaked mountains rose from the horizon like the dawning of a sun.

Sajinau, like Wangfujing, lay inside a massive fjord. But unlike Wangfujing, there were guard towers positioned at the entrance of the fjord, and she could see the smoke trailing from the flaming torches within them. The *Raven* was not alone in the water. Many junks came in and out, passing beneath the eyes of the sentinels guarding the way.

The inner chasm was broad enough for many ships to pass through side by side. Captain Guoduan carefully attended the tiller, and his pet raven squawked whenever another boat was seen. Anticipation bubbled inside Bingmei as they entered the fjord. She gazed up at the watchtowers, wishing she had wings like a raven's so she could fly up to enjoy the view.

A labyrinth of small waterways unfurled after they entered the fjord, weaving through the rubble of shattered mountains. But the captain knew his course. Quion worked closely with the crew still, and she saw the respect in the eyes of the sailors who had come to value his contributions. It made her smile.

Prince Rowen's looks darkened as they entered the shadows of the fjord. He was coming home. Bingmei sensed he had been gone for some time.

As the ship passed through the fjord, she saw additional guard towers built on the cliff walls. She wondered if there were ways to communicate between the towers, like signal fires, something to inform the whole kingdom of any invading forces. There were no houses or walls along the shore, nor was there room for them. The cliffs themselves provided protection.

When Sajinau came into view at last, Bingmei walked to the edge of the junk and gripped the railing in wonder. Her eyes feasted on the scene. The thick green trees and colorful gorse made the view particularly delightful. It was the largest city she had ever seen, dwarfing the size of Wangfujing. At the end of the inlet lay a wide, flat basin, around which the city and its palace had been constructed. Tree-covered mountains towered behind the city, providing ample protection there. In a distant valley, she saw a section of the Death Wall with its square turrets. She also saw evidence of a glacier in the range of mountains, feeding the fjord with ice and water.

Wooded hills engulfed the edges of the town, and the row of docks teemed with junks of all sizes and shapes. Now she understood why King Shulian was so respected. His kingdom enjoyed natural protections and was blessed with an uncultivated beauty that rivaled any in the living world.

The palace could be seen on a cleft of rock above the city, massive and ancient in construction. Yes, it was a good place to build a city, and it had gathered a population over the years that numbered in the thousands.

The harbor was patrolled by royal junks, and they were met by one of them and directed to a berth.

Damanhur prowled the deck restlessly. Mieshi watched him, her look impassive, but she smelled interested in him. He watched as the city drew near, his eyes furtively glancing to Rowen, who had seated himself beneath the pavilion and held his head in his hands. Most of Damanhur's ensign had survived the ordeal, but they all looked despondent about returning to Sajinau, as if doing so had brought dishonor to them.

As the ship approached the wharf, Bingmei saw a crowd had assembled. Some held banners with streamers, which fluttered in the winds. Bingmei noticed that the wharf they approached only contained royal ships.

Damanhur noticed it too. "Captain, what's going on? What did you tell them?"

Captain Guoduan frowned. "I told them about our cargo, and they directed me here."

"There are no merchants junks here," Damanhur pointed out.

"So I've noticed, Bao Damanhur."

The wharf was thronged with people. Not merchants but citizens.

Rowen stood from the bench. "I don't like this," he said worriedly. Bingmei could feel the tension emanating from him in waves. He remained within the shadows of the pavilion.

"They couldn't have known we were coming," Damanhur said.

"What if Echion is already here?" Kunmia suggested. She also looked troubled by the crowd that lay in wait. She had a worried smell, like wilting flowers.

"Turn the junk around," Damanhur said.

"I can't," the captain said. "There isn't room. And the royal fleet would only become suspicious. It could be nothing."

"I don't think it's nothing," Damanhur snapped back.

Mieshi gave off a fearful smell. She bit her lip.

"Look," Kunmia offered, pointing. "It's Jidi Majia."

Bingmei followed the line of her arm, but in truth, she did not need anyone to point him out. The man stood out of the crowd because, as Damanhur had told her, he, too, had the winter sickness. His hair was white as snow, his skin pale. He wore royal robes and the chains of office and held a ruyi with a tasseled end. That scepter was a mark of his power and rank.

After sidling up next to him, Bingmei asked Marenqo if he knew the famous advisor.

"I've never met him in person. Only Kunmia has. He looks . . ."

"Fat," Bingmei commented.

"If *I* were constantly surrounded by the delicacies of Sajinau . . . I would be too. That he's here on the docks is peculiar."

"Bingmei," Kunmia said, and the girl approached her master. "You will come with me as we disembark. Only you can know if Jidi Majia is real or an imposter. I'm worried we've come to a trap."

"Then we should turn while we still can," Damanhur seethed.

"If we try to leave, they'll launch the whirlwind trebuchets against us," Rowen said. "We wouldn't make it through the fjord. Be wary. If it *is* Echion, we cannot let him know we've unmasked him."

Bingmei had more than one wig, and so she'd already pinned the other to her hair. The experience she'd had in Wangfujing had left a bitter taste in her mouth, and she felt just as uneasy about approaching Sajinau as the others did. Worry bloomed in her breast. She turned and saw Quion coiling a rope around his arm, watching her. He set the rope down and stood near her, offering his silent support.

Captain Guoduan gave the command to dock the ship, and his crew acted with prompt obedience. Some dockmen on the wharf took the ropes and fastened them to the iron docking cleats at the bow and stern. Bingmei saw the crowd growing more eager, their faces aglow with wonder and joy. Jidi Majia stood at the forefront of the welcoming party as a plank was lowered from the junk and set carefully on the dock. Captain Guoduan went down first.

"Why the formal greeting, Jidi Majia?" the captain said, looking at the crowd.

Kunmia and Bingmei stood at the top of the plank. The smell of rotting salmon drifted up from the water, and she noticed a few dead fish bobbing on the surface. But that smell was mild compared to the hope and eagerness emanating from the crowd. These were not townsfolk, Bingmei quickly realized. They were all formally dressed in ceremonial clothes, many of them in great finery and silk.

As Bingmei fixed her gaze on Jidi Majia, she tried to catch his smell, but it was masked by the teeming emotions of the crowd. Kunmia gave her a quizzical look and Bingmei shrugged. She didn't know.

"Welcome home to Sajinau, Captain Guoduan," the counselor announced. "Your coming is a portent from the Dragon of Dawn."

"Is it? I bring a cargo of ground millet, peas, and lard."

Kunmia stepped down the gangway, and Bingmei followed, her skin tingling with dread. She still couldn't smell the counselor.

"No, Captain. You bring a much more precious cargo than that," Jidi Majia said. "You bring the lost son home. The prince's brother. Why should we not greet you and be merry?"

The voice didn't sound merry, though. It was calm and controlled. When Bingmei finally reached the dock, she could smell Jidi Majia at last. It wasn't the smell of corruption and murder. This wasn't Echion nor anything like him. He smelled tart, like the taste of unripe berries that were so sour they made someone's face turn grotesque. Bingmei's eyes watered at the overpowering smell. She realized, looking into Jidi Majia's blue eyes, eyes that startled and surprised her as much as his smell, that she knew what he smelled like.

It was the smell of unspeakable grief.

When he looked at her, just for a moment, that smell was honeyed with hope. His eyes widened as if he recognized her.

"You found her," he gasped. "You found the phoenix-chosen! It's not too late!"

杀雾

Jidi Majia led the way to the palace, his bulky frame keeping an easy pace. The walk had to be one of the strangest experiences of Bingmei's life. It felt as if time itself had slowed down and she was dreamwalking again. The passengers from the *Raven* were surrounded by courtiers from the palace. People cheered and waved pennants and poles. They smelled like flowers, a rich variety, and their joy was unfeigned and deep. A few were pungent, but the overall mix of scents made her heady. The trilling of musical instruments dashed through the crowd. While Damanhur basked in the unexpected glory, smiling and waving at the crowd, Rowen walked along with a haunted look on his face. She could tell the lost prince struggled with his emotions at the homecoming welcome.

Bingmei had no idea why they were being greeted in such a manner. Jidi Majia had called her the phoenix-chosen. Why? How had he known about her connection to the sword? As those words had left his lips, she'd felt a tingling down her back as if someone were about to stroke her neck.

Kunmia stayed next to her, eyeing the crowd warily. The exuberant welcome, as if they were returned war heroes, bewildered Bingmei. She'd even heard one person shout that the phoenix-chosen had come to save them. What did it mean? Bingmei had no Phoenix Blade, just an empty scabbard. Yet they cheered and sang and wept.

Guards with huge glaives, dressed in ceremonial armor and pointed helmets, held back the crowds as they passed. The studs on the leather breastpieces flashed in the sunlight, and the dragons decorating their uniforms reminded Bingmei of Fusang. The armor looked bulky and uncomfortable, but the soldiers stood tall, using their glaives to form a wall around them.

Bingmei craved answers, but it was too noisy to speak. Rowen looked back at her, his expression full of worry, but surely the situation wasn't too dangerous. The smell of this place was so different from Wangfujing, where she'd been despised and treated with contempt. But what did these people want from her? How could she save them?

The gates of the palace reminded her of Fusang as well, especially when she saw two stone lions, one with an orb and another with a cub, set by them. These weren't the massive bronze ones she'd faced outside the Summer Palace, but they were identical in style, including the slight tilt to the heads. Her heart quivered with fear as she approached them. But nothing happened to the guards as they walked past them and pushed open the heavy doors, revealing a vast courtyard. Inside, thousands of warriors were training. As Bingmei passed the stone lions, she smelled grief. A quick backward glance revealed Mieshi was glaring at the statues. The courtiers fanned out, giving them more space. Someone shouted a command, and all the soldiers hastily assembled into straight rows. They shouted back in unison, the sound crashing like thunder.

As they crossed the courtyard, someone else shouted, eliciting a loud response from the assembly. Bingmei felt small and insignificant behind the towering walls of the courtyard. A mountain loomed beyond the palace, adding to her sense of powerlessness. The huge palace loomed ahead, at the top of a sweeping set of stairs with a wide red carpet down the center. After they crossed the massive courtyard, they began to climb the steps, splitting into two groups walking to each side of the carpet. When Rowen tried to fall in with the ensigns, Jidi Majia shot him a look and nodded toward the carpet.

It was reserved for royalty.

Rowen sighed, his lips twisting into a grimace, and then he walked alone on the red carpet, climbing up the middle.

There were so many steps that Bingmei's legs began to burn. The voyage by ship had weakened her. She felt sorry for Rowen, walking alone on the carpet. When they were halfway up, she glanced back at the warriors assembled in neat rows, perfectly still, perfectly unified. They were a massive force, more than capable of handling armies of Qiangdao. And the fact that they seemed to be training for war also gave her some relief. Coming to Sajinau had been the right thing to do.

Someone was descending the carpeted part of the stairway from above. Bingmei realized with a start that it was Rowen's brother, Juexin. She could see the family resemblance, although Juexin was bigger and wore the bulky armor she'd seen among his guards. He had no helmet, and his hair was long and braided. Coming behind him was an elegantly dressed woman—the sister perhaps? She had the cold beauty of some sort of otherworldly creature. She did not look happy to see Rowen.

Juexin met Rowen on the landing below the top set of steps. Jidi Majia also paused, and those behind him were stranded on the steps, staring up at the scene.

Bingmei crept closer, shifting and climbing around the others. She needed to smell this man. She needed to know Echion had not yet infiltrated Sajinau. He looked nothing like Echion, but looks meant nothing. When she sidled up next to Kunmia, she was close enough to smell both the brother and the possible sister.

"You've returned," Juexin said, and Bingmei smelled the scent of antipathy coming from him. This was indeed a complex relationship. Past affection mingled with pain and disappointment. And there was even a hint of jealousy.

"I do not intend to stay," Rowen answered, keeping his composure.

"Father isn't here—"

"I know," Rowen cut him off.

"Please," the girl said, her voice edged with pain. "Let's not quarrel. Not here."

"How did you know I was coming?" Rowen asked, his cheek muscle twitching.

"Jidi Majia had a vision," Juexin said. "He foretold your return. And he said you would bring the phoenix's chosen servant with you. Which is she?" The prince looked at those assembled, but when his eyes rested on Bingmei, his lips parted, and a sigh came out. "Oh," he said, as if shocked. He scrutinized her more closely. "He said your hair would be like copper."

"It is," Jidi Majia said, bowing. "It is her."

"Then welcome, blessed of the phoenix. Slayer of dragons. You who will cross the Death Wall that we may live. Your sacrifice will be honored for generations."

CHAPTER
TWENTY-NINE
The Legend of the Phoenix

Prince Juexin's words were accompanied by the pleasant, floral smell of gratitude, but the sour weeds of worry he seeded spoiled the effect. There was no doubt he was sincere. There was no confusion as to his motives. He and, it appeared, the entire city were grateful she'd come. They did indeed look to her as someone who could save them from the terrors that were forthcoming. But at the cost of her life? Bingmei's entire soul recoiled from the thought.

"They are weary from their long journey, my prince," said Jidi Majia. "This is news to them. Come, Kunmia Suun. Bring your party into the palace for refreshment. You come bearing tidings, no doubt. But there is much you may still learn."

Bingmei looked into the big man's sad eyes, and her courage began to fray like a cloth being torn.

They climbed the remaining steps to the top of the palace entrance, and the courtiers assembled and bowed in respect as they passed. Bingmei felt the discomfort of being the center of attention. Stationed behind the courtiers stood a row of guards with polished glaives, standing at attention, eyes fixed with discipline. Shouts began in the courtyard below, and Bingmei turned before it was out of sight. The warriors had gathered into squares to recommence their drills. A breeze flowed by suddenly, carrying the pleasant smell of incense. She turned again, then entered the palace atop the huge rampart of steps. There was a threshold, similar to the one in Fusang, that she needed to step over.

Sajinau was a wealthy kingdom, far more so than Wangfujing, and the ornate decorations of the palace awed her. Fresh plants hung from the ceiling in elaborate pots. Decorative urns engraved with animal symbols, mostly lions, brightened up nooks and corners. The array of gleaming marble tiles and elegant curtains bespoke not ancient crafts-manship but recent embellishment. The walls had openings high up with lattice windows that let in the sunlight. It made the palace feel airy and alive. Bingmei craned her neck to see the tall pillars holding up the massive roof and the intricate footings that braced it.

"It has been many years since you last graced our beloved city, Kunmia Suun," said Jidi Majia as they walked.

"Too many years, sadly," she answered. "We have heard that King Shulian is on a journey."

"Yes," Prince Juexin answered. "My father has been away for some time. He will be saddened that he wasn't here to greet you in person. But I will perform the duties of hospitality. You are greatly respected, Master Suun. Though I must ask how you came to travel with my brother."

Bingmei saw Rowen's face tense. "Why not ask him yourself, *Brother*?"

"If I thought I'd get an honest answer, I would," Juexin shot back, revealing a glint of anger that boiled just beneath the surface.

Bingmei saw Jidi Majia's eyes crinkle with worry. She sensed that the advisor cared for both of the sons very much. Their squabbles were part of the pain he endured. The grief.

Kunmia plunged in before more sharp words could be exchanged. "We met up at King Budai's palace. Our ensigns joined for the assignment the king gave us."

"And what assignment was this?" Juexin asked with concern.

"He sent us to seek Fusang," she replied.

Jidi Majia nodded. He didn't seem surprised by the answer.

They had walked down the long corridor and entered a banquet hall. The servants had already arranged pillows around the circular tables. Steaming dishes of fragrant food waited at each table. Marenqo's eyes lit with excitement.

"Master Kunmia, you will dine at the prince's table," said Jidi Majia, taking her by the arm and directing her to the head table. Servants approached to escort the guests to their tables and provided them with steaming bowls and cloths to wipe their hands and faces. Bingmei was also led to the head table and was seated next to Prince Rowen and Kunmia. The woman whom Bingmei believed to be the princes' sister also joined them. Bao Damanhur, Mieshi, and the others were brought to a separate table.

"And you are Guanjia from Wangfujing," Jidi said, observing the other man. "Please join us as well," he offered with a gesture. Guanjia bowed in respect, but Bingmei could smell his disdain for the man's pale skin and snow-white hair, a sentiment she'd often smelled on him in response to *her*. It soured the wonderful scents of the meal. The dishes had been arranged on a wheel in the middle of the table, and Bingmei watched as the prince began to rotate the wheel, bringing the various dishes around to each person. There were two varieties of soup and several plates of seaweed and rice, which had been rolled up together and slit into logs. Fruit and vegetables were in abundance as well, each served in a syrupy sauce. The prince did not serve himself any food, strangely, and Bingmei wondered at the custom. Her stomach growled in anticipation. For too long, they'd subsisted on the most basic of food.

"So you were sent to find Fusang," the prince continued after they all had food on their plates. The noise of feasting and conversation from the other tables gave the illusion of privacy. "Were you successful?"

Kunmia nodded as she finished a bite of rice, then said, "We discovered it under a glacier in the northern rim. A fisherman had found a broken piece of the ruins in the bay while searching for crab. He brought it to King Budai."

A politic way of saying it, although Juexin was already shaking his head.

"He brought it to my brother, actually," said the prince. He glanced at Jidi, and the two shared a knowing smile. "It should not surprise you that we've kept watch over him from a distance. The Jingcha are quite adept at remaining unseen and learning the secrets others wish to keep hidden. Rowen has always been fascinated with the cult of the Dragon of Night." He gave his brother a meaningful look before turning his gaze back to Kunmia. Bingmei glanced at Rowen and wondered again how much he'd known about Fusang. Could he have warned them about the dangers they'd faced? Of Echion himself? "What you found was not what you expected, I should think."

"Indeed not," she replied. "The palace was perfectly intact, concealed beneath a sea of ice."

The prince nodded. "I've been to ice caves in the northern rim on a hunting trip. They're beautiful."

"Beautiful and deadly," Kunmia said. "The Qiangdao had already discovered the ruins. There was a band of them waiting for us, possibly two hundred or more. We killed as many as we could with our combined ensigns. But they lured us into the palace. We lost someone to the guardians at the gate."

"What kind of guardians?" the prince asked.

"Giant lions made of bronze or copper. Stone animals as well."

The prince looked at Jidi, who nodded knowingly. This only reaffirmed in Bingmei's mind that Sajinau knew much more about Echion than the other kingdoms did. What were they hiding? She remembered Rowen had said it was rumored the founder of Sajinau had possessed pale skin and hair, which was why the winter sickness was respected here. Could that ruler possibly be Echion?

"I will be brief, my lord," Kunmia continued, "since it seems you have information we do not. We entered the palace grounds. I've never seen such opulence. Fusang is larger even than this palace. It's a labyrinth, really, although the style is strangely similar. But we found a burial chamber. There were two stone tombs with effigies carved into the lids. One of a man, the other of a woman."

"Echion and Xisi," whispered Jidi Majia.

Kunmia's brow wrinkled. "How do you know of this?"

"Pardon me," Jidi said, shaking his head. He look agitated, nervous, full of dread and anticipation. "Please, go on."

"We opened the tomb of the man," she said. "There was a corpse inside, though highly preserved."

Prince Juexin put his fist on the table, his eyes full of worry. "And the phoenix-chosen revived him," he said in a low voice, his gaze turning to Bingmei. Despite his words, there was no accusation in his gaze. His sister touched his arm.

Bingmei nodded, her appetite beginning to shrivel. "I didn't know what I was doing, my lord," she said apologetically.

"Of course you didn't," Jidi Majia said mournfully. "How could you have known? There is no record of those rites. All knowledge of it is stamped in effigies. You were merely fulfilling your . . . role."

"If Echion has awakened," Juexin said, "then he will seek dominion of all the kingdoms." His eyebrow cocked as he glanced at Guanjia. "That you are here says misfortune has already fallen upon Wangfujing."

"It has," the steward answered. "My master is probably dead by now. Attacked by the mercenary captain he had hired to protect him. A man in disguise, we think. If the young woman here is to be believed, he was slain by the Dragon of Night himself."

Jidi Majia's brow wrinkled. "Murder and deception are his preferred tactics. We can expect nothing less."

Kunmia leaned forward. "How did you know we were coming, Jidi Majia?"

"Before I answer you," said the advisor, "can I ask another question? When you arrived at Fusang, did you find any carvings with images of creatures? Not decorations, like urns or vases, but in a plinth or wall of stone?"

"Yes," Bingmei said, nodding quickly. "There was a very long piece of stone, set into the staircase of one of the palaces."

"What was depicted there?"

Bingmei looked at Kunmia, who motioned for her to answer. "Mountains. The sea. And two dragons, coiled and entwined."

Jidi nodded. "I have been studying effigies like that one for many years," he said. "On my travels on behalf of King Shulian, I have seen them in faraway courts and realms. These images are not mere decorations." His eyes brightened. "They are *stories*. Retellings. For years I have wrestled to understand them. Why two dragons? Why the image of the phoenix? I have devoted myself to studying these images. To trying to understand their true meaning. I have traveled great distances and visited many forgotten quonsuun. And more palaces than you can imagine. I even went to the Death Wall."

The crown prince frowned at this, but he said nothing. Bingmei glanced at Rowen, whose every feature indicated his eagerness and interest.

"It is an immense and foreboding defense," Jidi said. "But from what? Whatever empire constructed it did so for a reason. But there is no record of when it was constructed or why. There are no records at all. Clues were left behind, but not the key that would unravel them. It is the same for all of the ancients' structures, including the palace around us. Why are there no settlements on the other side of the wall? There's nothing but trees and wilderness as far as the eye can see." He shook his head with despair. "Only animals seem to roam that land. Wild ones. Leopards and ice bears and huge elk with enormous antlers. I became obsessed with understanding these symbols. Why did so many seem to worship the symbol of the dragon? Was one dragon the Dragon of Night, the other the Dragon of Dawn? Were they at war or unified?"

Jidi shook his head, wiping his mouth as he frowned. "I meditated again and again, trying to discover the inner meaning of what I had seen. I visited a quonsuun that seemed to worship the symbol of the phoenix. It was at that quonsuun where I had my vision."

Bingmei saw that the prince had still not started eating. His eyes were fixed on Jidi Majia's sorrowful face.

The counselor cast his gaze down. "It was like nothing I had experienced before. I'd seen the symbols of the dragons and the phoenix in so many shrines, so many palaces, so many temples, but never before had they *moved*. The stone dragons quivered and flew. The waves carved onto the rock wriggled as if they were living. I stared in fascination at the images, and they revealed to me the story of the ancients.

"The story has been told in different times and different ways. In Sajinau, especially, these stories are whispered at night. Around fires. In children's ears. There are some commonalities across the tales. All of them tell of the wealth of the Summer Palace, of magic that doesn't call forth the killing fog, and of the pale king who used to rule all the kingdoms. But until I had my vision, I did not know what else was real. What I've learned comes down to this: the Dragon of Night exists. He is the first emperor. He is the last emperor." He looked up and gestured, palms up, at the dining room. "He is the one who built all of these palaces, including this one. He is the one who once enslaved mankind to build the Death Wall so that he might also rule over the dead in the Grave Kingdom. Balance is the only true ruler in our world, and in each incarnation of his empire, someone is chosen by the great phoenix to balance his evil with their goodness. But something went wrong ages ago. The balance was broken. Now, in each incarnation he kills the phoenix-chosen before they can defeat him.

"Whenever the Dragon of Night rises to power, he advances his kingdom until the people revolt and seek his downfall. Then he summons the killing fog to destroy the people, returns to his tomb, and waits for the phoenix to choose another to revive him from the Grave Kingdom. Each time he comes back, he is more powerful than the time before. The only thing that can stop him, the only thing that he fears, is the one the phoenix chooses to fight him.

"I saw in my vision that if the phoenix-chosen sacrifices herself by crossing the Death Wall before she is killed, then Echion and his queen will be destroyed in the end, the curse of the killing fog will end, and the people will finally be freed from their tyranny. It is the only way."

Great drops of sweat had appeared on Jidi Majia's brow as he related his vision. He grabbed a napkin from the table and mopped his face. "When the vision was finished, I was exhausted. I'd never felt so weak. I believe that if I hadn't visited so many places, I may not have gathered enough knowledge to trigger the vision during my meditation."

Bingmei sat in stunned silence. Her stomach felt sick. Her mouth was dry. This is what Prince Juexin had meant on the steps. The counselor was talking about sacrifice—*her* sacrifice—as if it were a given.

"I returned and shared the vision with King Shulian and Prince Juexin. The king went to the phoenix quonsuun himself, and he is there still. The one thing we did not know was *where* we would find the phoenix-chosen. And you, Prince Rowen, you have *brought* her to us!" Jidi Majia smiled with relief and exultation. "The vision was clear. The chosen must fly beyond the Death Wall for her sacrifice. Her death will bring life to all."

Bingmei's hands trembled, and she hid them in her lap. She darted a look at Rowen, wondering again what he'd known. He'd heard the legends of Echion, although it was clear he and Damanhur had not taken seriously the possibility that he might rise from the dead. Had they only been after his great wealth?

"Well, Brother," Prince Juexin said. "It seems you finally did something worth praising."

The smell of rage burned Bingmei's nose. Rowen set down his goblet, trying to master his fury. "How often I've disappointed you and Father. What a change."

The crown prince snorted. "I don't think you've changed at all, Brother. I don't think you *can* change. Our Jingcha spies at Budai's court informed me that you have already squandered the inheritance Father gave you. You're impoverished and without friends, save for that bragging swordsman over there." His mouth twisted with contempt. "I also learned that you intended to raise an army of mercenaries to challenge Father . . . and me."

Rage sharpened into the stench of fear. Bingmei stared at the brothers as they finally confronted each other.

"I wasn't—"

"Please," Juexin cut him off, shaking his head with disgust. "Do not foul the air with your lies. I see you, *Brother*, for who you really are. But I do not fear you. Neither should you fear me. I won't seek revenge. You see, I swore an oath to Father that if you came skulking back, I would greet you as an heir of Sajinau. That I would throw a feast for you and celebrate your return." He sniffed and controlled his emotions. "That I would protect you as if I were Father himself. But I do not trust you, Brother. You shattered that long ago. And I foresee that you will never change. You will never rise to become the man you *could* be. The man Father always hoped you would become. Just know that my men will be watching you. Always."

Bingmei felt the stink of humiliation coming off Rowen. These brothers had been rivals for many years. Any affection between them had been eclipsed by pain. And Bingmei smelled the sadness again rising from Jidi Majia as he stared at the intractable brothers. He mourned for them.

She stared at the advisor, at his wan face and the pain in his sad eyes. The advisor was an honest man, and she knew he believed everything he'd related about his miraculous vision.

But she also had no intention of fulfilling it.

CHAPTER THIRTY

Promises

The remainder of the feast went by in a blur as Bingmei wrestled against the information she had learned. It felt as if walls had suddenly sprung up around her, boxing her in. And then the walls had sprouted deadly spikes and begun to close in on her.

It seemed her every path led to death. *Her* death. A feeling of bitterness mingled with defiance rattled inside her chest.

After the meal, the courtiers of the palace led them to accommodations where they could rest from the journey. Bingmei quickly discovered that she had been assigned to share a room with Kunmia and Mieshi. The sleeping chamber was elegantly crafted, with three adjacent beds, cushions, a variety of chests in which they could store their things, and a private, screened area that contained a massive bath. When she arrived, a line of servants carrying pans of steaming water were filling the bath.

After so many weeks on ships and in the wild, Bingmei was grateful for the warmth and comforts of the palace. More comfortable than Wangfujing, it also lacked the omnipresent smell of greed in the air. The palace of Sajinau smelled like freshly cut wood and lacquer. Everything was orderly and refined, and the servants were cheerful and respectful.

They were as deferential to Bingmei as if she were some immortal to be worshipped. They acted in awe of her, which made her insides squeeze with the temptation to flee.

After they examined the chamber, Kunmia left to find and console Mieshi, allowing Bingmei the chance to bathe first. Bingmei had not seen Mieshi much since they'd arrived and suspected Kunmia would find her in Damanhur's company. The water was scented with fragrant oil. It felt overpowering at first, but after she stripped and entered the warm water, she found the eucalyptus smell soothing. A milky substance had been added to the water, making it translucent. She scrubbed and soaped her hair and skin and relished the feeling of being clean again. After this was done, she lingered in the bath, pondering Jidi Majia's vision.

There was no dishonesty in the man. He'd believed everything he'd told her about his vision. But did that mean she should listen? Perhaps his desperation to solve the riddle of the glyphs had led his mind to imagine or concoct a story.

Bingmei clenched her jaw, trying to calm the confusion in her mind and heart. In her short life, she had seen that the world was full of hate, pride, and jealousy. People did not trust each other, as a rule. Privy as she was to peoples' intentions, to their pettiness and jealousy, she understood why they were slow to trust. If someone dropped a coin in the street unwittingly, it would be snatched up and concealed. She'd seen it happen. She'd smelled the consequences. The greediness of the person who didn't care about another person's loss. The embarrassment and disappointment of the customer who tried to pay with a coin they no longer possessed.

Then there were the Qiangdao. Murderous thieves who would sooner kill someone than they would greet them.

The world was full of violence and enmity. Yes, there were good people, like Quion, whose innocence filled her with wonderment, and Kunmia, who was compassionate and respectable. But those fresh blooms were so rare.

The world wasn't *worth* saving.

That thought made her feel vengeful and petty, even to herself, but truth had deep roots, and she felt these wriggling deep inside her heart, inching into the darkest parts of herself.

No. She wouldn't do it. No one crossed the Death Wall. No one knew why. Maybe it was the source of the killing fog. Maybe it was a land full of ghosts. Maybe it was just a wall. But she could not take the chance.

"Bingmei?"

Quion's voice snapped her out of her reverie. Water sloshed against the side of the tub.

"I'm here," she answered quickly. "Wait a moment. I'm bathing."

She heard a little choking noise, and then he said, "I-I'll come back later."

"Stay. There's a robe behind the screen." She quickly left the tub and wiped the trickling water from her skin before thrusting her arms into the silk sleeves of one of the two robes the servants had left. She then leaned over the tub and squeezed her hair, watching the trail of water drip from it.

As she looked at her coppery tresses, still so strange and unexpected, she felt the spiked walls grind closer. She folded the robe over, tying the sash to keep it closed, and walked around the barrier. Quion was pacing, his expression anguished.

"What's wrong?" she asked in concern.

His eyes looked haunted, his lip quivering. "I just spoke with Marenqo," he said. He stepped toward her. Misery came off him in waves, stunning her.

"What did you hear?" she asked, her heart touched by the depth of his feeling.

"I don't know what to make of it," he said, shaking his head. His fingers clenched into fists. "Marenqo said he heard you were special. That you are the only one who can defeat Echion. But that it would kill you. That you'd *die*."

As he uttered that word, the smell of his misery smashed into her like a hammer. She took a step back, wincing.

"I'm sorry," he said, shaking his head. "I know . . . I know you can smell such things. I'm sorry, Bingmei. I'm so sorry. I should go." He backed away from her and turned to leave.

His concern for her was one of the sweetest things she'd ever smelled. It wasn't the same as Kunmia's scent or the tenderness of a mother's love. But it was close and it was sincere and it made her eyes burn hot in a strange way.

"Quion," she said. "Wait. Don't go."

He stopped but didn't turn around. "It's not fair," he said, shaking his head. "They shouldn't *make* you do something like that." He turned, his jaw quivering. His eyes were still haunted. She would remember that look for the rest of her life, however long that would be.

"I . . . ," she paused, struggling with her feelings, and swallowed. "I haven't decided yet."

He gave her a serious look, his eyes narrowing. "Are you going to run away, Bingmei?" he asked softly.

"I don't know," she answered.

He swallowed, his feelings shifting and changing, becoming stronger. What a mix of them. Her stomach fluttered inside. "I'd go with you," he said.

And she knew he meant it. His devotion gave her a little spark of hope. "Thank you," she said.

Kunmia appeared in the doorway, sweat trickling down the side of her face from her practice. She held the rune staff in one hand, her expression worried. "Go where?" she asked firmly.

Bingmei sighed. "Can we talk, Master?"

Quion ducked his head and left the room. Kunmia slid the partition closed behind him, then she stepped deeper into the room and leaned her staff against the frame of the bed. The look she gave Bingmei was suspicious, but she refrained from speaking.

"I would seek your counsel," Bingmei said. "I'm not leaving Sajinau . . . yet."

"But you *are* considering it?"

Bingmei felt her insides twist. "Master, you heard what Jidi Majia said. I'm supposed to sacrifice myself? He didn't say anything about it being a willing one."

Kunmia frowned. "I took his meaning to be just that."

"But how do you know?" Bingmei challenged. "He had a dream . . . a vision. But what does it really mean? How can we know whether there's any truth to it?"

Kunmia folded her arms, coming closer to Bingmei. "Are you saying that he deceived us?"

"I'm not," Bingmei said. "He's honest. My . . . instincts tell me he's a sad, grief-stricken man. Consumed by a sorrow I don't fully understand. But he's honest. I know that. He believes in what he saw." She licked her lips. "But what if he's wrong?"

Kunmia nodded in sympathy and put her hand on Bingmei's shoulder. "Let me be honest with you, Bingmei. I consider you my own daughter. I'm troubled by Jidi Majia's vision. As someone who cares for you deeply, I do not wish to see you suffer. My impression from what Jidi Majia said is that the sacrifice must come from you. You must *choose* it." She squeezed her shoulder. "I will not let them force you to do it."

A feeling of immense relief washed over Bingmei. "Thank you," she breathed.

"We will not make this or any decision rashly. I respect Jidi Majia's wisdom. You're right, though, sadness has ravaged him. The rivalry between the princes has caused a rift in the realm and in King Shulian's heart. I think Rowen had it in his head that he, the second born, would be chosen as the heir."

"Now part of him wishes to avenge himself on his brother for his being chosen instead," Bingmei said. She paused, then added, "You said you do not believe in revenge . . ."

She'd thought quite a bit about Kunmia Suun's story, and what it might mean for her personal quest.

Kunmia stared at the lamp, her expression soft. "No, I do not. There are some appetites that can never be satisfied. That is why I abhor revenge. It destroyed my grandfather, as I told you. And my father too, which is another story." She turned, giving Bingmei a sad look, which was chased by the subtle smell of grief. It wasn't overpowering. The master had long since mastered her own emotions.

"I know," Bingmei said.

Kunmia nodded. "That is why I chose to take up the staff instead. I wanted the cycle of revenge to stop there. I chose not to join it."

"But if that young man who wished to marry you became part of the Qiangdao, then he's possibly killed even more people!" Bingmei said. "Sparing him did not save lives, Master."

"I see that you disagree," Kunmia said with a kind smile. "But does that not prove my words are true? The craving for revenge cannot be sated. If my grandfather had killed the young man, perhaps it would have angered the boy's uncle. Or his mother." Kunmia walked over to the chest where she'd tucked away her belongings. She opened it and withdrew a clean set of clothes to wear in the palace. Clutching them against her chest, she said, "That is why, Bingmei, we have laws and rulers. Because the feeling of revenge cannot be sated, we must have just and wise rulers. They are the ones who execute justice. By not exacting revenge, I do not prevent justice. I am only unwilling to perform it for my own sake, to satisfy my feelings. When someone does wrong, they should be punished by those with authority. We should not take that authority for ourselves."

She stepped closer and ran her fingers through a strand of Bingmei's damp hair. That tender, motherly smell wafted over her. "King Shulian is a just and wise king. And his son will be the same. I do not believe they will compel you to make this sacrifice. And neither will I. But you must turn your heart and mind to answering this question: What if Jidi Majia's vision is true? What if you are the only person capable of saving us from Echion's power?"

The world wasn't *worth* saving. That cold, dark truth still lingered in the pit of Bingmei's heart.

"I will think on it," Bingmei said, bowing her head to her mentor, her friend. And she would. For Kunmia's sake.

While Bingmei dressed, Kunmia slipped off to the tub. After she was clothed, Bingmei tied braids in her hair and then stared at herself in the mirror. She looked different from everyone else, including Jidi Majia. Should she continue to disguise her strangeness? Or should she trust the people of Sajinau to see who she truly was?

Would they hate her even more than the hateful people who'd chased her out of Wangfujing if she forsook them and fled?

Her heart wrestled with pain as she fidgeted with one of the braids. She thought about Quion and his kindness and innocence. He had promised to go with her if she left. Should she do it? But where would they go? Where could a girl with copper hair hope to hide?

As she pondered that thought a moment, she suddenly felt the presence of the Phoenix Blade. Its power had been invoked, and she saw it in her mind's eye. The blade rippled with power. Her awareness was instantly linked with that of the Qiangdao leader who had murdered her parents, her grandfather. A man who still thirsted for blood. He was on a small fishing boat, entering the harbor at Sajinau, gazing up at the palace with a crooked smile on his face.

Hello, ghost girl, his thoughts seemed to whisper to her. *Found you.*

CHAPTER
THIRTY-ONE

Vengeance

Bingmei strode down the corridor alongside Kunmia. Dusk had settled over the palace of Sajinau, and the servants had lit torches and lamps to banish the falling shadows. Bingmei's insides squirmed with worry. She'd told Kunmia immediately about the preternatural warning she'd received, and they'd set off to warn Prince Juexin of the danger. While Bingmei could no longer see Muxidi in her head, she felt the blade's presence in the city. She was bound to it by invisible tethers that stretched but couldn't break.

Each corridor of the palace looked equally splendid, but Kunmia navigated past the servants without asking for help. The master's scent was troubled but still measured, like a pan of water with only a few bubbles seething at the bottom.

Turning another corner, they nearly walked into Prince Rowen. He looked agitated, not the expression one would expect from a man who'd been pardoned by a rival and forgiven by his father. Bingmei smelled his conflict, but he was driven at the moment by a different urgency. They locked eyes.

"Did you sense it?" he asked her seriously.

"What?" she demanded.

"The Phoenix Blade," he said. "It just arrived in Sajinau."

Kunmia looked at him in astonishment. "How did you know?"

He frowned. "The same way she does," he answered, gesturing to Bingmei. "It has a powerful magic. I was coming to find you both."

"We're going to see your brother," Kunmia said.

Rowen scowled. "Why him?"

"Because he's the ruler of Sajinau. He deserves to know."

"I was going to tell him later," Rowen hedged, "but why not get the sword first?"

"Let's be prudent, Prince Rowen," Kunmia said. "Your brother has thousands of troops at his disposal; he's in a better position to counter the Qiangdao."

Part of Bingmei agreed with him. She *wanted* the sword back. Logically, though, she knew its magic was leading Echion to them. To *her*. To pursue the sword would be to give him what he wanted.

"As you say," Rowen replied, bowing his head to her. And so he accompanied them down the corridor.

As they continued to walk, the prince asked in a worried voice, "Do you think Echion has come?"

Bingmei frowned. "I don't know. I felt the sword, and I felt the Qiangdao leader we lost at the glacier. Muxidi."

"Him? How did he get here so quickly?"

"By boat, probably," Bingmei said with a little burr in her voice.

He smirked at her jibe and remained silent as they continued to walk. Around another corner, they reached a huge door decked with golden knobs like the ones she'd seen in the lost palace. Four armored warriors stood guard outside it.

Kunmia paused in front of them and bowed her head. "We have urgent news for Prince Juexin."

"He is meeting with General Tzu right now," said one of the guards gruffly.

"Please advise him that this is urgent," Kunmia said.

The soldier snorted, but he nodded to one of his underlings, who slipped inside the room and shut the door behind him.

"How do you fare, Kunmia Suun?" asked the gruff guard.

"Well enough. Do I know you?"

"We've met. I served under General Tzu at a fight in the upper valley ten years ago. You were there. I recognized your staff."

Kunmia's brow wrinkled as she tried to remember, then softened again. Bingmei thought the man smelled like cooked tubers. It wasn't unpleasant, but it also wasn't sweet. There was no deception in him.

"We lost many good men in that war," Kunmia said.

"But we also slaughtered many Qiangdao and threw their bodies into the river. King Shulian fought with us then." His voice betrayed a tone of pride.

"Is your name Pangxie?"

The officer's eyes widened in surprise. "You remembered?" he said. "I was a young officer then." He smiled then, and the neutral smell of tubers gained a buttery warmth. It was a powerful smell, and it made Bingmei realize the power Kunmia's goodness, her kindness, had over others' emotions.

"It's good to see you again," Kunmia said.

The door opened again, and the soldier emerged. "If you please, Master," he said, gesturing for them to enter.

As they walked into the vibrant council room with the glittering vases and excellent woodwork, they saw Prince Juexin and his sister speaking in hushed tones to a middle-aged man in ceremonial armor. Although he was not particularly tall, he was trim and fit. He had a huge blade in a scabbard at his waist and a glaive strapped to his back. His plumed helmet was resting on a decorative table. Also with them was a spidery man with a long mustache and pointed beard, dressed in normal street clothes without any silk or design. Jidi Majia stood with them, head bowed in concentration.

Juexin's brow wrinkled when he noticed Rowen accompanying them. As they approached, he said, "If you wanted to see me, Brother, you need only have asked."

Bingmei caught the whiff of resentment exuding from Rowen, but Kunmia was quick to dispel it.

"We found him in the corridor, and I asked him to join us," she said.

Juexin pursed his lips. "What is it? You look concerned."

"There is reason to be," she answered. "I apologize for interrupting, but the matter is quite urgent."

"No apology needed, Master Kunmia," said General Tzu in a placid tone, giving a little wave of his hand. "As I was telling the prince, the Qiangdao have been restless. We've seen three raids in the last fortnight within our own borders. And that doesn't include the brazen attack on Wangfujing. Yiwu was also attacked two days ago."

"The Qiangdao are on the move," Kunmia said. "And one of their leaders has just entered Sajinau."

The spidery man crossed his arms and stepped forward, tilting his head. "I would have known," he said.

"Who are you?" Kunmia asked.

The man reeked of dishonesty. The stink lingered on him like smoke wafting off the clothing of someone who had stood near a fire too long. She sniffed loudly, trying to get Kunmia's attention, and fixed her eyes on the man. He wasn't Echion, but he wasn't good either.

"This is Jiaohua," said Crown Prince Juexin. "He's the head of the Jingcha. Why do you think the Qiangdao have arrived?"

"They didn't come in force," Kunmia said, "but one of their leaders has come for Bingmei. Let me explain, if you will. When we returned from a mission last year, at the end of the season of the Dragon of Dawn, we were ambushed by Qiangdao. The leader of that band wielded a sword with the crest of a phoenix on the hilt and the pommel. He attacked us and invoked the power of the blade."

"Did it summon the killing fog?" Jidi Majia asked, frowning.

"It did. The fog overcame the Qiangdao and even killed one of our own. We escaped back into the river, and when the fog subsided, I sent Bingmei to retrieve the weapon from among the sleeping dead."

The spidery man frowned, giving Bingmei a disdainful look. "Her?"

The crown prince looked at the man with arched eyebrows and a reproving glare. Jiaohua's expression was unrepentant.

"I believe the blade belongs to Echion himself," Kunmia said. "He used it after being revived. When it is near, Bingmei can sense it. And so can Prince Rowen."

Juexin frowned and looked at his brother.

"It's true," Rowen said. "I sensed it the moment it was brought here. It's in the city, and I feel it coming closer."

"My connection with it is stronger, I think," said Bingmei, asserting herself. "When he summoned its power to find me, I saw a flash of his face. I know the man." She allowed some of her anger to leak through. "He's the one who killed my parents."

Jidi Majia stepped closer, putting his hand on the table. "If he's brought that weapon into the city, it's a danger to everyone here. It could summon the fog."

"He must be killed," said General Tzu. "At once."

Juexin nodded in agreement. "If he can find you, Bingmei, then you can find him."

"We cannot risk her life," Jidi Majia said in concern. "Send the Jingcha after him. Send your brother since he, too, can sense the blade."

By the look on the crown prince's face, he didn't like the suggestion. There was a flicker of rivalry again as the brothers held each other's gaze.

"You cannot risk sending her!" the counselor implored.

Perhaps he was right—the man wanted her to come to him—but Bingmei couldn't bear to be left behind. "He's the man who murdered my parents. Killed my grandfather in front of my eyes." Despite the story Kunmia had shared with her, and even what her own heart told her, she still wanted revenge. She craved it. Perhaps Echion was counting on that.

The spidery Jiaohua didn't advocate one way or another. He waited for the command to be given. No doubt he would spin whatever choice was made to his own ends.

"Will you go, Brother?" Juexin asked.

"I already intended to," Rowen said, meeting his gaze.

The prince turned to the spidery man. "Take him, Jiaohua. Take as many men as you need, including Bao Damanhur. Bring this Qiangdao alive for justice if you can. But if not . . . do what you must."

Jiaohua grinned and Bingmei saw some ruined teeth in his smile.

杀雾

Night fell over Sajinau. Bingmei paced within the council room, awaiting news of the confrontation. General Tzu had related more details about the restless Qiangdao—the raids had worsened to the point that the general believed that the Qiangdao were massing to invade Sajinau. With the king gone, it would fall on Prince Juexin to protect the people. Bingmei still felt the presence of the sword, however, and her craving for it grew stronger in her breast, making it difficult to concentrate on the discussion.

The prince's sister approached, an elegant young woman in a beautiful green silk gown embroidered with golden thread, jade earrings, and a small tiara in a nest of luscious hair.

"I wanted to introduce myself to you, Bingmei," she said. "I am Eomen."

"I'm . . . I'm honored," Bingmei said, feeling a little callow in her warrior's pants and red shirt. She hadn't expected the princess to approach her. The young woman smelled of flowers and yearning. She, too, had a conflicted soul. It was clear she cared about both of her brothers and worried about them in different ways. That gave the flowery smell a musty edge.

"You are so young. This must be a great burden on you," Eomen said. "But can I speak freely and say that we are grateful you came to Sajinau. And *I* am grateful that you brought my brother with you. I've worried about him so." She touched Bingmei's shoulder as she said this, the gesture kind and solicitous.

"When did he leave home?" Bingmei asked.

"Several years ago. He liked to call himself Wuren even while he lived here. Do you know what that means?"

Bingmei nodded. "When we met him and Bao Damanhur in Wangfujing, that's what he called himself. But his exile is self-imposed, I think."

"It is, truly," Eomen said. "We want him home." She glanced at her brother, the crown prince, and something twisted in her expression. "Most of us do anyway."

A strange feeling washed over Bingmei. Her spine tingled, and she felt her legs crumple. Distantly, she heard Eomen call for help, but Bingmei was already somewhere else. The familiar magic had yanked her away from her body. In an instant, she was in a dark alley. The Phoenix Blade glowed a wicked green color as Muxidi stomped forward.

"You're a fool!" Jiaohua shouted. He stood behind nearly a dozen men dressed in normal street clothes, but Bingmei knew they were skilled officers in disguise. Rowen was beside him, eyes fixed on the Phoenix Blade, but his gaze darted up toward Bingmei's disembodied presence. Did he see her?

She had no time to think on it, for the killing fog crept down the alley from behind the Qiangdao leader, its hungry tendrils seeking the blade.

"Stop it! You're killing yourself!" said Jiaohua.

But the Qiangdao's eyes were unafraid. He yelled in challenge and rushed at the front men, swinging the blade at them. They brought up their weapons and defended themselves with skill, striking back quickly. She sensed their determination. They knew what was coming, but they intended to stand their ground. They honored their sacred duty.

The killing fog engulfed Muxidi's ankles, but nothing happened to him. The next man it touched shrieked in fear and pain. Bingmei watched in horror as the fog consumed him. He fell with a slump onto the pavement, eyes closed as if asleep. Dead.

Another man, caught in the grip of the fog, looked horrified, but the Phoenix Blade sliced through him before the killing fog could claim him. He, too, fell to the cobblestones.

"Run!" Jiaohua shouted. He raised a blowgun to his lips and sent a dart winging at the Qiangdao leader. Then another. But Muxidi's reflexes were too quick, and none of the darts hit him. He continued to advance.

The officers and Rowen fled down the alley, away from the menace. Bingmei watched the fog coalescing around Muxidi, who massaged his neck with one hand and spat on the ground as he walked. The fog had claimed two more men who couldn't escape fast enough.

Muxidi laughed harder as he sheathed the blade in the scabbard at his hip.

杀雾

Bingmei gasped, sitting up on the cold marble floor, struggling to breathe. It felt as if she'd been drowning. Faces stared down at her from all sides. Prince Juexin had squeezed her hand into a fist and gripped it, his eyes full of pleading. Jidi Majia looked confused and afraid, and she smelled the sadness exuding from his bones. Kunmia had been holding her, as if she were a child, stroking her hair.

"She's alive!" Eomen whispered in awe.

A painful tingling sensation filled her fingers and toes, but she ignored it. They needed to know what she'd seen.

Her breath was ragged. "They're coming back," she gasped. "I saw them. Muxidi . . ." She swallowed, her throat suddenly too tight to speak. She clutched her throat, gesturing for a drink, and someone fetched one quickly. She gulped it down.

"He's still coming," she wheezed. "He summoned the killing fog. And it didn't . . . it didn't even hurt him."

CHAPTER THIRTY-TWO
Shadows and Regrets

When Rowen and Jiaohua returned to the palace shortly thereafter, Bingmei was finally beginning to feel normal again. It seemed to take longer for her to recover feeling each time she slipped away from her body. Was leaving her body this way akin to dying? Perhaps the strange ability had something to do with Jidi Majia's vision.

Jiaohua's scent remained tinged with smoke, but he was bristling with anger and rage. He'd lost several of his men to Muxidi, and he wanted revenge. Rowen's eyes wandered the room until they landed on Bingmei. She sat on a small decorative sofa, Kunmia next to her, arm around her. His brow puckered with worry, and he approached them swiftly. He dropped onto his knee beside her. That pomegranate smell came again.

"Are you well?"

"I'm feeling better now," she said, but that was only partially true. Her body felt like it would never get warm again.

Rowen glanced at Kunmia with concern. "Did something happen?"

"She fainted and started to convulse," Kunmia said. "Then she stopped breathing."

Rowen's eyes widened.

"I'm all right," Bingmei said.

Kunmia hugged her closer. "When she revived, she told us about your confrontation with the Qiangdao. How the killing fog didn't harm him."

"I've never seen anything like it," Rowen said. "I . . . I knew you were there, Bingmei. I felt you."

Their eyes met. Neither understood what was going on. Whatever anger she'd felt toward him for keeping information from her and the others faded. She sensed he had his fated role in this mess, just as she did.

"It's something about the blade," Bingmei whispered. "It keeps drawing me toward it. You sensed me?"

He nodded. "I kept glancing around, expecting to see you. I thought you'd snuck off to join the fight."

"Part of me wanted to," she replied with a smile. "I don't like being left behind."

His gaze narrowed. "Did this also happen to you in Wangfujing?"

She blinked quickly, remembering the night she'd met him. "Yes."

He pressed his lips together firmly before speaking. "When Guanjia showed me the Phoenix Blade in the treasury, I felt like someone else was there, watching us. Was that you?"

Bingmei nodded. "The blade drew me away that time too. I was asleep in bed when I left my body. I could hear the two of you talking."

"Incredible," Rowen said. "But traveling that way kills you for a while. Right?"

"I think so." She looked at Kunmia. "It frightens me. I don't understand why it's happening."

"I think it's because you were chosen," Kunmia answered, stroking her cheek.

"But why *me*?"

"Master Kunmia?" It was Juexin calling to them. He was conferencing with his advisors and gestured for them to approach.

Kunmia rose, and Bingmei followed. "I don't like Jiaohua," she whispered to the master in a low voice. "He's dishonest."

"One doesn't need your power of discernment to recognize *that*," Rowen said with a low chuckle, coming with them. "He's the head of the Jingcha. He spends more time lurking in shadows than in the light."

"Why does your brother keep him, then?" Bingmei asked quickly.

"Every king needs a man like him," Rowen said as they arrived.

"Master Kunmia," Juexin said. He gave his brother a dark look before continuing. "Jiaohua's report matches what Bingmei saw in her vision. That Qiangdao was injured by the dart, which means he can be hurt and killed. General Tzu is stationing archers along the palace walls to defend the city, but we're concerned what may happen to the populace."

General Tzu nodded. While his face betrayed no emotion, Bingmei smelled his growing dread. "If you know your enemy and know yourself, you need not fear the outcome of a hundred battles. The Qiangdao are murderers—they are a threat we know. But we don't know what Echion is capable of. It may be his intention to summon the fog and slaughter everyone in Sajinau."

"I don't think so," Jidi Majia said, shaking his head. "A dragon seeks to rule others."

Juexin held up his hand. "I have disagreement among my advisors. General Tzu says we should begin evacuating Sajinau at once. Jidi Majia counsels caution. He fears we will be playing into Echion's hands if we empty the city for him. He suggested we send a team of Jingcha and ensign folk with Bingmei to the Death Wall at once. Master Kunmia, I would hear your advice if you'll give it."

"If we stand around too long debating," Jiaohua said with a nasty frown, "we may not have time to do anything. Let me hunt the Qiangdao leader first. If I put a reward on his head, every thief and qiezei will take a shot at him. Give me a thousand cowry shells, and he'll be dead before dawn. Why go to the Death Wall unless the girl is willing?"

"Be quiet a moment," Juexin said with a scowl. "I would hear Kunmia's advice."

Jiaohua scowled and gritted his teeth, his long mustache quivering with barely suppressed anger.

"It takes time to evacuate a city," Kunmia said. "And where would they all go? Enough food and supplies would need to be gathered first, or they'd starve. We need time. We must stall our enemy."

"You have faced Echion in the flesh," Jidi Majia said. "You said he claimed the right to rule the people. Do you think it's his intention to destroy everyone with the killing fog?"

"I don't," Kunmia said, "but while he professes benevolence, he seems to have no tolerance for opposition to his authority. He's very proud."

"Perhaps we should feign weakness," General Tzu said. "Pretend inferiority. Encourage his arrogance. You could offer to swear fealty to him, my lord?"

Juexin shook his head. "My father would not do that, and neither will I. I won't give up Sajinau without a fight."

"But what if this is a fight you can't win?" Rowen said. "We need more time to prepare. To learn his weaknesses . . . if he has any."

Juexin darted an angry look at his brother. "I won't surrender what Father has spent his lifetime building. *I* won't walk away."

Rowen's cheek twitched, and Bingmei smelled the fury concealed beneath his outwardly calm demeanor. "Of course you won't."

"This is not the time to argue," Eomen said, trying to play peacemaker. Bingmei sensed this was likely a familiar role for the princess.

"You're right," Juexin said. "It's time to *lead*. So, Master Kunmia, I understand from you that you don't think evacuating the city is the right course?"

"I don't. It would cause panic and a host of other ills. We don't know when Echion himself will arrive, but we can prepare for it. There is only so much time that he has to wage war before the season of the

Dragon of Night comes again. He may not be mortal himself, but his army is. They can freeze to death."

"Do you know that?" General Tzu said, his brow wrinkling. "What if he has an army of xixuegui that can fight without sleep? That are impervious to cold? We don't *know* what we are facing. And that, I fear, is why we will lose. If we feign submission, we'll buy ourselves time to learn more. Then, perhaps, we can discover how to defeat him."

"The general speaks reason," Rowen said.

"But reason alone won't save us," Jidi Majia said. "We must also decide with our hearts. And my heart tells me the outcome will be the same no matter what we do—enslavement and death. There is only one hope to defeat Echion. The phoenix showed me this in my vision." His eyes shifted to Bingmei, imploring her to listen. "You must save us from this fate. You were the one the phoenix chose to bear this awful task."

A sickening feeling crawled inside Bingmei's belly. Everyone was staring at her, their expectations weighing her down.

"You cannot force her," Rowen said, his tone fierce. "You said it was a sacrifice. Only she can decide whether to do it."

"What did you think we were going to do, Brother?" Juexin said hotly. "Tie her up and throw her over the Death Wall?"

Bingmei felt a shudder ripple through her. She sensed the presence of the blade coming closer to the palace. Maybe it would be best if she left Sajinau after all, just like she'd planned. The Qiangdao would follow her.

But would the prince and the others even let her go? She looked from face to face and felt a throb of anger at the unfairness of her situation. She was a warrior, trained to survive. The phoenix had chosen the wrong person. Bingmei didn't want to save the world. It was an impossible task.

"Please," Jidi Majia implored, the smell of his sorrow overpowering her.

"My lord," Jiaohua begged. "Give me a thousand cowry shells. My plan is the only prudent one."

Bingmei whirled and walked away, wiping her eyes as she went. They let her go, and she stormed out of the council chamber. She found Marenqo and Quion being held at bay by the guards, forbidden entrance into the chamber.

"What's going on in there?" Marenqo asked, quickly joining her. Quion followed him, his look worried. "The whole palace is in an uproar. Is Sajinau being invaded?"

"It's only a matter of time," Bingmei answered. "They're preparing for war." She pressed her lips, trying to quell the bitterness in her heart. "One they can't win."

杀雾

It was almost midnight. Bingmei was in bed, but she couldn't sleep. Every time she closed her eyes, she sensed the Phoenix Blade. It was somewhere to the west of the palace. Near, but not yet within the palace walls. Muxidi was biding his time. The constant awareness of it felt like the dull throbbing of a headache. It beckoned her to come, to claim it.

She sat up in bed, hugging herself, feeling her situation was beyond piteous. A small oil lamp burned on the table on the other side of the room. Kunmia and Mieshi were both asleep on the other beds, and Bingmei could hear the soft rhythm of their breathing. The rune staff leaned against the bedpost. Bingmei stared at the rugged meiwood that had seen so many battles. The glyphs and sigils were nicked and scarred. It held the power to drain the magic from other relics, but it, too, conjured the killing fog. All weapons of power did that. And the killing fog destroyed every living being it touched.

Until now.

Bingmei crossed her arms over her knees and sighed. Why couldn't she sleep? But how could she when it felt as if the weight of the world were crushing her shoulders? Staring at Kunmia, her master and friend, she felt a twinge of envy. Why hadn't Kunmia been chosen by the phoenix? She was just the kind of caring person who would have gladly sacrificed herself to save the world.

Her own smell made her sick.

Bingmei had always desired to emulate her master—except in that aspect. Kunmia had widespread respect, martial skill, good judgment, and loyal disciples. Her own quonsuun. Bingmei had hoped, with time, to establish those things for herself. She wanted to be so highly regarded that people would not think of the winter sickness as a curse but as something that made her unique. One day, *she* would be hired by the rulers of Sihui, Tuqiao, or Renxing to go on missions and defeat their enemies. The mere thought made her swell with ambition.

The other things a young woman might want had never appealed to Bingmei. She didn't want to marry, although perhaps part of her hesitation was that she didn't really think it possible. Who would want a wife who suffered from her condition, one that could be passed on to their posterity? Bingmei was fortunate that her own family had loved her in spite of it. Besides, she did not wish to bring an innocent life into the savage world.

No, she wanted only to be a warrior, a leader of men and women, but Jidi Majia's prophecy had taken her dream from her.

She wouldn't do it. No matter how Jidi Majia pleaded. Not even if every citizen in Sajinau prostrated themselves on the ground. She would not die so that people could go on robbing and deceiving each other. If the others could *smell* people like she could, no one would even suggest it. They'd know what she did—that most people were petty and jealous and small.

Her eyes drifted to the lamp's flickering flame. A feeling of dread bloomed in her breast, an instinct of warning that something was wrong. She sat up and slid her legs out from under the sheets, setting her bare feet on the floor. A prickle shot down her spine. A feeling of urgency tickled inside her. Without understanding why, she knew she had to hurry.

She walked across the floor and set her hand on the lattice of the screen door. The urge to open the door was strong. It didn't make sense in her head. But her heart screamed at her to listen to it instead. She tugged on the door, careful to make as little noise as possible, and gazed into the dark corridor of the palace. In her mind, she questioned going back for her boots, but the frenzied feeling of panic urged her to proceed without them.

She caught a whiff of sour-smelling air. Glancing both ways, she saw nothing. It felt as if something gave her a nudge from behind and pushed her into the corridor. The last time she'd felt such a strong nudge, it had been in Fusang. Dread filled her to bursting. What was happening? She looked back, expecting to see someone, but no one was there. A shiver tore through her. She was about to turn and close the door when the sour smell turned rancid. The smell came from the corridor behind her. She turned, looking into the gloom, and saw nothing.

But that smell was unmistakable. It was Muxidi.

Bingmei started to walk in the opposite direction. The smell grew stronger, wafting up from behind her like the wind. She could still sense the presence of the Phoenix Blade outside the palace walls. It hadn't moved or changed position. Then she realized, with horror, that the Qiangdao had left it there to distract her. To make her feel safe. He'd come for her without it.

Terror surged in her breast. She walked quickly, turning the corner. Pale moonlight spilling in from the upper windows was the only light. Her heart raced in her chest. This wasn't a nightmare. She could feel the weave of the rug on the soles of her feet.

When she reached the end of the corridor, it was a dead end. A set of heavy doors barred her path. She grabbed the handle and pulled, but it had been secured on the other side. Panic spasmed inside her. She could smell him following her.

The door wouldn't open.

CHAPTER
THIRTY-THREE

Hanging Trees

She had to hide because going back was unthinkable. He didn't have the sword with him, nor did he possess Bingmei's sense of smell, so he shouldn't have a supernatural ability to track her. When Bingmei turned, she saw a set of huge bronze decorative vases, each as tall as her. Two rings hung from the jaws of the beasts engraved on the sides. There were also the rafters above, but she didn't have the cricket charm with her.

She felt a little shove against her back toward one of the vases. Whatever force compelled her, she responded to it, because it had also warned her about the arrival of the Qiangdao. As quickly as she could, she climbed inside the nearest one and crouched within. It smelled musty, with a metallic tang from the bronze. Part of her wanted to stand up and face her enemy, but the instinct to hide had overpowered her. She waited, trying to calm her breathing so she wouldn't reveal herself.

The hideous stench slowly began to leach through the gaps in the bronze work. She bit her lip, staring through the small openings in the metal to see down the hall.

Three men appeared, walking quickly toward the doors. They were wreathed in smoke, which alarmed her. It was magic, pure and powerful, and the sight of it made her blood tingle. She recognized Muxidi in the forefront, but not the two dark-eyed men flanking him.

They reached the double doors and stopped, little curlicues of black smoke wafting from their bodies.

"I swear I saw her," said one of the men. They all reeked of murder. The smell made her gag.

"Maybe what you saw was a ghost," said the man she hated so much. Muxidi gazed at the door and then pulled the handle. It didn't budge for him either.

"She was in the corridor. I saw her turn down this way."

"I believe you," said Muxidi. He sniffed the air, wrinkling his nose. Bingmei quit breathing, gazing at him through the small gaps in the vase. "Where are you, little ghost?"

"She can't be far," said the other. "If we don't seize her before the Dragon Emperor's ships arrive, we'll be done for!"

"She's here," said Muxidi. "There are only so many places to hide."

She watched one of the men walk over to the other vase and look down inside. Apprehension rippled through her. Should she cry out for help? She was an able fighter, but she had a sense that the leader had brought some of his best men to abduct her. Three against one. She stared at him, trying to banish her fear with anger.

"She went through the door," said the other man. "Then she barred it. I think she knew we were following her."

Muxidi wrinkled his mouth into a frown and nodded. "You're right, I think. She's close. Come."

The Qiangdao leader bowed his head, and she saw the rippling smoke around him thicken. Then she watched in amazement as he walked *through* the closed door. Like he was made of smoke himself. The other two followed, the smoke dissipating after they had left.

Relief washed over her, relaxing her muscles. She hung her head a moment, grateful for the reprieve. It dawned on her that these Qiangdao were using magic artifacts without paying the death price. Echion controlled the killing fog, and he was rewarding his servants with magic. It was an unfair advantage. But now that she knew the extent of their power, she realized that she wasn't safe in the palace at Sajinau. If she stayed, it would only be a matter of time before they found her.

After waiting for a while to be sure they didn't come back the same way, she slowly climbed out of the vase. The metal vibrated when her foot struck it, and so she squeezed the material to dull the sound. There was some moonlight, enough for her to see the design on the bronze work. The elegant form of a phoenix in flight. A strange sensation shot down her back and nestled inside her stomach. Had the vase protected her somehow? How could that be?

She smelled the scent of smoke just before a hand grabbed her arm.

Bingmei whirled, thrusting the edge of her hand into Jiaohua's throat. He blocked it with his other hand and tightened his grip on her arm. She sidestepped around to lever his leg and flip him, but he moved in the opposite direction, putting them back to back. His reflexes were quick; hers would need to be quicker.

She drew her hand back to punch him in the stomach. He released her arm to block the blow, then stepped closer, his breath nauseating her, and gripped her wrist.

"Hold. I'm not your enemy," he said in a whisper.

"You attacked me," she said through gritted teeth.

"You mistake me, girl. You're a warrior. I was only defending myself. I was following three Qiangdao down the hall when I saw you jump out of the vase."

"You saw them? Or did you let them in?" Bingmei accused. "Let go of me!"

He pursed his lips and chuckled low in his throat. He gripped her wrist for a second more and then opened his hand. "See? I'm not a threat. Although it's insulting you'd accuse me of betraying King Shulian for *you*."

The smoky smell carried a tang of disdain.

"Then why not stop them?" she challenged, rubbing her wrist.

"They've already killed six of my guards tonight. And two soldiers patrolling the wall. They move like smoke and shadow. Looking for you, I imagine."

Bingmei could never trust someone who reeked of dishonesty. But there was also a smell of valor in him. Of bravery and cunning. He might look like a spider, but he could be an aggressive ally. One that bit with poisoned fangs.

"They were," she added.

"I heard them murmuring as I approached, but I couldn't hear what they said. Did you hear them?" It was a lie. Blatant. Maybe he was testing her.

"Echion is coming," she answered. There was no need to disguise the truth. It was frightening enough. "By sea."

Jiaohua nodded his head, and his emotions relaxed a bit. "Good. It's foolish to attack Sajinau by sea. They will lose many ships before they get near. I'll warn General Tzu."

She nodded and started walking away, but he walked in the same direction and kept the same pace. "What do you want?" She made no attempt to disguise her annoyance.

"The same thing everyone wants," he said. "The same thing *you* want. I want to live. You won't go to the Death Wall, will you? You'll run away and save yourself."

He was trying to provoke her into revealing herself. Bingmei felt his words like blows, but she didn't answer him.

After waiting a moment, giving her the opportunity to say something, he continued. "My duty is to protect Sajinau and the royal family. To keep peace in its streets. It's not easy. People steal from each other. Cheat. They kill out of anger. They abandon children. Someone has to deal with these tragedies. That is the role of the Jingcha. That is *my* role." He grabbed her shoulder once more, turning her around to face him, and raised a finger. "I will do *anything* to protect them. Don't try to escape Sajinau, young Bingmei. I'm watching you."

She struck him, palm first, in the gut, moving so quickly he didn't have the reflexes to block her move. His face wilting with pain, he removed his hand from her shoulder.

"Don't touch me again," she warned and then walked away.

杀雾

When dawn arrived at the palace, it found Bingmei in the training yard. She worked with every weapon they had, exercising her skills and testing her limitations. Every stance, every form blurred together. She relished the freedom her body gave her. Her muscles were honed and hard, her face dripping with sweat, but she continued to execute the forms with precision, flowing from one to the other, pausing to exchange a spear for a saber and then a chain. She'd practiced for hours, determined to calm her mind and decide what to do.

The murderous Qiangdao had not yet been found, although every member of the Jingcha sought them. She could still feel the itching presence of the Phoenix Blade, lurking beyond the walls. It was somewhere to the southwest of the palace.

Staying in Sajinau would be suicide. The rulers would try to coax her into sacrificing herself so that the Jingcha could continue ruling the streets. So that General Tzu could lead armies to spread Sajinau's dominion. So that King Shulian, whenever he returned, would rule a larger domain than the one his father had handed him. Meanwhile, her grandfather's quonsuun would remain abandoned and broken. Her purpose would go unfulfilled, her family unrevenged.

Why should everyone keep what they wanted except for her? The unfairness twisted inside her like a dagger.

At the end of her routine, she knelt on the floor for a moment, panting and covered in sweat, then returned the saber to its rack and refreshed herself with the towels and bowls of water that had been set out for that purpose. Not until she tossed the soiled towel on the table did she notice Prince Rowen leaning against one of the pillars, arms folded, regarding her.

Her mood soured slightly, but she didn't hesitate to confront him. "Have you also come to persuade me to die?" she asked as she walked toward his pillar.

Rowen chuckled and looked down. "No, Bingmei. I wanted to persuade you to see the hanging trees."

Her eyebrows arched. "Where criminals are killed?"

"No," he said, laughing harder. "No, it's the palace gardens. Plants *hang* from the trees. I think you'll like it."

"And why would I want to visit a garden?" she said, feeling that he wasn't being completely forthright with her.

He shrugged, his voice lowering. "Because that's how we'll escape Sajinau when Echion comes." His eyes glittered with determination. "My brother is a fool. And so are his advisors. Come see the hanging trees with me. We can talk more there." Now she smelled the truth. He meant every word.

A little smile crept onto Bingmei's mouth. "I'll get ready."

After bathing and changing into new clothes—the servants took her soiled ones to wash—Bingmei joined Marenqo and Quion at the feasting tables. She noticed Kunmia was speaking with Jidi Majia, their heads bent in conversation. The crown prince wasn't there, nor was the general or the master of the Jingcha.

"The boy tells me," Marenqo said in a sardonic tone, nibbling on a cube of purple dragon fruit, "that the people of Sajinau *trap* the fish here. Not with nets, but by building strange chutes. The fish swim into the trap, nearly kill themselves with the effort of climbing *up* the chutes, only to be caught at the top, killed, and sold. I've never heard of such lazy fishermen before. I'm astonished."

"I've not seen anything like it," Quion said in wonderment. "I know salmon go upstream to spawn, but this is made by *people*. There were so many fish. A net would burst. Ten nets would burst."

"Try the dragon fruit, Bingmei; it's quite delicious," Marenqo offered, gesturing to a silver platter that held an assortment of different fruits.

She took a tiny bamboo spear and stabbed one and ate it. It tasted like calmness smelled.

Bingmei smiled and nodded to Quion. "This isn't the first time we've tricked beasts into subservience. I imagine the first horse didn't relish a bridle."

"That's it precisely!" Marenqo said. "We use their instincts against them."

"Why did the ancients decorate everything with the shapes of animals, then?" Quion asked.

Marenqo raised his hand, looking sagely at the young man, then lowered it and said, "I have no idea."

Bingmei laughed and speared a slice of melon next.

After a lengthy pause, Marenqo looked at Bingmei. "So . . . what do you think of Jidi Majia's vision?"

She gave him an arch look. "Would *you* want to sacrifice yourself, Marenqo?"

"Not really, no. Actually, it would terrify me. I have a fear of death that is rather developed. Which is why I asked *you* the question."

Quion's countenance fell. He never had learned to hide his emotions.

"I'm still considering it," Bingmei said, although that wasn't entirely true. She had decided against it, more than once. "I don't think it is fair."

"It is not fair," Marenqo agreed. "But is it fair to let the world become enslaved?"

Bingmei snorted. "It already is, Marenqo." She cocked her head as she looked at him. "If I decided to leave . . . would you come with me?" She had always liked Marenqo, and his skills would be very useful if she escaped.

He looked down at his hands, and she smelled the mix of feelings within him. He wasn't disappointed in her request. Nor was he surprised. He was genuinely conflicted. It smelled like baking hot peppers. "I . . . I don't know, Bingmei. Kunmia is my master. I, her disciple. I don't think she intends to abandon Sajinau. When Echion comes, they will need fighters." The frown that had appeared on his mouth deepened.

"They already have an army," Bingmei pointed out. "We saw them training in the courtyard."

"Yes, but . . . their skills are not the same as those of us who have trained in a quonsuun." He glanced at her for a brief instant, then looked away. "I don't feel right about leaving my master. Mieshi is staying as well. I heard her say so."

"I hope to build up my own quonsuun someday," Bingmei said pointedly. She wasn't inviting him overtly, but she hoped he picked up on her meaning that someday she would.

She could tell he felt flattered, but loyalty bound more tightly than ropes. He simply nodded. "And you'll do well; I'm sure of it."

"Quion," she said, turning to the young fisherman. "I'm going to see the hanging trees now. Do you want to come?"

"They're beautiful," Marenqo said. "Especially this time of year."

"Yes!" Quion answered.

So Bingmei and Quion left the banquet room. She glanced over at Kunmia once again, feeling a pang of sorrow and also guilt. She knew her master would be duty bound to stay and protect Sajinau. Bingmei wished that the situation were otherwise, but secrecy was essential. Her heart ached at the thought of leaving Kunmia, not knowing when, or if, she'd see her again, but she didn't believe she had a choice. If she told her master she was leaving, then Prince Juexin might try to stop her—or send Jiaohua to do it.

She asked a servant for direction to the hanging trees, and the young man escorted them to the threshold. They passed beneath a beautiful meiwood arch, decorated with vines and the symbols of partridges and cockerels. The gardens opened up before them in an abundance of color. The scent was a delightful floral perfume.

The trees had been sculpted, the smaller branches removed, and only club-like joints remained. Bunches of blossoms of different mixes and varieties hung down from above, as if replacing the leaves that had been removed from the trees. She saw workers on short ladders tending to the arrangements. The path itself was overgrown with greenery, making it dense with foliage.

"Well, I've never," Quion said with an amazed sigh.

"I was worried you'd changed your mind," said Prince Rowen, stepping out from one side of the archway. Damanhur stood beside him, hand on his sword pommel.

She felt a little twisting sensation in her stomach.

Rowen walked up to her, holding out a little open sack. She saw a handful of brown pods within it. They had a waxy texture like a pepper, only the color was wrong. He dropped his voice low, proffering the bag to her. "Are you ready to leave?"

CHAPTER
THIRTY-FOUR

The Coming Fire

Bingmei took a brown pod. It was as large as her thumb, and she eyed it warily. Quion started to scowl, and the onion smell of distrust came from her friend in malodorous waves.

"Will this make my mouth burn?" she asked cautiously.

"Try it and see," said Rowen with a conniving smile.

Damanhur chuckled and shook his head, turning around and gazing at the gardens with a hint of impatience.

Bingmei raised the pod to her nose, but it didn't have an odor. "It's wrinkled like a fig," she said.

"It's not a fig," Rowen said.

Bingmei bit into the piece carefully. Its tough exterior was like dried meat, but sweet flavor exploded in her mouth as she began to chew. It looked like a dried piece of dung, but it tasted sweeter than any fruit she'd ever tasted. Her eyes widened in surprise at the texture and flavor. Then she quickly took another bite.

Rowen smiled at her reaction. "It's a delicacy in Sajinau," he said. "They come from the Namibu Desert far to the south. They're called medjool by the tribesmen there." He offered the bag to Quion, who took one and bit into the middle of it and winced. "They have long seeds," Rowen said apologetically. "I should have warned you about that."

Bingmei bit around the seed until it was exposed, then drew out the long wooden sliver. Quion did the same.

"Have you been to Namibu?" Rowen asked her.

"No. I've never been this far south before."

He nodded. "The town of Xidan is to the south on the coast. The junks from Namibu go there first before coming here to trade. They also go many other places, like Sihui. Depending on what happens, we may need to find shelter somewhere else. But this much is clear. If we stay in Sajinau, we'll lose any ability to maneuver. I hope I'm wrong and my brother is able to hold off Echion, I truly do." He paused, as if giving her time to judge his remark. She sensed he meant it, although his usual conflict regarding his brother was also present. "But if he fails, we cannot allow Echion to capture you, Bingmei. If he does, all is lost. We must leave now. Today."

"Why should she trust you?" Quion said.

"Why shouldn't she?" Rowen countered, giving Quion a look of annoyance. "Do you have another place to go?"

"He's coming," Damanhur muttered.

Rowen looked over Bingmei's shoulder. When she turned, she saw Juexin approaching with Jidi Majia and a few courtiers. Her insides clenched with dread. The sharp tang of hostility wafted off Rowen when he saw his brother.

Juexin motioned for the courtiers to remain at the archway, and he crossed with only Jidi Majia to greet them. When he arrived, he saw the sack of medjool and helped himself to one.

"Showing our guests the hanging trees?" Juexin asked.

"I was about to. Yes." Rowen's demeanor was courteous, but emotion seethed beneath the surface.

"These gardens are beautiful," the crown prince said. "Mother was fond of them. Wasn't she?" His eyes had an accusing look. Rowen bristled but said nothing.

Juexin bit into the strange leathery fruit and then tossed the seed onto the grass. "Bingmei, can I speak with you?"

It was just what she had been dreading. "Of course, Your Highness," she answered, feeling her discomfort grow at the tension between the brothers.

Rowen bowed his head in mocking deference, gesturing for Bingmei to accompany his brother. The prince led her to the left side of the gardens, not far from the others, but out of earshot.

"Kunmia has said you've never been all the way to the Death Wall?" he asked, clasping his hands behind his back. Despite herself, she admired him. He was a handsome man, full of vigor and strength. He walked with a sword buckled to his tunic, and the nicks and cuts on his knuckles indicated he knew how to use it. He was not a pampered prince—he had led his father's armies against the Qiangdao many times.

"No," she answered, fearing where the conversation was going.

"I have, several times. It's an arduous climb to get to the mountaintops. I've walked up and down the steps. I've shared meals with the soldiers garrisoned there. Some of them believe it is the entrance to the underworld. The Grave Kingdom. They're afraid to go there. A few claim they've seen ghosts on the other side. Others have seen poisonous serpents slithering around. Serpents that can climb trees." He chuckled, then stopped by a small koi pond where colorful fish flitted.

Still she waited, not wanting to encourage their talk any more than courtesy demanded. She glanced back at Rowen, who was watching them with a fierce, almost protective look on his face.

"Everyone is afraid to cross the Death Wall," he said, gazing at the water. "We've been taught to fear it. So I've been asking myself a question since you arrived." He looked at her seriously. "What would it take to persuade *you* to cross it?"

She felt her cheeks start to burn under his probing look. He was trying to bribe her to sacrifice herself. She turned away from him, trying to control her emotions.

"I cannot force you. No one can. The sacrifice must be willing. So I have an idea. A thought."

She bit her lip, knowing he would tell her whether she liked it or not.

"I would build a special quonsuun for you. Here, in the middle of Sajinau. One dedicated to the phoenix. I would set aside one day a week for the people of the city to visit the quonsuun to burn incense for you. Every week, they would remember your name and what you did for us. I would command that this practice would continue from now until the end of the world. I would appoint monks to officiate and tell your story. To be held in remembrance always. They will forget me someday, Bingmei. They will forget my father. But they will *never* forget you. The grounds of the phoenix quonsuun would be considered holy. This is what I would do to honor and respect your sacrifice."

Guilt squirmed inside her heart. What he promised was indeed an enormous honor. It would make her death mean something, which was rare in their world. How long would it last, though? How long before an unknown generation despised the tradition and mocked the girl they were forced to revere?

She turned to look at him. "If Jidi Majia had said that *you* must be the one to sacrifice your life, would *you* have done it?"

He stared at her with fixed attention. "Without hesitation."

"Because you care for your people," she said.

"I love my people," he answered. "I will not let them be enslaved."

She took a step closer to him. "But Sajinau is different than the rest of the world. Maybe there is more good in this kingdom. Maybe King Shulian has created something admirable here. But would you, Your Highness, give your life to save the Qiangdao? The murderers who seek to destroy us?"

His lips pressed together.

"I'm not sure you would. You fight them. You oppose them. Yet despite your father's talk of banding the kingdoms together, what has Sajinau done to defeat the Qiangdao?"

"You sound like my brother," he said, his voice tinged with resentment. It was a burning smell, like overcooked syrup.

"Maybe your brother has a point," Bingmei said simply.

Juexin controlled his expression, if barely. "You don't know him as well as I do, Bingmei. There's a reason my father didn't choose him."

"What if your father was wrong?" Bingmei asked. She felt impertinent asking it, but she needed to know how he'd react.

Juexin's nostrils flared, showing his offense, and his smell soured. "Kunmia has told me that you've fought the Qiangdao yourself. You don't lack for courage. The reason the Qiangdao have not yet attacked the city of Sajinau is because they know they cannot overpower it. We have enough food to withstand a siege for years, because my father has been wise enough to secure it. We can defend our walls with only a fraction of the soldiers it would take to breach them. But if we attacked the Qiangdao in their strongholds, in their mountain caves, we'd be slaughtered. It would take ten years or longer for us to overcome them, not to mention the loss of lives and treasure, and for what? To leave widows weeping for their husbands and sons? Sisters for their brothers? Whichever side attacks first loses. That is the argument against going to war. And if Echion seeks to defeat us here, then he will only succeed at a great cost."

Bingmei felt there was truth in his words. He believed them at least. She looked him in the eye. "The difference between you and Echion is that *he* is willing to endure the weeping widows and sisters. I've taken his measure, Prince Juexin. He does not share your qualms."

Juexin nodded at her words. "I don't doubt you. Echion is a monster. For a long time my brother has had an unhealthy fascination with the emblems of the Dragon of Night. He and Jidi Majia would discuss it often, trying to decipher what the carvings meant. And you're right. He doesn't share my qualms."

Did he mean Rowen or Echion? Or both?

That thought, grazing her mind, made her doubt Rowen's motives once again.

"I will let you return to your walk," he said, bowing to her in respect. "Consider my promise to you. I believe my father would have recommended the same. He and I think very much alike. Or so I flatter myself."

"Thank you for the generosity of your offer," Bingmei said, anxious to leave his company.

He escorted her back to where Rowen and the others waited. Jidi Majia gave Bingmei an earnest look, but she let nothing show on her face.

"Brother," Juexin said, looking at Rowen, his tone formal. "General Tzu has requested that you lead part of the army."

Rowen's surprise showed in his arched eyebrows. "He did?"

Juexin nodded. "You must help defend the city. I approved his request. This is your chance, Rowen." He looked as if he were about to say more, but stopped himself. "Eomen said she wanted to speak with you. Should I tell her you're coming after your walk?"

Rowen offered a pained smile. "Of course."

Juexin nodded curtly. He'd taken no more than two steps toward the arch, when a soldier with a shield emblazoned with the dragon emblem rushed through it.

The man bowed before the crown prince. "My lord," he said, huffing. "The fires in the watchtowers are burning. Enemy ships have been sighted."

"Where is General Tzu?" Juexin asked, his expression turning grave.

"He's preparing orders to defend the city."

"May the phoenix protect us," Juexin muttered and started marching toward the palace.

杀雾

When the entourage had finally withdrawn, Rowen continued to stare at the meiwood threshold. She felt the seething conflict within him, the resentment and guilt, the ambition. Even so, his exterior remained completely calm. This was something that had always troubled her about him. Juexin had no guile—the younger brother had inherited it all.

"I wish I didn't know about your power," Rowen said, turning to give her a slightly reproachful look. "It isn't fair."

"Sometimes it feels like a curse," Bingmei admitted.

"If we climb hard, we'll reach the top of the mountain before sunset. We'll be far away before the city falls."

"Then why are we waiting?" Damanhur asked with impatience.

Rowen turned to her. "Come with us."

"Even after what your brother said?" Bingmei asked.

"He's already expecting me to disappoint him," he replied darkly. "Why stop now? It's as I've told you—I fear they'll lose this battle. And if they do, I don't trust that you'll be safe here. Let's get away and plot our next move from a position of safety. There are other kings we can enlist to help. We should go. Now."

"I need my pack," Quion said.

Rowen looked annoyed. "We've already arranged for supplies."

Damanhur nodded. "My ensign has been gathering them since we arrived. I even had them get a new straight sword for you, Bingmei." He winked at her. "My men are slipping through the garden ahead of us. Let's go."

"I *need* my pack," Quion said forcefully, his voice breaking.

"Whatever you carried in that thing can be replaced," Rowen said. "If you are coming, then come now!"

But from the tortured look that crossed his face, Bingmei knew the prince was wrong. There was something sentimental in there, something he did not wish to leave behind.

"Delaying a few minutes won't hurt," Bingmei said. "And I promised I wouldn't go anywhere without him."

"He'll attract unwanted attention carrying that huge pack through the palace," Rowen said. "Come or stay. It's up to you, but we go now."

"I can't leave it," Quion said, giving Bingmei a pleading look. His smell of misery made her suffer with him.

Rowen seethed with impatience. "Come or stay," he repeated.

Quion's brow wilted. "I'll be quick."

Gongs sounded ominously from within the palace. Damanhur muttered a curse. "If we don't leave now, we'll lose the chance."

"We won't wait long for you," Rowen said to Quion, exasperated. "I just don't trust Jiaohua not to notice you, but the chaos in the palace might provide enough of a distraction. Catch up if you can. That's the best I can offer."

Quion nodded eagerly, looking at Bingmei for approval. She felt that Rowen was legitimately trying to be accommodating to her friend.

"Be quick," she told him, nodding.

He started running away from them.

"Quion!" she shouted.

He spun around, looking confused.

"Hurry . . . but be careful!"

He nodded in realization and then began walking vigorously back to the palace.

"Now can we go?" Damanhur said.

"Lead the way," Rowen answered.

The hanging trees were no less beautiful than they'd been when she first entered the garden, but Bingmei's heart shivered with dread. She kept glancing back on the path to see if they were being followed, but it was too soon for that. Too soon, also, for Quion to return. The trees provided a natural cover that hindered visibility. They passed little creeks and ponds and marble benches shaped like lions, as noisy birds called from the trees overhead, fluttering from branch to branch.

The gentle breeze rustled the branches, giving the garden an idyllic look that conflicted with the sound of another gong reverberating from the palace.

"Are the gongs warnings, then?" Bingmei asked.

"Yes," Rowen answered. "They warn the people to seek shelter. The soldiers will also gather in the courtyard to receive their orders. The fjords are the first line of defense. My brother's men are probably hoping they have days to prepare before the city is even breached. But I still don't think so." He looked backward as well, joining in her nervous habit. He had a sour smell, like bitter herbs, which she interpreted as self-loathing. The bitterness seemed to be familiar with him, but he marched on resolutely. "From what I have learned about the ancients, Echion has incredible powers. And access to magic that we simply can't match."

Bingmei caught the scent of another man up ahead, whose nervous energy radiated off him in waves of ginger, and Damanhur greeted one of the members of his ensign.

"Ah, Huqu," he said. Bingmei had traveled with him to the glacier and back, so he looked familiar, but she had never learned his name.

"The gongs have sounded," Huqu answered, gazing past them nervously. "Is that because of you, Master?"

"No, the Dragon of Night is coming," Rowen answered. "Do you have the supplies?"

"Yes, Master," Huqu said and retrieved a pack from its concealment in the bushes. Several more were hidden with it, and he tossed one to Rowen, one to Damanhur, and then found one for Bingmei.

"Where's the fisherman?" Huqu asked, grabbing a fourth bag.

"Coming up the trail behind us," Rowen said. He glanced back, leaning from side to side. "Hopefully."

There was a sword strapped to Bingmei's pack, a beautifully crafted saber with a meiwood handle. Her pack also carried clothes, a bedroll, and various other supplies.

Rowen pulled on a jacket over his silk shirt and quickly fastened the rope loops to close it. The rest of them changed, too, concealing the clothes they'd last been seen in. In a few moments, they were all garbed for the journey.

"What do we do with this one?" Huqu said, gesturing to the final pack.

"Leave it," Rowen said. "Let's go."

"Can't we wait here?" Bingmei asked, feeling anxious. She'd thought Quion would have joined them already.

Rowen shook his head no and touched her arm in a tender gesture. "He'll find us. I'm sure of it." He wasn't being intentionally deceptive, but she did smell his urgency.

The garden had been sloping upward, the foliage becoming progressively denser. Damanhur led the way, followed by Huqu. They were trailed by Rowen and Bingmei, and the steepness of the climb soon made it impossible for them to do anything but breathe fast and sweat. While she was wearied by the climb, it invigorated her spirits and helped occupy her mind. The trail was easy to follow, though narrow, and she knew that Quion would be able to pick his way up after them.

Another member of the ensign waited for them along the trail. He offered each a flask of cold water, which he'd filled from a tiny rivulet running down the mountain. It tasted delicious, but her thoughts strayed back to Quion. She stared back down the trail, listening for the sounds of her friend. If only she'd thought to give him her cricket . . .

Higher they climbed, straining as the trail grew even steeper. The trees grew larger and more wild as they climbed, and the flowers growing along the trail looked and smelled beautiful. She mopped her forehead on her sleeve, keeping pace with the men without difficulty. It reminded her a little of the trail from Kunmia's quonsuun to the top of the mountain where she'd first practiced with the Phoenix Blade. The memory brought another pang of guilt for abandoning her master in the face of an enemy. She'd broken Kunmia's trust in her—and she feared she'd never have the chance to make amends.

They reached the top of the mountain ridge before sunset. The air was colder up there, but it felt good after the long hike. Looking down, she could see the city of Sajinau nestled below, glimmering in the fading sun. The burning watchtowers inside the fjord were light stars against the dark wall of the cliffs. The city had siege crossbows and weapons for hurling stone down against the invading junks.

It still wouldn't be enough.

"Where are Batong and the others?" Damanhur asked, panting, hands on hips.

Huqu looked around, also winded. "They were supposed to wait for us up here."

And that was when Bingmei first noticed the insidious smell, which had been concealed by the abundance of wildflowers growing in the scrub on the ridge. The smell of death. The smell of murder.

The smell of Qiangdao lying in wait for their prey.

CHAPTER
THIRTY-FIVE

Jiukeshu

They had ventured up the mountain into a trap. The other members of the ensign had already been captured.

"Stop!" Bingmei cried out.

Damanhur turned to look at her with worried eyes. "What is it?"

"Qiangdao."

A blur from the sky hurtled toward them, and a weighted net slammed Damanhur to the ground. The rocks and scrub sprang to life as Qiangdao charged toward them, screaming in challenge.

Bingmei gaped when she saw their numbers, but she didn't hesitate. She drew her saber and reached into her pocket for the cricket. A net came flying at her, but she sprang free. As she soared through the air, she caught sight of the others. Huqu and Rowen drew their blades and were immediately surrounded, while Damanhur struggled against the weights of the net.

Bingmei landed abruptly in front of an enemy and sliced through his jacket and animal-hide armor. She kicked him down, only to find herself facing another Qiangdao who'd jumped over him. She ducked, spun around, and deflected his weapon. Another man was already grabbing for her arm. Her heart galloped in her chest as she spun, kicking him in the face, and knocked him down. Even with her blade whipping death, the enemy tried to swarm her. Summoning the cricket's power just in time, she leaped straight into the air and watched them collide beneath her. She came back down, landing on backs and heads, and deftly walked down their bodies to escape.

She darted a glance at Rowen, who was sawing at the ropes of Damanhur's net with his short blade. A Qiangdao tackled him from behind before he could finish. Frowning, she rushed toward them, dodging two men who tried to stop her, cutting at their legs and calves with her sword. The Qiangdao shoved Rowen's face into the dirt, then jumped to standing to meet her attack. She leaped at him, feet forward, and kicked him in the chest and then the face in a snapping motion, rocking his head and body back.

She landed near Rowen, grabbing his arm to help him stand. Someone tackled her from behind. Huge arms wrapped around her body, squeezing so hard she feared her ribs would break. She arched her head back to break the man's nose, but he was taller than she'd expected, and her head only struck his chest. With all her strength, she tried to squirm out of his hold, but his strength defied her.

Rowen plunged his blade into the man's thick leg. A grunt of pain, and then the man kicked the prince in the face, dropping him instantly. Blood dribbled from Rowen's nose as he slumped to the ground, unconscious.

Huqu was down, and several of the Qiangdao were stomping on him as he writhed in pain. Bingmei's heart shuddered with dread. Then she saw Damanhur rise from the nest of ropes, sword in hand, his eyes full of fury and the thirst for vengeance.

The Qiangdao holding her threw her down, and a huge rock caught her fall, knocking the wind out of her.

Damanhur rushed the man who'd attacked her and injured the prince, yelling in challenge. The huge Qiangdao pulled a chui from his belt. It had a meiwood handle, and the round iron orb attached to the end was engraved with sigils. The leader sneered at Damanhur, barking something in a language she didn't recognize.

Damanhur swung at him, and the chui was brought up to deflect the attack. The man was huge and quick and slammed his weapon into Damanhur's chest. Bingmei thought she heard the snap of a bone. Damanhur grimaced, but did not relent.

Bingmei struggled to her feet and saw several men rushing toward her. She still couldn't fill her lungs, and her arms were sore from being clamped by the giant man. The coppery taste of blood was in her mouth. Dizziness washed over her, but she was determined to fight on. She lunged forward, stabbing one enemy in the stomach with the point of her sword and then reversing the blow so the pommel hit another. She was about to mount another attack when someone grabbed her sword arm and wrenched it. Her fingers bent painfully. Bingmei struck out with her fist, knocking the man down, and then the blade tumbled from her hand and clattered against the rocks. Someone kicked her in the side. Pain blurred her vision. Another punch to her back made her stagger and cry out in agony.

Blinking the sweat from her eyes, she saw Rowen trying to lift his head, his eyes unfocused. Had he heard her cry out?

Another man kicked at the side of her knee, and she stumbled, planting her palm on the ground, her other arm torqued at a painful angle. Her chest screamed for air.

Confused, tortured by pain, she twisted her neck to see who'd attacked her. Instead, a sickly green glow caught her eye. The chui wielded by the giant Qiangdao was magic. Damanhur swung at him relentlessly, but the chui seemed to jerk of its own accord to deflect the blows. A primal sneer on the Qiangdao's face showed he knew the power he was wielding.

The men restraining Bingmei wrenched her arms harder. She cried out in pain and warning as the first tendrils of fog crept toward them, coming up from behind Damanhur. They came like snakes smelling rodents for food, hungry and greedy. As the fog touched the Qiangdao, she watched the mist shrink away from their legs, going around them to find the victims it desired. The Qiangdao were immune to it, just like Muxidi had been in her vision. Her heart skittered in panic.

She looked back, behind the Qiangdao subduing her, and saw more of the fog encroaching from that side. Panic filled her. There was no way to escape it.

Rowen was still trying to rise when a man kicked him hard in the ribs. He fell back down, groaning.

Blows from Damanhur's sword rained down on the massive Qiangdao, but the big man had no sense of urgency. So sure were they of the outcome, none of the other Qiangdao came to assist him in the fight. The other rogues were grinning at their victory, walking through the tendrils of fog. It seemed like a dream. No, a nightmare.

"Damanhur!" Bingmei screamed. "The fog!"

The swordsman heard her words and halted his attack. He glanced around quickly, seeing the thick, deadly mist converging on the chui gripped in the huge man's fist.

She saw the warring conflict on his face, the urge to kill and defeat his enemy. But he could not win. And if he kept fighting, the fog would kill Rowen, Huqu, and Bingmei. And then Damanhur himself. That was why the Qiangdao looked so smug. They knew there could only be one outcome.

She pleaded with him with her eyes as she knelt in the dirt and rocks, body aching, sweat and blood dripping from her face.

The look of conflict on Damanhur's face was terrible. He whirled around, taking in the full scene. The fog was nearly to Huqu, who lay unconscious. Almost as if the fog had already killed him. When Damanhur turned back to the giant Qiangdao, a look of revenge in his eyes, he did the only thing he could. He threw down his blade. It rang like a bell when it struck a stone.

The giant grunted with victory, grinning, and lowered the chui. The green haze around it subsided. The gathering fog became aimless, roiling in a frenzy as it lost strength and purpose. Bingmei watched it seep into the rocks and dirt and vanish.

Someone wrapped a rope around Bingmei's body, binding her arms to her sides. She felt a noose fix around her neck. She did not attempt to struggle. She tried to stand but wobbled and fell back down.

Damanhur held up his wrists to be bound, a symbol of submission. The Qiangdao grunted again, shaking his head. Then he gestured for him to follow on foot. She watched Rowen get tied up and Huqu as well. They were both carried while Bingmei was led by the noose after them.

She'd never been captured before. Always before, she'd found a way to escape. Dread filled her stomach, making it queasy. Her only hope was that these Qiangdao had no idea whom they'd captured.

杀雾

They were taken, bound as they were—save Damanhur—to a cleft on the other side of the mountain. The rest of Damanhur's ensign had been taken there. The horrible stench of the Qiangdao made Bingmei want to gag. The boulders formed the walls, and they were penned in like goats by a herdsman. The giant Qiangdao came with them but stood by the entrance, smiling at them in a way that made Bingmei sick.

"I'm sorry, Master," one of the prisoners said, bowing his head in shame. "They overpowered us."

"It's not your fault, Batong," Damanhur said bitterly. He turned around and looked at them all. Huqu was laid out, unconscious, though alive. Rowen was awake, but his eyes were wells of misery.

The giant said some unintelligible words, and a wiry man approached the opening of the cave, wearing beaver skin and a furred cap that flared open at his ears. He had stringy hair and a cunning look.

The wiry man bowed to the giant and then came into the little den made of stone and rubble. "Greetings," he said. "You have been captured by the mighty Jiukeshu, fiercest of the Qiangdao."

Damanhur scowled but inclined his head. That their lives had been spared at all surprised Bingmei. By reputation and her own experience, the Qiangdao relished plunder and murder, and these men smelled like they'd participated in both.

The wiry man nodded in acknowledgment. "My master bids me speak to you. I am his humble translator. I once lived in the city of Sajinau. I was captured, but I have made peace with the Qiangdao and am now one of them. The great emperor is coming to reclaim his realm. He will appoint those loyal to him to be his rulers. Now, my master bids me offer you all—"

He dipped his head at each one of them in turn, until he reached Rowen. His eyes widened with recognition. Bingmei smelled his sudden change in mood, and the dread in her heart deepened. He knew. The wiry man turned and began speaking quickly to Jiukeshu.

The giant stepped forward, his face twisting with confusion, then a broad, pleased smile brightened his face.

Damanhur's eyes were like daggers.

The wiry man spoke a few more words to the big leader, who nodded and gestured to where Rowen knelt, bound and still bloody.

"What is your name?" the wiry man asked, standing in front of Rowen.

The prince grimaced and said nothing.

"You are Prince *Rowen*," said the wiry man with eagerness.

"No, his name is Wuren!" Damanhur said angrily. "He's part of my ensign." The smell of the lie stung Bingmei's nose.

"Then he's deceived you," said the wiry man. "But I think not. You're lying. I know him. I know his face and his voice, if he'd but speak. No?" He snorted and then chortled. "Jiukeshu will take him to the emperor. He's coming to Sajinau, you know. He knows all the secret passes around the palace. We were set here to guard and prevent escape. How pleased Lord Echion will be to learn who my master has caught." He rubbed his hands together.

"What will become of us?" Damanhur said heatedly.

"You have a choice, bold one. My master respects you for your skill and courage. He could use you as a leader once you've proven your loyalty. None of your ensign will be harmed if you join us. Lord Echion will give us the cities he conquers. The Qiangdao will rule. Join us and partake. Or you'll be slaves working on the Death Wall." He shrugged. "It makes no difference to us."

"Tell your master," Damanhur said, "that I would come with him to greet Lord Echion."

The wiry man wrinkled his nose. He muttered some guttural words. Jiukeshu laughed and responded curtly.

"The great Jiukeshu says you have not earned the right to behold the greatness of Lord Echion. You have done nothing to prove yourself. Come, princeling. You will be quite valuable to our lord."

Rowen tried to stand, but his bonds made it difficult. The wiry man grabbed his arm and helped him. Damanhur, his face roiling with conflict, stepped forward. The huge Qiangdao leader did the same, bringing out the chui once more, his lips twitching with suppressed malice. Damanhur was weaponless, and there were dozens of Qiangdao outside. Bingmei could smell his intentions. Would he truly sacrifice himself to try to save Rowen, despite knowing he would fail?

"No, my friend," Rowen said, looking Damanhur in the eye. He shook his head slowly. "There is nothing more you can do for me. I will go." He swallowed. "I've always wanted to meet him anyway."

"A wise decision, *Prince*," the wiry man sneered. He shoved him toward Jiukeshu by the entrance. "Your friends would be wise to do the same."

Damanhur's fists were tight, and he trembled with rage. Rowen turned back and looked at him. He nodded, trying to convey with his eyes that it would be all right, even though they all knew it would not. Then Rowen looked at Bingmei, and she felt something leak from his normally clenched heart. He gave her a little smile, and she felt tenderness wash over her. He'd guarded this particular emotion when he was around her. It was strange to smell something like honey amidst so much violence.

Bingmei closed her eyes, feeling like weeping. Her own emotions were confused and conflicted. Why had he revealed himself at such a moment? Why had he shown her the tenderness he'd so strongly protected?

Echion was cruel and pitiless. He would have no mercy on someone like Rowen, for beneath all the prince's jealousy and bluster, she sensed he was *good*. As the prince left the cave, she felt in her bones that she would never see him again.

Alive.

CHAPTER THIRTY-SIX

Defiance at Sajinau

Darkness fell on the mountains, and with it came a bitter cold. Damanhur had been bound too, after the prince had been taken away. They were prisoners, caged by the rocky clefts and only protected somewhat from the wind. Qiangdao guards were stationed at the entrance, and food was brought to the guards but not to the prisoners.

A feeling of helplessness and hopelessness wrung inside Bingmei's heart. She struggled with the ropes at her wrists but could not get them any looser. They were tight enough to hurt. Now that the terror of the attack was over, the horrible consequences before them, she wondered what had happened to Quion. Had he followed them up the trail and avoided capture? Or had he been caught back at the palace? Or, even worse, had he been killed? The mere possibility filled her with a crawling feeling of unease.

The worry in her heart for Rowen was a constant torment. What would Echion do to him? What would Prince Juexin do when he learned his brother was in captivity? Would he assume the worst, that Rowen had gone over to the enemy willingly?

She regretted her decision to sneak out of Sajinau with the others. At least her wig still concealed her identity. But how long would that last?

It was a cloudless night, and soon the sky was thick with stars. She looked for familiar constellations and waited for the rising of the moon. Although she was tired from the climb up the mountain, she could not sleep. Her heart was too full of pain. She tried again to wriggle against the bonds, and again failed. She slumped back against one of the boulders, sighing.

"Bring us some food at least," Damanhur muttered in the dark.

One of the guards said something in response. They didn't speak the same language.

"Food!" Damanhur barked.

One of the guards called out, and the spidery man was summoned. He came into the area where they were bound.

"The guards wanted me to warn you that if you cry out again, you'll be beaten," he said.

"Why won't they feed us?" Damanhur said.

The man paused, then said, "The dead feel no hunger."

"You're going to kill us, then?"

"No, but they won't waste food on a corpse. After the city has fallen, you'll have the choice to join us. If you do, you'll be fed. Hunger may help speed up your decision." He chuckled darkly and left.

"I'm thirsty," Damanhur muttered. None of them had been given water either.

They remained in quietude and soon, one by one, they fell asleep. Bingmei listened to the whistle of the wind through the rocks and breathed in the noxious stench of the Qiangdao, somehow worse for the sweetness of the mountain flowers blooming in cracks in the rocks. She bowed her head and began meditating, trying not to shiver with the cold. Her pack had been stripped away and taken by the Qiangdao. Someone else was enjoying her new bedroll. The thought disgusted her.

As her thoughts faded to the background, she felt a flare of power in her mind. The magic of the Phoenix Blade was being summoned. It was still back in Sajinau, but she felt part of herself yanked away to the darkened palace. She saw Muxidi, blade in hand, roaming the halls.

The connection between them was weaker than before because of the distance. But she sensed he was following it like a spider creeping on a thread.

"Bingmei!"

She gasped, drawing breath, the connection severed. Damanhur had called out to her. This time, the strange prickling sensation in her fingers was a hundred times worse. She felt as cold as if she'd spent the night outside in the season of the Dragon of Night.

"Are you unwell? You stopped breathing."

She heard the guards grumbling, and one of them roused and stood. They'd been asleep on their duty. A shadow-faced man entered the little prison. He barked something and then raised a stick and started beating Damanhur. The master twisted and tried to keep the blows from landing on his head. She could do nothing more than watch, rage and helplessness coursing through her. This was her fault. Damanhur grunted as the wood struck him repeatedly, and then he collapsed on the ground. She smelled the outrage of his ensign. She shared it.

As the shadow-faced man retreated back to the opening, holding his stick on his knees, he hawked and spat. His face was just barely visible in the moonlight.

"I'm sorry," Bingmei whispered.

"Good. I'm . . . warmer now," Damanhur grunted. "I was . . . worried. Thought you'd died again."

"I did," Bingmei said softly. "The other Qiangdao is coming. The one with the Phoenix Blade. He knows where I am."

"That's bad news," Damanhur whispered back. "We have to escape."

"How?" Bingmei said with despair.

"I'm still working it out," he answered. "Now hush, before he gives me another round."

They fell silent, and she listened again to the lonely wind. And smelled the slumber of the Qiangdao and their fetid dreams. And felt the man with the Phoenix Blade coming for her.

杀雾

Bingmei did fall asleep eventually and awoke at the cry of a mountain bird. She saw through the gaps in the boulders the image of an eagle soaring past. How she longed to borrow its wings. Her muscles were cramped, her wrists swollen from the rough rope that bound them. The Qiangdao camp was rousing, and no one stood at the mouth of the cave. They were huddled together outside, eating strips of meat that had been cooked and cured. Some of the men had leather bladders they drank from, and her throat clenched at the sight of water dribbling off chins and falling wasted on the dirt.

In the light, she saw the scabbed faces of the other members of Damanhur's ensign. Huqu looked especially bad, although Damanhur had a bruise on his cheek. He glared at the men gathered outside, and she smelled the desire for vengeance in his heart, bubbling like a sour-smelling stew. She closed her eyes and tried to find the presence of the blade. She realized with dread that it was coming closer. She felt its presence on the mountain. He'd been picking his way up the trail in the dark.

She looked at Damanhur worriedly. "He's coming," she whispered.

Damanhur nodded. "You still can jump, can't you?"

She shook her head.

"Why not?"

"Because my hands are bound. I have a little meiwood charm in my pocket. That is what gives me the power."

"Then we need to get you loose," Damanhur said. "You'll have to leave the rest of us behind. If you die, we have no hope at all."

"I've tried. I can't loosen anything."

Damanhur frowned. "Shift so that you're facing the doorway. Huqu, wriggle up behind her. See if you can help. You're closer. Hurry."

After some grunting and movement, she felt Huqu against her back. She could see, from her angle, a portion of the Death Wall atop a distant mountain. It looked so far away. Not that she was thinking of going there. No, she regretted what had happened here, bitterly, but she still didn't want to die. She would hide in the mountains. Forage for food. And, above all, she would avoid involving anyone else. She didn't want anyone to be harmed because of her.

She felt Huqu's fingernail dig into the side of her hand, and she hissed in pain.

"Sorry," he said. Stretching the ropes binding his own wrists, he maneuvered his fingers around her bindings and scraped at them with a fingernail, like a mouse scratching with its tiny teeth.

The men gathered outside began to talk excitedly to one another. Then the spidery man appeared in the makeshift doorway, licking grease from his fingers. Bingmei pushed herself backward a bit, nudging Huqu. She felt his back stiffen.

"We can't let you miss the fun. Come and watch the fall of Sajinau. Lord Echion comes."

Several brutes entered the cleft and dragged everyone to their feet. Bingmei's bonds felt just as tight as before. As she staggered, her knees aching, she brushed her wrists against the jagged edge of the cleft wall. The prisoners emerged together, the breeze making Bingmei shiver with cold. A little blue mountain flower poked out of the ground ahead, lovely to look at, but it was trampled by the boot of a Qiangdao. Her heart ached as she passed the crushed petals.

The prisoners were walked, surrounded, up the slope a little way until they crested the pass. It was a beautiful morning, the dark green trees stark against the white patches of snow. She could see the entire city of Sajinau below, hazy with the morning smoke of a thousand cook-fires. The waters of the fjord were dark and deep, and looking down the edges, she could see the burning from the watchtowers. There were no ships in the fjord, not a single one. All had been moored at the docks of Sajinau.

"The fires are burning, and none of the ships have been destroyed," Damanhur muttered smugly. "He hasn't won yet."

A Qiangdao punched him in the ribs for talking. Damanhur grunted, but he didn't speak again.

The spidery man held up a single hand, palm outward. "There!" he pointed toward the fjord in the distance.

Bingmei squinted, not sure what she was seeing.

Until a ship sailed into view, rounding the edge of the mountain that dipped into the waters of the fjord. Her jaw dropped in awe and dread. It was at least six times larger than any junk she'd ever seen. There were so many masts she couldn't count them.

Damanhur let out a pent-up breath, and she felt his astonishment. His dread. The Qiangdao began chuckling, some laughing boldly, and they all pointed to the massive ship entering the strait leading to Sajinau.

In its wake came a curtain of fog.

All the way atop the mountain, she heard the boom and shudder of a catapult down below. A heavy stone flew from the tower nearest the massive ship. The stone fell short, landing with a huge splash in the fjord. She could almost see the ant-like men wriggling around in the tower, loading another missile. The mist-wreathed ship lumbered on, coming closer as they prepared another assault. A second stone was heaved from the catapult. She could hear the crack of timbers, the groan of ropes. The stone landed with a splash, missing.

And then she watched as the fog began to creep up the mountainside. She struggled against her bonds, gazing with horror as the fog climbed up the mountain, its movement and progression almost intelligent. The guffaws of the Qiangdao chilled her blood as they eagerly anticipated the defenders' deaths.

And then another set of sails appeared amidst the fog. If anything, this ship was even bigger than the first.

"Another one?" Huqu gasped.

The fog reached the first watchtower, and all fell silent. She could almost sense the deaths as they happened, the victims collapsing with a single sigh escaping their lips in unison. Their expressions placid in death. The first watch fire snuffed out, darkening the side of the mountain once again. The fog continued to swirl across the mountainside. It encroached on each side of the fjord, and one by one, she watched as the other watchtowers were overrun. The fires were all quenched. Not a single boulder had come near the enormous ships. There were three, then four. Sadness welled up in her heart. She felt like crying, but she held her tears back.

Prince Juexin had thought they could survive a siege for years. His heart had not understood the depth of evil they stood against.

The first titan ship approached Sajinau. The men on deck waved and cheered as they approached the shore.

"Look! Look!" the spidery man said, waving his finger. "They're too big to dock at the wooden wharves. Look! The stone wharves come to meet them!"

Out of the fjord rose an ancient stone quay, something that had been submerged for centuries. Even from a distance, Bingmei could see the magic rippling across the stone as the animal sigils came to life. The quay was on the south side of the city where only a few scattered homes dwelled. Vulnerable to the forefront of Echion's attack.

The first of the massive vessels came up alongside the stone quay.

Damanhur shoved his way closer to the spidery man. "You knew they were coming today?" he said, his voice throbbing with concern.

The fellow grinned. "Lord Echion said his arrival would be heralded by the lighting of the signal fires of Sajinau. He will give the people of

Sajinau a chance to be slaves. If they refuse, the fog will kill them all. And *we* will inherit the city, just as he promised."

Damanhur stared down the mountainside. He was trying to be strong, but she felt his composure cracking. He blinked, watching his city about to be overthrown. What would Prince Juexin do? What could he do? She wished she could reach into her pocket, that she could flee the scene unfolding before her eyes. The Qiangdao were all watching the tragedy unfold with open fascination. She could smell their greed, their desire for plunder, their desire to ravage and destroy. It made her sick to her stomach.

From the trail lower down, she saw three men struggling up the mountainside. They were dressed like Qiangdao. Her heart quailed. She tried to tug free of her bonds, but they wouldn't give.

"Who are they?" one of the Qiangdao men said, pointing.

The spidery man frowned and looked. "I don't know. It's not Jiukeshu. Ready your weapons!"

Her view was completely blocked by the guards, who pushed her and the others away as they brandished their blades, spears, and other weapons.

Bingmei could smell their hunger for violence, their rising desire to kill. The sight below had incited them.

"Who are you? Why are you here?" the spidery man demanded.

"I am Muxidi of the Phoenix Blade," said a gruff voice that Bingmei instantly recognized. Amidst the terrible smells, she could also smell a new strain of dishonesty. The newcomer reeked of it. "You are ordered to bring your prisoners down to Sajinau."

It wasn't the man who had killed her parents.

It was Jiaohua, the head of the Jingcha.

CHAPTER
THIRTY-SEVEN
Falling

Bingmei recognized the voice, could smell the lie, yet still she didn't understand what was happening. Was Jiaohua a traitor to his king? Had he been in league with the Qiangdao all along?

Or was it the Qiangdao he had deceived?

She could still sense the presence of the Phoenix Blade, but it wasn't near.

"Whose orders?" snapped the spidery man.

"What do you think, fool?" shouted Jiaohua. "Whose boats have come to seize Sajinau!"

"Lord Echion sent you?" asked the spidery man in confusion. "Why?"

"You are a dolt. Come down to the foot of the mountain. That is where Lord Echion will reward us all."

Bingmei smelled confusion and concern. The spidery man was distrustful. "My master Jiukeshu bid us to guard the pass. He was *ordered* by Echion to do so on peril of death."

"I am Muxidi, master of my own band. And *I* have orders from Echion commanding me to bring down your prisoners on pain of death! How could Jiukeshu have left such an idiot to stay behind?"

Bingmei could tell that Jiaohua was purposefully inflaming the spidery man's emotions with his choice of words. And she realized, through his guile, he was trying to rescue them. He was only acting the part of a Qiangdao. She felt a little spark of hope in her heart begin to flame.

"You are not in charge here; I am!" shouted the spidery man.

"Lord Echion is here, you idiot!" said Jiaohua. "The city will fall before night comes. I have my orders. I must bring the prisoners down."

"They are *my* prisoners."

"Send some guards down with us. I don't care. We must go down at once." His voiced dropped dangerously. "This cursed fog might not kill us, but I've seen Echion kill a man just by looking at him!"

The stench of the lie was overpowering, and Bingmei almost coughed in surprise. Jiaohua truly was a profligate liar.

The scent of unease began to overpower the spidery man's confidence. Hints of confusion and fear and offense battled for dominance. He was rattled, knowing he had to make a decision and knowing that a wrong decision could cost him his life. No doubt Jiaohua was gambling on that.

"There are five of us," said Jiaohua restlessly. "Send ten or twenty to accompany my people. The rest must stay up here and guard the pass. I don't care how many you send. Just choose quickly!"

"Twenty," said the spidery man in a shaking voice.

"Which ones? Hurry, man!"

The spidery man quickly counted off people and ordered them to go down with Jiaohua and the prisoners. Bingmei wanted to smile, she was so relieved, but she kept her expression dejected. She sidled up closer to Damanhur, who also kept a bland look on his face. But his command of his appearance was equally as good as his master's—she could smell his satisfaction and honeyed hope.

Surrounded by Qiangdao, they began the march down the trail. But Bingmei still sensed the Phoenix Blade coming toward them. The real enemy was on the way. Did Jiaohua know this? Was there any way to tell him without being overheard?

"Wait," said Jiaohua after they'd left the sight of the others. "The trail is steep. If their hands are tied behind their backs, they'll fall and kill themselves. Bind their wrists in the front instead."

The other guards did not speak his language. They looked at each other in confusion.

Jiaohua sighed and shook his head. "You're idiots too." He said something in a different dialect, one that sounded like theirs, then walked up to Bingmei, pretending not to recognize her, and untied the ropes behind her back.

"Like this," he said again, tying her hands in front of her instead. She watched him work and saw that he left the knot deliberately loose. He tugged on a firmer part of the rope to pretend it was tight.

The escort understood then, and soon all the members of Damanhur's ensign were bound with hands in front. Jiaohua looked her in the eye, frowning, then smacked her in the face. The stinging blow startled her, rocking her head back. He growled at her in another language, grabbing her by the arm and shaking her. The others backed away for a moment, surprised by his violence.

"Don't be insolent!" he snarled at her, then shook his finger at her.

Some of the Qiangdao chuckled, looking at each other in confusion. She wiped her burning cheek with her raw knuckles and glowered at him, wondering why he'd done it.

They proceeded to march down the narrow trail. Mosquitoes buzzed in the air around them. The trail offered a view of the massive ships, which were unloading soldiers on the edge of the city. Why were they coming back down the mountain *toward* Echion's army? *Toward* the evil Qiangdao with the Phoenix Blade? There was no way to ask her questions, but the sensation that they were approaching danger was enough to make her heart beat worriedly.

Climbing down the mountain took far less time than climbing up had. Soon they reached the edge of the wood of massive spruce and hemlock trees that grew lower down the slopes. The treetops obscured the view of the city below. She thought she heard the noise of fighting down below, the clash of arms that came and faded with the breeze.

"Faster," Jiaohua said angrily. "The battle is underway!"

They started to jog down the mountain, and worry bloomed in Bingmei like wildflowers. They reached a turn in the trail that was thick with boulders. She remembered the spot from the previous day's climb. Her sense of smell told her others were hidden behind the boulders. This was not the murderous stench of Qiangdao, but the smell of fighters, warriors. The scent had a distinctly fishy edge to it that she knew at once was Quion. She couldn't help but smile as they came around the corner.

The man next to her was struck in the neck by a poisoned dart. He hissed in pain, clutched at the area, and fell down. Chaos ensued. Bingmei pulled against her bonds, and the ropes sloughed off instantly. She was free. Cries of pain and shouts of alarm filled the air as warriors attacked the Qiangdao. Jiaohua had stationed men at this point on the trail and led them into the ambush on purpose.

She joined the fight, striking at the nearest Qiangdao. She disarmed him, throwing him face-first into a rough hemlock tree, and stole his battered saber. She freed Damanhur from his bonds. Once the rest of Damanhur's ensign was freed, they took their revenge and struck down the men who had been their captors. Huqu's scarred face twisted in triumph as he struck down one of his foes. The fight was over moments later.

Quion appeared from behind the boulders, and he hurried up to her, grinning with relief. His scent shifted, taking on hints of anger and concern, as he came closer and noticed her injuries.

"You're safe," he breathed with relief.

"Of course she's safe," Jiaohua said, coming up next. He gave her a scolding look and shook his head. "I told you we'd rescue her. Not that she deserves it. You shouldn't have left!"

Damanhur approached as well and joined them.

She smelled the conflict inside Jiaohua, but she didn't have time to argue or plead for forgiveness. "Where's Rowen?" she said, looking at him fiercely.

"Captured," said Jiaohua resentfully. "My orders from Prince Juexin were to rescue *you* first, then his brother. We don't have much time. I only brought ten Jingcha with me to rescue you, and the rest I sent trailing that giant of a man—what's his name? Jiukeshu?"

"Yes," said Damanhur. "He's bigger than an ox."

"A bear more like," said Jiaohua. "He passed us in the night. One of my men caught a glimpse of Prince Rowen. I sent three men to trail them, but they're down in the city right now. We have to go. Search the bodies and then conceal them in the rocks! Hurry!"

He was about to leave her, but Bingmei grabbed his arm.

"The Qiangdao with the real Phoenix Blade is coming up the trail."

He whirled, his eyes widening with fear. "How do you know this?"

"He and I are both connected to that sword," she explained. "He knows I've been captured, so he's coming up the mountain to get me."

Jiaohua's smell turned to worry. "He and the two Qiangdao who travel with him have been killing my men since they arrived in Sajinau. They have more magic than just the Phoenix Blade, as you know." He looked worriedly at his men. "I don't think we have the ability to kill them."

A searing pain shot through Bingmei's skull, and she felt a throb of warning. He was much closer, and he could sense her just as she could sense him.

"What's wrong, Bingmei?" Quion asked worriedly.

She looked frantically at Jiaohua. "Is there another way off the mountain? Another trail?"

Jiaohua shook his head no. "There are cliffs on either side of this trail. We can hide in the woods, but that won't help."

"We can't go back up," Damanhur said. "Those other Qiangdao are still blocking the pass." He shot a worried glance down the trail. "How far away are they?"

"I don't know," Bingmei said. She felt the throb of warning again, the urge to flee. "We have to go."

"Where?" Jiaohua demanded. "Even if we conceal ourselves, they'll still find you."

"It's *me* they want," Bingmei said, backing away from them. "I'll go alone. Bring them after me."

"No!" Quion said, shaking his head. "I'm coming with you."

"You can't," Bingmei said. "I won't let you die because of me. I'll go another way, make him chase me."

"You won't survive three nights in these mountains," Jiaohua said. "You'll starve to death, a bear will kill you, or you'll drink bad water and get sick. I've been charged by the prince of Sajinau to keep you safe! You aren't leaving my sight."

"What if you can't catch me?" Bingmei said, reaching her hand into her pocket.

Jiaohua grabbed her forearm, his eyes glittering with menace.

"Wait! I have an idea," Quion said firmly. "I've a lot of rope in my pack. We can climb down part of the mountain. They won't be able to follow us unless they have rope too."

Jiaohua looked at Quion in disbelief. "You have rope?"

"I have *lots* of rope," Quion said with a grin.

Bingmei's heart surged. "Let's go! We must get off the trail. Now!"

Jiaohua nodded firmly and released Bingmei's arm. As his men dragged the bodies off the trail into the brush, he barked out commands. Five of the men would accompany them, along with Damanhur's ensign, and the rest would conceal themselves and remain behind to warn others of the danger waiting in the pass.

"This way," said Jiaohua. "Be careful. Sometimes there's a cliff concealed by the brush. One wrong step could be your last."

杀雾

They didn't bother to conceal their trail. Branches of hemlock clawed at them, and dense moss covered the fallen limbs as well as healthy ones. Yellow skunk cabbage grew amidst the shaggy boulders and crisscrossed limbs. Small streams trickled down the mountains. As they clambered down boulders, Bingmei kept looking back over her shoulder. She felt the thrum of the blade's magic seeking her. It was behind her, behind and above. Muxidi was hunting her in the woods.

Someone cried out in warning from down below, and everyone halted.

A huge black bear and two cubs were foraging in the woods beneath them. The Jingcha's warning worked against them—the mother bear rushed toward them. There was hardly time to prepare before it slammed into the first man, one of the Jingcha, and slashed him with its knife-sharp claws. He cried out in pain and terror.

"This way!" Jiaohua said, pointing. She followed as fast as she could, trying not to fall and break her arm. The bear roared and attacked another man, who tried to jab at it with a short spear. A claw deflected the attack, and the bear knocked him over as easily as if he were a child, sinking its teeth into the man's shoulder.

Bingmei shuddered with dread and followed Jiaohua. They came abruptly to the edge of a cliff, and he pinwheeled his arms to keep from falling. Quion grabbed his jacket and pulled him back.

"Here's the edge," Jiaohua said, gasping. He looked back through the gorse, hearing his man's cries of pain. His face wrinkled with displeasure. "These mountains can *kill*. Get out your ropes, fisherman."

Quion was already pulling off his stuffed pack. He brought out a coil of rope and let it fall. The end only went partway down the cliffside.

Clamping the end in his armpit, he pulled out another. He quickly tied the two ropes together with a sturdy knot and let the end fall. Leaning over the edge, Bingmei saw the end coil on the ledge down below. Quion nodded quickly, then looked around for something to secure the rope. The bear continued to huff and thrash nearby. Groans and cries came from the fallen.

Quion chose a tree with sturdy roots and threw the end of the rope around it. "Who first?"

"The girl," said Jiaohua, nodding to Bingmei.

Quion wrapped the end of the rope around her waist and then, with a quick twist and tug, secured it with a knot. She tested it, and it held strong.

"We'll lower you down," Quion said. "Just hold on."

She nodded. Quion set his back against the rope and then created some slack in it. He looked at her. "Just step backward. Your feet toward the mountain. The rope will hold you. Be ready to push off when I let the slack go."

"I'll fall," she said worriedly.

"No you won't. Trust me." He smiled at her, and she nodded. She did feel safe in his hands, but when she looked back down the cliff, her stomach lurched.

"It'll hold you. Just lean back and push off against the rocks. Ready?"

She nodded.

"Jump," he said.

She gripped the rope with both hands, leaning back into the open air. She felt the wind rustle the wig. Her neck was slick with sweat. A little bubble in her stomach told her the idea was madness, that she should quit and run off by herself, but with all the men staring at her, she couldn't show fear. So she muscled down her terror and nodded at Quion.

"Now!" he said.

She jumped off the cliff as Quion let loose the slack.

CHAPTER
THIRTY-EIGHT

Traitor's Fate

The sensation of falling made her stomach lurch, her head grow dizzy, and then the rope went taut. She had just enough time to bring her legs forward and catch herself against the wall of the cliff before smashing into it. Pushing off the wall, she was suddenly falling again, the rope like water as she rushed down. The stop came faster this time, and it was easier to brace herself. The rope bit into her back painfully, but it was a solid support.

Looking up, she saw several faces staring down at her from above. Then she fell again, this time so far and fast her heart nearly came out of her throat. The fall stopped abruptly, the rope jerking against her ribs, and she gasped in pain. She dangled in the air, twisting slowly, and then the rope slowly descended until the scrub-covered ground rose to meet her feet. Once she was on firm ground again, she slipped out of the rope.

Jiaohua's voice called down to her. "Are you down?"

"Yes!" she cried back. The rope then whipped back up, stranding her on the ledge. There wasn't a trail, but the ground was traversable.

There weren't as many trees obstructing the view from this vantage point. She peered down into the valley and saw fighting in the streets of Sajinau. Echion's ships were disgorging more fighters into the fray. Ribbons of smoke rose from the outermost houses, and she could see at least one burning roof.

Small rocks pattered down on her. She stepped back, looking up and shielding her eyes. Jiaohua was being sent down. He grunted as the rope went slack and then suddenly taut, and her own ribs smarted for him in remembrance. The instinct that connected her with the Phoenix Blade thrummed as the weapon came closer. Its nearness made her anxiety grow more intense, her pulse pound. So many of them were still up there, including Quion. She would despair if anything happened to him.

The final plunge brought Jiaohua slamming into the ground. He nearly pitched over and fell, but Bingmei grabbed his arm and steadied him. Blinking and dazed, he wobbled a bit and then quickly pulled the rope loose.

"Up!" he shouted. The rope was whisked away.

Bingmei gazed up and waited in patient agony as the men from the ensign were lowered down. Several men had started working the rope, and the work became much faster. Yet in her mind, she could almost see Muxidi hunting her in the woods, eager to claim her and the reward he would earn by bringing the phoenix-chosen back to Echion. He was as intent on catching her as she was on escaping.

"Start heading down," Jiaohua ordered the others. "Scout ahead to see if more cliffs block the way."

"Yes, sir," replied one of the Jingcha. They began scrabbling down the mountainside.

Another came down. Then another. Anticipation churned inside Bingmei. How many were left?

After the next man landed, he said, "Two more. Just the master and the fisherman. The boy's hands are bleeding."

Bingmei gritted her teeth, looking up worriedly.

Then Damanhur poked his head over the edge. "We're both coming down together! Hold the rope!" It came sailing back down in a mass and struck Jiaohua on the head. He muttered a curse and then motioned for another man to help him. They wrapped the rope around their wrists and pulled against it.

Bingmei, stepping back a little, watched as they both climbed down, hand over hand. Damanhur slid down the rope quickly, wincing in pain, but he soon landed on the outcropping. Quion was much slower, and his huge pack tottered on his back. She heard some of the pots clanging like gongs.

Bingmei felt the Phoenix Blade right above her.

"Quion!" she warned. He was only halfway down.

He looked up just as a face appeared over the edge.

Bingmei bit her lip, staring up in suspense as Quion reached for the rocky cliffside, trying to find a handhold. The grim-faced Qiangdao leader gazed down at her with hate in his eyes. He'd murdered her parents. He'd killed her grandfather. She wished she had a bow and could have sent an arrow into his skull. Then, holding her gaze, he lifted the Phoenix Blade and sliced through the rope in one slash.

"Quion!" she yelled.

He didn't fall.

He managed to hold his grip on the rocks, dangling from them. The rope fell, whapping him as it did. He managed to grab the end before it raced by, but she felt sure he was going to fall.

Bingmei stared up at the Qiangdao, her heart flaming like a raging fire. Still Quion hung precariously, the tendons in his arm bulging.

"Drop the pack, boy!" Jiaohua shouted up at him.

Quion ignored him. He raised the rope and bit into it, then grabbed the wall with his other hand, sharing the weight.

"What? Can't you fly?" Jiaohua taunted the Qiangdao leader. "Come down here, brigand. If you dare."

He was trying to provoke the man, to draw his attention away from Quion's struggle for survival.

In amazement, Bingmei saw Quion's feet find little ledges to support his weight. He gazed off to the right, where a little knob of rock protruded from the cliffside. Holding firm with his left hand, he grabbed the rope from his mouth. Bingmei gazed at him in surprise as he formed a loop and a knot with one hand and his teeth. He then attached the loop around the knob and jerked on the rope, testing the strength. His whole body trembled with the effort, and he grunted, but he kept tugging until he was satisfied the rock would support him.

As Quion continued his climb, the Qiangdao leader shouted in outrage and threw a rock down from above. The rock slammed into his shoulder, and the young man began to slide down the rope, catching himself by squeezing it harder.

Jiaohua hurled an insult up at the Qiangdao. "You plague sore! Spread your pox down here!" He looked at Bingmei fiercely. "Get away!" he seethed.

"Not without Quion," she said with determination, staring at him.

The Qiangdao flung another rock down, but it struck the pack instead of him. Quion slid down the rope a ways before he managed to stop himself. She saw tears of pain coming out of his eyes. He gripped the rope, shuddering, still high over their heads.

"Lower, lad! Lower!" Jiaohua said.

Quion sniffled and slid down until his boot reached Jiaohua's upraised palms. A rock plummeted toward Jiaohua's head, but he sidestepped, and it crashed and shattered against the stones at his feet.

Quion released the rope, and the two men went sprawling against the rugged patches of ground and shrub. Bingmei hopped over to help Quion stand. His hands were smeared with blood and were red from the burns of the rope, but he was alive. She hugged him with gratitude and then helped him rise.

Jiaohua shook off the dirt. He glanced at Quion with a look of respect. "Well done, lad. Now let's get off this cursed mountain before something else tries to kill us."

杀雾

By the time they reached the palace at Sajinau, the air was thick with smoke. Chaos reigned. Some palace guards rushed them, mistaking them for Qiangdao because of their clothing, but Jiaohua was able to convince them of his identity.

"What's going on?" Jiaohua asked the armored soldier. The man had a gash on his forehead but otherwise looked healthy.

"The lower city is taken," said the soldier, looking miserable. "Prince Juexin opened the walls of the palace to the townsfolk. The Qiangdao rule the streets."

"Where is General Tzu?"

The soldier shook his head. "I don't know. I think he's with the prince."

A loud gong sounded, and the soldier lost color. "It's time to fight. Take what men you have and go to the courtyard to defend the palace!"

Jiaohua nodded, and Damanhur drew his sword. They entered the palace from the side gardens and found the populace of Sajinau cringing and huddling in fear inside. Families were gathered together, many weeping. The reek of their sadness and terror was overwhelming.

"This way," Jiaohua said, directing them to a side corridor. At the end, he pulled a rug away, revealing a golden grate on the floor. He bent down to pull it up. "Down!" he snapped. "Quickly!"

The group dropped down into the concealed passage. Jiaohua left one of his Jingcha above to conceal the way. The tunnel was narrow and small and very dark. It smelled of must and earth.

Jiaohua pulled on Bingmei's sleeve. "No matter what happens, we must get you out of here safely. The palace staff do not even know of these tunnels, or they would be clogged right now with people trying to escape. This way. Be silent. Bao Damanhur, protect her with your life."

"You're not coming with us?" Damanhur asked.

"Of course I am! You won't make it out of this palace without my help."

"Then show us the way," Damanhur said.

"I will." He shot a glance at Bingmei. "This tunnel leads by the courtyard. The water from the courtyard drains here during the rainy season. It may be raining blood on us today, but it's the only way out."

"Very well. Let's go," Bingmei said. She clutched Quion's arm, so grateful he had survived the experience on the cliff. His pack still rattled a little as he walked, but they'd done their best to stifle the sound.

The bigger men had to crouch in the tunnel, but Bingmei walked upright. The scent of worry filled the tight space. It was hard to understand how Sajinau had fallen so quickly. But she remembered all the soldiers training in the courtyard when she'd arrived. There would be a bloody battle. Or perhaps Echion would loose the killing fog on the populace? He'd already used it on the poor men and women in the watchtowers.

If the fog came for them, they'd be stuck in the tunnels, unable to escape. They had to get out.

After traveling some distance, she saw strips of light ahead. These were the grates Jiaohua had warned her about, the ones that connected to the courtyards. She saw the strips of sunlight streaming through the openings, revealing the slick, dark liquid pooling on the stones of the path.

Echion's voice.

Her blood froze in an instant.

Jiaohua paused at one of the grates, cocking his head to one side. "Who is that?" he muttered.

Bingmei frowned at him. "That's Echion."

"He's in the courtyard?" Jiaohua said, perplexed.

"Can we see what's going on up there?" Damanhur asked angrily.

"This way," Jiaohua replied. "There are grates we can see from at the edge of the courtyard. Hurry."

They marched quickly, the banging from the pans growing louder. Quion winced and used his hand to silence some of the noise. One of the Jingcha glared at him and reached out as if to rip the pack from him, but he'd stopped the noise. Bingmei patted his shoulder to reassure him. The tunnel branched off in two directions, and Jiaohua turned left. They came to a place where the tunnel floor began to rise, but the ceiling remained the same height. A row of grates came into view at eye level. There was enough room for all of them to find a place to view from. The grates themselves were narrow rectangles, wide enough to see through but not big enough to squeeze through. They were intended for rainwater.

Bingmei looked out and saw a pair of old scuffed boots in front of her. Shifting slightly, she saw a row of Qiangdao standing along the edge of the wall. Between the boots, she could see the interior of the courtyard.

Prince Rowen sat before Echion, who stood at the base of the steps leading up to the palace. His rancid, horrible stench trickled through the grate and into her nose. But she didn't need her nose to tell it was him. He stood in the same majestic form she'd seen rise from his desiccated body in Fusang, but this time he was heavily armored in an ancient style. Her heart quailed with pain. The prince was kneeling in forced submission.

Echion wore some ancient armor that was dark silver and wreathed in ivy-like designs intermingled with the symbols of dragons. The armor itself reminded her of dragon scales. He towered over Rowen, his pale hair gleaming in the sun, a braided crown around his head. His gaze was imperious, his look defiant and proud.

"This is my city, my land, my empire," Echion said with bold, strong words. "I am the sword of justice. I am the judge who condemns the guilty to die, princeling. Your brother is a traitor, and I condemn him as such. I have brought him so he might be executed for his crimes."

"Can we not bargain?" said Juexin.

She couldn't see him, but she imagined him standing on the steps. His voice came from that direction. She pressed her forehead against the slats of the grate, trying to spy him, but she could not. Looking back, she stared at Rowen, her heart panging with dread.

At that moment, he turned his head as if looking at her. Could he see her through the grate? Did he know she was near?

She smelled a flicker of him, of that flowery scent that had told her he was fond of her, but it was overpowered by the horrid stench of Echion and his murders.

"Bargain?" Echion said with contempt. "But what do you have that I could want? This is my city. I built these walls myself. The gate opened to me because they recognized me as their rightful master. Not you. I will not slay your people if they will accept their fate as our slaves. If not . . . the fog will rid me of your defiance. It is mine to command. So what is there to bargain for, princeling? I declare your brother is guilty of treason. And I will execute him as your weak-willed father should have done years ago. It is my will. It is my right." He drew his sword, which had glyphs fashioned into it. It seemed to crackle with energy.

Bingmei's heart felt as if it would burst. Would she have to watch him murder Rowen?

"Lower your head, you faithless boy," Echion said to Rowen. "That I might strike it from your shoulders."

Rowen did lean forward, dropping his head, exposing his neck.

"Wait!" Juexin cried out.

Echion sneered up at him, his pale lips cold and snarling. "You've pled for his life already, princeling."

Juexin stepped into view, clad in armor covered in bloodstains. He'd already fought bravely to defend the city. And he'd failed. His people cowered inside the palace. How many soldiers did he have left? Sajinau had been the strongest of the kingdoms, and yet Echion had toppled it effortlessly.

What hope did the rest of them have?

"I would trade places with him," Juexin said, his voice thick.

CHAPTER
THIRTY-NINE

Intercession

Bingmei could not believe what she'd heard, but there was no mistaking the smell that wafted down to her. It was a perfume of sincerity, compassion, and regret, powerful enough together to temporarily overpower Echion's stench. It came through the slats in the grate, stinging Bingmei's eyes, filling her with grief and admiration.

And guilt.

"An exchange of fates?" said the Dragon of Night with a sardonic chuckle. "How noble. And pointless."

"Do you think I would ever serve you willingly?" replied Juexin. "You say this is your kingdom, but it belongs to my father. Whatever right you had to it ended long ago."

"Bold words. Wrong, but bold."

"Brother, no," said Rowen, looking up at Juexin in horror. Bingmei could sense the emotions colliding inside him. He'd not expected this. He'd expected to die. He did not wish to be saved at such a price.

"Oh, if he *wants* to take your place, by all means, let him!" said Echion triumphantly. "If he thinks that sacrificing himself will alter the verdict, he's gravely mistaken. A life for a life. That is just."

"I will do it," Juexin said, coming down the remainder of the steps. From her angle, Bingmei caught a brief glimpse of Kunmia, Marenqo, and Mieshi standing in a group on the steps. Her heart twisted at the look on Kunmia's face. Her master rarely ever allowed emotion to play on her features, but her look was one of concern and dread.

"No," Rowen moaned, shaking his head. He was in agony. Bingmei's own heart throbbed in commiseration. She'd asked Juexin if, had the situation been reversed, he would have sacrificed himself. What had her question set in motion? The compassion she smelled from Juexin mingled with fear and dread. The emotions were so complex, so powerful, they sapped her strength. Jiaohua and the others were equally fixed on the scene, unable to tear their eyes away.

Juexin knelt by his brother, his face haggard and weary. He probably hadn't slept. He put his hand on his brother's shoulder.

"Why?" Rowen said in grief.

"I promised Father," he answered simply, his voice thick. "And he would have done the same for you." His lips firmed. "Go."

Rowen looked at his brother, tears in his eyes. There was a moment of shared anguish between them, one that tore down years of built-up resentment. Juexin pulled his brother up beside him. Again the smell of Juexin overpowered the stench of murder. It was rich and commanding, like a feast swelling atop a table. So many flavors, so many scents.

"Go, Brother," he said, glaring at Echion in defiance.

Bingmei's fingers slipped through the slats in the grate, squeezing them hard. Tears ran down her cheeks. Her grief was overwhelming, but it was mixed with respect and honor for the prince she'd scorned. Rowen bowed his head in defeat and walked the way his brother had come, trudging up the steps as if an impossible burden were lashed to his back.

The two men faced each other.

"You think to defeat me, boy?" Echion asked in a low, threatening voice. He still gripped his great sword in one hand. His pale hair was tousled by a sudden breeze.

Juexin's hands were clenched. His lips quivered with suppressed emotion. "I am a man of my word," he said, his voice thick. Gasps filled the courtyard as he dropped to his knees before his enemy, lowering his head and exposing his neck.

It happened so quickly, the sudden blur of movement, the sword coming down. Bingmei squeezed her eyes shut, but she heard the sound of the head as it landed on the stones. It was an awful sound. One that would haunt her dreams.

"So am I," answered Echion with a savage sneer in the sound. Gasps of shock and horror could be heard, as well as a few grunted chuckles from the Qiangdao observing the execution. Then Echion said mockingly to the corpse, "Serve me here or in my Grave Kingdom. It matters very little which you choose."

The horror of the moment made Bingmei want to shrivel in despair. Such an enemy could not be defeated. His power and knowledge and sheer age surpassed any resources they had. Her fingers were still hooked in the slats, her head bowed in reverence.

And then she felt the pull of the Phoenix Blade. Once again, it yanked her from her body. Death's compulsion was so strong, she couldn't resist it. The wrenching feeling drew her up through the grate, and she was suddenly aware, in her spirit form, of standing in the courtyard. Everything was awash in streaks of gray. It felt like her head had been plunged into a bucket of ice water.

Echion was there still, but behind him loomed the black dragon she'd seen at Fusang. Its power rippled, and its smokelike wings folded across its back. A low hissing growl came from it.

Bingmei.

Cowering in terror at the monstrosity, it took her a moment to see him. Prince Juexin, standing above his corpse, traces of golden light coming from his hair and his eyes. He *saw* her.

Bingmei, save us.

They came as thoughts more than words. His eyes implored her, and his hand reached out to her in supplication. And then she saw something tear him away—the claws of the dragon just barely visible through the black mist it rode in on. Like a piece of gossamer, he was snatched. He was being carried to the east, toward the mountains.

Toward the Death Wall.

She longed to pursue him, to *save* him, but she felt tethered to her body.

A man was crossing the courtyard toward Echion. Muxidi. Could he see her? Sense her? His face grim and determined, he held the Phoenix Blade. Anguish and grief shook her heart. She wanted to run, to hide. How could she feel so much more *strongly* in this state? It amazed her that her body, if anything, muted the strength of her feelings.

Echion turned and faced the newcomer, frowning with impatience.

"Where is she, Muxidi?" he asked with growing anger.

"She's *here*. Right now," answered the Qiangdao. He pointed at her.

Echion turned his head, his eyes bulging with rage. The dragon huffed, and bits of fog came out of its snout.

Bingmei felt terror freeze her, and then she recognized a familiar smell—the warm cinnamon porridge of Kunmia's regard for her. Kunmia Suun launched herself at Echion, the glyphs on her staff glowing as the wood struck him in the face.

No!

A wrenching feeling twisted in Bingmei's stomach, and she awoke with a gasp. She'd collapsed against the wall, her fingers still gripping the metal grid.

"Someone's down there!" called a voice from above.

Jiaohua was shaking her shoulders, trying to revive her. The pinpricks of pain came with harsh intensity up her legs, down her arms. She lacked the strength to unclench her fingers from the metal, but Damanhur pried them off for her.

Someone yanked the grate open, and an arm plunged down into the dark, groping at them. Jiaohua pulled Bingmei away. Her legs wouldn't work, and she struggled to breathe. Her chest felt like ice. Damanhur grabbed the arm and yanked it hard, smashing their would-be attacker's body against the stones above.

"Go! Go!" Jiaohua seethed. Quion grabbed her legs while Jiaohua hooked his hands beneath her arms, and they toted her back down the tunnel.

Bingmei's eyes were no longer used to the dark, and she felt dizzy and disoriented as they fled through the tunnels. Her heart panged with the knowledge that her master was facing the enemy. Kunmia had faced him once before while his power was still returning. He was even stronger now.

"How far is it?" Damanhur asked worriedly.

"Not far, but the exit may be guarded already," Jiaohua said. "He's anticipated us all along. We might have to fight our way out."

As they turned another corner, Bingmei began to reconnect with her body. Her fingers still didn't work, but she was trying to move them. The coldness inside her was all-consuming. She felt her teeth rattling. Kunmia couldn't die too. That wasn't possible. She could defeat anyone, couldn't she?

"Hurry!" Jiaohua grunted.

She sensed the presence of the Phoenix Blade enter the tunnels. There was no disguising its power, its luring magic.

"He's coming," she said in a choked voice.

"Can you run?" Jiaohua asked her.

"I can try," she said.

"Set her down, boy," Jiaohua snapped.

Quion obeyed. Bingmei felt herself wobble, but she felt steady enough when she gripped Quion's arm. They took a few steps and then broke into a run, but the sword was coming closer at a rapid rate. Muxidi was running too, and he was faster.

Another turn, another intersection. Still they pressed on. Bingmei would never have found her way on her own. She was hopelessly lost, but the Jingcha knew the tunnels. Light appeared ahead, finally, and they saw a metal gate. It looked out on a mess of foliage, but light from outside snaked through the growth.

"This is it," Jiaohua whispered. They all gathered up to the gate.

Bingmei could smell Muxidi. He was frantic and hateful and full of determination. He was so close, her skin crawled.

"I smell him," she murmured.

"Bingmei," Damanhur said, gripping her shoulder. "What about the other side? Is anyone there? We can't see past the thicket."

Bingmei turned to the bars of the gate, which were shaped like cranes. She gripped them, trying to smell past her pursuer. There were more Qiangdao outside, concealed.

She nodded bleakly. Surrounded, again.

Damanhur frowned and looked at Jiaohua. He drew his sword. "I'll hold him. Get her out of here."

Jiaohua nodded grimly and withdrew a key. He quickly inserted it into the lock of the gate and turned. The hinges creaked as they opened.

"Run!" he said to his men.

The ensign and members of the Jingcha rushed outside, weapons in hand. They were immediately set upon by screaming Qiangdao.

Bingmei turned as she felt the Phoenix Blade tugging at her soul. Muxidi slowed, his shadowy cloak making him nearly invisible in the dark. The vines and branches blocked the view outside, but she could hear the clash of weapons, the sound of fists smacking flesh. She could hear the groans of the injured.

So much violence. So much death.

Damanhur stalked back into the tunnel, sword held low. "Should have killed you on the beach," he said.

"Yes. You should have," came the taunting reply. "But you'll find I'm not so easy to kill."

Jiaohua let loose a foul curse. Gripping Bingmei's arm, he pulled her to the edge of the tunnel. He parted the leaves, looking outside, then swore again. "Too many," he grunted.

He released Bingmei's arm and withdrew his blowgun. He loaded a dart into it quickly and turned back to where Damanhur and Muxidi were fighting, although the fight was too fierce for him to have an opening. Quion held one of his fishing knives in his hand, his lips peeled back with anger, but he looked so helpless. The cries of pain from outside grew louder, drawing her gaze. The battle would be over soon.

It would not end in their favor.

She saw Damanhur fall in her peripheral vision, and when she turned her head back in shock and horror, Muxidi lunged toward her, his eyes raging. Jiaohua cried out in surprise and tried to shoot the dart at him, but the distance was too small. The Phoenix Blade whipped around, slashing his face. As Jiaohua cried out in pain, Bingmei grabbed Quion's shirt and pulled him with her out into the fresh air.

One of the Qiangdao grabbed her from behind, hauling her off her feet, but Quion smashed his fist into the man's head. The enemy dropped her instantly, stunned by the blow. Bingmei kicked him in the ribs and knocked him down. She sucked in a breath when she saw how badly they were outnumbered—at least four to one. Two Qiangdao rushed at her, and she launched herself at them, kicking one in the chest. The other lunged at her, trying to seize her, but she blocked his attack and grabbed his arm, flipping him hard onto his back.

Qiangdao charged her on every side, converging in a growling mass, and separated her from Quion. She could only hope he'd manage to protect himself, or run. Hand in her pocket, she summoned the power of the cricket and leaped high and away, coming down where some men were grappling with Huqu to subdue him. A quick blow to one man's knees shattered the hold, and Huqu was fighting again. She turned, dodging a fist that shot toward her face, and dropped into a sweeping kick that tripped her assailant backward. The Qiangdao were charging at her again, shouting in fury, but with the meiwood cricket, she leaped over them again. As she landed, she boxed down two more, feeling anger and fury build in her chest. She would not be captured again. Never again.

And then she caught a glimpse of Muxidi. He held the sharp edge of the Phoenix Blade against Quion's neck.

His lips twitched as he met her gaze. "You know I'll do it," he threatened.

"Go, Bingmei!" Quion shouted.

She stared into the Qiangdao's eyes. She smelled his intentions, his lack of any tender feeling.

A prickle crept down her back. An awareness tingled in her mind. It was familiar. She'd felt this same energy, thrill, and purpose while escaping Fusang. Power sizzled down her arms and legs.

"You have my sword," Bingmei said, reaching out her arm.

The blade was ripped out of Muxidi's hand and launched itself into hers.

CHAPTER FORTY
Phoenix-Chosen

As soon as her fingers closed around the warm pommel of the Phoenix Blade, she felt its magic ignite in her veins. Something within her altered. It was more a feeling than a physical sensation. She felt lighter, stronger, and full of purpose.

Quion slammed his elbow into Muxidi's ribs and broke out of his hold, flinging himself to the side to get out of the way.

"Get her!" Muxidi roared at the others gathered in the shadow outside Sajinau's walls. Bingmei dropped into a low stance, holding the blade behind her.

The murderous men stank up the area as they attempted to rush her once again. Without touching the cricket, she leaped, flipping backward, and came down in the midst of the rushing men. Power thrummed through her. Her blade swung almost by itself, striking and hitting a man with every thrust. She felt alive, thrilled, powerful—just as she had while escaping Fusang. Although she had done nothing to summon the power, nothing beyond retrieving the sword, it was heeding her anyway. At the moment, she didn't care how it did, only *that* it did. She dispatched five of the Qiangdao, then flew away before they could overwhelm her with their numbers.

That was the only way to describe it. The meiwood cricket gave her power to jump, but this felt entirely different. She whirled through the air, coming down again at the fringe of her enemies, and struck down another five. The others in the ensign were fighting again too. The tide was turning, the energy shifting.

Muxidi stepped in front of her, thrusting at her with a saber he'd claimed from Damanhur. She recognized the mark of the gorilla on the pommel, and sadness welled in the pit of her stomach. The master was not the contemptible person she'd originally thought him—he was arrogant, but also brave and devoted to his prince. She jammed the hilt of her blade down, blocking the blow, and then spun around to slice her enemy in half.

Only her blade went through shadows instead. It was like fighting smoke. He blinked back into being, corporeal once more, and she felt his fist crash into her cheek, rocking her head back. It hurt terribly and momentarily blinded her, but she kicked out at once.

Again, she met nothing but shadows.

"You cannot defeat me," Muxidi said with a wicked laugh. He vanished, only to reappear immediately on her right. She swept the Phoenix Blade at him and it sailed right through him. He vanished again, and she felt his blade slice her leg.

She jumped and felt her new power sweep her away from him. Her leg throbbed with pain, but it wasn't a deep cut. She blinked, trying to find him. The Qiangdao were smashing into the rest of their group. A few members of the ensign and the Jingcha were still standing, but their momentum was flagging. They were losing the battle once again.

Bingmei urged herself to fly into their midst again, and she did so, the power responding to her thoughts. Muxidi chased her through the overgrown fronds, but she dodged him, coming to the aid of her allies. She cut down several more Qiangdao.

"I will chase you, ghost!" Muxidi said, cutting down a member of the ensign as he passed, dropping him to the ground. He was mimicking her strategy.

She flew away from him again, going back to the wall. Soaring, she came up over the edge for long enough to see into the inner courtyard. The armored warriors of Sajinau were attacking the Qiangdao who had come to seize the city. Echion stood in the midst of the battle, deadly and unstoppable, cutting down warriors as if it were a sport. His cape fluttered behind him like dragon wings, tendrils of the killing fog converging on him. She couldn't see any sign of Kunmia Suun. The soldiers of Sajinau were dropping dead as the fog touched them, but not the Qiangdao. Sleeping corpses littered the courtyard. Bingmei's heart quailed with pain. Still, it was curious that the fog hadn't started coming for her after she'd invoked the magic of her blade. Echion must have meant what he'd said earlier—the fog was his to tame and command. He was directing it for a purpose.

"You cannot defeat us!" Muxidi snarled.

A feeling of overwhelming sadness flooded her, reminding her of Jidi Majia's smell. Had he seen the coming devastation in his vision? Was that why he had smelled that way? She grieved the loss of life and the fate of those who survived. Her grief turned to vengeance, and she lunged straight for Muxidi's heart.

His face grimaced with anticipation as she came at him, then he vanished into the smoke. She'd suspected as much—and prepared for it. When she landed, she spun the blade around, twirling it forward and back in a series of twisting loops in front of her body and then behind her back. She'd practiced this a thousand times with her grandfather's saber, the blade becoming a whirlwind of steel. Over and over, she spun it, and then she felt it embed in something behind her.

She turned her head, seeing the look of surprise on Muxidi's face. Her blade had pierced the shadows and found flesh. Blood began to patter on the ground. He backed away from her, withdrawing from her weapon, his face going pale with surprise. Anger burned away the vestiges of shock, and he struck at her again, overwhelming her with the stench of murderous rage. He was bleeding, the smoke of his cloak starting to unravel. He lunged at her again and again, and she retreated, blocking his blows. He cut at her legs, and she jumped. He tried to cut off her head, but she ducked. Their blades met during her retreat, and she continued to move backward, using the edge of her blade to protect herself—parry, swivel, parry, swivel—then she turned the tide and lunged at him.

The tip of the sword sunk into the flesh of his shoulder. He gasped in pain. The shadows were sloughing off him more quickly. She kicked him hard in the chest, then leaped, feeling the magic lift her up. Her other foot flipped up and kicked him on the chin.

His head snapped back, and he fell down, dropping his saber. When she landed, he rolled to the side, spinning his legs around to clip her calves. She bounded over them, amazed at his martial abilities, but then . . . he had once studied the craft himself, had he not? He'd been part of her grandfather's quonsuun. But he'd become a renegade.

Realizing he was vulnerable, he looked at her in panic and tried to lunge for his weapon. She kicked it out of his reach and leveled her sword at his throat.

Their eyes met. She could smell his fear and defiance.

"Kill me, then," he snarled at her.

She saw a brooch fastening his black cloak. The dark meiwood was engraved with a tarantula and bound in bronze. Muxidi swallowed, eyeing her and the blade at once. Breathing in, she smelled rancid deception. He planned to use her attack as an opening for his own.

She stepped back from him, lowering her sword.

A baffled look came on his face. "Kill me! Take your revenge!"

How she wanted to. Every instinct within her burned to end his life. She'd dreamed of it since she was a little girl. Hate was strong. It was powerful. But Kunmia's lessons hadn't been spoken to deaf ears after all. She found herself remembering what her master had said about its uselessness. About the unintended consequences.

Muxidi lunged at her suddenly, trying to catch her unawares. He grabbed the blade with his bare hand, cutting himself as he gripped it. Before she could shake him off, she saw he wielded a bear claw in his other hand, bound to a bit of metal. She had a split second to decide—if she pulled the blade out of his grip instead of defending herself from his attack, the claw would lacerate her.

She let go of the Phoenix Blade and used both hands to catch his wrist. The sharp end of the claw hovered near her eyebrow. Her legs felt the brunt of his next attempted blow in order to free himself, but she'd blocked it. Bingmei wrenched his arm and sent him face-first into the ground. Something sharp sliced his lip, and she saw him wrinkle his nose in pain. She torqued his arm even more, and the bear-claw weapon tumbled out of his reach.

Quion stepped forward from the fray, slamming one of his cooking pots against Muxidi's head. The Qiangdao slumped, no longer struggling, completely unconscious.

Her friend stood back, hefting the pot, and nodded in triumph. She let go of the arm she'd been twisting, then slid the blade from Muxidi's wounded hand. Crouching, she removed the spider brooch from her enemy's throat and stared at it a moment. She rubbed her thumb against it, like she did with her cricket, but nothing happened. So she slid it into her own pocket to examine it later.

She stood, breathing hard, and saw that the Qiangdao were fleeing into the woods. Only a few of the members of the combined group of ensign and Jingcha had been left standing, but they had won.

"You're bleeding," Quion said to her with a worried frown.

She looked down at her leg, barely remembering how she'd gotten the wound. Quion knelt by her and pulled off his pack again, looking through his supplies. He tore a rag to wipe away her blood and then bound the wound with strips of bandages from his pack. She saw more rope within, along with fishing hooks and other instruments. She tousled his hair as he tightened the knots on the bandages.

Jiaohua staggered out of the hollow then, pressing his injured face with his hand. He approached them, his frown growing deeper when he saw Muxidi lying prone. He drew a dagger without hesitation, and Bingmei's eyes burned at the smell of murder.

Bingmei rose and blocked him with her body. Emotion flashed through the Jingcha leader's eyes. "I'll kill him," he growled.

She shook her head. "We're leaving him."

"What! Don't be a fool! He's killed my men, murdered many in the city." He tried to go around her, but she intervened. His hate was almost as strong as hers.

"I know, Jiaohua," she said evenly. "He killed my grandfather. And my parents."

Jiaohua looked as if he'd explode. "Kill him, then!"

She gave him a defiant look. "Will killing him bring back my grandfather? Will it bring back my parents? Will it bring back anyone that you lost?"

"But he's a murdering Qiangdao! You *can't* let him live." Jiaohua trembled with rage.

"This isn't about what he's done," Bingmei said. "Look at what he's *become*, Jiaohua." She lowered her voice. "It's pitiful. I'm not sparing him because of mercy. It's not about *him*." She pointed at herself. "I don't want to be like him. Like Echion."

Jiaohua stared at her in surprise. She could smell a shift in his emotions, the hatred ebbing—slowly. "They're murdering my people," he said, his voice suddenly hoarse.

"I know," Bingmei said. She felt empathy for him, for this man who had tried his best to save the people of Sajinau. And failed. She knew he felt bound by duty to protect her, as he'd been commanded, but part of him wished to join the corpses in the courtyard. "Dying is easy. Living has always been the challenge. If we kill like they do, then we will become like them." Her heart panged with dread and sadness. "Echion will reclaim his kingdom, one city at a time, and our bitterness and anger will drive us into hiding. Maybe this is how the Qiangdao began?" She shook her head. "It took me long enough to realize it, but Kunmia was right. Revenge settles nothing. It only poisons those who carry it in their hearts." She swallowed, looking into his eyes. "I *know* how that man feels about himself, about others. He stinks with it. And I could not live with myself if I smelled that way. So we go, Jiaohua. We escape. We help others stand against Echion."

He stared at her. "Are you going to die at the Death Wall after all?"

She frowned at his words. She hadn't decided that. She wouldn't lie to him, but the truth was too painful to speak—she knew what she ought to do, what she wanted to do, but she still didn't know if she *could* do it.

When she'd watched Juexin offer his life for Rowen, she'd smelled a spice she'd never experienced before. It was a powerful smell—like cinnamon but with more of a sweet, potent bite.

"We'll see," she answered. "Where's Damanhur?" she asked worriedly. "I saw him go down."

Jiaohua shrugged. "He may have bled to death by now. The rogue cut off his arm, then took his sword. The only reason he didn't kill me too is because I played dead." He grimaced. "My face hurts. He may have taken my eye as well as Damanhur's arm."

"Quion, go check to see if Damanhur is still alive!" she said. Sadness pressed against her ribs.

"Yes, Bingmei," said the young man. Leaving his pack, he hurried into the tunnel. Bingmei gazed up at the wall. The magic that had flooded her was gone. It felt as if the earth were pulling harder at her boots than usual. She was exhausted. The sounds of fighting had dissipated. A deathly hush had fallen over Sajinau. A shiver went down her body.

Quion quickly ducked out again, looking relieved. "He's alive. Barely!"

"Let's bind our wounds," Bingmei said. "Then we must flee this place."

"Where will we go?" Jiaohua asked her.

They were both looking at her as if *she* were the master of the ensign. She gripped the hilt of the Phoenix Blade firmly. Perhaps she was. They seemed willing to follow.

"We'll go back to Kunmia's quonsuun. But I don't think we'll be able to stay there."

CHAPTER
FORTY-ONE

Escaping Sajinau

They came across the remains of another battlefield before sunset. The field was eerily quiet, save for the whip of the animal banners still fixed to broken spears. Even the horses were dead. It was not a battlefield full of blood. The corpses all appeared to be sleeping.

The fog had killed them all.

Jiaohua wandered among the dead, which Bingmei could see had been stripped of weapons. Some of the corpses no longer wore boots, and she could see their possessions had been rifled through. The vastness of the field, shadowed in the grass by the dark bodies, made her heart sink into her stomach. Thousands had been consumed by the fog, their lives snatched away by its misty tendrils. A large part of Sajinau's army had been wiped out in one swoop, their lives extinguished like lamp flames. So many dead. It was almost too much for her mind to take in, the sight made stranger by the tranquil death masks on the bodies.

The other members of her ensign stood around in disbelief. Damanhur looked weak from the loss of blood, his stump bandaged and strapped to his chest. She could smell his despair, but his desire for revenge was stronger still. Hate was keeping him going, forcing him to march his way out of Sajinau step by step. She could smell his hate growing stronger as he gazed at the vast ranks of the dead.

Jiaohua straightened after examining another corpse and rubbed his mouth. He had a bandage over his face, but dried blood stained his cheek.

"This was General Renmin's army," he said with bitterness. "I could barely tell, they've scavenged so much. He was holding the Xifu pass." He pointed to the mountains at the end of the valley. "It was the only pass that hadn't been attacked yet, so I thought it would be safest to come this way. I'd hoped he would give us fresh supplies and maybe a few more men." His lips squirmed with revulsion. "I just found his body. We'll find no help here."

"Do you think the Qiangdao who attacked them have moved on?" Bingmei asked.

Jiaohua nodded. "I think they're converging on Sajinau. They're probably already there. They just left the bodies here." He turned again and looked into the distance, rubbing his jaw. "We're too exposed. I think we should hide in the trees on that slope and wait until nightfall. If any of the Qiangdao have horses, we'll be vulnerable if we travel during the day. There's a village called Yonfeng on the other side of the pass. It's another day's walk from here. Maybe it's been destroyed too, but at least we'll find shelter. Maybe a chicken or two to kill for food. By land, Wangfujing is quite a distance. Are you sure you don't want to try and find a fishing boat?"

"We're not going to Wangfujing. It's overrun with Echion's men. The quonsuun is up in the mountains behind it. If we cross the mountains, we'll get there sooner."

"Or be eaten by bears," Jiaohua snorted.

"All the weapons have been taken," Quion confirmed, coming up to them. He was trying to be strong, but she could smell the devastation coming from him. The warriors had been caught and culled like salmon. "I don't see a single blade among them."

Damanhur grunted. "I noticed the same thing. They don't want to leave any weapons behind that could be used against them. Even the spear shafts have been snapped deliberately." He nudged one with the tip of his boot.

"Let's get out of the open," Jiaohua said worriedly. "This was about a fourth of Sajinau's warriors. Gone. Just like that."

Bingmei nodded, and the group trudged across the plains, careful not to step on the dead. When they reached the edge of the battlefield, Bingmei's sadness stretched as far as the distant hills. She didn't want to imagine what was happening back at the palace in Sajinau. Was Rowen still there? Her heart hurt for him, and for Prince Juexin. Had Kunmia survived her second battle with Echion? She hoped so, but her guts twisted with uncertainty. And what of Marenqo? Mieshi? The thought of losing all her companions was too horrible to bear. Inwardly, she grieved for them.

As they climbed, the trees grew closer together, thicker, and soon the horror of the plains was concealed. The group lay down to rest, and Jiaohua set guards to watch over them. Bingmei nestled in the scrub, sleeping on her arm. Quion looked pale and exhausted, and she watched him fall asleep almost instantly. And even though she was weary too, it took a long time before she fell asleep. Every time she closed her eyes, she imagined Juexin kneeling before Echion. Then she saw his ghost, his pleading look, and heard the petition he'd made before the Death Wall dragged him away.

Save us.

杀雾

She awoke when a hand shook her shoulder. Blinking, she saw Jiaohua crouching near her, his face full of concern. She heard it then—the moaning, the wails. It sounded like the wind through the trees, but the sound was made by humans, not the sky. It was the sound of mourning and grief. The sound of despair.

"What's happening?" she whispered, sitting up. Quion was still asleep next to her.

"The Qiangdao brought over womenfolk to bury the dead. Mothers and sisters. The aged. There are guards set over them, making them work."

She heard the crack of a whip cut through the groans. Jiaohua nodded. "Hear that?"

Bingmei nodded.

"We won't be able to slip away until dusk. We can move along the tree line to stay out of sight."

His whispers had aroused the others, who had been sleeping. Heads lifted, and then they, too, heard the sounds of mourning.

"I don't think we'll be sleeping anymore this night," Jiaohua said bitterly.

He was right. The noise made it impossible. When dusk finally settled over the valley, and shadows replaced light, they moved away from their makeshift camp and followed the uneven ground along the tree line. When it became so dark that the footing was treacherous, they emerged from the woods and walked along the edge of the plains, where the high grasses also helped conceal them. The ground turned rugged as they ventured up into the pass. Bingmei led the way, smelling the air for the stench of the Qiangdao.

When they neared the top, she still didn't smell anything, and so Jiaohua sent one of his men ahead to scout. He returned shortly with news that the pass was unguarded. They crossed it just as the moon started to rise. It surprised her how walking in the dark so long had heightened her sense of sight. The brightness of the moon almost hurt her eyes.

They traveled down the mountain into the valley beyond, keeping to the eastern edge rather than taking the main road. Once during the night, a group of torch-carrying horsemen—about a dozen or so—rode toward the pass along the road, but in the dark there was no way of knowing if they were friend or foe. The torches gave Bingmei and the others ample time to hunker down and conceal themselves.

Just before dawn, they reached the outskirts of the village of Yonfeng. Jiaohua led them to a spot in the woods to wait for sunrise. Bingmei and the others were tired, but they watched from their hiding places and saw that the village still had people inhabiting it. These were peasants mostly, with fraying boots and animal-skin jackets to ward off the chilly morning. Small cookfires began to appear, creating a little haze. A farmer came toward the woods with an axe, probably foraging for firewood.

"I'll go have a talk with him," Jiaohua said. "See what I can learn. Wait here."

Bingmei nodded and watched as Jiaohua slunk away from them, trying to keep his movement concealed from the approaching peasant. When the farmer reached the edge of the woods, Jiaohua grabbed him and pulled him into the brush. There was no sound of struggle.

Bingmei waited in anticipation, anxious for news. After a little time had passed, she saw the farmer walk back to the village, dragging a slender fallen tree with him. Jiaohua returned to them shortly thereafter.

Damanhur sidled close, his gaze intense. He smelled feverish and his eyes were glassy. Sweat dripped down his cheek. His wound was likely inflamed. If they didn't reach the quonsuun quickly, he was going to die. She was intent on saving him. On ensuring that one more death wasn't added to the day's tally.

"What did you find out?" Bingmei asked in a whisper.

The others huddled close, their faces intent.

Jiaohua rubbed his cheek. "He thought *I* was a Qiangdao," he said with a chuckle. "After I explained, he was relieved. He said the Qiangdao army came through here days ago. They stole much of the food from the village and nearly all the livestock. They told everyone they would not be harmed if they stayed inside. There are some Qiangdao there, about a dozen, and the villagers have to feed and shelter them. They say they are the masters now, and they eat the farmers' food."

Resentment chafed inside Bingmei's heart. "Maybe we should free them," she said.

Jiaohua shook his head no. "Riders come through regularly, and the Qiangdao give them reports. If we were to kill them, then the villagers would likely be put to death. They're slaves, but at least they're alive. They asked me for news from Sajinau and begged to know if King Shulian has returned to drive off the invaders. They believe the prince will send an army to free them. I didn't have the heart to say that no one is coming. They'll learn that soon enough."

Bingmei frowned and nodded in agreement. More and more she felt like *she* was becoming a Qiangdao. The situations had been reversed. Instead of walking the lands in freedom and respect, they were hunted.

"There's more," Jiaohua said, looking at her.

Her brow wrinkled.

"The farmer said the Qiangdao have offered a reward. They're looking for a pale girl with copper hair. Anyone harboring her or safeguarding her will be executed immediately. They're looking for you."

Bingmei nodded. But with the Phoenix Blade strapped to her back, they would have a difficult time finding her.

杀雾

It took another week to cross the mountains and the rivers of melting ice. They stayed in the hinterlands, forsaking the villages except to learn what news they could. The news, when it came, was always awful. Wangfujing and Sajinau had both fallen. Yiwu and Xidan had been taken as well and were paying tributes. The Dragon Emperor, Echion, ruled from the palace of Sajinau, where he gathered the wealth from his conquests. Soon the dark season would come again, and when it ended, his empire would spread to the western shores. They'd stumbled into a band of Qiangdao roving the woods and quickly dispatched them. The mountains had always been so dangerous, but they seemed quiet, abandoned—it seemed the Qiangdao had abandoned their caves and hidden lairs and come in droves to settle the land.

Each day made Damanhur sicker, weaker. He had a fever, but he was relentless in his determination to reach their destination. Thanks to Quion's skills, his wound wasn't festering, and the young man caught enough fish to feed them amply every day. There were also sweet mountain berries, bitter-tasting roots, and mushrooms in abundance. They even managed to find a deer with its antlers stuck in low-hanging branches and enjoyed sizzling meat that day. They were always careful with their fires and concealed their camps after they left.

Although Bingmei didn't say so to the others, she feared what they would find when they arrived. If the quonsuun had fallen, they'd need to find shelter during the season of the Dragon of Night. Maybe they could find a ship bound for Renxing, or Sihui, or Tuqiao? The rulers in each of those kingdoms would want to know as much as they could about Echion.

Or there was the Death Wall. When they reached the top of the mountain, she'd be able to see it again. Conflict roiled inside her. She wanted to live. She wanted to find another way to defeat Echion. One that did not require her to sacrifice herself. Why was that the only way? Or maybe they could find King Shulian. But she couldn't bear the thought of facing him.

When they passed Wangfujing, hiking along the mountain trails, they could see the city harbor was bustling with ships. It was tempting to send someone down for news and supplies, but the risk was too great. Bingmei stared down at it for a long moment, thinking of all the time she'd spent there, good and bad, and then Quion nudged her elbow.

When she turned, he showed her something in his palm. Her scorpion medallion, the one she'd yanked off in anger after being chased out of the city.

"You keep it," she said with a smile. She remembered showing him around Wangfujing after his father died. How long ago that felt. How much their world had changed.

The climb became more arduous, and the accumulation of snow on the mountainside grew deeper. Patches were still melting, and some would stay until winter came again. This land was familiar to her, achingly so, and she felt an urgent need to get to the quonsuun. To discover what had happened there. In their eagerness, they hardly rested.

When they rounded the corner, she saw the quonsuun still standing and felt tears of relief prick her eyes. The mountain air smelled fresh and inviting, but she was worried all was not as it seemed.

They stopped, everyone breathing fast. She felt a trickle of sweat drip down the tip of her nose.

"We made it," Quion gasped, leaning forward and pressing his hands against his knees.

"Who will go?" Jiaohua asked, wiping his mouth. "To see if it's safe?"

"We will all go," Bingmei answered.

He frowned but nodded. They would fight if they must. After resting and catching their breath, they trudged up the final slope of the trail toward the gate. She heard a voice calling out from the walls. A shout of warning. Then a cry of recognition. They demanded to know the watchword.

Bingmei answered with it.

As they approached, the main doors of the quonsuun were pulled open in greeting. Bingmei walked firmly, confidently, smelling the air for trouble. An oily, lemony scent flooded her with recognition. The smell of greed. And then Budai came hobbling forward, hand on a cane. He had lost some girth. A triumphant grin spread across his face when he saw her.

She smelled Marenqo before she saw him. When he did step into view, she saw he was gripping Kunmia's battered staff in his hands.

Her worst fear had been realized. She saw it in his face. Smelled it in his essence.

Kunmia Suun had crossed the Death Wall first.

CHAPTER FORTY-TWO

A Final Sunrise

Bingmei's sleep was fitful. Too many ghosts haunted her dreams. The quonsuun had always been a place of safety, of shelter, of defense against storms and the vagaries of life. Now it was a reminder, once again, of the fragility of existence. Death had claimed so many. But the harvest of souls was only beginning.

After resting for several hours, she rose from her bed and walked to the table with a basin and pitcher of water. She splashed some on her face and then stared at herself in the mirror. She'd hoped against hope that her mentor had survived Echion's slaughter at Sajinau. Pressing her lips together, she stewed in grief and misery, wishing she could rail against the evil she had unwittingly unleashed on the world. A glyph, drawn with a finger dipped in water, had started it all. If only she could undo it.

Tension mounted inside her. Her reflection brought the painful reminder that she was the phoenix-chosen. Her coppery hair was unfurling from the braids she'd coiled around her head. She sighed, untangled them with vigorous strokes of a comb, and then plaited them again.

Whatever fates had chosen *her* had chosen poorly.

She fastened the wig onto her head, disguising the bright strands. Her eyes looked hollow, her face wan and tired. There was no feeling of safety anymore, there or anywhere. She doubted there ever would be.

After changing into fresh clothes, she made sure the Phoenix Blade was hidden and then left her room and walked in the direction of the training yard. She passed a room, its door open, and saw Mieshi sitting on the edge of a bed. Damanhur was sitting up on it, his stump bandaged anew, and she was trying to feed him soup.

"No more," he said angrily, jerking his head away.

"Eat it. You need to regain your strength," Mieshi said.

"Would you stop pitying me?" Damanhur said.

"This isn't pity. It's compassion. Now eat the soup."

"I can *feed* myself!"

Bingmei passed quickly, anxious to be away from the strong, pungent smells coming from the room. Sometimes she hated her gift.

When she arrived at the training yard, she found Marenqo there, twirling Kunmia's staff in the basic sets they had learned at the quon-suun. She waited by one of the support pillars, watching him attack, stomp, swivel, and pivot the weapon. He'd never been their best warrior, but his form was good. When he reached the end, he was dripping with sweat. It was then he noticed her.

"Now I'm embarrassed," he said, chuffing, wiping his mouth. "The phoenix has been watching me."

"I'm not the phoenix," Bingmei said, stepping away from the pillar. "It made a mistake if it chose me."

"Undoubtedly," Marenqo said, agreeing quickly with a strident nod. "Why a fancy bird would choose someone so ugly and ill-tempered clearly proves it. But then again, a bird's brain is about the size of a pea, so we shouldn't be too surprised."

His jesting had always struck a little too close to the heart, and yet it was a welcome familiarity at the moment. She was grateful he and Mieshi had survived. "I've missed you, Marenqo."

He gave her a little shrug, but she smelled his pleasure at her compliment. "You made it out of Sajinau alive. I'm impressed." He hefted the staff and approached her. "Not many did."

"We learned from some of the villages we passed that Echion has defeated nearly all of the eastern kingdoms."

Marenqo nodded. "He made quick work of them. Mieshi and I left by boat, so we got here before you. Qiangdao are everywhere. Thankfully, they can't tell when someone is lying like you can. I bluffed our way out of several dangerous moments."

"Did anyone else come with you?"

He shook his head no. "Just the two of us." He pursed his lips. "Are you ready to hear how Kunmia died?"

Grief squeezed her heart again, making her gasp. "No, Marenqo. I don't think I'm ready yet."

He kept coming toward her, shaking his head. "It doesn't matter if you're ready. *She* thought you were ready."

Bingmei wrinkled her brows. "For what?"

"To take her place. This is yours now." He offered her the rune staff. Bingmei recoiled. "I don't want it."

"Her last command to me was to bring this to you, Bingmei. I will fulfill it, even if you don't want me to. Take it."

"Marenqo," Bingmei said, her throat thickening. But he shoved the staff into her hands. As her fingers closed around the scarred and battered wood, she felt something rip deep inside her.

He nodded firmly. "The ensign passes to you. She's been grooming you for it. I've already told all the servants. Haven't you noticed how they've been treating you since you returned? She had no children. She has no siblings left. She wanted me to give this to you and to tell you something."

Bingmei winced again, closing her eyes, dreading what was coming.

He put his hands on her shoulders. "Kunmia said, and I've heard her say this before while gazing up at the sky, that the most beautiful things in the universe are the starry heavens above us and the feeling of *duty* within us. She bid me tell you to do what you feel is your duty, no more and no less." He paused. "She supported your decision, Bingmei. Duty is a feeling that must come from within. No one can compel it on you. If you feel it is your duty to go to the Death Wall, then do so. If you feel it is your duty to do something else, then pursue it with equal vigor."

Bingmei opened her eyes, looking at him in surprise, feeling relief and gratitude for Kunmia's final words. She'd never heard Kunmia say it before, but the master's entire life had been lived according to that principle. When she made a promise she would do something, she always delivered on it.

Marenqo smiled at her, his face full of sympathy and pain. "I miss her," he admitted, his throat catching. "She was a sister to me. Mieshi, not so much. Zhuyi . . . well, I always liked her, but she never understood my humor. Damanhur lost his sense of humor along with his arm, poor wretch. You're the only one I would dare follow, Bingmei. If you take up this staff and all that it means, I'll be loyal to you. Assuming you don't make me clean latrines all day. And I'm pretty sure the fisherman's son won't leave your side either. I'm talking too much. I do that, I know. It's one of my many failings. I just want to know if you are *planning* to lead the ensign now. What do you think?"

Bingmei felt gratitude for his words and used the staff to tap his arm. "I do need someone who can speak many languages."

"I can babble in plenty of tongues, Master." He dropped down to his knees in a show of obeisance. "I will serve you, if you will have me."

"I will," she answered, nodding. He rose, then rubbed his hands together. "I think your first act as master of the quonsuun should be to order a large feast. If you've been walking all this way, and you must have because it took you so long to get here, then you're clearly famished. A feast would set you up just right."

"Why is it always about food with you?" Bingmei asked, grinning.

"When you never know which day will be your last, it's important to eat well every day. I try to take these words to heart."

"More likely, you take them to your stomach," she pointed out.

He laughed at that, just as she smelled Budai's approach. The scent came from behind her. Marenqo looked over her shoulder and muttered, "Speaking of feasts. Well, I'll let you deal with him. I have a feeling he is going to try and offer you a deal."

Bingmei nodded. "And tell the cooks to prepare a feast for tonight."

"With pleasure, Master," he said, bowing.

Bingmei turned, gripping the staff, and faced Budai as he approached her. Though he still smelled of greed, he'd been humbled by his near miss with death. The gnawing ambition had faded, and he was fixed on getting revenge and reclaiming his wealth. And it felt to her that he would try to use her to do this.

"So Kunmia wanted you to have the staff," he said, nodding gravely. She noticed a limp as he walked closer.

"How did you survive the attempt on your life?" she asked him. "When we fled Wangfujing, your steward said you'd been stabbed."

"Oh, I was stabbed," he admitted. "Thankfully, the blade didn't overcome my protection." He rubbed the lower part of his belly. "I feigned injury and escaped in the chaos."

"How did you climb this mountain?" Bingmei asked.

"Some of my faithful servants carried me up here on a litter."

Bingmei gaped, feeling sympathy for those servants. It was a difficult climb for someone with a pack, let alone for people carrying such a corpulent man. She smelled his offense at her reaction.

"You can't stay here," Budai said. "They will come looking for you."

"I know this already," Bingmei answered. She didn't feel he was trustworthy, but she'd hear him out.

"You need a place to go. And you need money. Not all of my treasures were kept in Wangfujing."

"Oh?"

"Indeed not. I knew there was a chance the Qiangdao would overrun the town, and I planned for it. That's how I escaped, through a back exit. I have a hunting preserve on an island east of Yiwu. It's not far, by boat, from the ruins of your grandfather's quonsuun. There's plenty of game there for those who stay to survive the season of the Dragon of Night." His eyes glittered. "Weapons. Armor. It's a start. Then we seek an alliance with another king."

Bingmei gave him a level look. "What do you want, Budai? You never do anything without benefitting from it."

She could sense an ulterior motive, although she couldn't root it out. But something didn't smell right, and it put her on her guard.

"I want to help you," he said, holding up his hands. He reeked of insincerity.

"The only person you've ever *wanted* to help is yourself," she answered.

"Of course you see me that way, Bingmei. You are young and still rather inexperienced in the ways of life. You need an advisor. Someone to counsel you. Of course, you will make all the decisions."

"Like Guanjia was to you?" she asked.

"Yes! Very much like that. I'll be honest, because I know you have a special gift. I want Wangfujing back. It's true. It was stolen from me. I was tricked and deceived."

"I do recall warning you," Bingmei said. "And you didn't listen."

"But I'm listening *now*. And I think, with a little help, this problem with Echion might be concluded in our favor. If that happens, I want your assurance that Wangfujing will be mine once again. I do not ask for favors. I'm offering you a place of refuge. A place no one else knows about. Everyone is looking for you. There won't be many places you can hide without being recognized. Let me help you hide. That is my offer. Will you accept it?"

She smelled his desperation like a rotting onion. There was a trick at play here, a deception she couldn't see.

Bingmei shook her head no. "I appreciate your offer, Budai." She started to leave and then paused, staring at him. "Oh, and now that I'm the master of this quonsuun, you will owe me for each day you have stayed here. The food you have eaten from my stores. The medicines and healing you have received. I will have Marenqo bring you the tally."

She watched his eyes narrow into slits and felt humiliation coming off him in waves. How many times had he done this to others? Taken advantage of their difficulties to bind their interests with his? He'd deliberately done this to Rowen.

"I . . . have no money . . . at the present," he said, his voice choking with anger.

"A pity," she answered dispassionately and left the training yard.

杀雾

Bingmei hiked up the steep trail to the top of the mountain. She had last been there with Kunmia, the day she'd practiced with the Phoenix Blade. The blade, strapped in a new scabbard to her back, bounced against her as she climbed. Her fur hat helped stave off the morning chill. Patches of snow blended in with the rocks and small scrub.

The feast at the quonsuun the night before would be remembered for years to come. After they had eaten, Bingmei announced they would be abandoning the quonsuun the next day. Although Bingmei did not want Budai's help, she agreed with his assessment—it wasn't safe to linger there. They would secure the doors and leave it to the elements, trusting that whatever strength had sustained it during the centuries would continue to do so. Maybe they would return.

There were questions about where they were going. Bingmei refused to answer them. Those who wanted to follow her would. But she wouldn't allow her whereabouts to be revealed to anyone after she was gone.

As she climbed, she thought of the look on Budai's face, his resentment and rage burning beneath the surface. He was not healthy enough to join her, nor did she want him to come. She'd rebuffed him. That would come with a price later on, she knew. Better to cut strings now instead of later, when he could do more damage.

She reached the little shrine at the top of the mountain and set her staff against one of the stone pillars. For a long moment, she stood there, hands on hips, catching her breath. The air smelled of sweet pine and spruce and the little bit of snow that crunched under her boots. A few shoots of wildflowers were blooming on the other slope, facing the sun. She even saw a black bear rooting in a berry bush, gorging itself.

The Death Wall loomed in the distance, the sharp lines of the wall starkly visible against the rock. She gazed at it, feeling a strange sensation ripple through her stomach. It was a feeling of longing. A sadness for those who had gone there before her—Grandfather, her parents. Although the sharpness of memories blurred with time, her feelings for them were still strong. Lieren had also gone before her. And sweet Zhuyi. Their lives had been snuffed out too soon. Prince Juexin's ghost-soul shimmered in her memory, his final words a plea for her to save them. But he, too, was gone to the Grave Kingdom. Kunmia Suun too. They'd all gone.

Bingmei pressed her lips firmly, staring at the morning sun as it rose over the Death Wall and stabbed at her eyes. Death was inexorable. It claimed the young as well as the old. What lay beyond that wall? What secrets were hidden on the other side? Echion knew. He had gone there and returned. He'd mastered death itself. How? She had a suspicion that he'd destroyed the knowledge of it deliberately, to prevent anyone else from achieving comparable power. All that remained of the ancients, and their knowledge of him, were the glyphs. And only he understood them.

Another memory flittered through her mind. Rowen's face. The warm, sweet smell of the feelings he'd finally revealed to her. Her own heart resisted the confusing emotions that suddenly swelled up. They'd not known each other very long. She'd asked Marenqo what had become of him. He didn't know, but he suspected he was one of Echion's prisoners. She shook her head. The prince had always been so full of contradictions. Irresolute yet determined. Poor yet ambitious. Unfaithful to his family, but devoted to his beliefs. It was dangerous to care for someone like Rowen. Yet she felt drawn to him. She wished for a moment that he were there, sharing this sunrise with her.

Where are you? she called out in her mind.

But there was no answer.

She heard the crunch of boots in the snow coming up the trail. With the breeze blowing into her face, she hadn't smelled anyone approaching. She turned cautiously and saw Quion ambling up the trail. A lean snow leopard padded behind him, not exactly stalking him but definitely following him.

Was it the one that had attacked him last winter?

She came away from the shrine and stopped, hands on her hips again.

"I've already given it three of the fish that I caught this morning," Quion said, looking back with a quirk of a smile. "I don't have any more, but it's still following me."

"Maybe it likes you," Bingmei said. "You saved it from starving."

"I can't make sense of it," Quion said. "I keep looking back, afraid it's going to pounce on me again." He wore his large pack, as usual, and the pots were jangling against it.

"It doesn't look hungry anymore," Bingmei said, folding her arms. She grabbed her staff from the pillar and sighed. "You followed me up the mountain?"

He nodded and looked a little sheepish. "Wanted to make sure you weren't . . . slipping away on your own. It looked like you were heading east." *Toward the Death Wall.*

"I'm not going anywhere near it," Bingmei replied. "I just wanted to see the view from the mountain one last time." She sighed. "I don't feel ready to be anyone's master. I've still much to learn."

"Oh, you're ready," Quion said, grinning. "You can handle anything, Bingmei."

His words smelled fragrant, and she appreciated his confidence in her. Her own self-doubts weren't nearly as pleasant. She saw that the snow leopard had paused, watching them both with an enigmatic look. It seemed only half-wild now.

She turned back one last time, gazing at the distant mountain. The wall. She turned her back then, and walked with Quion back down the other side toward the quonsuun they were about to leave.

杀雾

If you are patient in one moment of anger, you will escape a hundred days of sorrow.

—Dawanjir proverb

EPILOGUE

The Dragon Emperor

Rowen, like the other prisoners, had been herded into the throne room. A Qiangdao stood behind him, his saber resting on Rowen's left shoulder, the blade facing his neck. He could feel the tiny hairs on his skin prickle in awareness of the sharp edge. Kneeling in submission, as did the others, he waited his turn before the Dragon Emperor, Echion. His sister, Eomen, knelt beside him.

The fall of Sajinau was complete. Rowen had watched in horror as the killing fog decimated the soldiers. The bodies had already been carried out and tossed into the icy water, where they sank into the deep to feed the fish. All the weapons from the soldiers had been gathered and were being melted in the various forges throughout the city. Anyone who was not a Qiangdao would be put to death if they were spied carrying a weapon longer than an eating knife.

But Echion spared the lives of the common people of Sajinau. He had brought with him in the enormous ships huge casks of coins stamped with the symbol of the dragon. These were exchanged for cowry shells, which were fragile in comparison. Only the coin stamped with the dragon would be acceptable for purchasing food or paying bills. There were lines still as people came to exchange their shells. What became of the shells . . . Rowen had no idea.

Another man was dragged before the dragon. His armor had been stripped away, but Rowen could see his military bearing. His braided hair had been cut away since the loss of the battle. Every man in the kingdom had shorn hair.

"Who are you? What is your rank?" Echion asked from the throne of King Shulian, which had been built on stone plinths to make it higher. Even though Rowen had yearned to sit on that very throne, he resented seeing Echion up there, usurping his father's position.

"M-my name is Wuluju," stammered the man, his voice thick with fear. He dared not look up.

Echion stared at him, waiting.

"I am an officer in the army," he finished.

"Do you know where General Tzu is?" Echion asked. "That is why your life has been spared thus far. Do you have any useful information?" He sounded bored.

"I-I do," he replied.

"Go on," Echion said, gesturing for him to continue.

The man lifted his head slightly, but kept his gaze averted. "He was ordered by the crown prince to abandon Sajinau and rally the armies guarding the passes."

Traitor, Rowen thought with anger, glaring at the officer.

Echion sat in silence.

The soldier, emboldened, spoke more. "I believe he was planning to guard the Xishan pass first. He was ordered to mount a resistance. I heard the p-prince speak this. General Tzu left before the . . ." He gulped and swallowed and then fell silent.

"Your information was useful," Echion said, stroking his smooth chin. He wasn't wearing his dragon armor anymore but a costume of sumptuous silk, black with dazzling embroidery. His large sheathed blade was propped near him, and his other hand fondled the pommel.

"I need capable officers, Wuluju. You will serve in the Qiangdao army as an officer. I will give you some advice, if you will hear it."

"Th-thank you, great dragon!" sputtered the relieved officer. "I would hear anything you wish to tell me."

"This is not the first time I have ruled from this palace. I once chose a general to serve me here who was especially cunning. As a test of his leadership skills, I asked him to take command of my household of concubines and prepare them to march in the courtyard. He asked me to choose my two favorite concubines to serve as officers. I thought he was merely trying to ingratiate himself to me, so I named my two favorites, who were rivals with each other. He divided the consorts into two groups and explained the marching pattern to the officers who had been chosen. He then ordered them to march. They tittered and did nothing." Echion smiled in a wily way.

Rowen knew the speech was intended for everyone gathered there, not just the soldiers. He was teaching them what he expected of his servants. Rowen listened warily, expecting a dark ending to the tale.

"The general turned to me. If orders aren't obeyed, he said, it is the fault of the general. Perhaps he had not been clear. So he repeated his instructions, which were rather simple. Again he issued the order to march. Again the concubines tittered, mocking him with their inaction."

Echion's gaze swept the great hall. Rowen listened to the tale, riveted. Even though he hated the man, he was intrigued by the story.

Echion rose from the throne and stepped down the dais. He was impressive in size and strength. Rowen had not been there when Bingmei had revived him from his tomb. But he matched her description of him. Pale and powerful. He had the winter sickness, just as she did. Just as Jidi Majia did.

"The general then turned to me and said that if orders were understood but not obeyed, it was the fault of the officers, not the general. And the consequence for such disobedience should be swift death. He insisted they both should perish. Of course I remonstrated with him. We were all shocked. But I saw the wisdom in his counsel. If I failed to empower him, then he could not be trusted to lead my armies. My queen, my empress, was not wroth to see her rivals executed. And they were. Such a general. Such a man. Two more concubines were chosen as officers. And this time the consorts marched precisely. This was the man who built the Death Wall. Who devoted his full measure of strength and cunning to my cause. And now his bones lie buried under that sacred edifice."

He turned back and mounted the steps again. "Find General Tzu and bring him to me. I would have his service. Or, at the least, not his enmity. Begone."

Echion resumed his seat as Wuluju was hefted to his feet and taken away by his guard. The ancient ruler leaned back in his throne, gazing down at the prisoners. His eyes drifted past Rowen, who quickly looked down so as not to be caught staring at him.

"Jidi Majia. Kneel before me."

Rowen's heart clenched with worry. The pale-skinned advisor slowly rose, and the guard behind him butted him in the back with the pole of his spear. He looked weary and forlorn, but he shuffled forward and prostrated himself before the throne. Rowen turned his head and gazed at his sister. Her body trembled with fear, and although he dared not reach for her hand, he gave her a reassuring look.

"You served King Shulian and his eldest son."

"I did, dread sovereign," said Jidi Majia.

"I, too, respect and admire the role of counselor. It is a position of great power and honor. It was my greatest counselor who solved the riddle of immortality. Who learned the Immortal Word." Rowen stared at him, feeling a strange burn inside his own heart. He'd thought his ambitions lay in ashes, but there was a spark still. A little curl of smoke. What was this?

"Every person must serve a role," said Echion. "Some catch fish. Some harvest crops. Some provide order. Some execute the intransigent. One must learn their part and do it without murmur or complaint. Do you not agree, Jidi Majia?"

The wizened counselor gazed up at the dragon. "And what is the role you wish me to play, Your Highness?"

"First, I must see how useful you will be to me. The one I seek, the girl. The phoenix-chosen. Do you know where she is?"

Jidi Majia shook his head no. "I do not."

"Do you know where she is going?" Echion asked, seemingly unsurprised by the answer.

"I do not," said Jidi Majia.

"You disappoint me," said Echion. "I had hoped you would be more useful. But I still have need of your service. The Qiangdao are not learned. To work in my palace is a symbol of trust. You must sacrifice part of yourself. Take him away and make him a eunuch. When he has healed, bring him back for his role."

"Your Majesty!" Jidi Majia said, his eyes widening with horror.

"Begone," said Echion dismissively.

Rowen's stomach dropped, and he gaped in shock as the Qiangdao grabbed Jidi Majia by the arm and led him away. His insides squirmed with discomfort. Glancing at his sister, he saw tears in her eyes.

After Jidi Majia had left the throne room, Echion turned and faced Rowen. "It is your turn, princeling."

The man behind Rowen lowered the sword and grabbed his arm, yanking him to his feet. Rowen felt light-headed, queasy. His heart was pounding in his chest. He did *not* want to become a eunuch. Death was preferable.

When he was brought in front of the throne, his eyes were level with Echion's feet. The ruler wore sandals studded with gems. Rowen's ears were ringing with fear and dread. He dropped down on his knees and paid obeisance. Then he waited, breathless, worried.

"Prince Rowen. Or do you prefer Wuren?"

Rowen shouldn't have been surprised, but he flinched. His mouth went dry. "Whatever you would call me," he said in respect.

"Rise."

Rowen did so. He blinked quickly, trying to calm his emotions. To project a sense of ease. But he was terrified.

"I will ask you the same question. Do you know where the phoenix-chosen is? The girl called Bingmei?"

Rowen cleared his throat. "Yes."

A hush fell on the audience hall.

"That is useful," Echion said, sounding a little surprised. "I will tell you this, young man. If you do not assist me in finding her, then I will have your sister murdered in a most cruel, painful, and prolonged ritual, which, I assure you, will make her suffer beyond anything your puny mind can imagine." His eyes narrowed. "Now, where is she?"

The words sparked dark inside Rowen's heart. He'd just lost his brother. Although he hated the thought of putting Bingmei at risk, losing Eomen was unthinkable. He told himself that he was the only one who could protect Bingmei. That if *he* were sent after her, he might be able to help her and Eomen.

He tried to believe it.

"She's traveling, my lord," said Rowen. "Near . . . Wangfujing."

"And you know this . . . how?"

Rowen bit his lip. He swallowed, steeling himself. "Because of the Phoenix Blade. I can sense it. I know she has it. And so I know where she is."

Silence filled the great hall. Rowen stared at the sandaled feet, waiting, agonizing. But he didn't show his feelings. He didn't reveal the care he felt for the girl the Dragon of Night was hunting. His connection to *her*.

"That *is* useful. But I do not trust you, princeling, and I am not a fool. You will take a band of Qiangdao and find her. And you will bring her to me. Bring me the phoenix-chosen, and I will spare your sister. And you. I will reward you beyond your ambition's hunger."

There was a pause.

"Begone."

Rowen bowed again to the Dragon of Night. He had studied effigies of him all his life, but seeing him in the flesh had made Rowen shrink with terror.

Forgive me, he thought in his mind, feeling the tangles of loyalty ripping him apart.

There was no way to proceed without harming someone he loved. If only Juexin hadn't asked to take his place. The memory of sensing Bingmei, hidden behind the grate, stabbed him.

Forgive me.

CHARACTERS

Batong—八通—member of Damanhur's ensign

Bingmei—冰玫—orphaned main character, has winter sickness

Budai—布达—ruler of Wangfujing

Damanhur—达曼 回—leader of Gorilla Ensign from Sajinau

Echion—化身—the Dragon of Night, past emperor of the known world

Eomen—幽梦—King Shulian's daughter

Fuchou—复仇—ruler of Renxing

Guanjia—管家—Budai's steward

Guoduan—果断—captain of the merchant ship the *Raven*

Heise—黑色—captain from Tianrui, leader of mercenaries

Huqu—湖区—member of Damanhur's ensign

Jiao—狨—Bingmei's grandfather

Jiaohua—狨猾—master of Shulian's police force, the Jingcha

Jidi Majia—吉狄马加—Shulian's advisor, also has the winter sickness

Jiukeshu—九棵树—Qiangdao leader

Juexin—决心—crown prince of Sajinau, Rowen's brother

Keyi—可以—greedy fisherman

Kunmia Suun—群迷阿苏—owner of an ensign, Bingmei's master

Lieren—猎人—part of Kunmia's ensign, the hunter

Mao Zhang—毛长—businessman in Wangfujing, owner of fishing boats

Marenqo—马任可—translator for Kunmia

Mieshi—蔑视—member of Kunmia's ensign, sharp tongued

Mingzhi—明智—ruler of Tuqiao

Muxidi—木樨地—Qiangdao leader who murdered Bingmei's family

Pangxie—螃蟹—an officer in General Tzu's army

Qianxu—谦虚—ruler of Yiwu

Quion—球呢—fisherman's son who joins Kunmia's ensign

Rowen—如闻—prince of Sajinau, younger brother of Juexin

Shulian—熟练—king of Sajinau

Tzu—子—general of all of Sajinau's military

Wuren—无人—a man without a country, Rowen's disguise name

Zhongshi—重视—Kunmia's nephew, guards her quonsuun during absences

Zhuyi—注意—member of Kunmia's ensign, keen listener

Zizhu—自主—guardian of Bingmei's grandfather's quonsuun

AUTHOR'S NOTE

A few years ago, I visited the wilds of Alaska for the first time. The seed idea of this story came when we hiked to the Mendenhall Glacier, an enormous mass of ice that had carved between mountains and emptied into a bay. That was where I got the idea of Echion and his kingdom hidden beneath the ice. In my mind's eye, I saw a small group of people, treasure hunters and adventurers, who found his stone coffin. One of them revived him unwittingly, unleashing a powerful being on the earth. She was the only one who could turn back the tide, only it would require her to sacrifice herself, and she didn't want to. She wouldn't be Frodo and take the ring to Mordor. She'd want to get the heck out of there and just stay alive, thank you very much.

All these ideas came to me in a rush, and I jotted them down on my phone and filed it under the category "book ideas," where many of my ideas stew for months or years.

Then in early 2018 I was invited to visit China through the International Writing Program and my Chinese publisher, who had just released six of my books in Mandarin. It would be a month-long trip in the fall. Would I come? It turned out that the dates coincided with my kids' fall break from school. I said yes and brought my family with me. We visited the Great Wall, the Forbidden City, the Temple of Heaven, and even "Scorpion Alley" (Wangfujing).

To say that the trip inspired me is a complete and total understatement.

I learned a lot about Chinese mythology and culture, including how much of their past has been lost. As I studied the life of the First Emperor, I found he reminded me a lot of the ancient ruler I'd envisioned on that trip to Alaska, including his quest to find and gain eternal life. Suddenly these two ideas began to mesh together, and a new world was born inside my mind. Something a little different. Something new. As I visited the intriguing palaces and places, and tasted the amazing food, my imagination went into overdrive.

I hope you enjoy the Grave Kingdom Series. In it, we'll go to a place that my imagination hasn't taken us before.

ACKNOWLEDGMENTS

What I love so much about my team is their willingness to explore new ways and to brainstorm together ideas that are original and interesting. I never thought I'd use dragons in a book until this one. Everyone on my team contributes to the ultimate goal of making my novels the best they can possibly be.

When I pitched this idea to Jason Kirk, my editor at 47North, he was about as excited for the story as he was to learn it was something new. And he was very open to layering in an Asian flair that will hopefully resonate with readers around the world.

I also want to thank Angela, who helps improve the ideas already here and make them even better with her brilliant suggestions. She's an integral part of the team.

I'm also so indebted to my first readers: my wife, Gina, and my sister Emily. They got to be the first ones to jump into this story and provided helpful suggestions and feedback. To Dan and Wanda, who also help with the editing of my books and keeping them so professional and as free from error as humanly possible. To my street team: Shannon, Robin, Sandi, Travis, and Sunil—thank you! Your encouragement and early feedback helped give me confidence that this book, while a departure from my earlier books, was still a fun ride.

And finally, to my daughter Isabelle, who will get to read this when she returns from her mission around the time this book is published! Before she left, I started teaching her Shaolin kung fu, which I'd studied while in college. It was fun having a disciple after all these years, and I certainly enjoyed our early morning workouts with swords, staves, and fists!

And last, but not least, I'd like to acknowledge Sifu Kwong Wing Lam from Sunnyvale, California, who passed away in April 2018. I trained at his school in the early nineties and still practice martial arts today because of him.

ABOUT THE AUTHOR

Photo © 2016 Mica Sloan

Jeff Wheeler is the *Wall Street Journal* bestselling author of the Harbinger and Kingfountain series, as well as the Muirwood, Mirrowen, and Landmoor novels. He took an early retirement from his career at Intel in 2014 to write full-time. He is a husband, father of five, and devout member of his church. He lives in the Rocky Mountains and is the founder of *Deep Magic: The E-Zine of Clean Fantasy and Science Fiction.* Find out more about *Deep Magic* at www.deepmagic.co, and visit Jeff's many worlds at www.jeff-wheeler.com.